Jailhouse Doc

D1232273

By
John Avanzato

KCM PUBLISHING
A DIVISION OF KCM DIGITAL MEDIA, LLC

CREDITS

Jailhouse Doc by John Avanzato

ISBN-13: 978-1-939961-78-5
ISBN-10: 1-939961-78-5

First Edition

Publisher: Michael Fabiano
KCM Publishing
www.kcmpublishing.com

The Author

To the victims, wherever you are, whatever the color of your skin, whatever language you may speak, your suffering has not gone unnoticed.

Acknowledgements

Cheryl

Contents

"The only thing necessary for the triumph of evil is for good men to do nothing."

Edmund Burke
1729-1797

Jailhouse Doc

Prologue

The back of the van was dark and dirty. Fear permeated every inch of it. A young girl with short blonde hair and blue eyes huddled in one corner, tears streaming down her face as she contemplated the gravity of her situation. She glanced around furtively at the others. Barely fifteen, she knew she was in deep trouble. She had the luxury of seeing this kind of thing on television. The other children in the van looked Mexican. They were younger than her and not quite as scared. No, for some reason they weren't scared at all, but they did seem apprehensive. They spoke very little English and she spoke only the most rudimentary Spanish. A dirty-faced little girl no more than eight clutched a doll with a blue dress. Her name was Maria and she had offered her the comfort of her doll. One adult woman rode in the vehicle with them. She glanced nervously back and forth and made no effort to console any of them. Her main job, it seemed, was to keep them quiet. She wasn't mean, but neither was she sympathetic. At times, she seemed frightened herself.

The van rumbled along uncomfortably for several days, stopping only for gas and middle-of-the-night bathroom breaks, which consisted of supervised walks into the brush. Relieving themselves in full view of the leering drivers—swarthy, uncouth men who enjoyed the entertainment—was more than just a little humiliating. Glancing around during one of these breaks, she surmised they were taking the back roads wherever it was they were going. Meals consisted of bags of fast food handed out in the darkness. Although talking was forbidden, she had managed to exchange a few words here and there with Maria. Enough to figure out that no one knew their destination but the drivers.

The blonde girl cried a lot, much to the consternation of the others in the van. She had run away from her nice, suburban home just outside Dallas because she was tired of all the rules and needed to be free. She'd met a nice boy in Fort Worth who agreed with her views on personal liberty. They'd partied hard one night and the next thing she remembered was waking up in the van. Her name was Kayla and both of her parents were dentists. She had just finished her freshman year of high school, and she knew that she had stepped into the dark underbelly of society where unspeakable horrors lay ahead. She prayed that if she were ever reunited with her parents, she would never complain about rules again.

The other children were nervous but for a different reason. They were a long way from home and had never been separated from their families, but theirs was a good journey. They were being sent to live with affluent American relatives to become citizens of that great country. They would attend great universities and earn lots of money to send back to their impoverished families. At least that was what they were told.

Kayla knew better and had tried to escape once during a bathroom break only to be smacked so hard in the side of the head that her ear rang for hours. The good news was that except for the occasional grope, the drivers mostly ignored her. One of them had lifted her shirt once to examine her breasts but was sharply rebuked by the woman. The man slapped the woman, but he left Kayla alone after that. It seemed that wherever they were being delivered, the expectation was that they be delivered intact.

After three days and nights of travel without bathing or proper hygiene, the van began to stink, and just when she thought she couldn't take it anymore, the vehicle came to a stop. Doors opened, and she heard men conversing in Spanish and English. Shortly, the back of the van opened, and she saw white men, big white men with spider web tattoos on their necks and arms. She held her breath and her heart pounded as her fear grew. She glanced over at Maria still clutching the doll and watched her shrink back in terror. The men held flashlights and looked carefully at everyone inside the van. They seemed to be doing a head count or inspection. It was dark outside and she couldn't tell how many men there were. They smiled at her, but she instinctively knew things had just gone from bad to worse.

Her stomach churned as one of them extended his hand to her. He was a large, muscular, and dangerous-looking man wearing a T-shirt. His head was shaved, and he had piercing, black-as-coal eyes. Kayla was paralyzed with fear, and the man suddenly reached in and grabbed her by the arm, pulling her roughly out of the van. Falling to her knees in front of him, she yelped in pain and he slapped her, once, twice, three times. Her head swam with confusion and pain, and tears filled her eyes, but she made no further sounds.

The smile was gone from his face as he turned to the other men. "I got this one. You guys know what to do with the rest. I'll catch up with you later."

"Sure thing, Samuel."

Chapter 1

*D*oing my best not to appear nervous, I stared straight ahead and focused my energy on the desk in front of me, tapping my index finger gently and methodically to a private rhythm in my head as the jury filed in to read the verdict. I had worn my best suit with a dark navy tie and crisp white shirt, and thought that I looked pretty good—respectable anyway. My lawyer was big on appearances. His name was George Heath, but everyone called him George Teeth because of all the money he spent on dental implants to look good for prospective clients. I had wanted to wear jeans and a button-down shirt, but he had sternly warned me that would have been a bad idea. He didn't really say why. I mean, if the judge and jury were about to slam you, why did you have to look prim and proper? And if they were on your side, what did it matter?

As the foreman handed the verdict to the bailiff, who handed it to the judge, my pulse raced in anticipation. I wasn't upset, just concerned. George had told me not to worry and that although the jury was a tough read for him, he felt they were sympathetic to me. Traditionally, juries liked doctors so I remained hopeful and clung to the notion that my suit and tie would win the day for me. Then the verdict came crashing down on me like an avalanche: guilty on two counts of obstruction of justice for deliberately misleading a federal investigator. I held my breath and looked at George for support. I got none. All I saw was a statue focused stoically ahead. Twenty-five thousand dollars in legal fees and he had nothing to say.

Now I was upset.

Two weeks later, George had persuaded the judge that community service rather than actual time would be a better way for me to pay my debt to society. The judge wasn't as convinced of my good nature, but since it was my first felony conviction, we reached a compromise and settled for six months of community service and five years' probation. The sentence was to be performed on consecutive weekends as the on-site medical doctor at the Riker's Island detention facility in New York City. I would show up at 7:00 a.m. Saturday and stay until 7:00 a.m. Monday. I would see patients Saturday and Sunday from 8:00 a.m. until 5:00 p.m. with a one-hour lunch break. The rest of the time I would be housed in a cell wearing a Riker's throwback black-and-white prison suit and would be on call for medical emergencies during my stay. I would be subject to all the same rules and observances as an inmate while I was on the facility's grounds. I was not, I repeat, not to be regarded or treated as a civilian employee. In addition, my medical license was suspended, which meant thousands of dollars more in legal fees once I finished my sentence.

Riker's Island is New York City's main jail complex, as well as the name of the island on which it sits in the middle of the East River between Queens and the Bronx. Most likely the island was named after Abraham Rycken, a Dutch immigrant, who bought the island in 1664. His family sold the island back to the city in 1884. His descendants were notorious assholes and abused the fugitive slave act, selling hundreds if not thousands of runaway slaves back into slavery in the south. Riker's Island today is one of the world's largest correctional and mental institutions.

The jail complex, operated by the New York City Department of Correction, has a budget approaching $1 billion per year, a staff of 9,000 officers and 1,500 civilian employees, and an average daily population of 10,000 inmates. Riker's has a notorious reputation for abuse and neglect of prisoners as well as for numerous assaults by inmates on staff, often resulting in serious injuries. Riker's Island detention center is considered one of the most dangerous and violent places on earth to work, and has been ranked as one of the ten worst correctional facilities in the United States. This was my new weekend getaway for the next six months.

Great.

All this because I lied to an FBI agent about the whereabouts of a girl I believed to be innocent of any crime, but who turned out to be a homicidal maniac. Total bullshit. The judge was a jerk and my lawyer—well, one day they were both going to need a colonoscopy. I consoled myself with that thought. With my license suspended, I was unemployable as a physician and had lost my job as a staff gastroenterologist at St. Matt's hospital in lower Manhattan. I couldn't re-apply for my license to be reinstated until after I finished my sentence, so I needed a plan.

I had enough money in the bank to cover my rent for a while but living in Manhattan was expensive and my savings wouldn't last long. I had asked the judge how I was supposed to practice medicine at Riker's without a license and he worked a deal with New York State's Department of Higher Education that, as long as I confined my patient interactions to the correctional facility, it would be okay. No one seemed to care that I was a board-certified gastroenterologist and hadn't practiced primary care in almost a decade. The good news was that if I kept my nose clean, I was on my own from Monday through Friday.

Two months into it, and just when I thought it couldn't get worse, the doorbell to my third-floor Greenwich Village loft apartment rang. The first floor of the building was a Polish delicatessen, which specialized in house-made kielbasa and pierogis. The smokers in the basement were poorly ventilated and ran continuously, perfuming every inch of the building with the fragrance of Polish sausage. The second floor was storage. As a consequence, the third floor was a very private place, which was why I didn't mind being hijacked by the rent. I shared the space with Cleopatra, my 250 pound, rambunctious, fun-loving English mastiff, who woofed and jumped to attention as I went to answer the door.

It was Kelly, my betrothed, the love of my life, the mother of my children, and perhaps the only reason I hadn't jumped off the Brooklyn Bridge after my sentencing. She was black and beautiful, five feet four inches tall with big almond-shaped green eyes and a perfect figure. Her wavy brown hair swept over her shoulders and down her back. Apparently, she spent a lot of time and effort on her hair, but like most men I wasn't too concerned with the details of how a woman made herself look beautiful for me just as long as she did.

"Hi, John." She had a very serious look on her face, which made me apprehensive.

"Hi, Kel."

She walked past me and grabbed Cleo by her massive head, playing with her. Cleo knew Kelly well and almost knocked her down trying to get at her.

"Hey, what about me?" I asked.

She turned and slipped her arms around me, resting her head against my chest, hugging me tightly. She smelled great but something was wrong. I could feel it. It was Monday afternoon and I hadn't seen her since early Saturday morning when I kissed her goodbye as I packed off for Riker's.

Leaning down, I kissed her and tasted tears. I said, "Let's go sit down. Whatever it is, we'll figure it out."

Kelly was a nurse at my hospital and we had been dating on and off for a couple of years. She had twin girls just over a year old and had recently informed me that they were probably mine. Problem was that during the on and off again romance, Kelly had squeezed in an unsuccessful marriage to another man, Omar, an accountant, who had left her several months back. I had proposed to her and she had accepted pending the divorce. Then my trial came with the unexpected verdict, and we had been playing it day by day until my life settled down. I had decided to keep my apartment because of Cleo's enormous size and needs. She was a very gentle dog but still probably not a good idea to let her roam free around small children.

Kelly took a seat next to me on the sofa and Cleo sat on the floor in front of us whining for attention. "What's the matter, Kel?"

She stared downward as if she couldn't tell me while looking me in the eyes. "John—it's Omar."

"What about him?" I asked.

"I went to work Saturday morning and when I returned Omar was in the apartment."

Surprise and concern registered on my face. He had taken off one day and Kelly hadn't heard a word from him since. "He was? What did he want? How did he get in?"

She touched my hand gently. "Take it easy. He had a key. When he left, I never bothered to change the locks."

"What? Why?" I felt like kicking myself for not thinking of that for her.

"John, he left of his own accord. It was mutual—kind of—sort of. Besides, his name is on the lease so I didn't think I could keep him out anyway."

Rolling my eyes, I said, "Oh brother. Fine. What about the children? Are they okay?"

5

Nodding, she replied, "Yes, they're fine. They weren't there. Because I had to work all day, I had dropped them off at my aunt's in Yonkers."

"So, what did Omar want?"

"Well, he didn't just drop by to say hi. He came with all of his luggage." She hesitated momentarily, taking a deep breath and letting it out. "John, he moved back in. I didn't want to bother you with this while you were at the prison."

"What?! Can he do that?"

She nodded, teary eyed. "Yes. Yes, he can. I have no legal right to stop him. I never filed for legal separation or divorce."

"But he abandoned you and the kids."

"I can't prove that and since they are his kids..." She just let that one hang out there. I stiffened and she saw the color rise in my cheeks.

I retorted angrily, "They're not his kids, and if I have to beat him to death to prove it, I will."

She gripped my hands firmly and our eyes met. "John, I was married to Omar when the children were born. In the eyes of the law they're his children."

I turned my gaze away this time. Thinking it over, I said, "Maybe it's time to do a paternity test."

She shook her head. "Legally, I can't do that without his permission. The results would never be admissible in court without his consent. Trust me. I've been talking with my attorney all weekend."

"So, what are our options?" The bad news was coming at me so fast and furious, I hadn't had time to process its significance.

She drew another deep breath. "My only option would be to leave the apartment and take the kids with me. Technically, I would be kidnapping the children, and if I did that, I would run the risk of being arrested. If I wasn't arrested, I'd certainly run the risk of a massive custody battle. He made that clear. If

6

I stay in the apartment, I could file for divorce. In New York State, there's a mandatory wait period of about a year before the divorce would be granted. They want couples to think it over and not act in haste. You know, maybe go to counseling and try to work things out."

I could barely breathe. No, no, no. This couldn't be happening. "A year?" I was incredulous but then thought it over, calming down. "Well, Kel, what's a year? File the papers and let's begin the countdown." I was pleased with my maturity.

She looked down again. Now what? I asked, "Kel…?"

"It's a little more complicated than that."

"I'm waiting."

"Omar's been talking to lawyers too. He knows all about your felony conviction and has filed a restraining order for you to stay away from me and the children." She reached into her handbag and pulled out an envelope, handing it to me.

I took it but didn't open it. She continued. "It says you can't physically come within one hundred feet of us or the apartment nor can you contact me via phone, text, email, or Skype. It also says that because you're a convicted felon, you represent a clear and present danger to the welfare of the children and the family unit and if you violate the terms of the restraining order you will be in material and substantial breach of the terms of your probation and could potentially be subject to further incarceration."

I was dumbfounded. Who was Omar's lawyer, Johnny Cochran? She said, "John, are you okay? Did you hear what I said?"

I nodded glumly. "I heard."

"That's why I came here. I didn't want you to get this in the mail or by courier. I want you to know how sorry I am but I just don't know what we can do."

"What's this mean, really?"

She put her arms around me and gave me a gentle kiss. Her eyes were red and the dam would soon burst. "I'm sorry but I can't see you anymore. Omar would declare me an unfit mother and I would be in danger of losing the girls. I can't do anything to jeopardize them. I'll file for divorce right away but you and I need to stay away from each other. This will be the last time I come here and please don't call or do anything foolish. Omar is very serious. Have your lawyer read the restraining order. If he sees any loopholes, let me know, but for now we have to play by Omar's rules."

She stood to leave and I said, "That's it. You're just going to walk away—cold turkey?"

She pulled me up to her and hugged me tightly. She was crying. "Please don't make this any worse than it already is." After she left, I punched the wall and let out a primal scream.

Chapter 2

"So, what are you going to do, Cesari?" Vito asked. We sat across from each other at a wood table in the back of the *Chien Jaune* café on Bleecker Street sipping espresso. Chien jaune was French for yellow dog and had a decidedly European feel to it.

I spread homemade orange marmalade on a warm croissant and said, "I don't know. My lawyer says I'm fucked. I don't want to violate my probation and I certainly don't want to take a chance of hurting Kelly or the children so I guess I'll sit tight until something breaks in my direction."

Vito drained his cup and furrowed his brow in thought. Almost as if talking to no one in particular, he said, "You know, Omar disappeared once. Maybe he could just disappear again…"

I glanced at him sternly. "Get that idea out of your head. Kelly would never forgive me for that."

"How would she know?"

"She's not stupid and she knows me and you too well, so knock it off." Kelly was thoroughly familiar with my many nefarious connections and friendships, one of whom was Vito. She also knew I wasn't averse to engaging in street justice from time to time. But one of the terms of our love and mutual respect was that we would always be honest with each other and try to raise the children with the highest moral standards. I assumed that included not murdering her husband.

Vito grinned. He was a mountain of a man; well over six feet and close to 260 pounds with sharp, clean features and thick black hair with a spattering of gray at the sides. We grew up together in the Bronx and had been pals since the first grade. He ran the rackets in lower Manhattan with an iron fist, answering to no one but his own boss in Brooklyn. He just offered to eighty-six some guy for me the way you might offer to open the door for a stranger. The sick part was that it didn't even strike me as odd. In fact, given the context of our friendship it seemed rather natural. Such was life when you grew up in the Bronx.

He said, "Maybe we could just persuade him to go away peacefully. No one has to get hurt."

I put my hand up in protest. "Stop. Don't go anywhere near him, all right? Just put it out of your mind." The last time I saw Vito trying to gently persuade someone to do something they weren't inclined to, it involved multiple blows with a crowbar.

He was disappointed but relented. "Fine. How you doing for cash?"

"I'm okay in the short run. I've applied for several temporary jobs until I get my license back. I'm hoping one will come through soon."

"What does a doctor do if he can't be a doctor?" he asked with genuine curiosity.

"What does anybody do when they can't do their real job? They teach." I took a large bite of my croissant and chewed with enthusiasm. It was delicious.

He chuckled. "Teach?"

I nodded. "Yeah."

"Teach what? High school biology?"

"Close, but as a felon in the middle of his sentence, I'd never get a job in a high school. I've put together a course proposal and submitted it to a bunch of local colleges and universities. I'm hoping maybe one of the schools will see past my imperfections as a human being and appreciate the uniqueness of my idea."

Vito ordered a second espresso and said, "Tell me your proposal."

"Really?"

"Yeah."

I finished my coffee and dabbed my lips with a paper napkin. "Well, I outlined a one-semester course designed to introduce students to basic healthcare issues. Starting with general anatomy and physiology, I run through the more common diseases and medical problems people get, like high blood pressure, diabetes, heart disease, etcetera. I would teach them about the typical symptoms and manifestations of those diseases and treatment options. I was even thinking it might be kind of cool to teach the kids how to take blood pressures and use a stethoscope. From there, I would discuss the health-care system in its broadest terms, how health insurance works, and what to expect when they see a physician. Everyone should know what questions to ask about their own health, but almost no one does. I actually think it might be kind of fun."

The waitress placed Vito's espresso in front of him and he slurped it down in one quick shot, wiping his lips with the back of his hand. "I have to admit, Cesari, for a guy with no common sense, and who can barely manage his own life, this sounds like a pretty good idea."

"Thanks."

He glanced at his Rolex, adjusted his tie and said, "Well, I have to go. Unlike you, I have a real job that requires my attention, but before I leave, I brought you a little something to make your stay at Riker's a little more bearable."

I was puzzled. Vito wasn't the most caring human being I'd ever met. In fact, on a scale of one to ten thousand, he wasn't even number ten thousand. He reached down and picked up a small plastic bag that he had placed discreetly on the floor by his feet. It was from Walgreens.

He slid it across the table at me as he stood to leave. "You can thank me some other time."

He placed a twenty under his saucer for the coffees and walked away as I looked in the bag. What an asshole. In the bag were a large jar of Vaseline and a box of condoms.

Later that day, I settled down to review basic dermatology for internists. It was Friday and I was brushing up for the weekend. I had noticed right away that the inmates tended to have lots of rashes with which I was unfamiliar. It wasn't as hard as running blind but it was close. The general rules of dermatology were; if it was dry, keep it wet, and if it was wet, keep it dry. If it itched, use steroid creams and antihistamines. If it was on the feet or in groin, add antifungal medications. I smiled. They got paid six figures for that? My phone rang, breaking my concentration. I didn't recognize the number. Cleo woofed.

"Hello."

"Hello, is this Dr. John Cesari?"

"Yes, it is."

"John, this is Pam. Pam Gottlieb. I don't know if you remember me."

"Pam, of course I remember you."

"Thank you."

She was a psychologist on the faculty at NYU and had been contracted by my hospital a year or two ago to educate the staff on sexual harassment in the workplace. I personally had to go for extra counseling. She was a real dish if I recalled correctly. In fact, one of my counseling sessions was about not referring to women as dishes. "Women are not food or desserts for your dining pleasure," she had said. Damn, she was hot.

I smiled at the memory. "What can I do for you, Pam?"

"Well, John, I'm on the committee for curriculum development here at NYU and your course proposal came to our attention. To say the least, the members of the committee were intrigued and when I told them that I could vouch for you personally, they asked me to reach out. Are you still interested in developing this class?"

"Yes, I am, very much so; although, I have to admit that I didn't really expect to hear back from a university as prestigious as NYU. I figured one of the smaller, community colleges might consider it, but so far, not a nibble."

She sounded pleased. "Well, lucky for us. When can you come in for a face to face with the faculty? We'd like to get the ball rolling on this in time for the fall course offerings and we don't have a whole lot of time."

"How about Monday?" I asked.

She said, "Great. How about lunch at noon? I can meet you at Umberto's in Little Italy. That is, if you still like Italian food?"

I smiled. "Does the Pope wear a dress? Umberto's at noon will be perfect. How many faculty members are coming? Umberto's isn't that big a place."

"Just me. After lunch, we'll walk over to the Steinhardt building and meet the rest of them. I thought you and I should catch up first and that I should prep you a little on their personalities and what to expect."

"I appreciate that, but are you sure it's necessary? I'm a big boy."

"Well, I'd feel better. I think what won them over was your brutal honesty about what's going on in your life and we'll talk more about that over lunch. It sounds like you've been through a lot lately. But now that you're in the door you have to play by their rules. This is NYU and most of the faculty are—to say the least—quirky."

I smiled. She was being kind. Most of the faculty at NYU were out-of-touch whackos. Tenure did that to people. No one should be guaranteed employment without some sort of periodic performance review. "Sure thing, Pam. I'll see you Monday."

"I'm looking forward to it."

I hung up and looked down at Cleo lying beside me. "You know, Cleo, I think this calls for a celebration."

Sensing the excitement in my voice she stood, wagged her tail, and nudged me with her gigantic head. I walked over to the pantry where I kept doggie treats high up on the top shelf to prevent her from getting any ideas. When I reached for them, she knew what was coming and stood on her hind legs with her great paws leaning against my chest. Her head was at the same level as mine now and she almost tipped me over.

I reprimanded her, "Take it easy or I'll put them back."

She woofed and whined excitedly. I placed a large bone-shaped treat in her mouth and she got off me to chew contentedly. Now it was my turn. I opened the fridge and found a can of PBR. I popped the top and took a long swig while Cleo ate her doggy treat.

Things were looking up.

Maybe.

Chapter 3

I pulled into an empty space in the Riker's Island parking lot at ten of seven. It was a beautiful summer morning in mid-August, and my spirits were buoyed by the thought of a teaching gig at NYU. With any luck, I might even get approved for the upcoming semester beginning in a few weeks. I placed my cellphone in the glove compartment and frisked myself for any other contraband that might piss off the guards. No electronic devices of any kind were permitted. They didn't screw around here. Even a simple USB stick could get you a full body cavity search.

I entered the complex through an ordinary door, but once inside everything changed. Two-armed security guards checked my driver's license against their list of expected visitors, wanded me after I walked through a metal detector, and then opened a large metal gate. Five hundred feet later the procedure was repeated. Ultimately, I walked through no less than five metal gates, was wanded two more times, frisked and photo ID'd at least four more times before being escorted to the medical facilities by another two-armed correctional officers. Riker's was a multi-purpose detention center and housed a wide range of inmates, some of whom were quite violent. In general, New York State corrections officers were not armed because of the risk it posed to the officers themselves should they be overpowered, but Riker's was under the jurisdiction of New York City not the state and they followed a whole different set of rules here. This was a modern-day Devil's Island.

During normal hours of operation, six full-time medical doctors and three nurse practitioners managed the clinic. A variety of specialists who contracted with the city made scheduled visits on a weekly basis. They even had two operating rooms where they performed colonoscopy and other minor procedures. The full-time medical staff had given me the run down on policy and procedures. The doctor in charge was David Feldman, an internist in his mid-fifties and a real nice guy. He felt bad for me and was very supportive. To him I was a fallen angel. That made me smile. Me, a fallen angel? Too funny.

I was free to perform any procedures I felt comfortable with, including colonoscopy, but since anesthesia and nursing weren't routinely available on the weekends, that seemed unwise. I familiarized myself with the OR and equipment anyway out of habit more than anything. Other than that, I was pretty much on my own. The lack of nurses and other support staff made for a long and lonely day. Any emergency I couldn't handle had to be transferred to one of the city hospitals. Because I was technically a prisoner myself, I couldn't authorize that and had to call the chief medical officer, Dave, and discuss the case with him. If he concurred, he would pass the message along to the guards. Transferring prisoners off campus was a big deal and thoroughly discouraged by prison authorities. Once word spread amongst the prisoners that you were an easy touch, the place would be flooded with inmates feigning illness. No matter what they did to you on the outside it had to be better than sitting in your cell all day, so it was worth it. We called it R&R. If you were real lucky you might even catch a glimpse of a pretty nurse.

The building was old, damp, and gray. Paint peeled and water stained the ceiling. There were cracks in the cement walls. Riker's was in desperate need of maintenance, but try telling that to a cash-strapped city that was living off the federal dole to the tune of billions every year just to meet its payroll.

The clinic was comprised of ten medium-sized exam rooms, a central nursing station and multiple offices for the doctors and nurse practitioners. I was escorted to the office to which I had been assigned to set up shop. The guard unlocked it for me and I entered. There was a cheap metal desk and chair, a locker, and a small bookcase with a couple of outdated medical reference texts. A small window with bars allowed a glimmer of sunlight into the otherwise depressing room. I donned a white lab coat that was kept on a hook behind the door and smiled at the guard.

He smiled back. "Nice try, Doc. You know the rules."

He threw the black-and-white uniform at me, which I deftly caught. The button-down top had my identification number on it by the breast pocket. He handed me a plastic bag to place my civilian clothes in.

"What's the deal with these outfits anyway, Keith?" I asked. "Seems old-fashioned."

I was referring to the large, horizontal black-and-white stripes on the shirt and pants, which were popular in the earlier part of the twentieth century, but had since been replaced by orange jumpsuits almost everywhere.

Keith was a large black man, clean shaven, and just a bit out of shape. He'd been a corrections officer at Riker's for twenty years. He was in an unusually surly mood this morning and growled, "Just put them on and don't give me any sass. I told you once before I don't know and I don't care."

After I changed, they allowed me to make a pot of coffee in the break room. One guard stood behind me to my right and the other to my left as I made the coffee. I was now officially Prisoner 90157 until 7:00 a.m. Monday morning and they weren't taking any chances. They were armed with pepper spray, stun guns, 9mm Glocks, and really scary faces. They were each twice my size. I was no slouch at six feet, 220 pounds and in pretty good shape, but these guys were massive. We sipped coffee and waited.

The van with the prisoners arrived right on schedule and the buzzer rang, announcing today's morning panel of patients. Ten of the skankiest human beings I had ever seen shuffled their way into the waiting room, shackled together at the ankle and the hips. Four heavily armed guards complete with riot shotguns and metal batons watched them carefully and looked as if they were ready to pounce for even the slightest infraction. The prisoners lined up in front of a row of metal waiting-room chairs and sat in unison when instructed.

Keith greeted the leader of the new group of corrections officers and paperwork exchanged hands. They went over to the first patient, identified him together, and then released him from the group shackles. Now he just had handcuffs to contend with. He led him into the exam room and helped him up onto the exam table while I reviewed his paperwork. The guards stepped back but didn't leave the room.

I sat in front of him on a small stool with wheels. He was six feet four inches tall and weighed 280 pounds. Muscles bulged out of his neck and sleeves and I got the impression he could break his chains without working up a sweat. His chart said his name was Malcolm Steadwell and that today was his birthday. I would normally have wished one of my patients "Happy Birthday," but the medical staff had cautioned me not to be overly friendly or personal with the inmates. I was told to keep it strictly business. To me he was Prisoner 67729. African-American, forty-two years old, history of high blood pressure for which he was on Ramipril 10 mg daily, history of alcohol and drug abuse, convicted of assaulting his neighbor over a dispute about money and drugs. He was HIV and Hepatitis C negative at least for now. He was three years into a five-year sentence and now he was complaining of abdominal pain.

The inmates at Riker's were generally short termers, sentenced for a year or less. Many, like Malcolm, were waiting transfer to other facilities but the New York State prisons were so dangerously overcrowded there was often no place to put guys like him and so he languished here in purgatory.

I reached for a yellow legal pad and pen that was kept on the small desk. I crossed my legs clumsily and the stool I was sitting on rolled precipitously backwards. I almost lost my balance and Malcolm grinned broadly, revealing several missing molars. Recovering and without introductions I said, "So what can I do for you?"

"My stomach hurts real bad, Doc."

"Can you point to where it hurts?"

He rubbed a gigantic hand over the center of his abdomen.

"Can you be more specific about the pain? Is it sharp, dull, burning, cramping? Does it come and go or is it steady?"

He thought it over for a second. "I guess it's a dull pain, burns a little, gets worse from time to time. It's not there all the time but really bad now."

I jotted down notes while he spoke. "Okay. For how long have you had the pain?"

"Couple of days, maybe a week."

"Any nausea, vomiting or rectal bleeding?"

He shook his head no.

"Are there any other symptoms such as fever or sweats? Does anything make the pain better like a bowel movement?"

"Seems better when I eat."

19

"All right, just a few more questions. Have you ever had any abdominal surgeries such as gallbladder or an appendectomy?"

"I think I had my appendix out, but that was when I was a kid. I'm not sure. I got shot in the stomach years ago and had surgery for that."

"Have you ever had an ulcer?"

"Not that I know of."

I scratched on the pad again and said, "Okay, would you mind lying flat on your back so I could examine you?"

He sprawled backward and I extended the bottom of the table so he could rest his legs. I put the legal pad down and picked up the stethoscope lying on the desk. This was the part I hated. I would have to get close, very close, to examine him. Even handcuffed with two guards nearby he could seriously hurt me before they intervened. He would pay a heavy price, but so would I. As if they read my mind, the two guards snapped to attention.

I took his temperature with an electronic probe and then measured his blood pressure manually with a wall cuff. He was afebrile but his pressure was up a little. Nothing dangerous. His abdomen was tender but not terribly so. I examined him as carefully as I could and determined that he would not require surgery, at least not tonight. The rest of his exam was unremarkable and I concluded that he most likely had an ulcer.

I assisted him to a sitting position again and told him what I thought. "I'll order you a medication called omeprazole. You'll have to take it once a day for the next several months. If you don't get better we'll have to do more advanced testing such as endoscopy and maybe even a CT scan."

"Is that pill going to get rid of the pain?"

"If it's an ulcer, then yes. Maybe not immediately but certainly you'll start feeling better within a couple of days."

"And if I don't?"

"Then the guards will bring you back here for re-evaluation. Don't take any aspirin or ibuprofen for the next few weeks if you can avoid it, and if you notice any blood in your stool let me or the guards know right away."

He nodded as I filled out a form with my findings and recommendations and plopped it into a folder on the desk. Because of my unusual and temporary status, I wasn't allowed access to the prison's electronic medical records and would have to call the center's pharmacy personally with the prescription. And so, the morning wore on.

At noon, the guards escorted me to the cafeteria in one of the cell blocks. This was a fairly dangerous time for me. Being set loose, friendless and without allies into the general population even for an hour could have fatal consequences. I had tried declining lunch several times but the guards insisted that they were required to bring me there. The judge had a real hard-on for me and during my sentencing made it clear that I was to experience the full reality of prison life in all its glory.

Asshole.

I sincerely hoped that I ran into him again one day. I grabbed an old, beaten-up plastic tray and got in line at the buffet, sandwiched between drug addicts, thieves, wife beaters, and undiagnosed psychopaths. They watched me with curiosity. I was different—white, clean cut, healthy looking, sans tattoos. I didn't fit in.

The guy behind me said, "You a pretty bitch."

I tensed and abruptly turned to him. There was only one response possible. I snarled. "That's what I told your mother last night. Now fuck off."

He smiled and backed up. Slightly taller than me and missing his left ear, he chuckled. "Relax, white boy. Didn't mean nothing."

When my turn came, I asked for some pink stuff and a scoop of some brown stuff with a container of milk. The cafeteria was crowded and I was one of the last ones in. I searched unsuccessfully for an empty seat. Surly-looking whites were sitting at one table toward the back, hunched over their food. Most had shaved, tattooed heads and necks. Not my cup of tea. Shit, this was worse than high school. I was just about to throw my lunch out and lean against a wall when someone tapped me lightly on the arm.

"You look like you need a friend," he/she said in a falsetto. Short, nappy hair, dyed blonde, hoop earrings, ruby-red lipstick, and way too much make-up gave me a jolt, and I hesitated, taking in the sight.

She continued, "I'm Diamond. Why don't you sit with me and my girlfriends while you sort things out? I promise I won't bite."

She nodded toward a table with several other similarly adorned inmates, who watched with curiosity. I thought it over, nodded, and followed her slinking and strutting form toward the others. Sitting, I glanced around uncomfortably. There were six including me in the middle, our table positioned in the far corner against the wall. More than a thousand inmates were eating their lunch and yet, for some reason, I felt like we were all alone. It really did feel like high school.

Diamond said, "So, what's your name, honey?"

"Cesari. John Cesari."

"Well, it's a pleasure to meet you John Cesari. You are one heck of a good-looking human being. On your other side, there is Ruby. Say hi, Ruby, and across from you is Emerald. Say hi, Emerald." She continued to rattle off the names of precious stones until everyone had been introduced.

22

As we ate, Diamond led the chatter at the table. Several bites into the pink stuff on my plate she asked coyly, "So, are you attached?"

I looked up, taken by surprise and noticed everyone waiting for my reply. "I'm not sure what you mean?"

"I mean are you looking for a girlfriend?"

I shook my head. "No, I'm not."

She smiled. "Good, it's always better to play the field." She slid a hand onto my thigh, massaging it.

I noticed her biceps were bigger than mine as I gently and discreetly moved my leg away. "That wasn't what I meant."

She pouted but didn't in the slightest seem dissuaded. "Me and the girls can be lots of fun if you just give us a chance. You can be our white pony."

"I'm sure and thanks for the offer, but the reason I'm not looking for a girlfriend is that I already have one. I'm engaged to be married."

They all got genuinely excited and happy for me. Clapping their hands, Diamond and several others said, "Congratulations."

"Thanks."

"Well, maybe we could throw you a bachelor party someday. Honey, you ain't lived until you've had a lap dance by these girls."

"That sounds great."

Chapter 4

The last patient of the day was a wiry, pasty-looking, white guy with a spider web tattoo and bad attitude. Beginning at the level of his neck, the tattoo extended downward covering his back, chest, and arms. He had the obligatory shaved head and an unkempt blonde goatee. An inch shorter and considerably lighter than me by about thirty pounds, he was lean, hard, and had a sneaky, dangerous look to him I didn't like. He smiled like he was my friend. That "we white guys got to stick together" kind of smile. I wasn't buying it.

I read his chart. Duane Thompson, thirty-five years old, assault and battery, armed robbery, meth dealer. Nice. He was awaiting transfer to Sing Sing.

"So, what's wrong, prisoner?" I asked.

"Call me Duane, Doc."

"What's wrong, prisoner?" I repeated.

He grinned again and I noticed multiple rotting teeth giving rise to putrid breath, which made me wince when it reached me. "We've noticed that you've been ignoring your own kind. Probably not the smartest thing to do."

I glanced at the guards. They remained expressionless. Duane didn't represent any real physical danger to them or even to me. On the other hand, there was sort of an implied threat in that statement and I wondered if the guards noticed or cared.

I said, "If I was smart I wouldn't be here. Now would I? So, if you don't have a medical problem that you would like to talk about I'm going to have the guards return you to your cell and then I'm going to place a note in your file for the warden that you were a pain in the ass."

The guards definitely heard that and stepped forward bracing for a confrontation. I slid my chair back to get out of the way. Duane said, "Easy, cowboy. I do have a medical problem."

Everyone relaxed a hair. I said, "Go ahead."

"There's a sore in the back of my mouth and it hurts like hell every time I swallow."

Probably herpes, I thought. I stood up and retrieved a small flashlight and a tongue depressor. It was almost 5:00 p.m. and this guy was irritating me. Stepping close, I clicked on the light and said, "Open up and stick out your tongue." I was careful not to get within biting range.

As I neared, he suddenly inhaled with a grotesque snorting sound. I hesitated, confused, just inches from him, and he spit a large glob of mucous and saliva directly into my face. It hit me in the eye and some of it went into my mouth.

I yelled, "Shit!"

Before I could back away he launched a head butt at me catching me in the chin. I fell backward, tripped over my stool, and landed on the floor on my butt. I sat there stunned as the guards rushed forward with raised batons to subdue him.

He hissed, "That's just a warning, cocksucker."

I rose and staggered to the sink to wash my face and rinse my mouth to the sound of metal batons crashing down on him as he laughed maniacally. When they were done, they put a leather muzzle on him and half-walked, half-carried him away.

My chin sustained a small cut, which I washed and rubbed some antiseptic ointment on. It was starting to swell but I'd survived worse. At least I wouldn't need stitches. Keith returned and asked, "You going to be okay, Doc?"

"I'll be fine, thank you Keith. My pride hurts more than anything else."

Technically, I wasn't supposed to address him by his first name but given the circumstances, he let it pass. "We're going to have to fill out an incident report."

I nodded, "I understand. I will concur with anything you say." No one cared what happened to me but they were going to have to explain the beating they just handed out.

"Thanks, Doc. Ready to go?"

"Yeah."

I finished my paperwork and was brought back to the cell block, assigned a bed and left to my own devices. I was on my own until morning. I'd had enough excitement for one day so I decided to skip dinner. Arriving at my cell, I found a Mexican lying on the bottom bunk who barely noticed my arrival. The room was barely six feet wide by eight feet long with a small metal sink and toilet at the far end. The one act of mercy the judge had granted me was to order that I not be housed with a known violent offender. So my roommate was either a drug dealer, thief, or pervert. On the other hand, just because he wasn't here for a violent offense didn't mean that he wasn't violent. Taking his lead, I didn't bother with any small talk and climbed onto the top bunk.

The door to the cell wouldn't be locked until 10:00 p.m. so I needed to stay on high alert until then. I stared at the ceiling pondering my life and wondering where I went wrong to deserve this. I wasn't a spiritual man but I didn't rule anything out either. You never knew, right?

Maybe the Hindus were on to something, and I was being punished for something I had done in a previous life. I chuckled at that. That meant I was an asshole in two different lives. Thirty minutes into my musings, the metal door slid open. I looked toward it and saw three large skinheads standing at the entrance.

The one in charge said, "Pedro, beat it."

Pedro, if that was his name, jumped up and scurried from the room. The three guys came in and slid the metal gate closed. Why? I presumed to prevent me from leaving or anyone else from entering while they did whatever it was they came to do. My senses shot to attention and adrenaline surged throughout my body. I hopped down to the floor to face them. No matter how you cut it, this wasn't good.

I looked around. The only thing in my favor was that the room was so narrow they were forced to come at me one at a time and if one was guarding the entrance then I only had to contend with two of them.

I squared away at their leader. "What's up, guys?"

I noticed more spider web tattoos and a variety of body piercings. The guy in front of me was taller and more muscular than the ones behind. He outweighed me by twenty pounds at least and was clearly battle-hardened. His nose appeared to have been broken several times and reset the old-fashioned way without the benefit of medical assistance. Coal-black eyes dominated his aggressive features and I got the feeling that beneath the dangerous exterior, he was probably fairly intelligent. He seemed to be in charge. "Wasn't nice what you did to Duane today. He was just trying to make friends."

Bad news traveled fast.

"Like you're trying to do now?" I was playing a risky game and I felt my pulse race trying to decide what to do. They could be armed. If they wanted to talk, then let them. So I continued. "What do you guys want?"

"That's better," he said, relaxing a bit. "It's always better to be agreeable when you're in a strange place."

"I don't have anything."

He grinned. "I disagree. You have a nice ass. We'd make a lot of friends passing you around. Of course, we'd have to break you in first." He just let that one drift out there and I felt things tighten up. My eyes darted quickly from side to side, searching for anything I could use as a weapon.

He continued, "But that's not what we came for."

"I'm listening."

"My sources tell me you're only here on weekends, right?"

I was suddenly curious and nodded. "Yeah."

"Well, I need a favor, and if you help me out I'd consider it an act of friendship for which I'd be very grateful."

"What kind of favor?" I asked.

"I need to communicate with the outside."

"That's what phones are for. How long have you been in here, anyway?" I said sarcastically.

He hesitated almost as if he was suddenly unsure of my sanity. "Are you trying to be an asshole?"

"It comes easy when I'm around certain people."

His mouth gaped open in astonishment, but before he could respond I added, "Why don't you get to the point?"

"The point is the guards listen in on all my calls, and I'm not allowed visitors. Why is none of your concern. So I need you to deliver messages to and from a friend of mine on the outside."

"And if I don't?"

He smirked. "Are you fucking deaf? If you choose to decline my friendship then you're going to be the bitch of the cellblock. Your choice."

"I heard that was your job."

He nodded. "Okay wise guy, just picture yourself in here bent over the toilet with guys lined up all the way to the shower

28

room waiting their turn. Usually, I would charge a pack of smokes per pop but in your case, I might waive the fee as an introductory offer."

The guy behind him let out a nasty chuckle and chimed in enthusiastically, "Do it Samuel. Do it. Teach this piece of ass a lesson. Give it to him real good." He was practically salivating with excitement.

I zoomed in on pressure points and natural weaknesses; the larynx, the pinky, eyes, testicles, knees, and ankles. But the most obvious one that almost everyone overlooked was the solar plexus. It was a huge target and it was right in front of you.

Samuel looked at me long and hard before coming to a conclusion. Then slowly he began lifting his shirt, exposing ripped abs and bulging tattoo-covered sinews. There wasn't an ounce of fat on him and he looked like he worked out several hours a day.

But it was a stupid move, designed solely to impress me. As the shirt reached his face, I leapt into action, curling my right fist into a tight ball and using all my might and weight, launched a massive pre-emptive strike directly into his sternum. I gave it everything I had and felt his rib cage compress from the blow. If he was any less muscular, I might have broken several ribs. As it was, he gasped in pain but before he could react, I kneed him hard in the groin, and almost simultaneously, clapped his ears with as much force as I could muster.

He slid to the floor in agony, revealing the trouble maker behind him more clearly. Stunned by the sudden violence, he stood there slack-jawed and frozen in place as I leaned over his slumping friend and delivered a crushing blow into the bridge of his nose, breaking it and possibly his maxilla as well. He slumped backward into the guy behind, his nose flattened, and blood streaming down his face. The guy at the gate was now pinned behind his friends and wide-eyed, watching me, not sure what to expect next.

Before he could react, I climbed quickly onto the top bunk as he stared helplessly. I swung my legs around and launched a huge kick into his face. The back of his head clanged hard against the metal of the gate and his eyes rolled upward as he fell forward onto his companions. I looked down.

Samuel was on his knees, wheezing, groaning and clutching his balls. It was time to finish him off. I jumped on top of his back and locked him in a half-nelson, pulling back hard as he clawed weakly at me. In less than a minute, his strength gave out and he went limp.

I stood up. The only one of them who seemed even remotely conscious was the guy with the broken nose. Dazed and offering no resistance, he leaned back against the gate with his friend lying on top of him. On the other side of the entrance way a crowd of onlookers had gathered. News of the spectacle had percolated quickly. Nothing beat live entertainment.

I grabbed him roughly by his shirt and cocked my right fist, hissing through clenched teeth. "You wanted him to give it to me?"

The crowd roared its approval in anticipation of the coup de grace and I felt like a gladiator in the arena of ancient Rome. Blood ran down his face and barely audibly he whispered, "I'm sorry."

Whistles and sirens blared and the crowd suddenly dispersed as prison guards converged on my cell. Officers in SWAT gear approached my position.

One pointed a Taser at me and shouted, "Prisoner 90157, stand down!"

I dropped the guy and he collapsed to the floor.

"Prisoner 90157, turn around and get on your knees. Hands behind your head."

Chapter 5

For my own protection, I was placed in solitary confinement for the night and at 6:00 a.m., Keith woke me. "Rise and shine, Superman. Time to save more lives."

I sat up groggy and stiff. "You're awfully cheerful for a prison guard."

"I guess I like my work. You going to shower, Doc?"

"Not a chance."

He chuckled, "Probably a smart move. Breakfast?"

I was very hungry. "Yeah, sure."

"We got a lot more paperwork to fill out now because of you."

I grinned. "I didn't do anything."

"That's what everybody says. A hundred witnesses and they all say the same thing. Nothing happened. They all fell down by themselves."

I wanted to laugh but thought better of it. He continued. "Even the injured guys said that's what happened."

"Really?"

"Yup, but that's not a good thing for you."

I nodded. They wanted to keep this in house and take care of it themselves. Not good. "I didn't have many options."

"I bet. Well, from now on you sleep in solitary. It's the least we can do since you're providing a service that's for the benefit of the rest of them. Even if they don't appreciate it."

"Thanks, I'm glad someone cares."

"Okay, splash some water on your face and we'll get some chow."

The cafeteria looked pretty much the same as it did yesterday. Busy, noisy, a long line of guys in black-and-white pajamas snaked their way forward for breakfast that was marginally better than lunch. Watery egg casserole, spam impersonating bacon, soggy toast, and burnt coffee.

As usual, I filled my plate and looked around for a seat. The white guy table toward the back was missing a few guys. At least one would have had to have been transferred out to have his nose splinted and possibly to have his jaw wired. One had a concussion and may have required a head CT and observation. I saw the lead guy, Samuel, looking down as he ate his breakfast, plotting my demise, no doubt. I didn't see Diamond or her friends.

As I strolled down the nearest aisle scanning back and forth, I spotted a familiar face. It was Malcolm, my first patient from yesterday, the big guy with the ulcer. He nodded his oversized head at me and then pointed at the seat next to him. I wasn't sure what he meant since the seat next to him was occupied by an unfriendly-looking fellow with long dreads. Malcolm saw the confusion in my face and leaned over to say something to the guy with the dreads who either didn't understand or didn't respond fast enough, because Malcolm suddenly reached up with a colossal hand and grabbed a handful of his hair. With almost no effort he yanked backward and the guy fell off the bench onto the floor. Sitting there stunned, Malcolm took his tray and placed it gently on the floor next to him. No one said anything or even acknowledged what had just happened. Mr.

Dreads picked up his tray without protest and ambled away to another table as I took his seat.

If I anticipated some sort of welcome, I was wrong. No one looked at me and no introductions were made. Taking their cue, I ate in silence. I wasn't sure what was going on but I got the feeling Malcolm was sending Samuel some sort of message. Word spread fast and sides were forming.

Just as I finished my last bite and was about to leave, Malcolm turned to me. "You a tough little guy, aren't ya?"

I looked at him and shook my head as I stood. "Nah. If they had brought me flowers we'd be picking out baby names this morning."

He chuckled and nodded. "I'll keep that in mind."

The rest of the day ran very smoothly. A couple of rashes here, a headache or two there, minor cuts and bruises, a sore throat, an occasional toothache. I took care of what I could and made recommendations for the medical staff in the morning. Most of the prisoners were reasonable and just trying to do their time without getting in the crosshairs of your nastier elements, including foul-tempered guards.

At 5:00 p.m. sharp, we closed shop and I was escorted back to solitary. I had breakfast and lunch in the cafeteria but the idea of eating three meals there in one day made my stomach churn uncomfortably. I still wasn't sure what mystery meat I had eaten for lunch. Missing one meal here or there wouldn't kill me. I'd make up for it at tomorrow's lunch with Pam at Umberto's. The thought of fried calamari made me salivate. In fact, the thought of seeing Pam again made me salivate as well and I hoped she wore a short skirt like I remembered she was famous for.

My cell was a small, windowless room with a tiny metal sink, cot, hole in the ground for waste disposal and a roll of toilet paper. I peed into the three-inch hole and thought it was as accommodating as some of the shadier places I'd been to in Paris. Well, at least I didn't have to worry about unwanted guests here. On the other hand, I could drop dead from a heart attack and no one would notice until morning.

I lay on the hard cot and thought about Cleo. I had a grad student named Zach keeping an eye on her for me on the weekends. He was going for his master's in cyber security and it was the perfect way for him to pick up cash. He came to the apartment with his laptop and books, played with Cleo and studied all weekend. He was free to come and go as he pleased. He even slept over with his girlfriend and drank my booze. I didn't care what he did as long as he treated Cleo right. She was more human than dog and required lots of attention. So far, he was doing well and she seemed to like him.

At exactly 10:00 p.m. and without warning, the one light in the room went out and I was in complete darkness. The door wasn't made of metal bars like in the general cell block so there was no ambient light radiating in from the hallway. It was solid steel with two small rectangular openings with retractable coverings. One was at eye level for the guards to look in when they needed and one was just a few inches off the floor to pass food in and for the inmate to sit backward against with hands outstretched behind to be handcuffed.

I don't know how long I slept but I was awakened by a soft metallic scraping sound. It took me a couple of seconds to understand. Somebody was quietly unlocking the door. I held my breath and made no movement as my body roared to high alert. I wasn't sure what was going on but it would be better to keep the element of surprise on my side. I gently pulled my cover off to free up my legs. My heart raced and I tried to focus as best as possible in the gloom. Soon I heard muffled footsteps walking away.

Scared, I waited for quite some time, but heard nothing else so I stood up and went over to the door. This was uncharted territory for me. Why would anyone unlock my door? Were they trying to encourage me to escape? Escape to where? There was no way of getting out of here without a well-rehearsed plan and plenty of help. And why would I want to escape anyway? I was going home in the morning with their blessing. Something was wrong.

Shit!

It hit me like a brick. I was being set up. A rogue guard had unlocked the door. Unsavory visitors would soon be on their way. I needed to get out of there quickly. I leaped out of bed and ran to the door, opening it slowly and searching up and down the hallway. There was low-level lighting and I could see that the corridor was empty. I stepped into it barefoot and closed the door behind me. Not knowing where to go or what to do, I hurriedly walked down the corridor checking doors until I came across an unlocked cell and let myself in. Waiting in breathless anticipation for unknown assailants, my mind raced with possible counter measures. Having a guard on their side put me at a distinct and possibly insurmountable disadvantage.

In the still of night, every sound was magnified and so I heard the oncoming gentle padding of stealthily moving feet. Eventually, they stopped in front of my cell. I heard the door open and bodies rush in. Then I realized something. The doors had two kinds of locking mechanisms. A key lock and a sliding metal deadbolt on the outside. It was primitive but very reassuring for the guards to see the deadbolts engaged as they walked up and down the hallway.

Making up my mind quickly, I raced back toward my cell. The glimmering of a flashlight guided me and I heard frustrated and confused voices. Panting, I reached the door and slammed it shut engaging the deadbolt with a loud clang. Angry howling from within greeted me. I slid the metal peephole open and made out three skinheads and one flashlight.

I said, "Hi, Samuel."

He snarled at me. "You're going to get yours, asshole. It's just a matter of time."

I closed the peephole and sat on the ground, my heart pounding, trying to decide what to do next while they banged on the door and cursed. I didn't have many options so I curled up in a ball and waited until morning.

At 6:00 a.m., Keith nudged me with his night stick. I looked up and said, "Good morning, officer."

He shook his head. "Why do I get the feeling this is going to mean a whole lot more paperwork for me."

"I didn't do anything."

He chuckled. "I had no idea how much of a pain in the ass one little white doctor could be. Turn face down and hands behind your back."

He cuffed me and helped me to my feet. "So, if you're out here, Doctor, who is in there?"

"Take a look."

He did and his jaw dropped. Suddenly excited, he exclaimed, "Shit! How the fuck…? Cesari, get on the floor, back against the wall. Now!"

I did as I was told, and he got on his walkie-talkie, calling the alarm in to the main guardhouse. Through the peephole he shouted. "Okay, you three assholes. Get on your knees facing away and hands behind your heads. Do it now! The one closest to me. Back up slowly, sit your ass down and put your hands through the hole. Don't anybody say anything or move or I'll fill the room with tear gas."

Within seconds, guards filled the hallway to assist him. There was going to be hell to pay for sure. After the commotion settled down, Keith handed me my civilian clothes and I changed right there in the hallway. He questioned me about what happened, clearly intrigued by my narrow escape.

"Fuck, Doc, you got to be the luckiest son of a bitch I ever heard of. Look, this is a major breach so you're going to have to tell the story to the commanding officer, maybe even the warden. This isn't going to sail as just another unfortunate incident."

I grabbed a cup of coffee from a machine, choked it down and at 8:00 a.m. found myself sitting in the warden's office. I was in my jeans, short-sleeved cotton shirt, and loafers. I was no longer Prisoner 90157, at least not until 7:00 a.m. next Saturday.

At 8:15 a.m., the door opened and the warden entered. Short brown hair in a bob, maybe forty years old, Lucinda Maria Teresa Lopez was New York State's first Hispanic female warden. She was fit, lithe, probably ex-military, and very attractive. She wore a business-like, navy-blue pantsuit and matching flats. The slightest hint of makeup and tiny gold stud earrings were the only nod to her femininity. I started to stand and she waved me back down as she took a seat behind her desk. Shuffling through her papers, she eventually came across what she was looking for.

She said, "I'll be with you in a minute, Doctor."

"Thank you."

She looked up. "For what?"

"Calling me doctor and not Prisoner 90157."

She gave me the slightest grin and looked back down at her papers. Two minutes later she tucked them away and said, "So, what did I do in my previous life to deserve you?"

I smiled. "I really haven't been trying to cause you any trouble."

"Which is why I'm so upset. God only knows what you'd be capable of if you put your mind to it. Now tell me what happened from the minute you arrived Saturday morning and don't leave anything out."

It didn't take that long. She listened attentively, hands clasped. When I was done she let out a deep breath. "I read your file and think this is ridiculous that the judge ordered you to stay here all weekend. What did you do? Knock up his daughter or something? Don't answer that. It doesn't matter. I don't care. I can't have a doctor getting murdered in my jail while he's doing community service. We already have one of the worst reputations in the country and last night proves that we've got some serious internal problems to deal with. I'm going to call that judge today and let him know that from now on when you finish your clinic you're going home."

"Can you do that?"

Her face reddened. "This is my jail. I can do whatever I want. If I say you're out then you're out. We're dangerously overcrowded as it is and need the space. Besides, your presence is becoming disruptive, and that is something I will not allow."

"But he's a judge."

"He's an asshole and can suck my tit."

Definitely ex-military.

"Now, I hope that you will consider this act of generosity on my part as an apology for your recent negative experiences here at Riker's. I would appreciate it if you would refrain from repeating recent events to anyone outside this room including and especially the press."

"I can do that."

"Good. If you can do that then I'll see if I can refrain from charging you with assaulting three of my prisoners, one of whom is undergoing facial surgery as we speak. Do we have an understanding?"

"Totally, and blue is definitely your color."

"Are you flirting with me, 90157?"

"Me? Never. That would be presumptuous."

She curled her lip. "Just so you know, I eat guys like you for breakfast."

I chuckled. "What a way to go."

She shook her head in exasperation and then pressed the intercom button on her desk. "Sergeant, would you please escort this asshole out to the parking lot?"

"Yes, ma'am."

She turned back to me. "You have a nice day, Doctor."

I think she liked me.

Chapter 6

*U*mberto's Clam House sat in the middle of Mulberry Street between Broome and Grand in the heart of Manhattan's historic Little Italy. With its iconic blue awning casting shade over outdoor diners sitting at small white tables adorned with matching blue tablecloths, Umberto's set itself apart from the other restaurants that bathed themselves in the red, white, and green of the Italian flag. I had arrived a few minutes early, ordered a bottle of Lambrusco and parked myself just outside the entrance facing the sidewalk at a table for two. It was sunny and warm and the busy street overflowed with pretty girls in shorts and summer dresses, including Dr. Gottlieb who, at five feet six inches tall, with long brown hair and high heels, stood out as striking amidst a sea teeming with attractive sights.

I stood and extended my hand. "Hi, Pam."

She ignored that and planted a kiss on my cheek, European style, and in addition pressed herself into me, American style, just enough to remind me why women ran the planet. She smiled revealing beautiful teeth and full lips. "Hi, John."

Distracted ever so slightly, my eyes lingered just a little too long on her and she noticed. We sat down and I poured her a glass of wine. Clinking our glasses, I said, "Before we begin, Pam, I want you to know how sincerely grateful I am for your help."

40

"You're very welcome and I wish I could take credit but it was your introductory letter that did all the work."

"Well, I think you're being modest. In this world, it's usually who you know rather than what you know."

She nodded. "Unfortunately, that is more often the case than not. I must say you look well, despite everything."

"Well, I'm a glass half-full kind of guy."

She smiled as our waiter approached with menus. Pam ordered a salad with grilled salmon and I ordered fried calamari, chicken parmigiana with spaghetti, and an order of garlic bread. I hadn't eaten since noon yesterday and was ravenous.

She raised her eyebrows and grinned. "Are you sure that will be enough?"

"You're right." I called the waiter back and added an order of clams casino.

She laughed. "I see you haven't changed much. I still remember having lunch with you about a year ago and the waitress asked if you wanted anything else after we finished and you asked for another cheeseburger."

I smiled. "I'm still growing into my skin."

"Well, you don't seem none the worse for your—shall we say daring—diet. In fact, you look like you must be still working out regularly."

"Thanks, I try to stay in shape but it's mostly stress these days that keeps the weight off."

Curiosity got the better of her and she asked, "So, what's prison like?"

I sipped my wine. Light and crisp with just a little fizz, the way a good Lambrusco should be. It was a perfect summer wine. I don't know why so many people looked down at it. I said, "Well, I'm not really in prison. I'm doing community service at Riker's Island on the weekends."

"Yes, but you have to stay overnight there don't you? In a cell?"

"I did, yes, but that's going to change. They're probably going to let me start going home after clinic, beginning next weekend. I'm afraid there just isn't enough room at the inn for me. But to answer your question about what prison is like. Let's just say that the experience should be avoided at all costs."

She nodded soberly. "Are the prisoners more or less agreeable? The ones who come for treatment, I mean."

I thought about Duane. "Some got bad attitudes but most are just trying to survive."

She looked around. "It gets pretty crowded around here in summer time. Doesn't it?"

"In winter time, too. In fact, all the time. I used to live in a studio apartment just above that restaurant on the corner over there."

She turned to look in that direction. "Above the Grotto Azzurra restaurant?"

"Yeah, pretty famous place. Old blue eyes himself used to hang out there."

"Frank Sinatra?"

"The chairman of the board himself."

"How cool is that?"

"There are a lot of famous places down here. In fact, Umberto's is pretty notorious as well. A famous mobster, Crazy Joe Gallo, was murdered inside while celebrating his birthday."

"Really?"

"Yeah, right in the middle of his lobster fra diavolo, four hit men walked in and fired twenty rounds into him at close range. He was a tough son-of-a-bitch and managed to stagger out to the sidewalk before he collapsed, but that was a long time ago. We should be fine today."

Our lunch came and we started eating. Pam asked, "I hope you don't mind my asking, but are you in a relationship right now?"

"I don't mind at all. Yes, I'm engaged to be married."

She looked surprised. "Really?"

I swallowed a bite of chicken parm and chuckled. "You say that a lot."

"What?"

"Really."

"Well, you're surprising me a lot today. You're getting married was the last thing I expected to hear."

"Why does that surprise you?"

Laughing she said, "I apologize but you never struck me as the marrying kind."

"What did I strike you as?"

"You just seemed sort of a free spirit, not the settle-down-with-one-woman, two-point-one kids, one-car garage kind of guy."

Spearing a couple of rings of calamari with my fork, I said, "Well, I fool a lot of people like that."

"I bet. Well, congratulations. Who's the lucky girl?"

"Her name is Kelly and I believe you met her once."

"Kelly—I remember her. She's an OR nurse at your hospital, right?"

"Very good, Pam, but what has this got to do with anything."

"Just catching up. So, when is the wedding?"

"Just as soon as her divorce is finalized."

Putting her wine glass down, she looked at me quizzically. "Excuse me, did I hear right? She's married?"

"Yes, but she's filing for divorce so we can get married. It may take a while though because he's sure to contest it." I picked up a clam and scooped out its contents.

"Did she leave him? Is she living with you? How does something like this work?" she was suddenly animated, her interest now thoroughly piqued. Women thrived on this kind of stuff.

"No, she hasn't left him. It's complicated. In fact, we can't see each other at all because her husband obtained a restraining order against me. I'm a convicted felon and if I go near her or the children I could be arrested and she might lose custody of them."

"She has children?" Pam was so astonished she stopped eating and sat back.

"Twin girls. A year and a half old. Totally adorable. Their names are Beatrice and Gwendolyn."

Pam quietly contemplated the information.

I asked, "What are you thinking?"

"Can I be honest?"

"Sure."

"I mean really honest."

"Fire away."

"This sounds like one of the unhealthiest relationships I've ever heard of, fraught with risks for all involved. What kind of commitment do you have from Kelly? I mean how do you know she will follow through if you can't see her?"

I hesitated. The thought of her not following through had never entered my mind. "She'll follow through," I said, but once doubt entered the equation it permeated my expressions and my voice.

Sensing that, she added, "John, are you sure that you're really engaged or is this something you want so badly you're not willing to accept reality?"

Apparently, lunch had turned into a full-blown shrink session. "Thanks for the free psychoanalysis, but I thought we were going to talk about my potential faculty position."

She seemed surprised at my pushback. "That's exactly what we are doing. These are the kinds of things the faculty are going to ask you about. There is nothing off limits to these guys including your past, your present, your sexual orientation, and most importantly of all, your political leanings."

"Seriously?"

"Welcome to academia."

I took another slug of wine. "All right, fine. Geez, I thought questions like that were unlawful."

"They are in the real world."

I chuckled. "Please continue."

"Well, as long as the cat's out of the bag. Brace yourself. There are five other members on the committee you are going to meet today, three men and two women. Two of the men are openly gay and the third is bisexual and extremely proud of it. One of the women is a motorcycle racing, whiskey drinking, sailor-type dyke, who will probably challenge you to an arm-wrestling contest minutes after she meets you, and the other woman is a relic of the sixties. She doesn't believe in makeup, deodorant, shaving her legs, or letting men open doors for her. She thinks women's rights means that if you compliment her on her appearance you should be fired, arrested or at the very least, water-boarded."

I sat back in my chair. "I can't wait."

"Just don't lose your temper. Take everything with a grain of salt and remember that most academics associate exclusively with other academics. They have no idea how eccentric they are."

"How come you seem so normal?"

She smiled. "Thanks, I appreciate that and I hope that I really am. If one out of six NYU faculty members approaches what the lay population would describe as normal then we're batting a sixteen percent normalcy rate. That's not very good, but probably better than Harvard."

Smiling, I said, "So if I make the team that will increase your normalcy rate to two out of seven." I did some quick math in my head. "That's almost thirty percent."

"Or maybe you'll drop us down to one out of seven."

She was killing me. "I knew you were fun."

Becoming serious, she said, "You know, John, at one point last year I really thought you and I might have had some serious fun together."

I cleared my throat, but didn't say anything, and she suddenly looked uncomfortable, turning away in embarrassment. She said, "I'm sorry. That was inappropriate, to say the least. Please forgive me. I never could handle alcohol."

"You only had half a glass, Pam."

She giggled. "You're not going to let me off the hook, are you?"

"What hook? I thought you were preparing me for the committee. You know, just in case one of them propositions me."

"I didn't proposition you."

"You say tomato…"

"Oh, shut up."

I said, "By the way, you look great. I would have said that when you arrived but I didn't want to be inappropriate. However, since you broke the ice on that score…"

She blushed. "Thank you. Can we just pretend that I didn't breach protocol?"

I shook my head. "I'm afraid it doesn't work that way, Pam. Once protocol has been breached, it stays breached. Besides, what difference does it make if you say inappropriate things to me or if your faculty friends say inappropriate things to me?"

She hesitated, pursed her lips and said, "Touché."

"So there. I remain the victim of your sexual harassment. I demand an inquiry after lunch."

She found me very amusing and smiled. "Maybe I was wrong about you. You may fit in much better with the faculty than I would have guessed, but do yourself a favor. At all costs, steer clear of politics. They are all uber left and there isn't one of them who doesn't think they could run the country better than any elected politician."

"What makes you think I'm any different?"

She grinned. "You've been warned." Then looking at her watch, said, "We should get a move on. I'll fill you in more while we walk."

I paid the bill and we strolled to NYU together.

Chapter 7

We entered the NYU Steinhardt building on West 4th Street next to Washington Square Park in Greenwich Village just after 2:00 p.m. Pam looked mildly concerned when she didn't see a security guard in the lobby, but went ahead and signed us into a book sitting on the desk.

Walking toward the elevators, she remarked, "Maybe the guard needed to use the restroom."

I shrugged. "The building should be safe for the five minutes it takes him. This isn't the U.S. embassy in Beirut."

She agreed and we boarded the elevator to the sixth floor. Arriving at our destination, we were greeted by a mob of hysterical people, mostly students. Many were crying and hugging each other. Pam glanced at me suddenly apprehensive.

She tapped a girl on the shoulder and asked, "What's happened?"

The young brunette turned to us. Her eyes were puffy and red. "They found a student in one of the recording rooms. He may have overdosed."

We plowed through the crowd until we came to the room in question. It was maybe twenty feet by twenty feet and jammed with speakers and recording equipment. There was a young man lying face up in the center of the floor unconscious or dead with a security guard kneeling beside him. Several older men and women stood nearby anxiously. I surmised they were the faculty I was scheduled to meet. One of the men saw Pam and gestured to her, shaking his head. They all looked despondent. Ignoring them, I knelt down next to the student, across from the guard.

"I'm a physician. Tell me what you know," I said as I straightened the kid's legs and felt for a pulse.

"I just got here a minute ago. One of the other students found him and called downstairs. I came right away and called an ambulance, but he doesn't look too good."

He was right about that. The kid's lips were blue and skin color was pasty white but I detected a weak, thready, carotid pulse. I leaned in close with my face next to his and felt shallow respirations—barely. Lifting up his eyelids, I saw that his pupils were constricted. I checked his arms for needle marks but found none.

"Any drugs or paraphernalia lying around?"

"Haven't really had a chance to look."

I opened the kid's shirt, balled my right hand into a fist and rubbed my knuckles up and down his sternum. No response so I tried it again. Nothing.

"Everybody stand back." I said loudly and turned to Luther. "Do you know how to do CPR?"

He nodded yes.

"Okay, all this kid needs is oxygen. I'll start rescue breathing and will do it for as long as I can. Then you relieve me, okay?"

He nodded.

I arched the kid's head back, pinched his nose and prayed that he wasn't HIV positive as I delivered mouth-to-mouth resuscitation. Rotating with the security guard we delivered mouth to mouth for a solid fifteen minutes before city EMTs and police came crashing into the room to take over. They intubated him, hoisted him onto a stretcher and carted him away as the police took statements. I listened carefully. The student who found him initially said he came to the room to test out the sound equipment and saw him lying there at just about two o'clock, maybe a few minutes before. He called down to the guard almost immediately who responded within minutes and called 911. That was just about when Pam and I arrived. It sounded reasonable.

I turned to Pam, who stood toward the back of the room with her colleagues. She'd been crying and when I came close she put her arms around me, hugging me tightly.

"Is he going to be all right?"

The others came close and one patted me on the back. I said, "I can't be sure. It depends on what he took and how long he was lying there like that. I'm sorry."

A stocky woman with a crew cut, wearing a flannel shirt and jeans said in a rumbling voice, "You done good there, fella. You got good instincts. We were all just standing around pulling pud and then you came along. Good job. The name is Shawn Potter but everyone calls me Knuckles on account of I like to box bare fisted. As you can imagine it's a little hard to find sparring partners so if you're interested, let me know. I'm an associate professor in Women's Studies."

She extended her hand and I reluctantly disengaged from the warmth of Pam's embrace to grasp it. Her grip was firm and she squeezed my hand just a little too long and hard, as if testing my strength. We went around the group making introductions and then moved into a small conference room.

Understandably, it took a few minutes for everyone to get over the shock of what had just happened. They were just as Pam had described, almost caricatures of real people.

The two gay guys weren't just gay; they were way over the top. One wore a feather boa and the other wore leather pants and a flowered Tommy Bahama shirt unbuttoned to the waist. They were both married to two other guys, but from the way they were eyeing each other I got the feeling that they were more than just buds. They were Stan and Bob and they seemed genuinely nice. They were tenured professors in anthropology and political science, respectively. Bob had a beard. Not an ordinary beard mind you, but a perfectly manicured beard that came to a point at his chin and sported streaks of purple and blue. The last guy wore a three-piece gray suit with a handkerchief in the breast pocket and a red carnation pinned to the lapel. You don't see that much except at weddings and funerals. He sucked on an electronic cigarette as he studied me, apparently fascinated. He wore a wedding ring and his name was Todd. Todd was chairman of NYU's drama department at the prestigious Tisch School of the Arts. Maybe he had a right to be an asshole.

Last but not least was Liz. Maybe five feet one inch tall in heels, she had refused to acknowledge me until Pam had forced the issue by shoving her toward me. Her hair was short, brown, and unkempt. She was thin and wore mannish black-framed glasses, a tie-dyed T-shirt with a peace sign on the front, no bra, and faded blue jeans. She seemed very introverted, hostile, and likely to duck under the table at the first loud sound. In my considered opinion, she had more anxiety in her little finger than most of the psychiatric wards in Manhattan. She taught a course called the Art of Self Confidence for Modern Women. Pam had her hands full with this crowd.

It took me about five minutes to decide that I liked Knuckles the best. She started the questioning. "So, do you get horny when you're locked up?"

"I'm only in prison for two days a week."

"Still, I don't know if I'd last that long."

I tried not to laugh. "I manage to keep it in check."

She seemed to have a hard time wrapping her head around that. Todd decided to man up. "Studies have shown that prison life proves beyond any doubt that most of us at our core are bisexual. All it takes is the slightest of environmental provocations to bring it out."

Hmm. I needed the job so I decided to take the low road. "You may be right about that although I've never read those studies you speak of. Maybe you could show them to me some time."

Mistake.

He smiled. "I'd love to. Do you like sherry?" The twinks giggled. Pam cleared her throat. It was time to get down to business.

She said, "You've all had a chance to review Dr. Cesari's course outline and resumé. I think we are all in agreement that his personal experience and background are sufficient credentialing for a course such as this. I have discussed it with the registrar's office and they are willing to accept it as an interdisciplinary seminar under the general auspices of the social sciences department. We need to decide on a grading system and a volunteer to co-teach the course with him. Any ideas or volunteers?"

I raised my hand. She said, "You don't have to raise your hand, John."

"This is supposed to be a mellow course, right? So rather than have exams, I thought that maybe we could have the students write one or two-page position papers discussing that week's content. For example, suppose we discuss general health issues such as hypertension, diabetes, coronary artery disease, and screening guidelines for adults. Their assignment could be to write a brief paper on the current thoughts for management of high blood pressure or perhaps what the recommendations are for screening mammography and colonoscopy."

Knuckles said, "I like that." Stan and Bob agreed. Everyone nodded their approval.

I added. "I also think the course should be pass-fail. We'll probably attract more students that way and since we only have two weeks until the fall semester, we want to make the offering as appealing as possible."

Pam nodded. "I agree. How many days a week did you envision the class requiring?"

"I thought a two-hour seminar late afternoon, maybe three to five, once a week, would be best. Since it's an odd kind of course, I think it will be attractive to juniors and seniors looking to fulfill last-minute credit requirements for graduation. I'd like to make it as convenient as possible for them."

She smiled. "You have a knack for this sort of thing, John."

"Thanks. Now if only I had a knack for staying out of trouble."

Stan said, "If only that were true for all of us."

Knuckles added, "On the other hand, if you hadn't gotten in trouble, I doubt that we would have had the pleasure of meeting you."

I scanned around the table and felt it was time to address the elephant in the room. "So none of you have a problem with me being a felon?"

They all laughed at once. Everyone but Liz, that is. Todd said, "Heavens no. We love the idea of a big, dangerous brute on the faculty. Gives us street creds."

I smiled.

Pam corrected him. "Well, he's not actually on the faculty. His status is college affiliated, which is a euphemism for everyone will be keeping an eye on you, John."

I looked at her. "Do I get paid?"

"Yes, of course."

"Then I don't care what you call it."

She grinned, "There is a stipend pending approval, but that's just a formality. If the course is a success then we can opt to continue it in the spring. By the way, you also get a ten percent meal discount in the cafeteria and access to the gymnasium."

Liz who had been fidgeting quietly, said, "I did some research. This is the first time, not only in the history of NYU, but in the history of every major university I could find that a convicted felon actively serving jail time has ever been contracted to teach."

I tilted my head to see if I could make eye contact and she turned away. I said drolly, "Lucky you."

Still looking away she said, "Not if you commit a crime while you're here. Then we'll be the laughing stock of the city or worse, the subject of litigation."

Knuckles jumped in, "Oh please, Liz. Look at him. He wouldn't hurt a fly. Stop being paranoid, will you? For crying out loud, he just saved a student's life right before your eyes while you were shaking like a bowl of jelly. Never mind her, Doc, she has a pathological fear of men. She had to take an extra Valium just to meet you today."

I said, "I never would have noticed."

Liz turned to Knuckles clearly irritated. "Don't swing it around if you don't got it, sister."

Pam said, "Okay, ladies, I think we all got it. It'll be fine, Liz. Dr. Cesari has no intention of committing any crime. Besides, the crime he was convicted of was—well—more of a miscommunication than anything else."

Liz was indignant and had turned to stare at the far wall. "He lied to a federal investigator. Men always lie. That's the problem. They're animals."

Stan and Bob had enough. "Women lie too, Liz."

Todd concurred. "Men lie, women lie, we all lie. We're all pretending to be someone other than who we really are." He raised his eyebrows at me and concluded his statement by blowing a puff of water vapor in Liz's direction.

I admired his insight.

Knuckles said, "Fuck all this pansy-assed bullshit. I like him and I vote yea."

I whispered to Pam, "We're taking a vote?"

She smiled and leaned close to me. "She's speaking metaphorically. We've already agreed. You're watching NYU's finest in action."

I chuckled as Stan, Bob, Todd, and Pam raised their hands and said, "Yea."

After a moment, all eyes on the back of her head, Liz raised her tiny hand and reluctantly murmured, "Yea." I was sure she was rolling her eyes.

I looked at them.

"Yay!"

Chapter 8

*A*fter the meeting, Pam and I found ourselves alone in the small conference room. She said, "Go ahead. I'm sure you'd like to say something."

I smiled. "Well, that was interesting."

She chuckled. "I told you. It's a whole different world here."

"I get it."

"Do you?"

"I think so."

"Good. Then I'll push the paperwork through and we'll word of mouth the course to students. I think if you get at least three to five enrolled you'll be doing well. There's always a few scrambling around to fit extra credits in. By the way you'll need to come up with a text book you would like to use. There won't be any time for the university bookstore to obtain it, but the sooner you make it known the better, so the kids can get it online."

"It will be my highest priority and once again thank you. I think it will be a lot of fun. By the way, we never settled the question of who is going to co-teach the class with me."

Grinning from ear to ear she said, "Oh, I thought it was obvious. I volunteered."

I smiled. "This meeting really was a formality, wasn't it?"

"Mostly. You saw who I have to work with. I think it's good for them to get out and meet real people from time to time." She suddenly became serious. "I wonder how that student is doing."

"We can go check on him if you want. On the way out, we can ask the guard where they took him."

"You mean for us to actually go visit him in the hospital?"

"Sure, why not? I'm not doing anything and I'm kind of curious, too."

She thought it over. "Sure."

As she led the way to the elevator I couldn't help but study her figure. She had great legs and ass but it was her breasts I found terribly distracting. They were at least a 34D, maybe D and a half or even double D. I bit my lip and stared at the elevator buttons. Being engaged was going to be more difficult than I thought and I fought the urge to be my usual self as we descended to the main floor. She must have noticed my reticence and asked innocently, "Are you all right?"

I looked at her. "Couldn't be better."

Pam persisted and I wondered if she was taunting me. "You don't seem right. You look as if you're having some internal quarrel."

"Well, I haven't had any alcohol since lunch and my body might be rebelling against such austerity."

She smiled and looked at her watch. "It's almost four. How about we go see the student and step out for a drink afterward?"

I smiled. "As long as you promise to keep it professional."

Cocking her head slightly and grinning, she said, "I think I can handle that."

We waved to the guard and as Pam signed us out, I asked him, "Can you tell us which hospital they took that kid to?"

"They took him to St. Matt's on Third Avenue. It's the nearest hospital. Hope he's okay."

"Me too. We're going to check on him. I'll let you know."

"Thanks."

As we turned to leave, I hesitated and turned back to him. "Say, does everybody have to sign in?"

He nodded. "And sign out."

"Is it possible for you to tell me when that kid signed in? I was wondering how long he might have been up there."

"I don't see why not." He picked up the sign-in book and turned a few pages until he found the signature he was looking for. "He signed in last night at 10:00 p.m."

I was surprised. "He signed in last night? Is that normal? I mean for a student to be here all night?" It hadn't even occurred to me that the building would be open twenty-four hours.

"Normal's a funny word around here, Doc. But yeah, you're right. All night would be a little unusual but not that much. Kids keep funny hours, especially the artistic ones."

"Is there a security guard here all night as well?"

"Of course."

I nodded trying to piece it together. Something didn't add up.

Pam nudged me. "What are you thinking about?"

"I don't know." We said goodbye to the guard and left the building, deciding to walk to the hospital rather than take a cab. It was just a few blocks away.

"Pam, does that make sense to you? That a student would sign in to use the building's recording equipment at ten o'clock at night and no one would check in on him until two in the afternoon the next day?"

"Well, if you put it that way, it does seem odd. What are you getting at?"

"I don't know. I just don't like it when something should be simple but isn't."

"Maybe you're making it more complicated than it needs to be. Kids overdose all the time."

She was right about that. It was a sad reality of modern times. I said, "Still, I wonder if there was anyone else in the building with him last night. We should have asked. There was the guard on duty, of course, but he would have stayed in the lobby, wouldn't he? Or would he have wandered up there just to make sure everything was all right?"

"Good questions, although I'm not sure where you're going with all this."

"I'm not sure where I'm going with it either. Remember, you're talking to a felon."

We walked and talked like that until we arrived at the hospital's front entrance, found the elevators, and headed up to the ICU. A nurse buzzed us through the electronic doors and we asked to see the student. Pam had found out that his name was Justin Delrosa, and he was a twenty-two-year-old grad student from upstate New York studying audio engineering and advanced classical piano.

His nurse recognized me. "Hi, Dr. Cesari. It's good to see you. I'm so sorry to hear about all your problems."

"Thank you, Regina. I appreciate that. How is the NYU student that was brought in?"

She frowned. "Not good. He's still intubated. His vitals are rock stable, and he's oxygenating well but hasn't responded at all to Narcan or gastric lavage. His toxicology screen was negative. The initial report from the ER is that his head CT is negative also and we're waiting for the neurology consult to see him. The intensivist managing him here in the ICU said that he's very worried about his lack of responsiveness this many hours after an OD. The family has been notified and they're on the way from Buffalo. It's so sad. I guess they didn't get to him in time. The odd thing is that not only is his tox screen negative for narcotics, but we couldn't find any track marks on him. I suppose he could have ingested or smoked some new type of poison that's just starting to hit the streets. Why are these kids so stupid?"

Damn.

Pam gasped and clutched my hand. I said, "Regina, can we see him?"

"Sure, he's in room six. There's a friend of his in there now but I don't think he'll mind. How do you know him?"

"Pam here teaches at NYU and we were there earlier when they found him."

She turned to Pam. "I'm sorry."

Pam replied, "Thank you."

We walked into the room and were greeted by the sights and sounds of modern medicine; the rhythmic hissing of mechanical ventilation, the beeping of his cardiac monitor and the monotonous drone of cable news from a mounted television in one corner of the ceiling, just in case he was listening. A large man faced away from us, looking down at Justin as he lay there motionless. Except for all the tubes coming out of him, he appeared to be having a restful sleep. He looked like a nice kid. Clean cut, short brown hair, thin build. His parents were surely going to lose it when they arrived.

I cleared my throat to announce our arrival and the guy staring at Justin swung around abruptly. Pam and I stepped back in surprise. He was at least twice Justin's age, unkempt beard and hair, wearing a dirty T-shirt underneath a jean jacket.

I said, "Hello, we were at the scene when they found Justin. I understand you're a friend of his. My name is John Cesari."

I proffered my hand and he just looked at it and then at me through icy, suspicious eyes, and then brazenly ogled Pam, checking her out from top to bottom.

He said, "Yeah, sure. I was just leaving."

As he turned and walked quickly past us I noticed something peculiar but couldn't quite place it.

After he left, Pam said, "That was odd."

"To say the least. Well, this is what a typical ICU looks like and tomorrow it will be filled with the sounds of distraught parents."

Pam sniffled and buried her face in her hands. I didn't mean to be unsympathetic but I was preoccupied with the guy who just left and then it clicked in my head what bugged me about him. He had a spider web tattoo that crept up past the neckline of his shirt. It reminded me of the ones I had seen on those jerks at Riker's Island. Spider webs must be all the rage these days.

I put my arm around Pam to console her. She stammered but the words wouldn't come out. I said reassuringly, "He's young and healthy and things can look really bad before they start to turn around. It's too early to think the worst."

She sighed. "This is so awful."

"Yes, it is. Maybe coming here wasn't such a good idea after all."

"No, I'm glad we came. Who knows? Maybe he can sense we're here to support him."

I nodded. "You're right about that. You never know. That's why they keep the TV on."

We stayed for a few more minutes and then took a cab over to The Mercer Kitchen on Prince Street for a much-needed drink. The Mercer Kitchen was an upscale restaurant in the Village that was dark, cool and very avant-garde. There was lots of wood and leather. We sat at the bar and I ordered a 25 year old Macallan neat, ice on the side. Pam ordered a Hendricks gin martini, dirty with two olives. In a place like this, I figured I was already in for close to a hundred bucks.

I studied her profile as she sat cross-legged next to me admiring the wall coverings and room furnishings. She was in her mid-thirties, never married, Ph.D. in psychology and tenured professor at NYU. In addition, she was a babe. Light brown, shoulder-length hair, big eyes, high cheek bones, and full lips, she could have been a model. She was letting me get a full view while she pretended to be interested in a row of bourbons. I loved this game of cat and mouse that men and women played, and wouldn't have it any other way.

I caught her eyes in the mirror behind the bar watching me watch her and she smiled. Our drinks came and we settled down. She looked like she was trying to get something off her chest.

Finally, she said, "I don't know—I just feel like hugging you right now."

I swept the room with my eyes and said, "There's no one here, so go ahead."

She laughed. The room was packed and we just barely managed to get the last two bar stools. With her leg extended, she gently tapped me with the tip of her shoe. "My apartment isn't that far from here and I have scotch."

I swirled my Macallan, looked at it and took a sip enjoying its smooth, rich texture. So there it was for all the world to see. When I was in school an older friend had once counseled me. *John, he said. Men and women can never be friends. It's all about sex. Don't ever kid yourself about that. It's hardwired in our brains that way. So why do they get married? I asked. Because women got the bigger brains.*

Our eyes met. I said, "Um, Doctor?"

She smiled broadly. "Yes, Doctor."

"If memory serves me correctly I believe that I may have mentioned that I am engaged."

"Yes, you did and I truly believe that you believe you are. But to clear the air I was not suggesting any change in our status. It's just that it's been a long, stressful day and I'd rather sit on a comfortable sofa than an uncomfortable bar stool for the next two hours."

I thought it over. "So no change in status? Just friends?"

"Of course. We have to maintain professional standards if we're going to work together effectively."

"Do you have food?"

She grinned. "My home is made almost entirely of ginger bread and candy. You can literally eat the furniture."

That made me laugh. I always liked the story of Hansel and Gretel. This was a new form of psychological warfare I wasn't used to. I had to admit she had game. I said, "Well, if I'm Hansel, then that would make you the witch, but you don't look like a witch."

"That's why we're so dangerous. We're very tricky so don't get too close to the oven."

I was going to have to remember that.

Chapter 9

*T*wo hours later, we lay on her sofa, tangled in each other's arms. A half empty bottle of Johnnie Walker Blue sat on the coffee table nearby. Lying on top of me, her long hair fell down around us like a canopy of fragrant silk. Our lips were locked and her tongue was deep inside my mouth probing and searching for something. My hands gently caressed her butt and I was debating whether to reach under her skirt. We had been going at it strong ever since the third glass of scotch, and I could feel her heart pounding next to mine. Her excitement was palpable. When she finally came up for air, I said, "That's the last time I fall for the old gingerbread-and-candy house routine."

Her eyes were glazed and hungry. She whispered hoarsely, "By the time I'm done with you, you're going to beg me to put you out of your misery."

"But, I'm engaged," I whimpered.

"Oh please…"

"You don't understand."

"I understand that you're whining like a little girl." She grabbed my head and looked deeply into my eyes.

"What are you doing?" I asked.

"I'm trying to see if there's a man in there somewhere."

"That's not fair." I objected.

Her response was to wiggle her tongue into my mouth again. When she was done, she said, "Tell you what. Why don't you call your little cupcake and tell her you'll be right over... Oh, wait a minute, you can't do that because she'll have you arrested." She thought she was real funny and giggled. "You know, as a trained psychologist, I've heard some good ones before but I've rarely heard a story quite as delusional as yours. I almost feel like writing it up for one of the medical journals as a case study. Hey, I have an idea! Can I bring you to one of the psychology conferences so they can interview you? I'd like to show you off. There's free food."

"I think you're drunk, doctor."

"I know I'm drunk—and horny." With that said she slid a hand down and grabbed my crotch. "Well, well, well, what do we have here? Is this that famous Italian sausage I've heard so much about or is it just a little wiener?"

I flinched and chuckled. "That's it. No more scotch for you. Look, I didn't say I wasn't attracted to you. It's just that, how can I be sure you'll respect me in the morning? Women are always calling me names like man-whore."

She started laughing out loud so hard she almost slid off me onto the floor. "I promise not to call you a man-whore, okay?"

"Or hound dog or slut."

Still chuckling, she said, "I didn't know guineas were so sensitive about their reputations."

I shook my head and grinned. "Well, we are and that was very racist."

She thought it over but didn't apologize. "How about Casanova? That's pretty harmless and since he was the most famous Italian man-whore in history, you might even take pride in it."

I snorted but couldn't come up with an adequate response. That was the problem when you argued with smart women. "Casanova's okay, I guess."

She was on a roll and sensed an opening. "Look, I don't know what turnip truck you fell off but if you want to go back to your imaginary fiancée in the morning, that's perfectly fine with me just as long as you take care of business right here and now because I can't even begin to tell you how long it's been for me." To emphasize the point, she pressed herself into me even harder, grinding her hips and sticking her tongue in my ear.

My desire for her overwhelmed me. She was driving me crazy and I was ready to explode. I let out a deep breath and went all in. "I can't take it anymore. Here or in the bedroom. Clothes on, clothes off, I don't care."

She smiled and ordered, "Pull down your pants and let me see what you got. I'm pretty thirsty."

She and I both frantically yanked my trousers off. Then she got on her knees beside the sofa grabbed her scotch glass off the coffee table and chugged the remains down. Our excitement was almost at critical mass when her cellphone rang. She ignored it as she unbuttoned my shirt while I caressed her breasts through her blouse. Her phone started ringing again and she again ignored it. I kissed her and said, "Maybe it's important."

Her face was flushed and she could barely breathe. "It can wait. Oh my, look at you. Yum." She ran her hands over my chest as I unbuttoned her top, staring at her cleavage. I waited eagerly for what I was sure was going to be the experience of a lifetime.

She looked down at Mr. Happy who was showing off what he was capable of and playfully flicked him with her index finger. Smiling, she leaned in for a closer inspection, whispering softly, "Lean back and don't say another word."

Just as she was starting, the phone rang insistently for the third time. Annoyed and muttering under her breath in frustration, she reached into her bag on the floor nearby. I lay there awkwardly in anticipation.

"Knuckles, what is it and make it quick!"

She listened and her features changed from irritated to consternation. "Oh my God. I can't believe it. We just saw him. They told us everything was stable."

Silently listening, her eyes grew wide as she looked at me. "John? He's here with me…That's none of your business what we're doing. Yes, I'll put him on."

She handed me the phone and said, "It's Knuckles. The student died this afternoon. She'd like to talk to you."

I sat up, taking the phone from her. "Hello."

"Man, Doc, you're good. You bagged Pam and classes haven't even started yet. I had a bet with the twinks that she'd at least hold out until mid-terms."

I cleared my throat. "I'm not sure what you're talking about. I'm engaged. What's going on? The student died?"

"Yeah, the kid died suddenly a few hours ago. They're not sure why. It's a mess. The family was in transit and no one had a chance to call them. When they got here, he was already in the morgue. Because he was just brought in today, he was still a police matter so the staff had to call five-o to let them know what happened. The nurse who spoke to them happened to mention that you and Pam were there for a visit. During the course of that conversation it came out that you were a felon serving time at Riker's. This got them itchy in the nether region and now they want to talk to you. I didn't know how to reach you so I called Pam not realizing you two were already getting nasty."

I let that last part slide. "It's 10:00 p.m. When did you find out?"

"Ten minutes ago. It took the New York Pussy Department that long to figure out how to reach one of us. Makes you feel real safe, don't it?"

"Did the police say anything else that I should be concerned about?"

"Not about you per se, but they wanted to know if anybody took anything from the room. When they found the kid at Steinhardt, his backpack was empty and they didn't find any personal effects like a cellphone or a laptop. They said that he didn't even have any apartment keys on him. Look, that's all I got."

"Okay, thanks for the heads up."

"One more thing, Doc."

"What's that?"

"Wear a condom. Pam's a friend. Who knows what you caught over there on the rock."

"I'll be careful."

I handed Pam her phone and slumped back on the sofa. She sat down next to me, tears in her eyes.

"I'm sorry, Pam."

She just nodded. "This is so awful. His poor parents."

She was right about that. There is no greater grief than to lose your child at any age for any reason. We sat there for a few minutes lost in thought. I didn't like the feel of it at all.

"Pam, do you think you can get me that kid's school records in the morning? I'd like to get to know him a little better."

She looked confused. "Probably, but why?"

"I'm curious about what kind of student he was. You know, if there had been any problems or reprimands for misconduct. Something to suggest drug use."

"What does it matter now?"

"I just want to know what happened. A healthy young kid shouldn't have fallen off a cliff like this. There will probably be an autopsy. I'll see if I can find out the results of that. I still have friends in the pathology department."

She smiled. "I can see why you became a physician. You like to get to the bottom of things." She had an interesting way of phrasing things, especially with me being a gastroenterologist, but the mood had shifted dramatically, and this was no time for jokes. I looked down at myself and suddenly felt a little silly sitting there naked. My pride and joy was already at half-mast and sinking fast. She noticed and added wistfully, "I guess we're done for tonight?"

From the moment she answered the phone I knew the answer to that one, but I figured I'd give it the old college try. I glanced at her, cleared my throat and said demurely, "I'm sure with some gentle coaxing we could bring him back to life."

Not a chance.

"I don't know, John. I feel so bad, all I want to do is throw up or something."

Great.

That was a deal killer for sure. Maybe it was for the best. I was engaged, after all. Besides, my mind had just lurched in a different direction. "I understand. Well, I think I'll be going then."

Misunderstanding me, she said, "John, don't be like that."

I smiled and kissed her gently. "I'm not. I'm fine, really, but this whole thing has got me unsettled. There are too many unanswered questions, and I want to go back to the Steinhardt building to talk to the night security guard there."

She looked astonished. "Now? But we're drunk."

Laughing, I said, "Speak for yourself. My liver is doing just fine."

"Well, I'll come with you. You won't even get past the front door without an ID. I'll grab coffee from a Starbucks that's on the way. Put your clothes on while I go splash some water on my face and change into jeans."

Twenty minutes later, cool night air and black coffee brought us both back into focus as we walked past Washington Square Park. The Steinhardt building was just ahead and Pam asked, "What are you hoping to find out, exactly?"

"I don't know. Maybe nothing. As you mentioned earlier, kids OD all the time, and you're right. I just don't like it when it happens around me. Besides, he was medically stable in the ICU, so what the hell happened? Might as well start here."

She swiped her ID against the electronic receptacle and the door unlocked. We walked up a short flight of stairs and were greeted by a uniformed security guard sitting at his desk. He was in his mid-thirties, muscular, white, and a little on the scruffy side in appearance. He could use a shave I thought.

Pam introduced us and asked if he'd mind answering a few questions. He nodded confidently. I asked, "Were you the guard on duty last night when that kid signed in?"

"Yes, I was. Just for the record, the police have already questioned me."

"They did?" I was surprised because he wasn't the guard on duty when we found the kid.

"Yeah, routine they said."

"I wish to reassure you that you're not in any trouble. We're just trying to understand a few things. You can imagine how upsetting this is to everyone here. I don't know if you heard but he passed away just a few hours ago."

He nodded. "Of course, I heard. That's why the police were asking questions. That's too bad. Go ahead."

"Thanks. Were there any other students who checked in with him last night, or was he by himself?"

Without any hesitation he answered, "No, he was the only one here all night."

"Don't you want to check your records?"

"I told you I already spoke to the police. They asked the same question three different ways and no, I didn't go up there to check on him. That's not my job nor is it my concern what they might be doing up there. I get paid to watch the door and that's what I do."

Fair enough. He was a little testy but I guess that was understandable given the circumstances. "All right, fine. Are there any other access points to the building?"

"Of course. Maintenance has their own entrance in the rear of the building and there are two emergency fire exits besides the one you came through. The head of maintenance has already given a statement to the police that none of his men were here last night and their door has an electronic lock that also requires an ID like the one out front, so if anyone had accessed it there were would be an electronic record. The fire doors are always locked from the outside. So there you have it. The kid was alone, except for me that is, and I'm under constant surveillance by the camera mounted on the wall behind you."

Pam and I looked up at the surveillance camera he motioned to as he continued. "The police are reviewing the tapes but won't find anything except for me closing my eyes for a few minutes here and there sitting at this desk and a five-minute trip to the john to pee and that would hardly have been enough time to make it upstairs to the sixth floor, kill a healthy young man without trace of a struggle, and get back to my chair."

I nodded in agreement. This was an old building and even though this was my first visit I noticed how slow the elevators were. Could he have run up the six flights, done the deed, and made it back in five minutes? Doubtful.

"What time does your shift end?"

Behind him and overhead was a large old-fashioned wall clock with an hour and minute hand. He looked up at it reflexively, and as he stretched, his collar dragged down, revealing a spider web tattoo creeping into view. I suppressed an urge to comment. This was becoming too much of a coincidence.

"At 8:00 a.m. sharp. Three twelve-hour shifts per week. This is my third in a row and then I'm off for a few days."

"Thanks for your help. Do you think we could look around a little while we're here?"

"Sure, Dr. Gottlieb is faculty. She can look around all night if she wants, but you'll both have to sign in. There's no one else here tonight so far."

Chapter 10

*O*nce on the sixth floor, we did our best to retrace the student's steps and possible activities while there, including bathroom trips. The layout of the floor was pretty straightforward. There were multiple recording and sound rooms, depending on your purpose. Several academic and administrative offices were nearby in addition to a classroom and a break room with a water fountain, table and coffee machine.

We entered the room where Justin was found and the vision of him flashed in front of me. He lay sprawled on his back in the middle of the room with his legs bent at the knees. The mixer and chair were at least six feet away. No signs of a struggle. Nothing amiss in the room. His empty backpack was carted away by the police. I looked at all the equipment surrounding us. There were at least twenty speakers of various sizes and sound ranges mounted from floor to ceiling in every position possible.

I said, "It could get pretty noisy in here, I bet."

She said, "Oh yeah. That's why all the rooms are soundproofed and sound canceling headsets are mandatory for everyone who uses these rooms. The school provides all that." She pointed to the desk where two pairs of headsets rested. They looked exactly like the kind you might see at a gun range.

"You really can't hear anything outside the room?" I asked.

"Theoretically, no, but I can't say for sure since I've never stood outside the room when someone cranked it up."

"Or screamed for help."

She thought about that. "Are you suggesting that he was murdered?"

"It can't hurt to let our minds wander outside the box."

"But there wasn't anyone else around to hear him scream for help."

"Let's pretend for the sake of argument that he was murdered and it wasn't the guard. That would mean there was at least one other person up here the guard didn't know about and if there was one other person then there might conceivably have been more. Follow me?"

She nodded slowly.

I continued, "Why was he in the middle of the room? Didn't that strike you as odd? Think about it. The kid comes up here, puts on some music, gets high and overdoses with whatever it was. I would have thought that he would have been chilling out in that comfortable leather chair over there, maybe playing on his phone or laptop. Which brings me to another point. They didn't find a laptop or cellphone. That doesn't make sense either, and then there's something else..."

Pam's features clouded and I could see she didn't like where this was going. "You're scaring me, John. What else is there?"

"That guy in the hospital room. Did he really look like he might be a friend of this kid?"

She shook her head. "No, not really. He almost looked like he might be homeless, but I'm not sure it's fair to judge the man."

"I'm not that nice. He was a piece of garbage, but that's not what bothers me. He had a spider web tattoo crawling up his neck. I don't know if you noticed it."

She nodded. "I did."

"Well, the guard downstairs had a similar tattoo. I saw it when he turned to look at the wall clock. I've seen those tattoos before. There's a gang in Riker's I had a couple of run-ins with. They had the exact same tattoo."

Her eyes went wide. "What are you saying?"

"I'm saying that I don't believe in coincidences. Something happened here and it wasn't as simple as an accidental overdose. And I don't believe for a minute that a student could check in and stay all night without a security guard being in the slightest bit curious if he or she was okay. It's possible, but you'd have to be the most callous asshole in the world not to be concerned."

Pam was visibly shaken. "You're making me upset."

"I'm sorry. It's just the way I think." I turned my attention to the audio equipment. "Do you know how to use any of this stuff?"

She shook her head, "No, I don't." I walked to the console and examined it. There were way too many buttons and switches for me to comprehend. I had seen professional mixers before but never thought about how they worked. There had to be some way of plugging in an external source to play back.

"Do you have any music on your phone, Pam? Something we can listen to through the sound system here?"

"I subscribe to an internet radio service if that's what you mean."

"That should work."

I searched the walls and desk filled with unfamiliar electronics and eventually came across what appeared to be the main power switch and flicked it. The apparatus lit up across the board in response and I felt pleased with myself. Any eighteen-year-old could probably walk in here blindfolded and start jamming to his favorite music and I was happy I found the power switch. Another five minutes brought me to an auxiliary port with a wire hanging out from it. The free end appeared to be similar to any typical standardized audio cable you might see on a set of headphones.

"Turn on your phone's radio and hand it to me."

Soon, tinny rock music from some '60s station was playing through the phone's speaker. I plugged the cable into her phone and the music went dead. Searching through the panel, I eventually came to a series of switches that appeared to control which input played through the room's speaker system. I selected the auxiliary switch without thinking to check the master volume. I flipped it and the explosion of sound sent us both reeling backward clutching our ears in pain. I quickly grabbed the phone and yanked the jack out and we bent over trying to catch our breath. My heart raced from the sudden adrenaline surge.

I said, "Oh my God."

Pam said something which I couldn't hear clearly and I wondered if I had burst my ear drums they hurt so much. I looked at her and mouthed the words *are you all right?* She shook her head no and clutched her ears.

It was a full five minutes before we could reasonably converse again. I said, "I'm sorry, Pam. I should've checked the volume before I flipped the switch."

She nodded. "Hence the sound-cancelation headsets."

I nodded. "Man, I wonder how much wattage they can pump through these speakers."

"I guess the answer is a lot."

I looked for the volume control switch and saw that it wasn't even close to being on maximum.

Damn.

"What were you hoping to accomplish by that?" she asked.

"I'm sorry. I just wanted to see how truly soundproofed the room was. I thought we'd have time to walk outside. I had no concept of the power of this system, but I guess the pair of twenty-four-inch woofers in the corner over there should have given me a clue."

Our ears were still ringing but gradually improving. She said, "Experiment over?"

"Yeah. The room would necessarily have to be soundproofed pretty well to withstand that or everybody on this floor would be incapacitated."

She laughed. "Well, at least I don't feel drunk anymore."

"Thanks for not being upset. That was pretty stupid of me. Let's take a walk. There are a couple of more things I'd like to check out."

We went down the stairwell to the main floor. The door opened into a side corridor out of sight from the security desk. We walked around, inspecting the emergency exits the guard had mentioned. There were big signs with arrows overhead identifying them and signs on the doors themselves stating that they were for emergencies only and would trigger an alarm if opened. Back in the main lobby we signed out and said goodbye to the guard.

We walked down the five steps to ground level and were just about to leave when I noticed a door off to one side. "Where's that lead to?" I asked.

She shrugged. "The basement?"

I tested the handle. It was locked. Looking back, I realized that I was now out of sight of the guard and the camera. That was interesting. Apparently, the camera's sole purpose was to witness who signed in and got on the elevators. If you walked in and had a key you could go into the basement completely unseen. But still, you would need an electronic ID to get in the front door so one way or another there would be a record of who came in.

I was curious and went back to the guard. "I just noticed the door down there near the entrance way. Where's that lead to?"

"The basement, you know, maintenance stuff. The furnace, a/c units, plumbing and electrical grid are all down there."

"Anything else?"

He shrugged. "A couple of bathrooms, closets, storage rooms."

"Do you think we could take a look?"

He hesitated, clearly unsure of himself, looked at me and then looked at Pam. Strumming his fingers slowly on his desk he finally said, "Sure, why not?"

He pushed away from the desk, got up and led us back to the door, opening it with his key. "Have fun."

The light switch on the wall turned on a series of fluorescent lights illuminating the way and we walked down ten cement steps, made a right turn, walked down another five steps and found ourselves in a cold, bare cavern of cement, exposed pipes, and cinderblock walls. The harsh robotic sound of machinery, humming and hissing, accompanied us as we toured the bowels of the building.

We passed a unisex bathroom and several large rooms housing the furnace and air-conditioning units, just as the guard had said. The pipes, the walls, and floor were neatly painted in battleship gray. The electrical room fascinated me. There were dozens of circuit breakers, computer boards, cable modems, wires, and conduits leading in and out of the room with red and green blinking lights managing incoming and outgoing signals.

At the far end of the basement was an over-sized door leading outside. It had an industrial-strength look to it. It was self-locking with a metal bar that you pushed on to open it. There were no signs saying that an alarm would be triggered by opening it. I stood in front of it with Pam by my side.

Before she could say "Don't do that," I pushed the door open and we were enveloped by the night. Pam cringed, waiting for an alarm to sound, but none did. Outside, adjacent to the door was the electronic receptacle for the employees to swipe their ID's. We stood at the rear of the building looking out onto Washington Place across from the park. I looked at Pam.

"Interesting."

"What?" she asked.

"If there's no alarm on this door then someone could potentially have left the building without anyone knowing. C'mon, one more thing to check."

Pam was brooding. "So it's possible that if someone killed Justin they could have escaped undetected through this door, which means that if there is no medical evidence that this was a drug OD the police should be looking at this as a potential homicide and the family should be made aware of that."

I nodded. "Well, we'll have to see what the autopsy shows first. His toxicology screen being negative doesn't necessarily mean he's not an OD. There's all sorts of crap that isn't routinely tested for and all sorts of things we don't even know to look for. Then there's always the possibility that he died of natural causes like a brain aneurysm, pulmonary embolus, or cardiac arrhythmia."

"When will the results be ready?"

"Officially, probably not until next week, but the examination will most likely be performed tomorrow morning. I'll drop by the hospital and see what I can dig up. I have a few favors I can call in."

As we talked we eventually came to the elevators and I pressed the up button. "Why not take the stairs?" she asked.

"I just want to see if what I'm thinking makes any sense. If the elevator can go up and down freely then it's perfectly plausible that someone could have escaped through the basement without the guard knowing. There are no cameras down here either. I don't know if you noticed."

She looked around for herself and agreed. "And then what?"

"I guess we go to the police and let them know we have a situation on our hands."

Suddenly a gruff voice from behind us announced that we weren't alone. "What are you two doing?"

Pam almost jumped out of her skin as we both spun around to face the security guard. Standing up, he was a lot bigger; at least two inches taller than me and much heavier. He didn't look happy. Pam could barely breathe she was so startled. I said, "We were tired and decided to take the elevator up."

"Well you can't, at least not without a proper access code. Didn't you notice the key pad over there?" He pointed to a small keypad off to one side of the elevator doors. We hadn't noticed. "The same is true coming down. You can only go to the lobby without an access code. There's another keypad inside the elevator. They don't want the kids fooling around down here. But that's not what I meant when I asked what you're doing. Someone opened the access door. It signaled me upstairs."

Pam recovered from her fright. "I needed some fresh air. I was feeling a little claustrophobic down here. We were just leaving."

He didn't say anything and just stood there staring at us. I noticed he wore a metal baton at his side dangling from his belt. He didn't smile and he didn't frown. He was trying to make up his mind. Pam's fear was palpable and my mind raced at what to do should this scene take a turn for the worse. He was big but I've gone against bigger. Guaranteeing Pam's safety would be very difficult once the action started and I hoped it wouldn't go in that direction.

Suddenly he said, "Okay then. Let's go." Abruptly, he turned around and we followed him up the stairs.

Outside Pam nearly collapsed into my arms. "Oh my God. I don't think I've ever been that frightened."

I grinned. "You haven't spent enough time with me."

We walked back to her apartment building and I said goodnight outside. She was taken aback and disappointed. "You're not going to come up?"

I shook my head. The moment of weakness had passed. I liked her—a lot—but I had made a commitment to Kelly however crazy it seemed to Pam. Besides, I had to get back to Cleo. Zach had watched her today for me but he left at five and now it was closing in on midnight. She might need me.

"I have to get going, Pam. I have a dog I have to check on."

She pouted but didn't argue. "Cleopatra? I remember her. Big dog, right?"

"Very big dog. You have a good memory."

"She's hard to forget. A real sweetheart if I recall correctly."

"That's her."

We stood there uncomfortably under a streetlight making small talk the way people do when they don't want to address the real issue. I said, "Pam…"

She shook her head. "You don't have to say anything else. You have a dog. I understand … and a fiancée. Well, I'll be going. It was a fun night, wasn't it?"

I smiled. "Yes, it was."

"Who knows? Maybe there'll more fun nights."

"You never know."

I watched her walk into her building before heading off to my apartment. Cleo greeted me energetically when I entered. I checked her water bowl and rubbed her head.

"How've you been girl? I know I haven't spent too much time with you lately. I'm sorry."

She whined in response.

I sat on the sofa and she jumped up beside me, licking my face. I kissed her once and then got her to settle down. I was troubled by the guard and this spider web tattoo business. Who knew what that meant? The one thing I knew for certain is that no one entered or left the building without the guard at the desk being aware of it.

Chapter 11

I devoted the next morning to quality time with Cleo. We played and exercised in Washington Square Park for a couple of hours. I wore shorts, T-shirt, and sneakers and jogged around the perimeter with her several times. She was a big dog and when she tired, she just stopped and dragged me over to a shaded area.

I purchased a bottle of water from a beverage cart by the central fountain and drank half before giving Cleo the rest. By 11:00 a.m. the temperature had reached eighty degrees and she was panting heavily. We had both worked up quite a sweat.

"Okay, girl. It's time to go home. I have work to do."

She woofed in agreement. She was getting hot.

Arriving at the apartment, I found an envelope that had been slipped under the door. It was addressed simply, *John*.

In it were a folded note and the diamond engagement ring I had given Kelly. It was a two-carat, oval, flawless white diamond set in a six-pronged platinum band. Forty-five hundred big ones. Not good, I thought as I read the note.

John,

I love you with all my heart but I'm afraid our love is simply not meant to be. You and I are like the two lovers in Dante's Inferno, damned to forever circle each other, but never to touch. I cannot in good conscience keep this ring knowing the uncertainty that lies ahead. Omar has insisted on marriage counseling and I feel I owe him that much. You are a good man and I want to be truthful about what is going on. Know that you will always have a special place in my heart and that I cherish every moment we ever spent together.

Kelly

I slumped on the sofa massively depressed and stared at the ceiling. A goddamn Dear John letter. Fuck, I thought that only happened in the movies. I couldn't believe it. I felt like the rug had just been pulled out from under me and the air had been sucked out of the room. Wow! Pam was right. I really was delusional. I doubted that I could feel much worse than I did right now. The finality in the note's tone really shook me up and I was tempted to take a cab to St. Luke's hospital where Kelly worked, but I decided against it. After indulging in self-pity for a few minutes, I showered and pet Cleo goodbye. "You be a good girl, all right? Zach is coming by this afternoon."

By the time I hit the street it was after twelve o'clock and I was starving and upset. I grabbed a couple of hot dogs and a soda off a street vendor and ate while I walked. On Ninth Avenue, I stopped at the small jewelry store where I had purchased the diamond from my friends, Avi and Hesh. They were twin brothers in their eighties sporting gray beards and yarmulkes.

They'd been in the diamond business for three quarters of a century.

Avi saw me first and smiled. "Hello, young man. It is so good to see you."

Hesh also seemed pleased. "So tell us; was your sweetheart pleased with the diamond? We haven't seen you in quite some time."

I cleared my throat. "Well, yes actually. She was very pleased at first but maybe not as pleased now."

Avi and Hesh glanced at each other. Avi said, "Oy vey! This doesn't sound good."

Hesh concurred, "Not good at all. What happened or should I say, what did you do?"

I said, "I didn't do anything in particular. It's just that … well, for the moment our wedding plans have been put on hold while she sort of … re-evaluates things."

They nodded in unison. Hesh said, "Love doesn't require re-evaluation, young man."

Avi said, "Nope. She definitely doesn't love you. I'm sorry."

Hesh added wistfully, "A girl once re-evaluated me three times before she decided she didn't love me."

I took a deep breath. The situation was way too complicated to explain. "At any rate, I was wondering…?"

Avi said, "What were you wondering?"

Hesh chimed in, "I'd kind of like to know as well."

"I was wondering if you guys had some sort of—return policy?"

They looked at each other again and then at me. Avi shook his head. "I am afraid not. In the diamond business, all sales are final. We wouldn't last very long if we took returns."

Hesh agreed, "We wouldn't last long at all. Girls are always re-evaluating things."

Avi added, "That's right. My brother is wise. Girls are always re-evaluating things. The one thing you can count on with girls is that no matter what they say, they will re-evaluate it later. Sorry."

Hesh said, "You're lucky she returned the ring. Usually when they re-evaluate things they flush it down the toilet."

They both nodded vigorously.

I said, "I had a feeling. Just thought I'd ask. I guess I'll just keep it in case I fall in love again."

The two old guys gave me a big smile and said in harmony, "That's the spirit. There's always more gefilte fish in the jar."

I looked at them as I conjured up that imagery, then said goodbye, and headed over to St. Matt's to see if the autopsy had been performed on the kid. I was dressed neatly in beige khakis, loafers and a cotton dress shirt. I blended in nicely in the bustling lobby and nobody questioned me as I took the elevator down to the pathology department. I opened the main door and entered, waving to a young lab tech I knew.

"Hi, Steve. Is Dr. Van Nest in?" The lab had several long rows of black countertops with small sinks and several offices with closed doors around the perimeter for various other sub-departments such as microbiology, cytology, chemistry, and hematology. There was a distinct odor in every pathology department I had ever been in. It was combination of antiseptic chemicals, stains used in histology, and preservatives such as formaldehyde. It was slightly nauseating on a stomach full of street dogs, sauerkraut, and onions.

"I believe so, Dr. Cesari. He might be dictating his report. He did an autopsy this morning and the police and family were very interested in the results."

"Thanks, Steve."

I walked through the lab and knocked on the door.

"The door's open," a voice called out.

I entered and Harry's eyes went wide as he stood to greet me. "Cesari! Well of all the people I didn't expect to see this fine morning. Come on in." He came from around his desk and shook my hand warmly. "Come in. Come in. You must tell me everything that's going on. You've been the talk of the town for months."

I closed the door behind me and sat down as he reclaimed his seat behind his desk. His office was painted plain white and he had a few diplomas on the wall. On his desk was a microscope, a pile of papers and a box of histology slides. I hadn't seen him since before the trial. I said, "Not much to tell. I'm a convicted, out-of-work felon, but I'm trying to maintain a positive attitude."

"Did you do it? Did you really lie to a federal agent to protect some girl? Can I assume she was a great lay and worth it?" He was working himself into a lather. Nothing beat salacious sex rumors as a topic for hospital gossip.

"We were involved, yes, but that's not what it was about. I was just trying to do what I thought was the right thing at the time."

He shook his head in frank admiration. "You're legendary, Cesari. Did you know that?"

I chuckled. "A legend in my own mind maybe. Look, Harry. This isn't just a casual, let's catch up visit. I was hoping you could tell me what the autopsy showed on that NYU kid. I was there when they found him."

He looked surprised. "Damn. I just did it an hour ago and have already received no less than four phone calls about it and now you. I haven't even finished dictating the report I've been interrupted so much. Who was this kid anyway?"

"That's what we're trying to figure out. Right now, all we know is he was an NYU grad student from Buffalo. So what did you find?"

"Not much at all. Preliminary toxicology screen was negative and physically there were no signs of violence or drug abuse. I couldn't find a single needle mark on him. His heart and lungs looked okay too. No physical abnormalities and no signs of drug or alcohol abuse, but that doesn't rule out a sudden arrhythmia. Pretty normal exam."

"No evidence for a pulmonary embolus?"

"Nope. The only strange thing I found was that he had perforated ear drums bilaterally."

"Perforated ear drums?"

"Yes, kind of a strange thing to find. In fact, I can't remember the last time I performed an autopsy and found both drums perforated."

I thought about that and asked, "Could loud music do that? He was found in a recording studio at NYU."

"Any really loud sound could, or a blow to the side of the head causing a sudden increase in air pressure within the canal." I thought about how I had clapped Samuel's ears in Riker's.

"Not the cause of death I gather?"

"Not a chance. It's just an interesting finding. At this point, I favor a cardiac arrhythmia of one sort or another as the cause of death. He probably had some underlying electrical abnormality in the wiring to his ventricles and for some reason it chose to blow at that moment. It happens all the time unfortunately to both the young and the old. Every time you hear about a kid dropping dead at a football or little league game that's usually what it is. He probably went down with the music on loud and his drums perforated after the fact. There's no way of knowing for sure. Alternatively, he could have perforated his drums the day before. It's impossible to tell and like I said I don't think it matters. People don't die from perforated ear drums."

I nodded, soaking it all in. A healthy young kid suddenly drops dead from an arrhythmia. It happens all the time. Maybe that's all it was. On the other hand, people get murdered all the time too. Harry saw the skepticism on my face and said, "You're not buying it, are you?"

I shook my head. "No, I'm not. This thing smells. I just can't figure out what it smells like."

"Well, that's all I have, Cesari. If something changes I can always give you a call."

"Would you do that?"

"Sure."

"Well, thanks, Harry I appreciate your time."

"Are you going to be coming back? I mean ever."

"That's the plan, but there are a lot of ifs in between then and now."

"I'll bet."

I stood up and we shook hands. "Thanks again, Harry. I can find my way out."

"Try not to find your way back in, like in a body bag, all right? Riker's is a dangerous place."

"I'll do my best."

It was almost two when I left the hospital. I called Pam and filled her in on the autopsy report. She was in her office on the tenth floor of the Givelber building doing paperwork. The Givelber building was part of the massive NYU complex surrounding Washington Square Park and devoted itself to the advancement of humankind's psychological well-being.

"Is this good or bad?" she asked.

"Not sure. If he died of natural causes then I guess it's good for him, but there's some odd stuff going on around here. Did you get a chance to pull up his records for me?"

"I can pull it up on my computer but I don't have permission to print anything out for privacy reasons. To my eye, there's nothing here. He was a good student with no blemishes. You can come up and look at it if you're nearby."

"I just left the hospital. I can be there in ten minutes."

The building was a stone's throw from Steinhardt and just a few blocks from her apartment. At first, NYU can seem huge and intimidating but after a while you began to realize that everything revolved around the park. It was the sun in NYU's universe.

In fifteen minutes, I knocked on her door and let myself into her spacious office overlooking the park. Floor to ceiling windows gave her a magnificent view of the city. She had a large mahogany desk, leather furniture, and a collection of oils on canvas decorating the walls. I had been here once before for sexual harassment counseling and remembered it well. She stood up from her chair to greet me.

"Good afternoon, Doctor," I said.

"Good afternoon, Doctor." She was a little stiff and I hoped she wasn't holding a grudge about last night.

I pointed to an object on her desk. "Is that a new bust of Freud? I don't recall that from the last time I was here."

"You are very observant, Doctor."

Right now, I was observing how well she filled out a yellow sundress. I said, "It depends on what I'm observing."

"I have Justin's records pulled up for you. You can sit in my chair to look at them."

I walked around the desk and came close to her as she made room for me. Her hair was in a ponytail and she smelled nice. She looked at me intently trying to figure out where she stood. By all traditional standards and norms, I should have at least given her a little peck on the cheek. It was an awkward moment for sure. I had decided not to mention Kelly's *Dear John* letter. For the moment, I thought it would be better to let sleeping dogs lie. I extended my right hand and she stared at it astonished.

After an uncomfortable second or two, she grasped it and pulled me forcefully toward her. Not expecting that, I stumbled forward, pushing her back onto her desk. She didn't smile or frown but took the opportunity to wrap her arms around my neck and kiss me. Not in the European way. More like in the southern California porn industry way.

She said, "Sorry, but shaking hands just didn't seem appropriate."

"And wrestling me onto your desk did?"

She laughed and pushed me back. "Now you can do your work."

I said, "Geez, isn't this the office where you counsel people on sexual harassment?"

"Just do what you came to do. I'll be fine now."

That was the problem with women. If you showed weakness once, you became a sitting duck the rest of the time.

Chapter 12

The records were very complete including a blurb about his family, his demographics, course transcripts, and professor's notes but other than that I didn't learn anything more than he was a model student. His parents were humble hard-working citizens of western New York. His father worked in a ceramics factory and his mother was an LPN at the Erie County Medical Center. Solid middle-income people. He had earned a modest academic scholarship, which paid for part of his tuition, and the rest he paid for with student loans and personal income. He lived off campus in an eastside apartment and had registered his car so he could park in one of the University's parking lots.

I paused for a minute thinking about that. Why would he want a car living in the city? It's quite an expense if he didn't use it other than to drive home a couple of times a year. Maybe he was a momma's boy and drove home every weekend? Still, between rent, tuition and food, it seemed an unnecessary expense.

"Hey Pam, it says here that he had a car but it doesn't say the make or model. Where would I find that information?"

She looked at the screen with me then took the mouse and clicked a few times eventually bringing me to the car's registration screen. She said, "There it is."

I read with curiosity. Now that was very interesting. He owned a one-year-old silver BMW Alpina B7. I looked at Pam. "This can't possibly be right."

"Why not?"

"It's a hundred and fifty thousand-dollar car, that's why not. He took out student loans to pay his tuition and even that doesn't cover the full cost. This doesn't make sense. His parents are average middle-income people, so there's no way they could have given him this car as a present." I tapped my fingers on her desk. "How can we check up on this?"

"I don't know. The school doesn't provide for long-term parking so he would have had to have it privately garaged."

"That would have cost a pretty penny, too." I wrote his apartment's address down on a piece of paper I found on her desk. "Feel like doing a little investigating?"

"Sure, it's a beautiful day and you've made me curious, although I suppose a rich uncle could have gifted it to him."

"A rich uncle would have done better by paying for his tuition instead of a car he didn't need. Don't you think?"

She nodded as we left her office.

He lived in a two-bedroom apartment on East 7th Street near Avenue D very close to the Eastside Drive. We took a cab there and observed that it was a pretty nice neighborhood with lots of trees and high-end cars parked on the street. The door to the apartment building was locked and I rang every buzzer until one eventually responded.

"Who is it?" crackled an old woman's voice over the intercom.

"Hi, I'm Dr. Cesari. I live in apartment 2B. I was in a rush this morning and forgot my keys on the kitchen counter when I left for work. Could you buzz me in please? I'm sorry to inconvenience you."

There was silence as she thought it over. "You forgot to lock your apartment?"

She was sharp, that's for sure. New Yorkers never forgot things like that. "I was very distracted when I left this morning. There was a sick patient in the emergency room waiting for me."

"I have a .357 magnum loaded with hollow points and I'm not afraid to use it. You've been warned."

Pam raised her eyebrows. I responded soothingly, "I assure you that I have nothing but gratitude on my mind but thank you for the warning."

There was a sharp buzzing sound and the door unlocked, allowing us to enter. He lived on the fourth floor and we jogged up the staircase, our excitement building. Pam was clearly having fun.

When we reached his apartment, we paused to collect ourselves. She looked at me and smiled. "This is exciting. I feel like Nancy Drew."

I nodded. "Just remember to stop me if it looks like I'm going to commit a felony."

She whispered. "You mean another felony?"

Chuckling, I said, "Yeah."

I rang the doorbell and waited. His school records couldn't tell us whether he had a roommate or not, and I was mildly concerned about that. No one answered. We looked at each other and I knocked loudly three times and waited. Again no one answered.

Pam asked, "Now what?"

I reached out and tested the doorknob but it was locked. It never hurt to try. I looked up and down the hallway and then at Pam who was starting to get a little apprehensive. Maybe she saw something in my eye that said, *now would be a good time to stop me.*

I pulled out my wallet and retrieved a credit card. "Keep an eye out for me." I grabbed the doorknob and wedged the credit card deftly between it and the door jamb, jiggling it with a persistence born of experience with unlawful entry—much experience. After a while the card slipped through the lock mechanism and the door swung inward.

The apartment was a mess and had been systematically ransacked. The contents of the kitchen drawers and cabinets lay sprawled all over the floor. The sofa and chairs were overturned, their pillows and cushions shredded and the stuffing removed. Pam grabbed my arm. "I'm scared. Maybe this wasn't such a great idea after all?"

I disagreed. "How do you figure? At least we have some hard evidence that all is not what it seems with Justin. Somebody was looking for something. C'mon, let's check the bedrooms."

The first bedroom was a mess also. The mattress was overturned and cut open, night tables were on their sides, closets wide open. As we entered the other bedroom Pam gasped in horror. The room was in the same disarray as the last but on the floor at the foot of the bed was a girl in her teens, naked, bloodied, and disheveled. She was motionless.

I raced to her and felt for a pulse. Weak but definitely there. She was still breathing. I stretched her out on her back and elevated her feet with a couple of pillows. "Pam, grab a blanket and help me cover her. She's still alive."

She grabbed bed sheets off the floor and we tucked her in. The girl moaned and her eyes fluttered briefly, but she remained unconscious. She had been beaten pretty badly; her eyes were deep purple and swollen. She had a cauliflower ear on the right and was missing her left thumb. Multiple other bruises and cigarette burn marks decorated her body. Thankfully, the thumb wound had coagulated, but she had lost a lot of blood. Pam started crying and slumped to the floor next to her.

I took out my phone and called 911. While we waited I searched the apartment but couldn't find any identifying information. There was no bag or purse with a driver's license or credit card. She made a sound and her eyes fluttered again. Pam held her hand and the girl gripped her weakly.

Pam whispered reassuringly to her. "It's going to be all right, honey. Help is on the way. Just rest. We're friends."

The girl moaned and Pam called me. "John, I think she's trying to say something."

I knelt down next to her and said softly, "Hi, I'm John Cesari. You're going to be okay. Just rest now. We won't leave you."

I picked up her other hand, the one missing its thumb, and held it gently just so she could feel another human. She opened her mouth and I saw she was missing her two front teeth. Barely audible, she whispered, "Maria..."

Pam said, "Is that your name? Maria?"

In response, she said, "The toilet."

Pam and I glanced at each other and she said, "Do you have to go to the bathroom, Maria?"

Weakly, she shook her head no and closed her eyes. She was quiet for another minute and then when she gathered enough strength said ever so slowly, "It's ... it's in the toilet."

Pam looked at me and said, "Maybe she's just rambling? She's been through so much trauma it wouldn't be unusual."

I nodded and asked, "What's in the toilet, Maria?"

It was no good. She lapsed into unconsciousness again and couldn't answer. I said to Pam, "I have no idea what she's talking about, but I might as well check it out."

I rose to go inspect the bathroom as sirens announced the arrival of emergency vehicles on the street outside. The bathroom was small with a shower stall, sink, vanity and normal toilet. The mirror above the sink had been smashed and the contents of the cabinet below had been tossed on the floor. The toilet seat was closed and I lifted it. Nothing, so I rolled up my sleeve and plunged my hand into the cold water, fishing around, but came up empty. I dried my arm off on a bath towel and looked around. Nothing.

It was then that I noticed a peculiar sound emanating from the porcelain tank. It was the gentle sound of running water. The gasket inside the porcelain tank wasn't sealing properly, preventing the tank from filling completely. This was a very common and ordinary household problem especially in these older buildings with ancient plumbing. Usually, you just wiggled the gasket and it corrected itself. If not, you called a plumber to replace it.

I stared at the tank and just as I heard EMS and police entering the apartment, I lifted the cover and looked in. The reason the gasket wouldn't seal was that there was a string tied to the metal mechanism above dangling into the mouth of the drain below preventing complete closure. This slight opening allowed water to drip through causing the noise I heard. I reached in and pulled the string out, discovering a condom on the other end with an electronic car key wrapped tightly inside. I quickly removed it and hid it in my pocket, replacing the tank cover.

I joined Pam and greeted the police and EMS team, introducing myself. Pam and I gave them a joint statement with some minor tweaks. I told them we were faculty at NYU and that we weren't sure if Justin had a roommate or if anyone had informed him or her of his status. We came for that purpose, found the door wide open and based on the appearance of the apartment, had reason to believe that an injured person may have been inside, prompting us to enter. They took our names and phone numbers down and mentioned there might be a follow-up phone call.

We left together and I held Pam tightly as we walked. At the end of the block, we stopped to regroup in a coffee shop, ordering a couple of mugs. The mood was somber. Pam said, "John, that was horrible. What happened?"

"I can't be sure but I think Justin may have been mixed up in something way over his head. Somebody was looking for something and got pretty upset when they didn't find it."

"That was so terrible. That poor girl. Was she his girlfriend?"

"I hope not. She looked pretty young."

She nodded. "That she did. Maybe his parents will know who she is?"

"They might even be on their way to the apartment to collect his stuff right now. Speaking of which..." I reached into my pocket and pulled out the condom with key in it.

Pam shrank back. "Eww, what's that?"

"I found it in the toilet tank tied to a string. I don't know if that's what the girl was referring to but it certainly seems like she wasn't babbling as much as we thought."

As we spoke I tore open the condom and took out the key. It was the key to his BMW.

"What are you going to do with that?"

"Find his car, of course."

"Why?"

"I don't know. He must have hidden the key for a reason."

"Maybe that's what they were looking for?"

"Maybe."

"Wouldn't she have told them?"

"Maybe they didn't ask."

"Well good luck finding it. There about a million parking garages in New York and what if you do find it? Then what?"

"There might be a million garages but an almost new Alpina B7 should stick out like a sore thumb and I know these parking garage guys. They know their high-end cars. We'll start nearby and fan out. If we get lucky and find it, we'll give it a quick search. If there's nothing in it, we can cross that off the list."

"I guess I'm not totally clear as to what is going on. The autopsy result suggested his death was from natural causes, right? But now this seems to suggest otherwise unless this was just a coincidence. Maybe she was the victim of an unrelated break-in."

I shook my head. "Not a chance. First of all, the autopsy couldn't confirm a cause of death and the conclusion the pathologist was leaning toward was that it must be from natural causes such as an arrhythmia. That's a long way from saying beyond a shadow of a doubt that's what it was. Secondly, in my world, when a young guy is found dead and his girlfriend is found beaten half to death and their apartment is ransacked there is a 100 percent chance the two events are related, and I don't care what the coroner says. Let's finish up and start looking for the car. We'll start with the closest garages first."

She cleared her throat. "Don't you think we should let the police handle it from this point? This is getting a little hairy. There are obviously some very dangerous people involved in this, and I'm not sure I want to get to know them better."

I sat back in the booth as I thought about that. She was right. She had no business getting involved with this on any level. Hell, I had no business getting involved in this. I liked being around her, but I didn't want to lead her on either. Kelly's note had put me in a foul mood and it wouldn't be right. This was no way to begin a relationship.

"You're right, of course. This is what happens when I have too much time on my hands. I get myself in trouble. I'll walk you home if you like. The Ninth Precinct is on the way if I recall correctly. I'll stop in and give them the car key. I'll tell them I picked it up out of curiosity and just forgot I had it. Besides, they wanted to speak to me anyway about our little trip to the ICU last night."

She stared at me suspiciously and pursed her lips. "Just like that. You're not even going to pretend to argue about it?"

I was hurt. "No, why would I? When you're right, you're right."

"You're good that's for sure, but remember, you're talking to a trained therapist. I listen to people lie all day long for a living."

"Lie? There's no need for that. I'm trying to be reasonable."

"Reasonable? After what you did to me last night you think you're a reasonable person?"

I was confused. "What are you talking about? I thought we had a great night."

"You left me hanging to go take care of a dog. That'll look great on my resume. I don't even rate as high as a dog."

The gloves were off now. No one goes after my dog. "I left you hanging? You're the one who wanted to throw up while I was sitting there with my pocket rocket out, ready for blast off, and I do have a dog and I thought you understood."

"What? You couldn't give me a few minutes to get over it and I understood nothing, other than I was up half the night thinking about you."

I folded my arms and looked out the window. I didn't have an answer to that. I hated when women acted like this. If they didn't get their way 110 percent of the time, they got pissy. It's as if a guy isn't allowed to say no once in a while. Maybe it was in some rule book they never showed us. Lots of girls say no to me and not nearly as nicely. You didn't hear me whining. I wasn't even sure what we were arguing about.

I cleared my throat. "Well, I'm glad we cleared the air on that subject."

She rolled her eyes. "We haven't cleared the air on anything. I could barely think straight this morning either."

"I appreciate your frankness."

"You don't appreciate anything. Do you think I throw myself at just any guy that walks by?"

"I'm guessing no."

"That's right."

"Well, Pam, I think we officially have what can only be called—a situation."

"I guess we do."

We sat across from each other, arms folded, staring. Let's go over the positives—she was attractive, intelligent and about my age. I wasn't 100 percent sure about the age thing. I asked, "How old are you?"

"What's that got to do with anything?"

"Just curious."

"I'm thirty-four."

Just a little younger than me. Good. Attractive, intelligent, similar age. All positive. Now the negatives. A little pushy sexually, perhaps. Doesn't seem to care that I'm engaged. I wasn't, but she didn't know that. Did that make her a home-wrecker? I didn't like being bullied into someone's bedroom either. It was a self-esteem thing.

She asked, frustration in her voice, "What are you thinking about?"

"When we kissed earlier you said you'd be fine."

"I was fine—for about half an hour. The effect of a kiss only lasts a finite amount of time. As a man of science, you should know that. The endorphin rush that a human experiences following a kiss has a half-life of approximately twenty to thirty minutes. Let's see. You kissed me at two and it's now after five." She started counting her fingers and appeared to be doing a calculation in her head. "Any positive feelings generated wore off hours ago."

I nodded, coming to a conclusion. "Okay, Pam. Have it your way. Your office, your apartment, or right here on this table? I'm going to count to five before I change my mind. One…"

"The table!"

Chapter 13

We decided to hold off on having sex on the table and walked back to her office. It had always been a fantasy of hers to do it up there with the city visible in the background. It would have been nice to wait until it got dark but she didn't think she could hang on that long. There was a Chinese take-out place on the way and we planned on picking up dinner there. On East 5th Street between First and Second Avenues we spotted the Ninth Precinct, and I said, "Would you mind if I stopped in and dropped off the key?"

"Yes, I would mind. I don't think you understand. I can barely function. I need to get this over with."

Jesus!

I almost asked if she was ovulating. "Pam, it'll take less than five minutes. I'll just leave it at the front desk. I promise I won't let you down. I don't want to have to come back."

"You're killing me. Go ahead. I'll wait out here on one of those benches." She pointed to a wood bench under a tree across the street from the station house. "Hurry up."

I walked into the police station and found the information desk. There was a uniformed officer behind bullet-proof glass. He acknowledged me and I in turn identified myself and stated my reason for coming in, passing the BMW key to him through a slot beneath the glass. He asked me to wait while he checked with a senior officer for advice.

A couple of minutes later, a door clicked open and a big, ruddy-faced guy with a handle-bar mustache and wearing a baggy brown suit walked in and asked with an Irish brogue, "John Cesari?"

I turned to him. "Yes."

"I'm Detective Kilcullen. May I have a wee word with ya?"

Out of the corner of my eye I saw two uniformed officers take up position by the entrance behind me, dashing any thought I may have had of refusing. Suddenly, I had a sinking feeling that Pam was going to have to start without me. I said, "Sure."

"Come with me then if you don't mind."

He took me to a small office with white walls and a frosted glass door. His desk had piles of papers on it as well as three half-filled cups of coffee. The metal file cabinet off to one side was about a hundred years old. A plaque on his desk said his name was Terrence Kilcullen. A framed picture of him shaking hands with the mayor hung on the wall behind him. Motioning me to sit in an uncomfortable, flimsy folding chair, he walked around to his side of the desk. He was six feet two inches tall, fifty years old and about 240 pounds with light brown hair, blue inquisitive eyes and a .44 magnum in a shoulder holster. I wondered how many pints of Guinness a day he consumed. He took his jacket off, sat down and looked at me.

"So, where's the kid's car, Johnny boy?"

He got right to it. No small talk. I shook my head. "I don't know."

"You don't know or you don't want to tell me."

I loved his accent. It was melodic and whimsical. I felt like I was talking to a gigantic leprechaun. "I don't know."

"Then tell me what you do know. Let's start with the victims. How do you know them?"

"Victims?" It was a subtle point. Unlike the rest of society, the police generally did not consider a drug overdose a victim other than to their own stupidity.

"Yes, the victims. Justin Delrosa and the girl in his apartment."

"I thought Justin was just an OD and I already gave a statement as to why we were at the apartment. By the way, her name is Maria."

"By the way yourself, her name is Kayla. She woke up briefly but long enough to identify herself to one of my officers. Her name is Kayla and she's from Dallas, but that's all we know. So unless you think one of my men is lying, we're going to stick with that. Now, are you going to cooperate or not?"

That surprised me. Who was Maria? Maybe she really was just babbling. "I'm trying."

He suddenly got annoyed. "Okay, listen up, Dr. Cesari and let me explain a few ground rules to you. You are a convicted felon serving time on Riker's. You're only doing weekends now and are on five years' probation. You fuck with me, laddy, and I'll make sure you spend every day and night there for the next five years not just weekends, understand?"

I nodded. "I want to cooperate but maybe you should give me a clue as to what you're expecting from me."

"I expect the truth and as a sign of goodwill any regarded opinions you might have. I spoke with the coroner this afternoon and he told me his theory about death by natural causes and I don't believe t'at any more than you do."

"How do you know I have any opinion about that at all?"

"Because your friend, the pathologist, told us you were there to find out the results of the autopsy and had your own doubts. I want to know why and don't get yourself all fired up. He's a law-abiding citizen who was informed that t'is a felony to withhold information or deliberately mislead a law enforcement officer. Something you are somewhat familiar with."

I didn't say anything. I was getting the feeling from his tone that not only was Pam going to have to start without me but that she was probably going to have to bring it on home as well.

I instinctively looked at my hands wondering why I wasn't already in cuffs. He noticed that and smiled confidently. "You're not under arrest, son. We're just having a nice chat, see?"

"Should I call my lawyer?"

"Only if you want to make this more complicated than necessary. Listen to me, Doctor. I like guineas. I really do. Your people have made some great contributions to the world order. Pizza, gelato, I really love gelato, Gucci. I've seen the Godfather a thousand times meself. Great stuff t'at. Keep your friends close and your enemies closer." He paused to chuckle and then continued. "How great is t'at? You know, I've always believed that the Irish and Italians have a lot in common."

"We do?"

"For sure. People are always pre-judging us. We Irish are drunks and you guineas are greasy, over-sexed, thievin', throat-slittin', murderin' pimps. T'at sort of stuff."

My eyes went wide and he continued. "Relax, you know t'ain't true and I know t'ain't true but try telling that to the rest of America. What I'm getting at is that I want to give you a fair shake. Understand?"

"I'm beginning to."

"Good. Then let's take it from the top, starting with your relationship with Samuel Archer, the skinhead you slapped around last weekend in Riker's."

My jaw dropped at that. "What's he got to do with anything and how did you know about that?"

"Samuel Archer is a degenerate of unparalleled proportions serving time for dealing crack, heroin, and meth. He was convicted of t'at but guilty of much worse t'at couldn't be proven, such as rape, murder, and trafficking. I know because I'm the one t'at put him away. He's awaiting transfer to Attica where I hope he gets a well-deserved shiv up his arse. So tell me what you know and don't leave anything out. I can smell a lie the way you can smell a pepperoni pizza."

He sat back in his chair, hands clasped in front of him studying my body language as I spoke. He interjected from time to time to clarify a specific point or two. After forty-five minutes, I had brought him up to speed on everything I knew or suspected.

He nodded and I said, "Now it's my turn. What's going on? Are these guys Aryan Nation or some other type of supremacist group?"

"No, they don't have any grand vision or plan for a new world order. Are they racists? Oh, I have no doubt about t'at, but t'at's not what drives them. They're greedy street punks that have learned to organize and follow a command structure. Most criminal acts today are random or the results of relatively small groups acting in unison. There aren't any national organizations like the mafia anymore. They've been greatly diminished and reduced in size and scope."

I smiled inwardly. "Are you sure about that? Maybe they've just learned how to play according to the new rules. You know, maybe they've learned to live symbiotically off of their host like a well-evolved parasite."

"Maybe they have, but the Spiders as they call themselves, and you probably noticed the tattoos, are a different kind of threat to society. These guys have the potential to cause a new type of chaos and using your example if they're not stopped they will most definitely kill their host organism. They're flooding the market with cheap, addictive drugs, undercutting their competition and reaching new markets. They're losing money by doing that, but they're successfully driving their competition out of business. They're organized, structured, and their soldiers are loyal, which is bad for us. Even when we catch one, they're hard to turn."

"Is it fair to assume that Samuel is some type of head guy?"

"*The* head guy in New York, t'at's for sure. So far, we believe the Spiders are primarily located in the city but we know they're spreading. At last count, we estimate there are three hundred strong in their rank and file. Our latest concern is the raging epidemic of drug use on the campus of one of our major universities. Everybody knows kids play with drugs. It's almost a rite of passage these days but what people are unaware of is that the Spiders have *deliberately* infiltrated NYU in order to distribute their poison."

"You mean like the security guard at Steinhardt?"

He raised his eyebrows. "You know about him? Well, this has led to rates of drug use, overdose, and application for rehabilitation that are nearly five times the rate of any other comparable university. The Spiders are all over NYU in various forms; security guards, janitors, electricians, etcetera. We watch as many as we can but there are too many of them. We've focused our attention on Steinhardt but so far, we can't figure out how they're getting the drugs in, and the money out. Needless to say, the Spiders are building up a solid head of steam and are getting ready to break out and go city-wide, maybe even nationwide. They have a good system and they've been fine tuning it at NYU. In addition, we think they have their hands in various other enterprises such as prostitution, extortion, and may even have started dabbling in the supply side in order to cut out the middleman. We suspect they're involved in human trafficking as well."

I nodded. Damn. "How does the dead student figure in?"

"Good question. We've never so much as seen the guard smile at him or shake his hand in the last three months."

"But you do believe he was involved with these guys?"

"Don't be stupid. Of course, he was and obviously they had a misunderstanding resulting in his tragic death. I don't know how they killed him but I'd bet a pot of gold on it. Personally, I'd like to go there and strangle the bastard of a guard meself."

"But that wouldn't stop anything."

"No, it wouldn't. So about a year ago we decided to go whole hog after Samuel. We listen in on all his calls and strip and cavity search anyone who comes to see him. He's not allowed conjugal visits. No one talks to him and he don't talk to nobody unless we know about it. We sent one of our best guys in undercover and it took him nearly a year but he finally worked his way into a position of trust with Samuel. Do you know how he did t'at?"

I shook my head no and he continued, "We had another undercover agent stage an attack against Samuel and when my lad went to his defense he took a four-inch shiv made of broken glass in the abdomen. This is not an exact science and the blade nicked his spleen. The poor bastard nearly lost his life but when he got out of the hospital he was suddenly in Samuel's inner circle."

I let out a deep breath wondering where he was heading with this. He continued, "This is where you come in."

"Me?"

"Yeah, you. So, after a whole year of risking his life for the greater good some guinea arsehole by the name of Cesari breaks his nose and jaw." He opened a desk drawer, retrieved a 5x7 inch photo, and tossed it at me. I picked it up and my heart sank. Clean cut, in full dress blues, smiling ear to ear, receiving a medal from the police commissioner was prick number two in my cell last weekend. He was the one standing behind Samuel.

He added, "Just a wee bit embarrassing for the Ninth Precinct's boxing champ."

I protested weakly. "But they were going to run a train on me."

Kilcullen's ruddy face turned eight shades of scarlet with anger. "He was just role playing, you dumb fuck. He never would have let it get that far. He's done that routine a dozen times to get information out of people. His name is Patrick Lutz and his great grandfather came from county Cork same as mine and now his mouth is wired shut so tight the doctors say he might never be able to lick his wife's pussy again."

I stammered, "I'm sorry. I didn't know."

"Well, now you know. The question is what are you willing to do to make up for your asinine behavior? We have a drug epidemic infecting the city's most prestigious university. It's on the verge of becoming institutionalized, and you just set the investigation back a whole year. You, son, need to make restitution to society."

"What can *I* do?"

"I thought you'd never ask. When you're in Riker's you make nice to Samuel and apologize for your bad attitude. Tell him you didn't know who he was and how important he was. Stroke him. Tell him you're now receptive to acting as his courier like he asked."

"Are you out of your mind?! He'll never go for that. He'll kill me before I get the words out."

"Not if you're convincing. Remember, he's desperate to communicate with the outside. Like it or not, he needs you the way you need me. If you don't cooperate I'll make sure you're charged with assaulting my officer. I guarantee you that will not play out well in court especially when they hear what he was doing in there. By the way, did you happen to notice all the medals on his chest in that photo there? Patrick was a rising star in the department and our best undercover officer."

I sat there speechless. This was about as dangerous a game as I'd ever been asked to play only I wasn't being asked. I was being ordered.

He said, "Think it over, lad. I'll be in touch."

I left his office a full two hours after entering and was surprised to find Pam waiting for me on a bench in the foyer. She looked very worried as she approached.

"Is everything okay?" she asked.

"Yeah, let's get out of here. Thanks for waiting, Pam. You didn't have to."

"What was I supposed to do, leave? No one would tell me anything."

We left the building. It was after 9:00 p.m. and dark out. She said, "What did they want?"

I turned to her and our eyes met. "My soul."

"What does that mean?"

Ignoring the question, I wrapped my arms around her and kissed her long and slow. When I was finished I said, "Let's go to your office. I need a woman real bad."

"Really?"

"Yeah, is the light still on in the motel?"

"Oh yeah. C'mon let's hurry."

"Your desk or the couch?"

"No way. It's up against the window time. I want to watch the city."

Jesus!

Chapter 14

$\mathcal{N}$ ow that Pam and I had crossed the Rubicon sexually, I felt somewhat self-conscious about misleading her. For her own safety, I couldn't tell her or anyone else about what the police wanted me to do and she was under the impression that I had let go of my own personal desire to investigate the student's death. But after meeting with Kilcullen, my curiosity had been stoked to fever pitch. I was at a disadvantage because I had surrendered the key to the BMW to the police but where there was a will, there was a way. Besides, I counted on the fact that if the car was parked in a garage, they would have a second set of keys.

Pam and I had slept in her office on the couch and woke to a New York sunrise blaring in through the windows. We went to our respective apartments to clean up and I assumed she was now back in her office doing paperwork and humming the way women do the next day. I, on other hand, was busy on the phone.

"Okay, Knuckles, are we clear about what I want you to do?"

"Roger that, macho man. This here's a rubber duck." I smiled. She was using CB call signs that truckers used. "We fan out from the kid's apartment and go to every garage for a ten-block radius. We're looking for a silver BMW Alpina B7, license plate DOME69." She laughed. "The kid had a sense of humor."

"Yeah, and don't do anything foolish like go near it. It might be under surveillance or even worse, booby-trapped. Just locate it and let me know where it is. There are a lot of parking garages in that neighborhood and this may take a while. It might not even be here at all or the cops may get to it before us. Is the gang all in?"

"Oh yeah. They're upset about that kid and want to help. Besides, they haven't had this much fun in decades. All except Liz, that is. She thinks you want to rape her and that this is a plot to lure her out into the open."

"What?! Why does she think that?"

"Because you have a loud voice and exude sexuality from every pore, but don't take it personally. She thinks that about every man she meets. It doesn't mean she won't help us. It just means that she'll be looking over her shoulder for you wherever we go so don't sneak up on her unless you want to be maced."

"She carries mace?"

"And a stun gun."

"Fine, I won't sneak up on her." What the hell was wrong with this city? I've been threatened twice with physical violence in the last twenty-four hours by women I hardly knew. I thought they were the weaker sex. When I was in training, one of my mentors was a married guy with kids. I remembered him telling me horror stories about his wife's PMS and her bouts of explosive anger and mood swings. He told me that he had considered sprinkling antidepressants into her morning coffee but was afraid that if she ever found out she'd kill him for real. I'd never seen a guy that scared of his own shadow. I was beginning to understand how he felt.

"Knuckles, one more thing. Can you guys keep this between you and me? I'd prefer if Pam were not involved."

"Uh oh. Trouble in paradise already? What's going on and why's Pam out?"

"We had a really bad day yesterday and finding that girl really shook her up. I kind of promised her I'd drop the whole thing and let the police handle it and…"

"And since you're trying to make babies with her you'll tell her anything she wants to hear. Got it and totally approve of the strategy. She needs the lovin'. She was acting like a bear before you came along. I'll spread the word to the rest of the Mission Impossible team. Say, Doc, can I ask you something personal?"

"Go ahead?"

"What razor do you shave with?"

It was a little early for Christmas. "Why do you ask?"

She lowered her voice. "There's a guy at the gym. He's been giving me some—you know—supplements. Anyway, I've been starting to see the effects and was wondering…?"

"It's called the Gillette Fusion and uses five-blade technology. Gives a very smooth and comfortable shave, but I have to tell you I don't approve of anabolic steroid use unless under the supervision of a physician. They can be very harmful to your health."

"I know. I'll be careful and thanks. Maybe you can show me how to shave properly someday? You know … a little demo."

I smiled. "Sure, but why are you doing this?"

"Doc, if you have to ask, you'll never understand."

"All right, we'll make a date. Now let's go, and mum's the word."

"Roger that. This here's a rubber duck."

She was killing me. I put my phone away and entered the first garage I saw. Since his apartment was as far east as you could go on Manhattan Island we only had three directions to cover, north, west and south. I went north alone; Stan and Bob went west, and Knuckles and Liz took the southern route. Todd was picking out window dressings at Macy's with his wife. It was 10:00 a.m. We kept a record of which garages we investigated so we didn't overlap and would stay in touch by phone planning to regroup at 1:00 p.m. to compare notes and strategize if we didn't find the car by then.

I proceeded in a zig-zag pattern up eighth, down ninth, up tenth, down eleventh. I made notes of which garages were closed so I could come back later. The attendants were helpful and really didn't seem to care that I couldn't remember which garage I had parked my car in. A twenty-dollar bill got me full access not only to their office records and key boards but a full tour of the lot itself. Trouble was that by noon I was almost out of twenties and stood exhausted at the corner of East 13th Street and Avenue C. I had searched twelve parking garages and had only covered about a third of my designated area.

My phone rang. I said, "Hi, cupcake."

Pam giggled. "Pet names already?"

"Sure, why not?"

"What are you doing? Feel like having lunch?"

"I'm kind of tied up at the moment. I was heading to the library to review anti-social behavioral disorders and other maladaptive manifestations of incarcerated patients and their treatments. It's a big deal in prison."

"I bet. Well, that's too bad. Maybe later we could meet for dinner?"

"That sounds fabulous. Where'd you have in mind?"

"How about Wolfgang's Steakhouse? It's all the way over on the West Side. I heard it's wonderful."

"Sounds great. Would you mind taking care of the reservations? I might forget."

"Not at all. Is seven good for you?"

"Seven is perfect."

"John...?"

"Yes?"

"I've been thinking about last night over and over. I can't get it out of my head."

A second call buzzed through on my phone. It was Knuckles. "Pam, can you hold that thought for a minute. I got a call from the prison coming through."

"The prison? Why are they calling?"

"Hold on, Pam." I switched calls. "Hey, Knuckles, any luck?"

"You can bet your sweet loving ass." I could feel the excitement in her voice. "It's in a long-term parking garage on the corner of East Houston and Avenue B. You can't miss it. What do you want us to do?"

"Call off the twinks but don't do anything else. Just stay put. I'm on the way." I hung up and returned to Pam as I hailed a yellow cab. "I'm sorry. Where were we?"

"I was telling you how much I enjoyed last night."

"Yeah, me too. It was great."

A taxi pulled over and I entered, whispering the directions to the driver as I held my hand over the receiver.

"It was better than great. It was like the Fourth of July fireworks over the harbor."

"You really know how to flatter a guy, Pam."

"I mean it. I feel hormones and emotions surging and pulsating in parts of my body that I didn't even know those things were allowed to enter. I feel incredible today. Is it like that for you?"

I didn't like these kinds of questions. Men weren't like that. For men, it was a gigantic explosion, a few minutes of afterglow and then, "Could you hand me the remote, there's a show I wanted to watch and by the way do you think there's any leftover pizza in the fridge?" That is, of course, if we managed to stay awake that long.

I said, "That's exactly how I feel. Absolutely incredible. I'm surging everywhere too. Well, I'm glad

I lived up to expectations. I was a little nervous about that."

She laughed. "Yeah, you lived up to expectations and more." She lowered her voice as if someone were eavesdropping. "I didn't know men liked to put their tongues there."

"Well, I was like that once but prison has really changed me."

Again, she chuckled, "Stop it—I think I'd like to do that again. Can you arrange for that?"

The cab pulled up in front of the garage and I spotted Knuckles and Liz standing outside on the sidewalk. I was silent for a moment as I threw my last twenty at the driver, mouthed a thank you and exited.

"I think it's doable. Let me check." I waited for a second and said, "Yup, I just asked my secretary. She said I'm allowed to do that twice per week so we're good to go."

She burst out laughing on the other end. "Oh my, you are fun. So, my office after dinner?"

"The window again?"

"Yeah, that was amazing. Looking down on the park, my face... my nipples pressed up against the cold glass while you..." I could hear her breathing heavily into the phone.

I cleared my throat. "Pam, are you all right?"

She whispered, "I don't know. Are you sure you can't come here now?"

"I'm really tied up. Be patient, please."

"I'll try. Well, I'll let you get on with your studies."

"I'll see you later."

117

Chapter 15

As I walked up to greet Knuckles and Liz, another taxi pulled up and the twinks spilled out wearing matching Hawaiian shirts, straw hats, and sunglasses.

I said, "Hi, Knuckles—Liz." Liz had her back to me and didn't say anything. Knuckles said, "Hi, Doc." Stan and Bob said, "Hi." I noticed they were holding hands.

I didn't mean to be peevish but Liz was frustrating me. I walked around to face her. She wore gym shorts, a loose tee, and black, ankle-high Keds sneakers. If it wasn't for the cynical lines around her pouty lips, she could pass for sixteen or seventeen. She looked down and I repeated myself. "Hi, Liz."

She said, "I have mace."

"I know, so either use it or say hi."

There was an uncomfortable silence as Knuckles and the boys took a step back—just in case. I surmised that they'd seen her in action before. Slowly, without looking at me she said, "Hi."

Everybody breathed a sigh of relief and I turned to Knuckles. "So what have you got?"

"You got balls, Doc. I'll give you that. The car's somewhere inside there. The attendant looked up the plate and model number. He wasn't here when the kid checked in but he remembered hearing the other guys talking about it. Apparently, it impressed them all. Trouble is we don't have a claim ticket so they can't let us near the car."

I nodded. That made sense. I took out the remaining cash I had in my pockets. All I had left was two five-dollar bills. I said, "How much money do you guys have?" They all reached into their pockets and came out with varying amounts, but the sum total was less than a hundred dollars. That wasn't going to be good enough.

Looking down both sides of the street, less than half a block away, I spotted a bank and figured they might have an ATM. I told everybody to wait and I jogged down to it. There was an ATM in the vestibule and I withdrew $500 and hoped it would be enough. I jogged back and told everybody to walk one block down Avenue B and wait for me on the corner.

I walked up to the attendant, a heavy-set guy with a Russian accent and three days' growth of beard. He sat inside a small office chewing on a salami sandwich. He eyed me, suspicious that I was about to interrupt his meal.

I said, "Hi. I understand that you have a BMW Alpina B7 lodged in here somewhere?"

His eyes narrowed. With a mouthful of bread and salami, he said gruffly, "No ticket, no car. I already told others."

"I understand. Allow me to introduce myself. I'm John Cesari." I extended my hand and he reluctantly took it. "My crew and I are in the middle of filming a documentary on the cars of New York. You know, like 'Humans of New York.' We've set up shop a block away and we were hoping that you— or I could just drive the car around the block once or twice so we could catch it on film. I'd be happy to mention you in the credits for being cooperative."

I caught his attention and he stopped chewing. "You are from Hollywood?"

"No, no, nothing so glamorous. We're a small independent production company based here the city. The film will be shown locally and hopefully make it to the Tribeca film festival with any luck. But you never know with these things."

He nodded. "You never know."

I repeated, "One trip around the block."

"Why is car so important? Lots of pretty cars in New York."

"It's the exact same car, make and model Robert DeNiro drives. We have a DeNiro lookalike who'll be having a cup of coffee at a diner when the car pulls up. He'll get up and walk toward the car. We're going to film it at such an angle that no one will know it's not him."

He smiled and nodded some more. "I see—Hollywood."

I grinned. "Hollywood."

As he thought it over, I reached into my wallet and showed him a crisp one-hundred-dollar bill. "One trip around the block."

He looked greedily at the bill. "One trip—but I come."

I took out another two hundreds. "One trip, and you stay."

Staring greedily at the money, I could see his wheels spinning. "How do I know you bring car back?"

I played my last card and took out the last $200 and handed all five bills to him. "You don't, but cars go missing all the time and you're just one of many attendants who work here. You can't be held accountable—especially if there's no record of this transaction."

He held the $500 in his hands and stared at me, motionless, for a full minute as he made up his mind. Without a word, he pocketed the cash and reached into a key cabinet behind him, searched around for a few seconds and found what he was looking for. He placed the keys on a small desk in front of him but just out of my reach. "I go bathroom. If you no here when I return, I no cry."

"But…?"

"Upper level." With that, he turned his back to me and walked away.

I quickly grabbed the keys and raced up the stairwell across from his office. The smell of grease and gasoline permeated the building and I wondered what kind of chronic diseases one could get working here.

The garage had only four floors. I reached the top quickly and perused the rows of cars as I ran up and down each aisle. I found it at the far end of the second row facing out. It was a gorgeous metallic silver sedan with twenty-one-inch high-performance tires and a beige leather interior. Shiny and almost new. I let myself in, quickly buckled up and started the engine. The 600 horsepower V-8 engine sprang to life, rumbling like a male lion on the African plains. I raced the engine like a teenager and its deep baritone response told me it was ready for action. Examining the cockpit, I saw all sorts of buttons and accessories I wasn't sure of, including one that said night vision. There was a full tank of gas. My plan was to take the car somewhere safe where I could examine it at my leisure and then return it in the morning.

I turned on the air conditioning and left the garage uneventfully, noticing that the attendant hadn't returned. On Avenue B, I spotted the gang waiting patiently at the corner next to a bus stop. Pulling up to the curb, I found the window controls and lowered the passenger side.

"Hey guys, hop in."

They saw me and came close, admiring the car. Knuckles said, "Now that's fine."

Even Liz seemed interested. Stan said, "What are we going to do with this?"

Bob opened the rear door and said, "Let's get in and find out."

As they were starting to enter, I noticed in the rearview mirror two guys shouting and running in our direction. They were about half a block back. My first reaction was that they might be trying to hail a cab but I didn't see one anywhere near. Knuckles got in the front and Liz squeezed into the back with the boys. The men were closing in fast and their agitation appeared to be reaching the boiling point. Twenty feet away, one stopped, reached behind his back and came out with a small hand cannon. The metal barrel glinted in the sunlight as he took aim and I realized it was the car he was after.

Yelling, "Hold on!", I slammed the car into gear and pressed the pedal to the metal. The car screeched, burned rubber, and rocketed into the intersection just as the light turned red. Cars honked their annoyance and New Yorkers flipped me the bird as they dodged the 5,000-pound bullet heading their way. In the mirror the two guys stopped, the one put his gun away and they both piled into some type of black SUV that had pulled up beside them.

I was going too fast to worry about what was going on behind me. For safety, I slowed down to just ordinary speeding and turned right with a squealing sound onto East 4th Street. Liz screamed and Knuckles clutched the dashboard. I wanted to get away from city traffic and made my way over to the FDR highway.

Looking around the cabin, I saw everyone frozen with fear. Knuckles said, "Doc, are you kidnapping us?"

Liz said, "I knew it," and started crying.

"Everybody relax. No one's being kidnapped. There were guys with guns approaching the car. I saw them in the rear-view mirror. Sorry, I didn't have time to explain." We were doing 45 mph on a 30, should be 20, street. Sooner or later I was going to get into an accident or pick up a cop so I brought the speed down.

Bob said, "Guns!? Oh my God!"

Knuckles turned around. "Take it easy everyone. The doc knows what he's doing. Liz, take a deep breath and put the mace away. This would not be a good time to incapacitate the doc." She turned back to me. "You know what you're doing, right?"

"Sure."

"So, who were they? The same guys who iced the kid?"

"Probably."

"And this is their car? You might have mentioned that."

"I didn't know it. It's registered to the dead student."

Liz screamed, "Watch out!"

I was making a left onto Avenue D when a black Ford Bronco blasted by and almost clipped my front end. It was them! They must have surmised my plan to get on the East Side Drive and sought to cut me off. They realized they overshot their quarry and came to a screeching halt. Smoke filled the air from their burning tires. I floored the accelerator and took off in the opposite direction as they made a U-turn, cutting off traffic. I was just a few blocks from Houston. If we could make it there we should be able to get on the highway. I had no doubt that on the open road the BMW would easily outperform the Bronco.

I saw them coming up quickly, recklessly weaving in and out around other motorists. They were three vehicles back and I was approaching a red light on East Houston. I held my breath and clenched my teeth as I swerved into the opposing lane, cut off traffic on Houston, honked my horn at pedestrians and made perhaps the most dangerous left turn of my life. I slammed the pedal and found the entrance to the FDR northbound to the Bronx while everyone in the car shrieked and rolled back and forth with every maneuver.

They were still behind me but had lost ground in the chaos. Neither one of us was paying a whole lot of attention to traffic laws at the moment. Every car, stop sign, or cyclist was an obstacle to be overcome without regard to etiquette or safety.

Traffic was light on the FDR and I let her rip. Zero to sixty in four seconds. Not bad for a sedan. I reached eighty and left it there. Going any faster would be unnecessarily hazardous. This was an old highway with potholes and merging traffic, not the Daytona speedway. For the moment, I couldn't see the Bronco and let out a deep breath through my teeth.

"We in the clear, Doc?" Knuckles asked.

"I doubt it. They can't be that far behind and I can't maintain this speed for long." I looked in the mirror and didn't see them. Maybe they got stuck in traffic or with any luck got pulled over by a cop. Wouldn't that be convenient?

"Where are we going?" asked Stan.

"Nowhere in particular, Stan. I'm just trying to get away from them. The further out from the city, the better chance we'll have." I crossed the Willis Avenue Bridge into the Bronx, merged into heavy South Bronx traffic meandering my way to my old stomping grounds. I was hungry and thought it was time for a pit stop. I was thinking about taking my gang, as I now thought of them, out to lunch on Arthur Avenue, the Bronx's version of Little Italy.

They all stared out their windows at the desolate, burnt-out neighborhoods we drove through. Whole blocks of wasteland, empty lots and boarded-up buildings. If they were scared before, they were pissing in their pants now. I stayed on Third Avenue all the way to restaurant row and never caught sight of the Bronco again. This buoyed all of our spirits. Once on Arthur Avenue I parked on a small side street in back of my favorite restaurant *Zero Otto Nove*. It was 1:00 p.m. and I was famished.

I said, "C'mon guys. Lunch is on me."

Chapter 16

We sat at a large round table in the center of the dining room, Knuckles on my right, Stan on my left. Bob and Liz on the other side. The waiter opened the bottle of Chianti I had ordered and everyone studied their menus.

Bob said, "I can't read the menu. It's in Italian."

Knuckles asked loudly, "Is this place mobbed up?"

The waiter and some guy sipping espresso by himself in a corner raised their eyebrows and glared at her.

I raised my hands. "Whoa! Take it easy with that kind of talk around here." Turning to the waiter I added, "She's a big kidder."

He nodded and filled our glasses. I leaned close to Knuckles. "They take this stuff rather seriously in these neighborhoods."

She whispered, "So I see. Are we going to make it out of here in one piece?"

I smiled. "I'll see what I can do."

She grinned back. "You're one of them, aren't you?"

I looked over my shoulder and then back at her and said dead-panned. "I'll never talk."

She started laughing. "Jesus, you had me going."

Stan cleared his throat. "If somebody doesn't help us with the menu, we're going to be eating breadsticks for lunch."

I said, "How about I order for the table? I get the feeling you guys don't eat much real Italian food other than pizza. I'll get a mix of plates to share."

"There he goes taking over again. I don't need anybody making decisions for me," whined Liz.

Stan, Bob and Knuckles closed their menus and agreed in unison. Liz rolled her eyes and said, "Fine."

I raised my glass and they followed suit. "Salute, everyone. Here's to good health and new friends. I'd also like to thank you for helping me today, and I'm sorry about all the excitement. I'll try to keep it down from now on."

I ordered a large platter of antipasto for the table with prosciutto, assorted salamis, clams oreganata, eggplant rollatini, marinated artichoke hearts, fresh sardines, stuffed mushrooms, and house-made mozzarella drizzled with extra virgin olive oil and aged balsamic vinegar. A loaf of warm, crusty Italian bread completed the first course. For entrees, I ordered three extra-large plates to share; penne vodka, risotto with shrimp and crabmeat, and sautéed sweet sausage with butternut squash and gorgonzola. A helluva carb load but worth it.

Knuckles was practically salivating. "Doc, you really know how to live."

Liz rolled her eyes again and I wanted to go over there and shake her. I said, "What now, Liz?"

"Are you trying to give us all heart attacks?"

Bob interjected. "Not everyone, Liz, just you." Everyone at the table burst into laughter. Liz folded her arms and pouted, shifting her body away from the table.

Our food came and we got to know each other on a very different level that only a good meal and wine can facilitate. When Stan and Bob excused themselves to go to the bathroom together Knuckles shook her head. I said, "What's up?"

"Those two are going to be the death of me."

"Why is that?"

"Bob's husband is insanely jealous and Stan's wife is also crazy nuts. If they ever catch them it's going to be a war zone."

I thought about that. "So, if Stan has a wife and Bob has a husband then Stan must be the man and Bob must be the woman in the relationship."

Liz choked on her penne. "Are you for real?"

Knuckles laughed and slapped me on the back. "Doc, you're a riot. It's not quite like that, but if that helps you keep it straight in your head then don't worry about it or as they say in a joint like this…" She leaned close and lowered her voice. "Fuggedaboutit."

Liz said, "It's rude to talk about people when they're not present."

Knuckles and I looked at each other and started laughing again. I turned to Liz. "It's even ruder to not look at someone when you speak to them."

Knuckles said, "Take it easy on her, Doc. She's not so bad. She's got PTSD or something. That's all I know because she won't talk about it."

"You know what, Knuckles? I don't give a damn what she's got. I'm tired of people making excuses for their bad behavior. I've been crapped on my whole life and I don't take it out on anyone."

"I can hear every word," Liz interjected.

Ignoring her Knuckles added, "I hear you, but not everyone has the same coping skills that you do."

I softened up at her logic, took a sip of wine and said, "Maybe you're right. I'm sorry, Liz."

She had turned her seat away from the table and held her plate on her lap. With a mouthful of risotto, she said, "The only thing ruder than talking about someone when they're not there is to talk about someone when they are sitting right there."

Bob and Stan returned to the table. "Did we miss anything?" Liz said, "Knuckles filled him in on you two."

Stan replied, "Who cares? Doc, pass the sausage, please?"

As I handed him the plate, Knuckles commented, "Hey, Doc, you got a pair of guns, don't you? Even with a long-sleeve shirt it's pretty obvious. You must work out."

"Not as much as I should. When I was younger I was a gym rat. I'm getting soft these days."

"You ever use the juice?" she asked referring to anabolic steroids.

"No, never. I'm strictly a natural guy. I don't believe in artificial enhancements of any kind."

Knuckles and Liz started giggling. Knuckles said, "Then you'd better not ask Pam about her breasts."

My jaw dropped and it was obvious I didn't know. I said, "I don't believe you."

She added, "Liz and I drove her to and from the hospital."

I was still speechless and Knuckles slapped me on the back. "Must have been a pretty good job if you didn't notice. Either that or you haven't even gotten to first base and I find that hard to believe. She told me her plastic surgeon is a genius. I guess she was right."

Bob and Stan finished off their wine. "All right, leave him alone. Can't you see he's in shock?"

I turned to them. "You guys know, too?"

"Oh, please."

Liz's shoulders were shaking uncontrollably as she tried hard to suppress her laughter. "What's so funny, Liz?" I asked.

She shook her head back and forth giggling quietly. "You thought those 34 Ds were real?"

I needed some fresh air. I don't know why but I felt a little off balance by this news. I was being silly and I knew it. So she had breast implants. So what? How could I have not known? I suddenly felt vulnerable. Was there anything else about her that I didn't know about? How much plastic surgery has she had? Who knew? I loved her ass and her legs. Were they real? Her lips? Was she a man? Oh my God! It was dark last night. How could I be sure?

I suddenly felt very hot and excused myself to go to the men's room. The dining room was separated from the main entrance and bar area by a short narrow hallway where the bathrooms were. I relieved myself, washed my hands and splashed cold water on my face.

When I came out, I noticed a guy at the bar with his back to me chatting with the bartender and showing him photos. He was in need of information. There was something familiar about him and then I saw the bulge in his back under his windbreaker. It was the guy with the hand cannon in the Bronco. How the hell did he find us? It dawned on me. The BMW must have a GPS tracker in it that activated when I started the engine.

Shit!

Did he know what we looked like? Maybe. The twinks wore brightly colored Hawaiian shirts and Knuckles was Knuckles. They were an eclectic group for sure. See them once and they'd be indelibly imprinted in your brain. I had to assume the worst. What were those photos he was showing? Probably the car.

Returning to the table, I signaled the waiter for the bill. I didn't know how much time I had. Knuckles said, "Hey, Doc, we decided in your absence that from now on, you're Jim Phelps and we're the IMF team."

I was distracted. "I'm who and you're what?"

"We're the IMF team— 'Impossible Mission Force' —and you're our leader, Jim Phelps. C'mon you must have seen the movies? You know…" She lowered her voice. "As always, Jim, if you or any member of your team are caught or killed, you will be disavowed."

Before I could respond Liz said, "I don't see how he could lead anything. He can't even tell fake boobs when he sees them."

I liked it better when she didn't talk. I answered Knuckles, "I saw the first movie. I know what you mean."

I handed my credit card to the waiter. "Guys, don't freak out but we have a bit of a problem."

They suddenly got serious and focused their full attention on me, even Liz. I said, "Those guys that were following us, one is in the bar out front."

Liz gasped and the boys went white as sheets. Knuckles said, "How are we going to get out of here?"

I looked around and didn't see any other exit other than the way we came in. There had to be fire codes about this stuff but older buildings frequently bypassed the rules until they got caught. Maybe I was overreacting. He may just ask a few questions and leave. That still left me with the problem of getting out of here with my IMF team unseen. Once we were on the street, we would be sitting ducks.

I said, "I'm thinking about it."

I snapped my fingers. "The kitchen. There has to be a way out from there. There always is."

The waiter returned my credit card and I asked him where the kitchen was so I could compliment the chef and he pointed to a swinging door at the far end of the room. As we stood up to leave two things happened: One, the guy with the large handgun behind his back entered the dining room; and two, Liz screamed at the top of her lungs and pointed at me. I looked down. My fly was open.

The entire room turned in our direction, including the guy looking for us. Recognizing us immediately, he made a bee line toward the table. I turned to them. "Knuckles, the kitchen now! Get them out of here."

130

She and the others ran toward the kitchen behind us while I held my ground. People sat around slack-jawed trying to understand what was happening. When the guy was within a few feet, he began to reach around his back for the weapon. A waiter at the table next to me had just finished setting down a large bowl of steaming hot cioppino. He was frozen in place as was everyone else.

I grabbed the bowl off the table, hurled it into the guy's face and he howled in pain, clawing at scungilli and mussels. The gun was still holstered in the small of his back and I charged him like a linebacker. He fell backward onto the floor with me on top. I grabbed his shirt collar with both hands and banged his head onto the hardwood floor. Once, twice, three times—that was enough. He lost consciousness. I rolled him over and took his pistol.

Full blown panic swept the room at the sight of the gun. People screamed and dialed 911. Running through the kitchen, I tossed the revolver into a large stock pot simmering with tomato sauce. Outside, I caught up with the others standing nervously on the sidewalk in the rear of the restaurant and quickly hustled them to the car half a block further down the street. We sped off to the wail of approaching police sirens.

Chapter 17

"There's must be some type of GPS tracking device linked to the car's ignition," I explained as we drove.

"Knuckles asked nervously, "What are we going to do?"

"We're going to die, that's what," Liz chimed in.

I didn't argue the point with her because it was entirely within the realm of possibility. "Relax, everybody. I have an idea."

I drove the car to an old chop shop I frequented as a misguided youth on the corner of Morris Park Avenue and Eastchester Road. It had been a long time since I'd been there and wasn't even sure if they were still in business, but it was worth a try. If I remembered correctly, they had a massive underground parking garage they would store the cars in until they were ready to dispose of them.

I pulled into the nondescript entrance and signaled a mechanic. A guy with dirty overalls approached the car and said, "You gotta park on the street. You can't leave the car here."

I responded, "Does Vinnie still work here?"

"Sure does. He owns the place now. You want I should get him?"

"I'd appreciate it. I'm in sort of a hurry."

He sized up the car and its occupants, perceived no threat and went into the back office. A couple of minutes later a rotund, clean-shaven man wearing a black three-piece suit and alligator shoes, sporting a large diamond-and-onyx pinky ring, appeared. Vincenzo Terranova, all-state offensive tackle for five straight years at my high school, a holy terror both on and off the field, had finally come into his own.

I got out of the car and shook his hand. He was at least 300 pounds. I said, "Vinnie, it's been a long time. You look like you've lost weight."

He chuckled. "My wife and I do Weight Watchers. Thanks for noticing. How've you been, Cesari?"

Two sentences in and he was already walking around the car inspecting it. I said, "I've been good. The car's hot."

"I figured as much. I thought you became a doctor or something?"

"I am a doctor, a gastroenterologist."

He stuck his big head in the open driver's side window and inspected the passengers as well, while I stared at his fat ass. He came out and said, "How much do you want for it?"

"It's not that simple. I need to keep it for a day or so but I got a big problem right now. It's got a GPS tracking device hardwired to the ignition and there are some nasty guys following us. Can you fix that?"

"Fuck, Cesari. That should have been the first thing you said, not the last. You're slipping." He turned to the guy in the overalls. "Tommy, take the car to the basement and find the damn tracking device. Do it now." He opened the driver's side door and ordered everybody to get out.

Turning to me he said, "Let's go to my office."

His "office" was in the rear of the garage and was barely ten feet square with a small laminate desk piled high with invoices, receipts, catalogues and porn magazines. We crammed in and he said, "The basement is reinforced with cement and heavy-duty steel. They'll lose the signal down there. We've been playing this GPS game for a while now. Tommy will find it. He's a mechanical genius. So how's life been treating you? You look well enough. Introduce me to your friends. Anybody want I should make coffee?"

I went around the room making introductions. His rapid-fire style of speech didn't throw me off too much. That was his trademark even as a kid. I said, "Congratulations, by the way, on taking over the business. How is Pops? Having fun in retirement, I hope?"

"If being under ground in a $10,000 silk-lined coffin wearing a $1,000 suit you never would have worn when you were alive is having fun, then I guess he's having a ball."

I remembered his father well and did a quick calculation in my head. He would only have been in his early sixties at best. "I'm sorry, Vinnie. I didn't know. What happened?"

"One too many plates of lasagna, that's what happened. He had a massive heart attack."

"I'm sorry. How's your mom?"

"She's doing time at Fishkill."

"What!?"

"Well, dad decided to have his heart attack while he was getting his knob polished by his girlfriend, Delilah, right here in this office and mom decided that if Delilah cared for him that much she should join him in the afterlife. It was a mess, Cesari. I'm scarred from it."

"I'll bet."

"It's no joke. I'm telling you. Right after that, I went on a diet and broke up with my girlfriend, both of them. Trying to live right, you know? Me and the wife, we go for walks. It's tough. I live in Scarsdale and there are gelato and pastry shops on every corner and the sex is so—boring. I mean, marriage is to sex what a bucket of cold water is to fire. You know what I mean?"

"You got to fight it, Vinnie. You're doing the right thing."

Knuckles, Liz, and the boys looked at each other. They were afraid to speak. He said, "So what's with the BMW? You gonna sell it to me? I'll give you fifteen grand. No questions asked."

I thought about it. I could use the cash. The car was worth a lot more but beggars can't be choosy. "That's a generous offer. Give me twenty-four hours, all right? I need the car for a while."

When the GPS unit was removed, I offered to compensate Vinnie but he waved me off. "Fuggedaboutit." Knuckles no longer thought the expression was quite as funny as she had.

We left the garage and drove to a row of abandoned store fronts on Allerton Avenue. I pulled into a narrow driveway between two small, boarded-up, brick buildings until the car was out of sight from the main road.

Knuckles and I got out of the car and went to the back of the vehicle and I popped the trunk. It was filled to overflowing with tightly wrapped bags of a white powder, probably heroin. Knuckles was shocked. I wasn't but it was nice to have proof. I still didn't understand the mechanics of the operation though. How did the transactions take place, the exchange of money and drugs, and basic communications? Other than that, it seemed like a straightforward dope-dealing business.

"How much is all that worth, Doc?"

I picked up one big bag and counted twenty-five smaller bags wrapped inside. There were thousands of bags each with single dose contents of narcotics. At ten bucks a hit, that translated into a lot of cash. I said, "I can't be sure. Maybe a couple of million. Maybe more."

She said, "Enough to die for?"

"Not enough for me to die for."

Knuckles said, "Yeah, but you're a doctor. A student might see things differently."

"What do you mean?"

"Are you kidding? Undergraduate tuition at NYU including room and board, books, laptop, and other supplies is easily over $60,000 per year. These kids are getting reamed."

"Really? I had no idea it was that much."

"And no guarantee of a job when you're done."

I mulled that over, trying to see it from a different perspective. "I take it back then. This must have seemed like the mother lode to him."

"Hell, it seems like the mother lode to me."

"Still not a good reason to die."

"He probably never thought that was going to happen."

I nodded in agreement. People who deal or use drugs never think the worst is going to happen. I closed the trunk and asked everyone to get out while I performed a detailed search of the entire vehicle inside and out. I crawled underneath to inspect the chassis and Knuckles helped me get to my feet when I was done, she said, "Jesus, Doc, where'd you learn all this stuff?"

"Right here in the Bronx. Before I saw the light."

I didn't find anything else and was disappointed. Although Knuckles' point about tuition costs being outrageous made sense, it seemed a ridiculous reason to die for. Then again, people died for much less reason all the time. I consoled myself with that thought as I rummaged through the interior one more time. In the glove compartment, I found the invoice to the car, its registration and owner's manual. They seemed in order and unrevealing. That is, except for all the yellow highlights on the invoice and in the manual. I looked at them a little more carefully but couldn't find any pattern or relationship. I made a mental note to examine it a little more carefully later.

"Okay, guys, I got to get you back to Manhattan. It's almost five and I have dinner plans with Pam." I regretted saying that immediately.

Stan and Bob giggled, "We knew it."

Knuckles said, "Of course you knew it. I told you."

"We knew it before that."

Liz said, "You'd better not rape her."

I gave her a severe look. "Would you stop that?"

"If the shoe fits."

I bit my lip and drove them back to Manhattan, dropping them off in the vicinity of NYU. They all lived relatively nearby. I parked the car in a garage by my apartment, grabbed the owner's manual and invoice and went upstairs to change. Cleo nearly knocked me over in joy as I entered the apartment and I hugged her tightly. Zach was sitting at the kitchen table studying and stood up to greet me. He was shorter than me, thin with long, wavy brown hair, and wore black-framed eyeglasses.

"Hello, Dr. Cesari. I just walked and fed her. She's had another great day in the park. She really loves it there."

I smiled. "Thanks, Zach. I really appreciate you taking care of her. School going well?"

"Oh, I love her. I'd be happy to take care of her every day if you need. She's wonderful, and yes, school's fine."

"Glad to hear it about school and I'll keep you posted on the other. She seems to really like you too."

I paid him and he said goodbye to Cleo. I showered, pranced around in my Fordham University boxers for a few minutes humming Sinatra's "That's Life," and then changed into dress slacks and shirt for my big date. I splashed on some after shave and by 6:30 p.m. was in a cab heading over to Pam's.

She opened the door, checked me out, sniffed me, and pulled me into the apartment. Once the door was closed, she pushed me back against it, threw her arms around my neck and kissed me.

She sighed deeply. "It's been so long."

"It's just been a few hours, Pam."

"Yeah, but you're going back to prison."

"But I don't have to stay overnight anymore so we can still see each other at night."

"I guess I'll have to be satisfied with that. Today was just torture. I looked at the clock every five minutes."

"C'mon, Pam, I'm not that good."

She smiled, "It's not quality that matters. It's the size."

I snorted. She was killing me. "You look great." She did, too. She wore tight jeans and a light-colored top with heels, gold dangly earrings, and a braided gold chain necklace. Out of the corner of my eye, so as not to be caught, I studied her breasts trying to see if I could tell. I couldn't, but that was no excuse for last night's failure. "We should get going or we'll be late for our reservation."

Looking at me seriously, she said, "I wouldn't mind skipping dinner and getting right to the main course."

I'd had a big lunch but the idea of missing a steak dinner was intolerable on so many levels I didn't know where to begin. I said, "I perform better on a full stomach."

She laughed. "Then let's go."

Wolfgang's Steakhouse was an old-school place in Tribeca on the west side. You could practically see the water of the Hudson River from where we sat. The waiters wore black, with white aprons. Every woman who entered the place no matter her age was handed a long-stemmed red rose. I ordered a hundred-dollar bottle of Robert Mondavi cabernet and thought I was getting away with murder when I perused the full wine list. There were half-bottles going for five hundred or more.

We sipped the delicious nectar and nibbled on warm bread as we waited for our twenty-ounce rib eye steaks and creamed spinach. I studied her features through the candlelight. Her lips were full but not botoxed, I surmised. Her nose looked natural though if her plastic surgeon was that good, how would I know? My eyes drifted down to her breasts again, only this time she caught me and smiled approvingly. I bet she did. Those guys were there for one reason and one reason only. To lure fools like me into the tender trap.

"What are you thinking about?" she asked.

I rested my chin in the palm of my left hand while I wiggled my wine glass on the table with my right. I said, "How beautiful you are."

She liked that and gave me a big smile. "Thank you. You're not so bad yourself."

Our steaks came and we began eating. The creamed spinach was probably the best I ever had, seasoned with plenty of fresh nutmeg. "So how did your studying go today? Did you learn a lot?"

"Oh yeah."

"What about?"

"The art of deception…"

"Oh really, and what exactly did you learn about it?"

"That I should never underestimate a person's ability to deceive others about who they are emotionally, mentally, and—physically. It's a big issue in the prisons."

She sipped her wine and I took a bite of steak. "Wow, sounds like you spent the entire afternoon in my field of expertise. We should just have studied together. It would have been fun."

She was good the way she side-stepped that one. "It might have been difficult studying with you if you were clock-watching all day."

"Did I mention the fun part?" she said smiling ear to ear.

She ate about half of her steak and I ate most of mine. The rest we boxed to go and caught a taxi to her office. I was anxious to get up there and do a real examination before I committed myself to intimacy. I wanted answers and I wanted them tonight.

We entered her office at just after 10:00 p.m. and I flipped on the overhead lights as she tugged at my clothes. She looked at me puzzled and flipped the lights back off.

She said, "I'd prefer the lights off if you don't mind."

I smiled. "I wanted to see you better." I flipped them back on.

She took a step back studying me, slightly confused. "I understand, but I want you to throw me up against the window like you did last night, and if the lights are on, half the city will see us." She flipped the lights off again.

She was good.

"Can we fool around on the couch first? You know a little foreplay before the main event. Then we can turn them off and I'll throw you anywhere you want."

"You're going to make me wait? Are you kidding?"

"Some things are worth waiting for."

"Yeah, but I've been waiting all day. Fine, but there's a floor lamp we can use next to the sofa. The lighting won't be as harsh."

I compromised. "Okay."

Ten minutes later, we lay nestled on the couch. She was down to her panties and I was in my Fordham boxers, which made her laugh. "This is what you wear on a date?"

"What's wrong with them? I'm very proud of the education I received there."

"They're kind of sexy, I guess."

"Hey, you really want to have fun?"

"What do you think?" She asked hugging me and kissing me on the neck.

"Let's play doctor."

"What?"

"You pretend to be my patient and that you've come for a complete physical exam."

"Seriously? What do I have to do?"

"Just lie down and let me take a look at you. You won't regret it."

Giggling she said, "All right, but I still want to do it by the window—and the tongue thing."

She lay flat on the sofa and I pulled the floor lamp in as close as possible. She covered her eyes and said, "What's with you and the light?"

"A good doctor needs to see everything."

"Fine."

I got on my knees and started with her face. I looked closely as she watched, grinning from ear to ear. "What are you doing?"

Without responding, I continued to check her out. There were no obvious signs of surgery. Her eyebrows, nose and lips looked real. I put my face close to hers and looked into her eyes. I could feel her breathing as I brushed my lips against hers. She moaned and tried to pull me down to her. I pushed her arms down to her side. "There'll be plenty of time for that when I'm done. Now be a good patient and don't move."

"That's not fair," she pouted.

I shuffled down to her feet and examined them including each pink-painted toe, one at a time. She liked having her feet caressed and I lingered there, happy to oblige her. There were no signs of binding or other intervention. Her calves were smooth as silk and I ran my hands gently up and down to check for implants and then came her thighs. I placed my hands around each thigh starting at the knee and slid them up until I reached her lace panties. Purple. Not my favorite color for ladies' undergarments but I supposed I shouldn't complain considering what I was wearing. At the top of her thighs I reached around to feel her bottom searching for irregularities and signs of surgery. Her breathing came in short heaving bursts and her excitement grew as I slipped my hands inside her underwear. I wasn't trying to torture her but it couldn't be helped. This had to be done. It was all part of the process.

I gently pulled her panties down and she made a whimpering sound. I examined this area most carefully of all. I had never been with someone who'd had a sex change operation and wasn't sure what to expect. If she did, how should I react? If I didn't care, did that mean I was gay? Good questions. The area was shaved smooth and as I got close she arched upward, receptively. With my tongue, I explored her for taste, texture, and authenticity as she reached out to play with my throbbing member. Suddenly climaxing, she moaned hoarsely, "Oh my God."

She passed inspection on all counts, and by the time I finished, I was satisfied she was a real woman. I said, "No noise please. You'll break my concentration."

"You bastard," she panted. "Come over here."

"I'm almost done." I pulled her hands off me and placed them back at her side, pissing her off.

"Take me now," she pleaded.

Ignoring her, I placed my hands on her abdomen, watching them rise and fall as she breathed heavily in and out. She had a dangly type belly ring that I kissed over and over to her satisfaction. I looked at her breasts, now arched high off the sofa. They were perfect in every way. Symmetrical globes with soft, erect nipples—they were amazing. I couldn't even find the scars no matter how hard I looked. I felt each one carefully trying to discern by tactile sensation if I could tell, but was disappointed. They passed the taste test, the twirl test, and the tug test. Her surgeon was a genius. She started to moan again.

I kissed her on the neck and could feel her carotid artery pounding ferociously. A moment later, I gave her a small peck on the cheek and then a more serious one on the lips. She purred her approval and this time I allowed her to pull me on top of her as she wrapped her legs tightly around my waist. Our lips met passionately. We were two people on fire and in danger of being consumed by the flames. She reached down and found me, guiding me into her. We both arched into each other at the same time as we lost control.

She panted, "Can you just stay in there forever?"

"Sure, why not?"

Later, we pulled the sofa over to the window, and as she sat on my lap with her arms around my neck, we looked out at the Manhattan skyline.

Life was good today.

Chapter 18

*I*t was Saturday and Riker's sucked more than usual. The inmates were all being assholes and the guards were unusually surly. The morning was grueling and tedious. It seemed like everybody had a head cold or sore throat. I was going through the motions and was preoccupied with my mission as outlined to me by my new boss, Detective Kilcullen.

I watched the clock, filled with dread, as noon approached. Racked with anxiety, my heart raced as I entered the cafeteria with a sense of doom and foreboding. Espionage or undercover work or whatever you wanted to call it wasn't my strong suit. I was much too direct a guy. The room was filling up fast as 1,500 guys shuffled in, beaten down by life. I got in line with my plastic tray, got a bologna sandwich and container of milk, and came out the other end looking for Samuel.

Diamond waved to me to come sit at her table and I politely pretended I didn't notice. I spotted Samuel ten tables back right smack in the center of the room, surrounded by a sea of his spider web tattooed goons. I walked slowly up the aisle toward him reviewing in my mind the possible combinations of responses I might receive to my overture. Most of them weren't good and I couldn't blame him. I reached the table, hesitated and walked down the row until I was in the center opposite him standing behind a nasty looking guy shoveling food into his mouth as fast as he could. He had a crucifix tattooed on his head.

Samuel looked up at me as did several of his guys. We made eye contact and I said, "May I join you?"

He was silent as he stared at me. I waited an uncomfortable minute and repeated myself. "May I join you?"

Slowly, his gaze drifted down to the guy I was standing behind who had stopped eating. Samuel signaled him to move and without a word he picked up his tray and left the table. I sat in his space and nodded at Samuel.

No one said anything and I began eating my sandwich. Samuel watched in silence, with no emotion, not even curiosity, on his face. He studied me like I was a lab rat and I ate like I didn't care. I was sure he would have loved to jump across the table and tear my heart out but in Riker's, in full view of the guards, that would put him in solitary for weeks if not months, which could hurt business, or even worse, his standing with his men.

Lunch ended quietly enough and I felt good that I hadn't sustained severe injury as a result of the experience. Unfortunately, I didn't accomplish much either. He didn't say a word and neither did I, so I was still at square one until tomorrow, when I would try again. Now all I had to do was make it until five and then I'd be free to see Pam.

Thinking about her lifted my spirits. Damn, she was wild. Afternoon clinic started off with a guy having rectal pain because he shoved a six-inch wood dowel up his ass and accidentally let go of it. I shook my head as I talked to him. Some of these guys were so far out there you needed a telescope to see them.

"How bad is the pain?" I asked.

"Pretty bad."

His vital signs were stable and he didn't have a fever. His abdominal exam revealed moderate tenderness in the left lower quadrant without evidence for peritonitis. Good.

I turned to Keith who was apparently my personal prison guard as he seemed to be assigned to me and the clinic every weekend. I didn't mind because he was basically a decent guy. If you didn't mess with him he left you alone. I said to him, "There are two ways we can handle this. I could have him transferred to Queens County hospital for a colonoscopy, which would cause piles of paperwork for you, or you could let me take him to the OR here and perform a sigmoidoscopy on him to get this thing out."

Keith rubbed his chin and said, "Let me call the doctor in charge and you can tell him. If he says it's okay then it's okay."

He took out his cellphone and made the call, spoke for a minute and handed me the phone. I said, "Hi, Dave, sorry to bother you."

"No problem, John. What's going on?"

"One of the inmates lost a six-inch wood dowel up his rectum."

He chuckled, "You're kidding? Where'd he get it?"

"He made it in the woodshop."

"Is he okay?"

"He's uncomfortable but yeah, he's okay. Your call."

"You don't need anesthesia or a nurse?"

"No, it's down low in the rectum. I can practically feel it. If I can't get it out then we'll transfer him."

"Isn't this going to hurt without sedation?"

"I won't feel a thing."

He thought I was funny and laughed. "Go ahead, give it a shot. Put Keith on and I'll tell him."

Thirty minutes later, I had set up the equipment in one of the ORs and had him lying on his left side facing away. I generously lubricated the tip of the colonoscope and inserted it. He flinched, recovered, and remained still.

"Okay, just relax now, all right? There it is. See it? This will only take a minute." Barely a couple of inches in, one could easily see the rounded end of the wood dowel. I had pre-opened a large metal snare and inserted it through one of the channels on the colonoscope. When it appeared on the screen I looped it around the piece of wood and asked Keith to tighten it from his end.

He looked at me uneasily. "You didn't say anything about this part, Doc."

"I'm sorry. It didn't occur to me. Look, it's not that hard. See the white plastic handle? Just pull the round part out until it won't go any further and I'll do the rest. Just hold onto it tightly is all I need you to do."

With reluctance, he did as I asked and I gently withdrew the scope hanging onto the wood dowel until it rested safely on the exam table in front of us. The inmate breathed a loud sigh of relief. He ought to have kissed my ass because I've seen situations like this result in perforations and emergency colectomies.

The guy said, "Thanks, Doc. I owe you one."

"You don't owe me anything, but do yourself a favor and get a girlfriend."

Keith chuckled at that.

The rest of the afternoon passed uneventfully and when the last patient left I had mixed feelings. I was glad to be going home yet I was sort of disappointed that I hadn't made the connection with Samuel the way I had wanted. Still, no one could fault me for that. There was always tomorrow.

As I straightened out the room, the two guards took up position on opposing sides of the door the way they always did when they were about to escort me to the cell block. That struck me as odd, since my next stop was supposed to be the parking lot. I finished what I was doing and turned to Keith and stood there waiting for my civilian clothes.

He looked at me and signaled me to start walking toward the cell block. I was confused. "Aren't you going to give me my clothes?"

He looked at the other guard and then back at me. "Don't give me any trouble, Doc." The other guard stepped forward in an aggressive stance.

Alarmed I said, "I thought I was going home tonight?"

"Doc, I don't know anything about that. Now step forward right now or things are going to start getting real serious in here." He reached for his baton.

My heart sank. What was happening? "But the warden said..."

He squared off in front of me. "I'm going to count to three. One..."

I started walking and when I was done, I found myself in the cafeteria again in line behind 200 other guys trudging forward. My brain raced frantically to understand. Did the warden forget to tell the guards? Or maybe she changed her mind? Or maybe—just maybe that prick, Kilcullen, talked her out of it so that I could spend more quality time with Samuel. Could he do that? And if he could, then what other surprises were in store for me?

I took a slab of meatloaf with gravy, some peas, and a couple of slices of white bread and made my way into the dining hall. Samuel's table hadn't quite filled up as I meandered toward it. Might as well give it another shot while I was here. This time he watched me intently as I approached. The seat next to him was open and I didn't bother asking permission this time as I sat and started eating.

Every eye at the table was burning a hole into me and I could feel Samuel's hot breath on the side of my face. In a low, menacing voice, he hissed, "What the fuck do you want?"

Without skipping a beat or looking at anything but my food I replied, "A chance to apologize."

There was a long pause as he digested that. "And why would you want to do that?"

"Last week, I didn't know who you were. My bad."

"And how do you know me now?"

"I have friends on the outside who've heard of you. People in the business, you know? People who admire the way you operate and would like to maybe do business with you sometime. When I told them what happened last week, they came down on me real hard and told me to suck it up and do whatever it takes to make it right. You need something done just name it. I'm very sorry about our misunderstanding."

"Just like that? I lost one of my men permanently, the other's still having headaches and I couldn't hear right all week because of you and I'm supposed to accept an apology?"

"No, of course not, but I owe you for my disrespect. All you have to do is give me a chance to prove myself."

He thought it over as everyone else had resumed eating their meals and pretended not to notice our private conversation. I was sure he would have preferred to pummel me and be done with the whole Cesari situation but he needed to communicate with the outside and I was his best option, so he tempered his primal impulse.

"You said you have friends on the outside who want to do business with me. What kind of friends?"

I lowered my voice to a hush, looked all around and whispered, "Italian friends."

He didn't say anything but he nodded his head at the implication. In his little pond, he was the big fish but with the right backing he could go prime time. He said, "The wops want to do business with me?"

"They've been watching your operation at NYU and they want in. So far you're small time and some of your guys are sloppy like the security guard at Steinhardt. They spotted him a mile away."

This caught him completely off guard and I saw the color rise in his cheeks. He hissed, "Fuck."

"Look, I don't expect you to trust me. I understand, but hear me out. My friends can help you grow your business. They got the money and connections. They like your system and don't want to step on your toes. They just want a piece of the pie."

"And what will they do for me?"

"First of all, they make problems go away—permanently, like your competition. Secondly, they have connections at NYU…"

He interrupted me. "We got that part covered."

"Fine, but there are other campuses. Think big, Samuel. These guys can bring the junk in bulk probably ten times the amount you can. My friends have friends in places you don't. You'll know what the cops are thinking before they think it. No more looking over your shoulder."

"How do I know you're not a cop?"

I laughed. "Be real. I put two guys in the hospital who didn't even lay a finger on me. That's two to five years for aggravated assault right there."

"Still…"

"Look, I understand your concern. Go ahead and ask around on the street. Do a Google search. Do whatever you want. I'm not a cop. I don't care. You want to vet me, vet me."

The buzzer screamed overhead signaling the end to dinner, and the inmates started filing out. Samuel was quiet for a while before turning toward me. Staring at me through narrowed eyes, he said, "We'll talk more."

Chapter 19

*M*onday morning, I sat in Detective Kilcullen's office. There was an open bottle of Jameson's on his desk and I wondered what he was sipping from the large coffee mug he held. He was pleased I had made contact with Samuel. "You done good, lad. I was sure you'd be in the morgue by now. I'm impressed."

"Thanks, but I think you made a mistake by keeping me confined there all weekend. It would be better if I could travel freely with his messages. It would be more productive, don't you think? Certainly faster."

He strummed his fingers on his desk. "Maybe. I'll think about it. So where do we stand in the trust department?"

"He gave me some type of coded message to deliver to the security guard at Steinhardt. I'm sure it's just a test, his way of vetting me, so I'll deliver it and see what happens."

He took a swallow from his mug, winced, and shook his head. "Tell us the message, lad."

"He told me to tell him. *Feeling blue. Bring your friends.* He said the guard would understand. He also gave me a code to use to identify myself to the guard."

"And that is?"

"The guard says, "Latrodectus and I respond, Hesperus.""

Kilcullen repeated softly, "Latrodectus Hesperus? What the hell does that mean?"

"It's the Latin name for Black Widow spider."

"You don't say?" he chuckled.

"Simple but clever."

"Well, good work. You made that look easy."

"Not really. He gave me a task to perform to prove my offer of friendship is genuine. There's an inmate that needs to be taken care of and I have to take care of him."

"What exactly does he want done?"

"Wants him beaten—badly. Wants to send a message to the guy's friends and everyone else in the cell block. Tensions have been a little high as of late. He doesn't want to get involved personally because he can't afford a month in solitary."

"And you can?"

"That's what I told him. He also knows that if I start a fight and injure someone it'll ruin my chances of getting out of there in six months. He doesn't care. Fortunately, I didn't cross paths with the guy all weekend. I told him that I would think of something and fix his problem by next week."

"Who's he want beaten?"

"That's problem number two. The guy's name is Malcolm Steadwell. He's a six foot four-inch black guy who weighs 280 pounds. I've been treating him for an ulcer. Even worse is the guy sort of did me a good turn last week. I think that's the real reason Samuel wants to go after him, to set the record straight as to whose side I'm on."

Kilcullen whistled and sat back in his chair. "Well, we knew there was going to be a price to pay, but how you pay it without getting killed is the question."

"Or spending the rest of my life in Riker's?"

"Exactly."

I said, "Well, I've been thinking about it. If I don't start the fight and I'm only defending myself then I can't be charged with assault and I'm pretty sure that I wouldn't be in violation of my probation. I'll need to discuss that with my lawyer."

"Still, the guy sounds like he's twice your size. Not to mention, I'm sure he has friends."

"This is where you come in. How badly do you want this?"

He raised his eyebrows. "What did you have in mind?"

"Offer him something. Maybe shave some time off his sentence or instead of sending him to a maximum-security prison like he's scheduled for, put him someplace light where he can relax a little. Tell him all he's got to do is pick a fight with me and let me win. Take a few punches, you know, make it look good. Some blood's going to have to be spilled of course, but I think he can take it. You'll also need to talk to the warden and explain what's going on so I don't wind up in solitary."

"You really thought this through haven't you, boy? Well, I'll have to talk to the D.A. about this. A lowly detective like me can't make offers like that."

"Stress makes me creative. Go ahead and talk to the D.A. but if he says no then make the offer anyway. How will Malcolm know the difference?"

He chuckled. "You're a dangerous little greaser, aren't you? I love it. I think I like that even better than going to the D.A. at all."

"One more thing."

"Go on."

"When I was pitching the deal to Samuel, I mentioned that I had contacts in NYU's hierarchy and he told me that he had that part covered. I didn't press him on what he meant by that."

Kilcullen hummed as he thought that over. "Okay, Cesari. So far, you're earning your keep. I'll be thinking about your problem. Stay in touch."

I called Pam on the way to my apartment. "John, what happened? I've been worried sick." I had called her from Riker's Saturday night and explained that there had been a change of plans and that I had to stay the night. I kept it brief, which only increased her anxiety.

"It's complicated, Pam. All sorts of legal mumbo-jumbo. I'm hoping it will be cleared up by next weekend."

"Are you all right?"

"I am, thank you. Just very tired. It's hard to sleep well in there, and I stink because I'm afraid to use the showers. I'm going to my apartment to clean up, walk the dog, and take a nap."

"I've got some good news for you. I received word this morning that your course has been approved. Welcome to NYU."

I smiled. "That is good news. When do classes start?"

"Two weeks."

"Great."

"When will I see you?"

"I'll call you when I wake up, okay?"

Late afternoon, the sound of someone entering my apartment permeated my subconscious. Cleo barked, and through groggy eyes I looked at the clock on the night table. It was 4:00 p.m. I rubbed my eyes, got up to investigate, and saw Zach playing with Cleo in the living room. I yawned loudly announcing my presence.

"Hi, Zach."

"Hi, Dr. Cesari. I called but you didn't answer. I thought I should check on Cleo."

"Thanks, Zach. I appreciate that. I turned my phone off to take a nap. Make yourself at home. I'm going out soon anyway. You want some coffee?" I moved to the kitchen to put a half pot of Columbian on in the Mr. Coffee machine.

"No, thank you. I'm all coffeed out today."

While the coffee brewed and they wrestled, I turned on my phone and saw two missed phone calls and a couple of texts from Pam since I spoke to her this morning. Geez. She had Cesari fever bad. I sat on the sofa and dialed her number.

"Hey there. You've been looking for me?"

"Yeah, it's four o'clock. I thought you were going to call me?"

I yawned again. "I just woke up."

"Really? Wow, you were tired."

"You didn't believe me?"

"I believed you. It's just that…"

"Are you staring at the clock again?"

"Well, it's been two whole days."

"Has it been that long?"

The coffee machine beeped and I got up to pour myself a cup. I leaned against the counter and smelled it.

"Yes, and I can't believe you've done this to me. I feel like a barn cat in heat. I'm afraid I'm going to start screeching for you."

I sipped the coffee and it rushed right to the back of my eyeballs causing them to pop open. "I didn't do anything. In fact, I tried to keep you at bay but no, you wouldn't listen."

She laughed. "I admit it. You did try to warn me. Let's just go with the flow."

"Fine with me."

"Feel like coming over?"

"The apartment or the office?"

"The apartment. I'll make dinner. Say six?"

"Say seven and I'm in."

"Seven it is. Don't be late."

I finished the coffee and shook off any remaining drowsiness. "Hey, Zach, can I ask you a couple of questions? They're kind of personal and you may not have the answers but that's okay."

He stopped playing with Cleo and sat down at my kitchen table. "Sure thing."

"It's about drugs on campus. If you don't feel comfortable answering, that's fine. All right?"

"Got it."

"Suppose I was a student and I wanted to experiment with heroin or meth, where would I get it?"

He raised his eyebrows. "Oh, those kinds of questions. Hmm. Well, since I don't use drugs I'm not a hundred percent certain but it's not really that hard. Pretty much everyone knows who the users and who the dealers are. Don't ask me how they know. It's sort of an unwritten code on campus."

I thought about that. I guessed that made sense. They probably had a certain look to them. Word of mouth was also the most common way this stuff got around. It was like that with wise guys and hookers too. You just knew by looking at them most of the time.

"Okay, let me put it another way. How would I purchase drugs on campus if I wanted them?"

He rubbed his chin in thought with one hand and cuddled Cleo's head with the other. "That's a difficult question. Most of the time it's one student talking to another student or maybe some guy shows up at a party with goodies and everybody gets to meet him. You're sort of out of the loop. I'm not really sure. I suppose you could start by just asking around."

I sipped some coffee, thinking about that. "Wouldn't that seem a little strange?"

"Asking about drugs at NYU? I doubt it." He chuckled politely. "College campuses have changed a bit since you attended. Nobody cares."

Nobody cares?

Seriously? For some reason that comment made me sad. Deep down I knew he was right. It was probably the single biggest problem facing our country and perhaps the world. Nobody cared anymore—about anything. We were infected by a malaise of the spirit. We accepted mediocrity, violence, and moral decrepitude at every level of society. Disrespect for our fellow man had become the new norm. Of course, nobody cared. Why should they? If we, as a society, didn't strive to be the very best we could be, then what were we? Then it hit me. We were devolving back to the Stone Age, but who was I to judge? I was just a man-whore serving time on the rock.

I said, "Thanks, Zach. I'm going to head out now. Have a good time with Cleo." I turned to Cleo and gave her a big hug. "And you be a good girl for Zach."

I left the apartment and headed over to NYU. Samuel told me to pass the message to the security guard tonight. His name I learned was Lester. I thought I'd go over now and do a little reconnaissance. I was sure that I was missing something so I thought I'd check the log records before meeting Pam for dinner.

On the way, I called Knuckles and asked her to meet me at the entrance to let me in. As luck would have it, she was just around the corner in the bookstore and agreed. As she approached, I suppressed a smile. She wore jeans and a leather biker jacket with a red bandana and dark Ray Orbison-type sunglasses. She looked the part for sure; short and stocky, with a take-no-prisoners look to her.

I said, "Hi, girlfriend."

"Don't even think about it. What's up?"

"I need to get in here and look at the log records at the security desk. It shouldn't take too long."

"Roger that."

We entered, approached the guard and identified ourselves and our purpose. He shrugged and handed us the log book. The first thing I did was look for Justin's name, page by page, day by day, and week by week. I was curious. I discovered that he came to Steinhardt every Sunday night at roughly the same time, 10:00 p.m. and then generally signed out around midnight. I looked through the records for a two-month period and it was the same thing every time. Okay, now we had something—a pattern.

Just for fun, I flipped through the pages back to a random Sunday night a couple of months earlier and found his name again logging in at night. What were the odds of that? I looked at the guard and said, "Thanks. Say, is there any record of who the security guard is on any particular night?"

"I suppose the main administrative office has all that. Is there anything in particular you're interested in? Maybe I could help you?"

I looked at his name tag and said, "Thanks, Tim, I appreciate it. I was just wondering if you guys rotated or if you had some sort of standing schedule."

"Well, there are five of us in total. Four of us rotate because everyone hates the night shift except for Lester, that is. He's sort of a loner and likes the night solitude. He volunteers to work almost every weekend. I guess he doesn't have much of a life. The rest of us are glad because that's three less nights we have to cover and nobody wants to work weekend nights anyway so we don't ask questions."

Outside, I thanked Knuckles for her time and she invited me to work out with her in the morning. She wanted to see how much I could bench press.

Chapter 20

Pam greeted me in a sleeveless top and long, flowing skirt, wearing a big smile and an apron that said *Kiss the Chef.* We kissed and I said, "Nice look."

"Thanks. I thought about wearing nothing under the apron but I didn't want to scare you off. I figured it would be better to get you into the apartment before I revealed my true intentions."

She closed the door behind me and I chuckled. "Well, I'm trapped now. Reveal away."

She laughed. "You must think I'm terrible."

"Don't be silly. It's not a state secret that some women enjoy the company of men, Pam."

"Thank you for putting that delicately. So, you don't think I'm—bad?"

I grinned. "Since when is nymphomania bad?"

She punched me playfully. "That's what I mean. I'm not usually like this."

"It's not your fault. No woman can resist Cesari charm. It's been a curse on the men in my family for centuries."

She laughed. "I'll bet."

Changing the subject, I said, "Something smells great."

"I made salmon."

"My favorite, but I was talking about you. What is that?" I placed my face close to hers and sniffed.

I got too close and she kissed me again. "Thanks, it's Fendi. Do you really like it?"

I made a purring, growling sound. "I love it." And then I pretended to bite her on the neck.

She laughed, "Fendi is trendy. I'm glad you're in such a good mood. How about opening the bottle of wine on the counter and pouring us each a glass? Dinner is nearly ready."

There was a bottle of Pinot Grigio and a corkscrew on her countertop. I opened it and filled two nearby glasses. I sipped mine and held hers as she withdrew a baking pan with a long salmon filet covered with herbs and thin lemon slices. On the stove top, I saw green beans with garlic slivers in a sauté pan. There was a baguette in its white paper sleeve sitting on a cutting board and I offered to slice it.

"If you trust me with a sharp knife, I'll take care of the bread?"

"Thanks, there's one in the drawer right in front of you."

As I sawed through the bread on a bias, she did some last-minute checking on her masterpiece. The small kitchen table was set with a blue, patterned tablecloth, a small vase with pink carnations, and a candle waiting to be lit.

"John, could you bring the plates over from the table? It'll be easier to serve the salmon here on the counter."

"Sure thing."

As I returned the plated meals to the table, she dimmed the lights, lit the candle, and turned on soft music. She had thought this through. Just go with the flow. This kind of spoiling could grow on a guy. We sat, clinked our glasses, and began eating.

"Pam, this is absolutely the best salmon I have ever had."

She smiled. "You don't have to say that but thank you."

"I mean it. It's great. What's in the topping?"

"It's so easy; chopped Italian parsley, scallions, fresh dill, extra virgin olive oil, salt, pepper, and lemon juice. That's it."

"Well, the flavors blend well together. I really love it."

"Thank you. So, I know you don't like to talk too much about what goes on at Riker's but did they give you any hint as to why you had to stay at night when the warden told you otherwise? That kind of frightened me when I heard."

"I'm sorry. I didn't mean for you to worry. I think it was more or less a paperwork thing. I've been reassured that they're working on it."

She nodded. "Unbelievable how cavalier they can be with someone else's life."

I agreed. "No one cares, unfortunately, about anything or anyone. Don't lose sleep over it. It'll get it straightened out."

"On a lighter note, isn't it exciting we're going to teach a course together?"

"Yes, it is. I'm truly looking forward to this."

She thought about that and said, "Given everything that's going on in your life you probably won't think it's a big deal, but we should really start preparing a course outline and pick out reading material."

"I agree. We could start tonight after dinner."

She nodded and we made small talk like that enjoying each other's company until the bottle of wine was empty and every last morsel was gone from our plates. She was a tremendous person; well-read, with many interests outside of her profession. Not very athletic, though. Her idea of exercise was walking through the mall searching for the perfect pair of shoes. We'd have to work on that.

After dinner, we cleaned up the table and did the dishes by hand. She washed and I dried. She asked if I wanted to open another bottle of wine but I declined. I had things to do tonight that she didn't know about and I didn't want her to know about. I smiled as I watched her. She was about as happy right now as any woman I had ever seen. I knew we were moving way too fast but how on earth do you slow things like this down? Men have probably been asking themselves that question since the beginning of time.

And then there was Kelly. I wasn't past her and maybe never would be. I'd have to accept that, I guessed. Sooner or later I was going to have to tell Pam she was right about that. It was almost 9:00 p.m. I said, "Do you have a yellow pad and some pens? We could get started on the course outline."

"Sure, you want coffee?"

"That would be great."

We spent the better part of an hour and a half brainstorming the class structure and jotting down thoughts. She was better at details because of her experience as an educator. She knew right away what would work and what wouldn't. We sat on her sofa with two legal pads and a couple of coffee mugs on the table in front of us. At 11:00 p.m. she suddenly stretched her arms over her head and yawned. She sat back in the sofa and tossed her pad onto the table.

She said, "Okay, teacher, I think we've done enough homework for tonight. I didn't make you dinner so you could put me to sleep with paperwork."

I smiled at her. "I hope you're not expecting anything from me just because I've been nice to you."

"Oh, but I am." She took the legal pad and pen from me and placed them on top of hers. Then she got on her knees beside me on the couch, wrapped her arms around my neck and pressed her breasts into my face. She used those guys like they were weapons of mass destruction.

I lifted my head upward to take a breath. She looked at me seriously, lowered her face to mine, and kissed me. When she was done she inhaled deeply and let it out. She whispered, "It's time. Let's go to the bedroom."

"I guess no isn't an option."

She shook her head. "No only means no when a girl says it."

I chuckled. She was right about that. I stood and scooped her up into my arms as if she were a child causing her to giggle. I carried her into the bedroom and said, "You'd better not tire me out too much. I'm working out with Knuckles in the morning."

She snorted. "Get out of here."

"It's true. I really am."

"Oh my God. I don't believe it."

"Believe it. She wants to see my muscles."

"I'll bet. What time are you supposed to meet her?"

"I was thinking about ten or eleven. I need a chance to get back to my apartment and check on Cleo."

She smiled. "So you're going to stay? That'll make three times you stayed all night. Are you sure you're ready for a commitment like that?"

Funny girl. I hadn't thought about it in that way and said, "The first two times were in your office, so in my mind, they don't count, but since you want to be a wise guy…"

I tossed her on the bed and she rolled over squealing with delight. Sitting up, she shook her tousled hair and looked at me with a big grin that let me know she was ready. "Hey, you can't just throw me around like I'm a rag doll."

"That's what you get for calling me names."

"I didn't call you any names."

"Yeah, but you were thinking it."

Giggling she said, "Man-whore?"

She was really getting into it. "Yeah, that's the one."

"But you are," she laughed.

"That did it. Now you're in trouble."

She watched me carefully, tracking my every movement. Her eyes grew wide as I slowly and dramatically pulled my belt off. "What do you think you're going to do with that?"

she asked, concerned yet aroused at the prospect of a new adventure.

"Something that should have been done a long time ago if you'd had proper parenting."

She caught her breath. "You wouldn't dare."

"Come over here."

***

I looked at my watch. It was almost 1:00 a.m. and Pam lay sleeping peacefully in the crook of my arm, her head on my chest. As I listened to her gentle breathing, I wondered how much longer I would last at this pace. It occurred to me that I may have finally met my match. She was so wound up with sexual energy, I thought she'd never fall asleep.

Gently, I removed my arm from her shoulder and slid slowly, little by little, out from under her. She wiggled a little adjusting herself into her new position but didn't wake. I had left all my things in a pile by my side of the bed and quietly dressed in the dark.

In the living room, I picked up the yellow pad and wrote a note telling her that I got worried about Cleo and went to check on her. It was lame but at least it would keep her from worrying if she woke up and found me missing. I placed the pad on the night table. She had left her bag on the kitchen counter and I rummaged through it until I found her apartment keys and NYU ID, which I pocketed.

I walked quickly over to the Steinhardt building thinking over what I would say. Unfortunately, the ball would be almost entirely in the other guy's court, but I would do my best to sound convincing. I needed coffee and picked up a cup at an all-night diner on the way.

I arrived there at 1:30 a.m. and let myself in with Pam's ID. The guard looked up as I approached. I saw his name tag and said, "Hi, Lester."

He was bored and nodded. If he recognized me from when we met a week ago he didn't let on, so I decided to let sleeping dogs lie. He said, "I need to know which floor and room you'll be going to. New rules."

"I came to see you, Lester."

He looked up suddenly interested. "Have we met?"

"I don't think so. I'm friends with Samuel."

Surprised, he was silent for a moment. Then he said, "I don't know anybody named Samuel."

"He sent me to give you a message."

"Why should I care if somebody I don't know wants to give me a message I don't care about?"

I was a little taken aback by this unexpected response but maybe he was just being cautious. "Have it your own way, but when I see him at Riker's this weekend, he won't be pleased."

He thought it over for a moment and said, "Latrodectus."

I replied, "Hesperus."

Even though we were completely alone, he looked in both directions before saying, "What is it?"

"Feeling Blue. Bring your friends."

He stared at me as if I had two heads and for a brief moment I wondered if I had got the message wrong. He said, "Are you sure?"

I repeated it. "Feeling Blue. Bring your friends."

"All right. Tomorrow night. Meet me at the portico of Washington Square Park at midnight and don't be late."

I tried hard not to let my surprise show. Samuel didn't let on to me that I was supposed to be involved in anything other than the transfer of the information to the guard. I said, "I'll be there."

We maintained eye contact for a few more seconds and I said, "Is that all?"

"Midnight, tomorrow."

I nodded and left. What the hell did that mean? Back in Pam's apartment, I returned her keys and ID to her bag and got back in bed. I was tired and soon passed out with one thought on my mind.

Feeling Blue. Bring your friends.

Chapter 21

The next morning, I checked on Cleo, packed some work-out clothes in a gym bag, and caught up with Knuckles at the entrance to the NYU fitness center on Lafayette Avenue.

"Good morning, Doc. Hope you brought your game."

"You better take it easy on me, Knuckles. I haven't worked out in a while."

"Making excuses already? Geez, how about we get started first before we start crying?"

I changed in the locker room and met her on the gym floor by the free weights. She was stacking small metal plates onto a bench press bar. I said, "Slow down, tiger. I need to warm up first."

She looked at me and shook her head. "Man, Doc, you really are a bit of a pansy."

"I'd rather be a pansy without any injuries if you don't mind."

I walked over to a corner of the room, found a floor mat, and started stretching. The place was enormous and seemed like it could easily accommodate 500 people. A boxing ring dominated the center of the room, and I suddenly remembered why Knuckles was called Knuckles. It was 10:00 a.m. and the place was mostly empty with just a few young women on treadmills and stationary bikes wearing earphones and staring out the window onto East 4th Street.

A couple of skinny guys in pristine outfits gently pumped iron with light weights. No real heavy hitters like I was used to back in the Bronx where guys lived for their work-outs. They would come in with torn and ripped T-shirts and sweat pants, muscles and veins bulging, faces beet red before they even touched the weights. And once the work-outs began, they would go on for hours until they could barely stand. They weren't famous, they didn't care who noticed or admired them. They were committed and self-motivated, but most of all, they loved it. Once I saw a guy throw 300 pounds on a bar, do ten squats followed by two sets of twenty-five pull-ups and then walk out of the gym. I asked him where he was going and he said this was his rest day but that he just couldn't stay away.

Wearing cotton gym pants and a sweatshirt over a tank top, I fit in okay in this place. I had a routine of stretches that I performed on the mat, gradually increasing the intensity as my muscles responded. From there, I progressed to push-ups, deep knee bends, and light dumbbells. When I felt fairly warmed up, I took my sweatshirt off and found a dip and pull-up station and did a few sets to get the blood rushing into my joints and sinews. Having worked up a light sweat and a little bit of a pump, I joined Knuckles at the bench press.

She had about a hundred pounds on the bar and had done a few sets. Not bad for most girls. She watched as I approached, staring unabashedly at my biceps and chest.

"Wow. Now, that's what I'm talking about, Doc. C'mon, you must be on the juice?"

"I told you I don't believe in that stuff. Just work hard and eat right, and you'll get there."

"Are you ready?"

"Yeah, help me change the plates."

"How much do you want?

"Strip the bar down and put two big plates on."

She was astonished. "Fuck, two big plates? On each side? The 45 pounders?" She did a quick calculation in her head. "With the bar that's 225 pounds. Maybe you should warm up?"

I laughed at her sudden concern. Exercising with women, no matter what their flavor, was always amusing. "That's exactly what I'm about to do."

"Jesus. Okay, let's go for it. Should I spot you?"

"Sure, but don't drip sweat on me, all right?"

I positioned myself on the bench, grabbed the bar overhead, stared at the ceiling and took a deep breath, hoisting it in the air. I paused for a second to stabilize it and then effortlessly performed ten repetitions, replacing the bar onto the holders at the end.

A little short of breath, I sat up and waited for my heart rate to come down. Knuckles said, "Man, that was something. You might be the strongest guy I've ever seen in here."

I smiled at her. "Then you better take a picture. It'll last longer."

There were at least ten squat cages, ten more benches, several platforms for deadlifting, and thousands of pounds of free weights; all very suggestive that some very large men visited this place, but no signs of it right now.

"I'm serious."

"Who uses all the heavy-duty equipment over there?"

She looked in the direction I had pointed and shrugged. "No one as far as I know. I come here five days a week and have never seen anyone over there."

I found this hard to believe. "Seriously? Then why did they buy all of this expensive stuff?"

"It's a recruiting tool for the university. It looks good to parents and students when they come on their tours."

I shook my head and sighed at that revelation. Everything these days was smoke and mirrors. I thought about what Zach had said. Nobody cares—about anything, especially reality. I sighed and put it behind me.

We worked out for another forty minutes and then headed to the lockers. She stopped and turned toward me. "Feel like showing me how to shave? You promised."

I had forgotten. "Now?"

"I brought the razor and some shaving cream."

I thought about it for a moment. For the first time, I noticed the peach fuzz on her face. I considered lecturing her about the risks of anabolic steroid use but decided against it. We were bonding. Maybe later. I said, "Why not? But you come into the men's locker-room. I don't want to get caught in the women's room."

She chuckled. "I'll get my stuff and meet you in there."

I had to admit, she was growing on me. She was refreshing like an ocean breeze. She was who she was. You didn't have to like it. In fact, it didn't really matter what you thought.

A few minutes later, she knocked politely on the door and entered. I was the only one in the locker-room. We went into the bathroom together and I checked out her equipment. She brought a can of shaving cream and the razor I had recommended loaded with a fresh blade. She also had a small bottle of after-shave. I laughed when she placed it on the counter and she gave me a look.

I said, "I'm sorry. Okay, the key to a good shave is preparing the skin properly and to do that you have to open up your facial pores. So turn on the hot water and let it run a bit. I'll shave at the same time so you get the idea."

She turned on the hot water and we waited. There was a pile of wash cloths stacked neatly on the counter and I took one and soaked it under the faucet. Then I placed it on my face enjoying its warmth. She followed suit and we stood there with our faces buried in wash cloths. After a minute, I said, "That's enough. How does it feel?"

"Great."

"Splash a little hot water on your face to keep it moist. That's right. Just like I'm doing. Now, we take a little dab of shaving cream and work it into the skin. Just a little, okay? The idea isn't to look like Santa Claus."

She turned to me all lathered up and said, "How am I doing?"

I suppressed a chuckle. "Great."

"Okay, I'll start since we only have one razor. I always rinse it under hot water to heat up the blades before starting." I began at the low point on my neck and gently stroked upward, clearing a path to my chin. I repeated the process another two times and then rinsed the blade, handing it to her. "Your turn. Press the blade gently but firmly and don't try to do too much at once. Be extra careful around the turns. We'll save the upper lip for last since that's where most guys cut themselves."

She didn't do too badly for a first try and was happy as a clam. She'd only made one small nick on her lip and proudly left the men's room with bloody tissue paper on it. I smiled as I changed into my jeans. I had fun.

Outside on the street, I asked, "You doing anything tonight?"

"Doc, I already told you I don't swing that way. Don't make this anymore uncomfortable than it already is. Capeesh?"

She was killing me. "I understand. Are you still interested in finding out what happened to that student?"

"Definitely. I'd like to pop someone in the nose big time. What's going on?"

"I could use some backup tonight. I'm meeting some guys who might be able to shed some light on the situation."

She suddenly got very serious. "What do you want me to do?"

"Just watch. I need a pair of eyes keeping a look out for me."

"Where and when?"

"Midnight at the entrance to Washington Square Park."

"Should I notify the team?"

"I don't think it's necessary unless you want company. I just want you to watch."

"Nah, I'll be fine. The park is always crowded at midnight during the summer."

"Thank, Knuckles, I appreciate your help."

She swiped her hand over her fresh-shaved chin.

"Ditto, Doc."

Chapter 22

*L*ater I took Cleo for a walk down Fifth Avenue. She wanted to play with everyone we met and by the time we reached East 12th Street she had become a local sensation with strolling New Yorkers. At noon, I bought us a couple of hot dogs. She wolfed hers down in one gulp and stared at me as I ate.

I said, "Forget it, dog."

By the time, we reached the Union Square Station I was ready for a rest and parked myself on a bench facing the statue of George Washington with Cleo by my side. I had a lot to think about, not least of which was Pam. Almost as if she read my mind, my phone buzzed.

"Hi, Pam. I was just thinking about you."

"You were?"

I smiled. "Yes, I was."

"Good thoughts, I hope."

"Naughty thoughts for sure."

She laughed. "Oh, my goodness. What are we going to do? This situation is getting so out of control."

"Just keep going with the flow I guess. No point in fighting Mother Nature."

She lowered her voice. "Yeah, but now we're into belts."

"We're just making memories, Pam."

She snorted. "I can't believe I like this stuff. I never would have thought it. What's next, handcuffs and paddles?"

"That's for me to know."

"That's not fair. So how'd the gym go with Knuckles?"

"It went well. She's growing on me. We had a good time. I have to get you started."

She chortled. "Ha, don't count on that. I'm a girlie girl and proud of it. Sweating is for peasants."

That made me chuckle. "You never know until you try it. Look at last night."

"I still can't get over what we did. Where did you learn this stuff, or do you just conjure it up?"

"In prison, it's see one, do one, teach one."

She laughed out loud this time. "Stop. Are you free for lunch?"

"I'm in Union Square with Cleo. We just had hot dogs."

"You gave her street food? That's not good for a dog."

"It's not good for a human either."

"No, it's not. Later then?"

"Sure, I have a bunch of things to take care of and then I'll call you."

"Have you heard anything about that girl, Kayla, from the other day? The one we found in Justin's apartment."

"I know she's still hospitalized but that's all I know. I was planning on looking in on her this afternoon. I'll let you know."

"Okay, I await your call with bated breath."

"Let me guess, you like Shakespeare?"

"Oh, my goodness. You got that. That's pretty good for a felon."

Ouch.

"Shall I bend low and in a bondman's key,
With bated breath and whisp'ring humbleness, say this..."

"Okay, Dr. Cesari, now I am totally impressed."

"*The Merchant of Venice* was my favorite play. You see, there's more to me than belts and a gigantic..."

"Stop! You're killing me."

"Hey, that's my line."

"Anyway, I love *The Merchant of Venice* too, although the rank anti-Semitism in it was appalling."

"Yeah, I know. I've read that the Nazis loved that play because of that but scholars are still debating whether Shakespeare truly intended to promote anti-Semitism or to highlight the endemic and pervasive nature of it at the time. Remember, in the play Shylock only wanted his pound of flesh because of how poorly he had been treated at the hands of Antonio, the Christian merchant. In some ways, you could sympathize with a guy who had been pushed too far."

"Wow. You really know your Shakespeare."

"I told you already, I know stuff."

She giggled. "Yes, you do. Well, I'll let you go. Call me."

"I will."

I hung up and looked at Cleo, saying. "Do you think I have a Pam problem?"

She shook her big head and stood up. I laughed and guessed it was time to go. I dropped her off at the apartment and headed out to St. Matt's to check on Kayla. I had a lot to do today including taking a closer look at the BMW's owner's manual, call Detective Kilcullen, and figure out what to do with a car whose trunk was filled with drugs. That last was a particularly difficult question because I couldn't just return it to the garage and I couldn't just remove the drugs and dispose of them.

I had a lot on my mind as I entered St. Matt's and asked the woman at the information desk which room Kayla was in. She was still in the ICU. Not unexpected considering the condition we found her in, but not good.

175

At the nursing station in the ICU, I was greeted by the secretary. "Hello, Dr. Cesari. What brings you here today?"

"Hi, Norma. I'd like to say hello to Kayla. I don't know her last name. She was the girl brought in last week; the victim of a brutal attack. I was there when they found her."

"You mean Kayla Schmitter. Poor thing. She's in Room 10. Jessica is her nurse. She's doing much better and may be transferred to a regular floor bed today. Her family just left. Nice people. They're handling this as well as can be expected."

I nodded. "Thanks."

I walked into the room and was relieved to see that she was awake and breathing on her own. Always a good sign in an ICU. The swelling in her eyes had gone down considerably, but her broken nose had been splinted and her entire face was black and blue. She was still missing a thumb and I surmised that the hand surgeons got to her too late. An IV poured antibiotics and pain medications into her bloodstream.

She looked at me as I entered the room. I smiled and said, "Hi, Kayla."

With great difficulty and in tremendous pain, she slowly opened her mouth and whispered, "Hi."

"Kayla, I'm Dr. Cesari. I'm the one who found you in Justin's apartment last week and called the police."

Slowly and painfully, she said, "Thank you."

I pointed to chair next to her and asked, "May I?"

She nodded, then coughed and grimaced. Probably had broken ribs. I sat down next to her. "Can I ask you a few questions about what happened, Kayla? I know the police have already talked to you and I won't be long."

She nodded again.

"Can you tell me who did this to you?" I asked softly.

She shook her head. "I already told the police I can't remember anything."

176

I took a deep breath. "Nothing at all?"

"Nothing. I'm not even sure who I am. An hour from now I might not even remember my own name. The doctors said I have brain swelling and that I'm lucky to be alive."

"I'm sorry, Kayla."

"Thank you."

"Would it be okay if I came back in a couple of days to say hello?"

She nodded and did her best to smile but wound up looking sadder than ever. I stood to leave but then remembered something. "Kayla, when I found you, you said the name Maria. Who is she?"

She thought about it for a moment and then shook her head. "I don't know. I'm sorry."

"It's okay. You just get better, all right?"

"Yes."

As I turned she suddenly grabbed my arm with surprising strength. Her eyes glared ferociously. She yelled loudly, "Find her! You must find her!"

"Who?"

She swung her other arm around to grab me and now had me firmly in her grip. I tried to disengage myself without hurting her but she was clawing at me desperately. Her face was contorted in pain and rage. I called out to the nursing station. "Help! I need help in here!"

Kayla shouted, "Chip ... No! Please don't!"

Her nurse Jessica came rushing in holding a needle. "Calm down, Kayla. He won't hurt you."

She quickly injected the contents of the needle into the IV and then helped pull Kayla off me. Within seconds, Kayla relaxed and quietly lay back down onto her pillow. Jessica made sure that she hadn't disconnected any of her tubes and then gently stroked the girl's head, whispering soothingly, "There,

177

there. You poor thing. You've been through so much, but it's going to be all right, honey. Try to sleep now."

Kayla looked at her and nodded as tears streamed down her face. Jessica signaled me to follow back to the nursing station. As we left the room, I looked back and saw that Kayla was already asleep.

"Are you okay, Doc?" Jessica asked, taking a seat across from me.

"She's pretty strong."

"You're telling me. We wrestle with her like that two or three times daily. I carry a syringe loaded with Valium all day just in case. They say it's frontal lobe trauma leading to emotional instability and erratic behavior. Her parents are putting up a strong front but they're devastated inside."

"I'll bet."

"She was saying stuff about finding 'her' and somebody named Chip. Does any of that make sense?"

"Beats me, Doc. We're talking about a fifteen-year-old girl who's been beaten, raped, tortured, and now has brain trauma. I wouldn't be shocked if she thought she was the queen of England. The good news is that when she wakes up later she won't remember any of it."

"Fifteen?"

"Yeah, she's a run away from Dallas. Can you believe it? So sad, but you know something. At least she's alive. She's got a chance and that means something."

"Yes, it does mean something. Say, Jessica, I know a lot of what she says is probably just rambling but have you ever heard her say the name, Maria?"

"All the time, but that's it. She'll say something like you just heard about finding Maria or helping Maria or something, but nothing more specific, and ten minutes later can't remember saying it. What do you think happened? Was she shacking up with that college kid doing drugs, and things just went sideways?"

Letting out a deep breath, I said, "Certainly, seems like it. I'm going to take off now but I'll come back in a few days if it's okay with you guys."

"Sure, always like seeing you. Stay out of trouble, hear?"

I smiled. "Too late for that."

I left the hospital and hoofed it down to Mulberry Street as I called Vito.

He answered on the third ring. "Cesari, how's prison?"

"About what you'd expect. Where are you?"

"I'm in my apartment. Why?"

"I need a favor."

"Oh yeah, what?"

"Are the Feds still listening in on your calls?" He'd been under constant surveillance by the FBI for years for various violations of the RICO act.

"Probably. Let me see. Fuck all you guys." He was then quiet for a second and laughed. "That'll teach them."

"I'll be in your apartment in ten minutes."

"Sure, but hurry up. I got things to do."

His apartment was above the Café Napoli on Mulberry Street and when I arrived his guards were expecting me but still patted me down. Friend or foe, no one entered the king's quarters packing heat. They buzzed me in when they were done and I found Vito sitting at his desk on the phone. There was a new bottle of Glenlivet on a credenza nearby. I picked it up and examined it. It said 1973 Cellar Collection on its label. I looked at my watch. It was five o'clock somewhere so I opened the bottle, poured myself two fingers into a crystal tumbler and took a seat on the leather sofa opposite him.

179

He finished his call and glared at me. "Fucking Cesari. That was a $2,000 bottle of scotch you opened without permission. My men just gave that to me to wish me good health."

I smiled and couldn't care less. This guy owed me for all the jams I'd gotten him out of—and into over the years. I raised the glass and said, "Here's to your health."

He laughed. "The least you could have done is pour me some." With that he stood and filled a glass half-way up, came over and plopped on the other end of the sofa. "So, what's up?"

"Is it safe to talk?"

"Yeah, I sweep the place for electronics every morning. Go ahead."

I filled him in on my troubles at Riker's and how it had led me to Kilcullen in the Ninth Precinct. He chuckled. "Let me get this straight. You have a stolen car with a trunk full of smack garaged somewhere that belongs to this Spider gang. You pissed off the head Spider in Riker's and now you're working for the cops. There's already two casualties and the Spiders want to meet you somewhere in the middle of the night. Damn, Cesari, being a snitch in prison is dangerous business."

"I'm not a snitch. I'm working undercover."

"Are you getting paid?"

I shook my head.

"Then you're a snitch."

"Whatever. My problem right now is that I'm supposed to meet with these guys in Washington Square Park at midnight for purposes unknown and I'm very uncomfortable with it."

"Then tell your pal Kilcullen about it, and he'll send guys over to keep an eye on you."

"I'm afraid to do that. Surveillance cops are about as subtle as an icepick in the eye. If these guys smell a rat I might as well be signing my death warrant when I go back to Riker's."

He nodded. "This is true. So what do you want from me? I hope you don't think I can send guys down there with the FBI watching every move I make? I got enough problems without mixing it up with these Spider punks. Besides, there's no gain in it for me." I loved his logic. We'd known each other since grade school and had risked life and limb for each other on numerous occasions, but here he was telling me that he couldn't help me because there was no gain in it.

I said, "No, of course that's not what I meant. I need a gun and intel."

"What kind of gun and what kind of intel?"

"A .38 special. Hollow points would be nice if you have them."

He nodded. "And intel?"

"Find out what you can about the Spiders and particularly this guy Samuel Archer."

Chapter 23

*B*ack in my apartment I made a pot of coffee, fed Cleo, and placed Vito's .38 special on the table. It was 4:00 p.m. As I sat on the sofa, I sipped from a mug and opened the BMW's owner's manual and invoice I had taken from the car. There were multiple yellow highlights on the invoice and in the manual, but no matter how many times I looked at them I couldn't see any pattern. After an hour, I was almost ready to give up. Maybe it was nothing.

I examined them one more time. I had the invoice unfolded lying on the coffee table and flipped through the manual in my lap. For the first time, I noticed that only numbers were highlighted on the invoice and only letters and groups of letters in the manual. I got excited. That was something, wasn't it?

There were sixteen numbers in total on the invoice highlighted in pairs of two. The letters in the manual were also highlighted in groups of two. I wrote down all the numbers and letters just as I saw them on a legal pad and stared at them. What did it mean?

Concentrating hard, I lost track of time and almost jumped out of my skin when my cell phone rang. "Hi, Pam."

"Did you forget me?"

I looked at my watch. It was 6:00 p.m. "I'm sorry, Pam. I got tied up."

"I'm getting hungry."

This was starting to get uncomfortable. I had too much to do to go out to dinner and I needed to think before I met these guys tonight. She wasn't going to take this well but I needed some space. "Pam, I've got a lot of work to do here in my apartment. I know I promised to meet you but I'm swamped. Can we get together tomorrow night?"

"No problem. I'll come over there. We can order pizza. I'll bring my paperwork and stay out of your hair. I promise. Besides, I haven't seen Cleo in a long time. It'll be fun."

"Pam…?"

"Yes, John?"

I didn't know what to say. "What toppings do you want on your pizza?"

"Mushrooms and eggplant are yummy. You know what? I have to pass John's pizzeria on the way to your apartment. How about I pick up a pie there? This way you can keep on working. Are you okay with mushrooms and eggplant? Do you have wine?"

"Mushrooms and eggplant are fine with me and yes, I have wine."

"See you soon."

Clicking off, I sat back. Geez. It was like a hurricane had entered my life; a very nice hurricane but a hurricane nonetheless. Oh well, at least she was fun. I've dated hurricanes who weren't.

I hid the .38 at the bottom of an umbrella stand by the door. Vito was nice enough to provide me with a clip holster so I could carry it in the small of my back. It was a black, hammerless, snubbed-nose Smith and Wesson, with a laser sight. Very sexy.

My real problem was how I was going to get out of the apartment in time to make my rendezvous with the Spiders. I was only five minutes from the park entrance but Pam had boundless energy. If she didn't fall asleep on schedule I would be late, and I couldn't afford to screw this up.

I looked around the apartment, thinking. My wine rack had a variety of vintages and I was sure I could drink her into a coma but I couldn't afford to be impaired myself when I went to meet Lester. That would be too big of a mistake. Wine would take too long anyway.

I needed some way of getting her stupid drunk while I remained sober without her knowing it. I snapped my fingers and opened my liquor cabinet. Perfect. There was a full bottle of Grey Goose vodka and some dry vermouth. I placed them on the kitchen counter and retrieved two martini glasses and a cocktail shaker. I found some olives in the fridge and most importantly, a bottle of water that I placed on a shelf under the counter out of sight.

To complete the plan, I emptied the twenty-four-bottle wine rack and hid the bottles in a large suitcase, which I shoved into a closet. That should head off at the pass any discussion about how well wine and pizza pair. No wine, no problem. We'll have martinis. If I wasn't so sore from working out with Knuckles this morning I might have attempted to pat myself on the back. I couldn't believe I over did it trying to impress a dyke. Sometimes I think we should all be neutered.

Close to 7:00 p.m., the doorbell rang and I let Pam in. She was smiling from ear to ear holding a large pizza and, unbelievably, a bottle of wine. My heart sank. Okay, plan B.

"Hi, Pam. You brought wine?"

"It's just an inexpensive chianti. It's been lying around my apartment for years. I figured it was time to drink it. Hi,

Cleo." She had come to the door and was now starting to prance around us.

"Well, here, let me help you before she gets at the pizza," I said kissing her. I grabbed the pizza with one hand and the wine with the other. I set the pizza down on the coffee table, and walking to the kitchen with the wine, pretended to trip. I stumbled awkwardly, flinging the bottle of wine forward and watched it bounce along the hardwood floor. It slid harmlessly into the kitchen unbroken. Cleo barked and Pam shouted concern.

"John, are you all right?"

Goddammit!

"Yeah, I'm fine. Just a little clumsy tonight. Good thing that bottle is indestructible."

"Yeah, good thing is right. That would have made a terrible mess."

She picked up the bottle and noticed the martini set up. "What's going on here?"

"After we spoke earlier, I realized that I didn't have any wine. I figured we'd have a nice romantic martini."

"Aww, that's kind of sweet, but martinis and pizza? Yuk. It's a good thing I brought a bottle. Wine and pizza pair so well, don't you agree?"

"Totally agree. Well, I'll open it." I pulled a corkscrew from a kitchen drawer. "There are plates in the upper cabinets and napkins on the counter. We can eat in the living room."

I uncorked the bottle and poured a couple of glasses. I sat beside her and handed her a glass. We clinked and she said, "Here's to good health and good pizza."

She sipped her wine first, winced and ran into the kitchen to spit it out. "Ugh, don't drink it. It's turned to vinegar."

I sniffed my glass. She was right. Talk about good luck. I dumped the bottle in the sink and said, "I guess we're having martinis after all."

"I'm sorry about the wine."

"You messed up bad this time, Pam," I said smiling.

She snuggled up close. "Yeah, I'm a really bad girl."

Definitely killing me. "Go sit and I'll make us a couple of martinis. We'll have a great night. Grey Goose is the best."

She went into the living room and I dumped some ice into the shaker, poured a hefty amount of vodka in with a splash of vermouth, shook it up really good and filled her glass. Her back was to me and I filled my glass with water from the bottle I hid under the counter. I skewered some olives and tossed them in both glasses.

She called to me. "If I open the pizza box will Cleo attack it?"

"Probably, I'll put her in the bedroom while we eat. She won't like it but this is my apartment."

I led Cleo into the bedroom and warned her to be good. I sat next to Pam and placed her martini in front of her. She picked it up and said, "Let's try that again. Here's to good health, good pizza and good martinis."

We sipped and smiled. We were back on schedule again. She opened the pizza box and placed a slice on each of our dishes. "How's your martini?" I asked.

"It's very good, but these glasses are so big. I'll probably be drunk half way through."

I looked at my watch and smiled. "Take your time."

"What?"

"I meant, pace yourself and you'll be fine."

"Oh my, isn't this pizza great?"

"Yes, it's a New York classic. Actually, the vodka goes pretty well with it. Don't you think?"

She looked at me as if I were crazy. "If you say so. A few more sips and I won't care any way. By the way, did you go see the girl in the hospital?"

"Yes, I did. Her parents were there but I didn't get to talk to them. Not sure if I even wanted to. She's a runaway from Dallas. Physically, she's coming around but she suffered traumatic brain injury and only time will tell whether she'll recover fully. She has amnesia and her behavior is very erratic. She's young. Hopefully with time, she'll make it back."

Pam nodded and looked genuinely concerned. "That's so sad. Hey, what's that? Did you buy a new car?" She pointed to the coffee table. I forgot to put the BMW invoice and user's manual away.

I replied, "I found them on the street when I was walking home from the gym today. There was no name or phone number. I hadn't decided what to do with them yet."

"That's too bad, but I guess whoever lost them could always get new ones."

She picked up the manual and underneath spotted the legal pad I was taking notes on. For some reason, she found this more interesting and put the manual aside as she looked at the pad with the pairs of numbers and letters.

"What's this?"

I swallowed the bite of pizza in my mouth and said, "Sort of a puzzle I've been working on. Want to help me with it?"

She nodded. "Sure, I love puzzles."

"Great but first you have to catch up to me with the martini. You're falling behind."

"Oh, so this is a drinking game type of puzzle? Does it involve clothes coming off?"

"Naturally. Okay, let's start with the numbers. There are sixteen of them in pairs of two. Our job is to figure out what possible relationship these numbers have if any. Same thing with the letters."

"What's the prize if I get it?"

I thought it over and then leaned close, whispering in her ear. She giggled. "Okay, but you better not make promises like that unless you intend to keep them."

"You look at the numbers and I'll refresh the martinis."

When I returned with the drinks she said, "So what is this all about?"

"It's a brain teaser game we play a lot at the hospital. Somebody gave it to me a while back and I saw it lying around so I thought I'd give it a shot."

She sipped her martini, studying the page in front of her intently as I grabbed another slice of pizza. Cleo whined from the bedroom. She picked up the pen lying on the table that I had been using earlier and started playing with the numbers.

After a while she looked at me. "There is an answer, right?"

"Yes, there is."

I hope.

An hour later, I finished my second full glass of water and she was almost done with her second martini. I put the leftover pizza in the refrigerator and let Cleo join us. Pam was clearly inebriated but not even close to passing out. It was after eight, and still a little early so I didn't offer to make her a third drink yet. I'd wait a bit.

She raised her glass and giggled. "It's almost empty. You're not a very good host."

All of a sudden vodka and pizza seemed to pair well. "Let's work on the puzzle a little more before we get too hammered."

By 10:00 p.m., many sheets of discarded yellow paper cluttered the coffee table and floor as we tried various combinations of the numbers and letters hoping to come up with a solution. We used our phones to do internet searches on numerical combinations. Many hits came back but none that were relevant to us. Most of those involved biblical references to the end of times.

She sat back, crossed her legs, and gave me a sultry look. "I've been working on a puzzle of my own."

I looked at her. "Go ahead."

"I've been trying to figure out how you did this to me."

"What did I do?"

She shook her head, grinning. "You know exactly what you've done."

"How about I make you another martini?" I looked at my watch. It was almost time to go to bed.

I started to rise and she grabbed my arm pulling me back down. "I wasn't done talking."

Oh boy. Female empowerment was about to run over me like a freight train. "I wake up in the morning and I think about you. I go to bed and I think about you, and every minute in between. I feel like I'm sixteen years old. I'm a mature, educated woman; I don't have time for this. I have responsibilities. Classes start in less than two weeks, I have patients to see, papers to write, and deadlines to meet. I give lectures on feminism to rooms full of sane professional women who would eat me alive if they knew how I've been regressing."

I sat there silently, staring at her with my best deer-in-the-headlights look, not sure how to respond. She continued, "Well, do you have anything to say for yourself?"

I stammered. "How about that martini?"

She laughed. "That's it? I should take that belt and spank *you* with it tonight. Seriously, do you see where I'm going with this?"

I really didn't but felt that would be too insensitive to say out loud so I nodded and waited expectantly. "John, I am in danger of losing self-control. I can't let this happen."

Probably too late, I thought. "What do you propose?"

"A moratorium on our relationship."

"A what?"

"A temporary suspension of—this." She waved her finger at me and then back again at her. "We'll sleep together tonight but then I suggest a cooling off period of say—a week. Okay, no sex for a week just so I can get my equilibrium back. We can see each other and talk but—you know what I'm saying. I think I'll take that martini now."

I walked into the kitchen to fix her another cocktail. She needed it badly now. She had worked herself up pretty good. I wasn't sure yet whether what she had said was good or bad. It certainly raised the question in my mind of whether every woman was crazy or was it just the ones I was attracted to. Maybe this was a good thing. If we started tonight then I could make my meeting and save some vodka. I doubted she would go for that but it would be worth a try. I looked at my watch again.

I returned to the living room and found her busy staring at the numbers. She took her glass and chugged a big sip down smiling broadly as if nothing had just happened. My instincts told me that if I tried to throw her out now she'd be hurt and it would be interpreted as rejection and invalidation of her feelings. I took a big breath and let it out.

I said, "I need a drink," and took a long swallow of my water martini. She agreed and matched me.

A half hour later, we were well into the fourth round of martinis and she was slurring her speech badly. She tried to get up to go to the bathroom, staggered and almost fell. I walked with her and helped her back. For some reason, she was obsessed with the numbers on the page and despite the fact that she could barely see straight, insisted on trying to solve the riddle.

At eleven I poured the last of the vodka into her glass straight from the bottle bypassing the shaker. She chuckled. "If I didn't know better, Dr. Cesari, I'd think you were trying to get me drunk."

She went to pick up the glass and knocked it over on the coffee table. Fortunately, it didn't break. This made her laugh uncontrollably. I grabbed a towel from the kitchen and wiped up the liquid. She watched me through glassy eyes and whispered, "It's time."

Shit.

I had a very narrow window to work with. I needed her asleep no later than 11:45 and it was already after eleven by a few minutes. If we went at it now she'd wake up. Women always did for some reason. She rose clumsily to her feet and started unbuttoning her jeans.

I said, "Whoa, Pam. How about we go into the bedroom first?"

"But I want to show you what I wore for you."

Jokingly, I said, "I know, but the dog's watching. You can show me in there."

She pouted. "Okay."

I put my arm around her and we careened off into my bedroom. She threw her arms around me and pressed her lips into mine looking for my tongue. I said, "Pam, you know what would turn me on right now?"

"You can tell me anything."

"I would love to give you a back massage."

She stepped back surprised. "Really?"

"I've been dying to. Would you let me do that?"

She nodded gleefully. "Of course. As long as it has a happy ending if you get my drift?"

"It will," I lied.

I looked at my watch as she undressed and lay face down on the bed. I needed to speed things up. Time was becoming an issue. "That's a beautiful thong, Pam." God, she was gorgeous.

She hugged the pillow, with eyes closed and barely audible whispered, "Thank you."

I turned off the light, sat on the side of the bed next to her, and starting at the small of her back, ran my hands upward in a smooth rhythmic motion. With each stroke, she purred ever so slightly. I squeezed her shoulders gently fanning out to her biceps and triceps. The key to a good massage was rhythm and appropriate use of strength. I'd had some massages that were so rough that I'd felt like I'd been used as a punching bag. I looked at my watch. Hurry. It took twenty minutes but the purring eventually stopped, and from her relaxed features and open mouth I could tell that she was out cold. She was on top of my bed sheets so I retrieved a blanket from the closet and covered her up.

Watching her lie there, I smiled. They should call me the girl whisperer. Before leaving I tore a page from the legal pad and wrote her another lame note about a distraught friend calling me for help in the middle of the night. I read it over and even I didn't buy it but it was the best I could do on the spur of the moment. I left it on the night table, retrieved the .38 special from the umbrella stand, and hit the streets with just a few minutes to spare.

Chapter 24

*A*t five minutes of twelve, I stood at the entrance to Washington Square Park as I had been instructed. It was a balmy late August night and the New Yorkers were out and about. People conversed, laughed, smoked pot, skateboarded, and played chess on cement tables. The park was well lit and I could easily see Knuckles sitting on a bench fifty feet away listening to music on her iPod. I had told her to sit tight and under no circumstance approach us. If she felt I was in immediate danger she would call the police.

I wore a light windbreaker to conceal the weapon in the small of my back and leaned against the massive arched portico that led into the park. At exactly midnight, the black Ford Bronco that had pursued us the other day pulled up and a big guy wearing sunglasses got out of the passenger side. He looked around, spotted me, nodded, and opened the rear door.

It was my experience that getting into cars with guys I didn't know wearing sunglasses at night was never a smart idea. I glanced quickly at Knuckles who had snapped to attention. I was told I was going to meet someone or some people. No one told me I was going for a ride. Making an executive decision, I took a deep breath, and to Knuckles' great distress, went to the Bronco and got in. I was sure I had just given her a massive heart attack.

In the backseat was another guy who nodded but didn't say anything. He frisked me and took the .38, making no expression when he found it. Without a word, he threw a burlap bag over my head and the Bronco lurched forward. It was hot in there and I sucked air in through the heavy weave. Moderately concerned but not panicky, I thought through my options. None were very good but I was all in at this point so I tried to relax.

Fifteen minutes later, we pulled to a stop and I was escorted out. The room was cool, the floor felt like cement, and their steps and voices echoed. I suspected I was in a warehouse. They sat me in a metal chair and roughly secured my hands behind my back. No one said anything directly to me but I heard them greet others. My instincts told me I was in the company of someone higher up the food chain who didn't wish to be seen. A chair scraped close in front of me and someone sat down.

"Who are you?" he asked.

"John Cesari. Do you think we can take the bag off? It's really hot in here."

Ignoring my request. "Tell me how you know Samuel."

I gave him the abbreviated version and stayed as close to the truth as possible to withstand any fact-checking. There was silence when I was done as he thought it over. "You're a real doctor?"

I nodded. "Yes."

"What did you do to wind up at Riker's?"

"I lied to a federal investigator."

"And just like that Samuel decides to trust you? Doesn't that seem odd to you? Because it does to me."

"I think Samuel is desperate to communicate with the outside and saw me as a viable alternative."

"That's exactly why I don't like it. Desperate people do stupid things. Like talk to law enforcement plants."

I didn't say anything.

He continued. "You see my dilemma?"

I nodded. "I'm not the cops or the Feds. The people I represent are in the same business you're in. If you're not interested, fine. No harm done."

He laughed loudly. "Well, isn't that mighty white of you?" He had a very cultured voice and I suspected he was very educated. This wasn't some street punk I was speaking with.

"Repeat the message Samuel gave you. I don't wish to have any misunderstandings."

I said slowly and deliberately. "Feeling blue. Bring your friends."

"Do you have any idea what that means?"

I shook my head. "Something bad, I gather?"

"For you, yes."

I was getting a sinking feeling in my stomach. "It means that Samuel isn't at all sure if you are to be trusted and would like you to undergo extreme vetting before advancing our relationship."

Extreme vetting?

"I assure you that is not necessary."

"My men are going to start interrogating you now. If at the end, I determine that you are being untruthful your body will be dumped into the East River in such a condition that not even your own mother would recognize you."

Oh shit!

I braced myself for the worst and prepared answers for some very difficult questions. I also said a silent prayer to my maker just in case. I felt my heart rate and breathing pick up speed.

195

Suddenly and without warning I was punched in the face and my head snapped back. Before I could even register pain, another blow was delivered to my abdomen and I lurched forward short of breath. I sat there, bent over trying to recover, when another blow to the side of my head knocked me and the chair onto the floor.

I was hoping that sooner or later they would start asking me questions. At least then I would have a chance. No such luck. They didn't even pick me up. They kicked and stomped on me for a solid five minutes before they returned me to a sitting position. Woozy, I nearly lost consciousness.

All was quiet except for the sounds of heavy breathing from my assailants. They had worked up quite a sweat. I was bleeding from a split lip and tasted my own salty blood. It hurt to breathe and I suspected I had a minimum of several bruised, possibly fractured ribs. I suddenly vomited into the burlap bag and started gagging and choking on it. I became acutely distressed in a way that even they understood could possibly be fatal. Aspirating my own vomit would be a brutal way to die.

We hadn't reached that decision point yet so the one in charge said, "Take the bag off and clean him up so we can get started."

The bag was rudely yanked off and I suddenly realized that I could only see out of one eye because the other was swollen shut. With the bag off I gasped and sucked in fresh air, wheezing and coughing, the smell of vomit on my face and clothes perpetuating my nausea.

I eventually settled down and looked around the room with my good eye, which was blurry at best. I made out the three Spiders that brought me here and one other—a tall, lanky guy with red-framed, round sunglasses wearing an Irish walking hat and a tweed sport coat. I couldn't make out his features well, but he was at least six feet five inches tall and seemed to be the nerdiest guy I had ever seen. He was in charge of the Spiders? On a small card table nearby, I spotted a 12V car battery and jumper cables. Not good.

I was in danger of passing out, but one of them dragged a hose over and sprayed ice-cold water on me, soaking me to the bone. Revived and drenched, I sat there waiting. A strip of duct tape was slapped across my eyes as a metal chair scraped along the floor in front of me and someone sat down.

The one in charge said, "Are you ready?"

"For what?"

He said, "I ask a question and you answer it immediately. Understand?"

I nodded and he continued, "I don't mean to be rude but I'm going to give you a test dose to make sure the battery has a full charge and for you to understand what's coming your way if I don't like your answers."

I was too weak to protest and suddenly, two of the Spiders at my sides ripped open my shirt and he clamped the jumper cables to my nipples. I winced. They stepped away and I screamed and writhed in pain as he applied the charge. After a few seconds, he turned it off, satisfied that everything was in working order.

He interrogated me for about an hour like that. It could have been longer but I lost track of time. He asked me all sorts of background questions including things I could not possibly have known the answers to, simply to see if I would lie. I know he asked me if I was a police informant several times but I have no idea what I told him because I kept passing out.

I must have passed the test because the next thing I remembered was being rolled out of the Bronco onto the curb outside Washington Square Park at four in the morning. I lost consciousness again and when I next woke I was in the ICU at St. Matt's two doors down from Kayla Schmitter.

Disoriented, my good eye fluttered open and I noticed that I wasn't in pain anymore which seemed strange until I spotted the IV pole with a small bag of Toradol piggy backed into the main line of saline.

As my vision came into focus, I spotted Pam and Knuckles sitting at the foot of the bed. Sensing me rouse they stood and came over to me. They both looked exhausted.

I said to Pam. "I'm sorry."

She'd been crying and her eyes were red. She put her index finger in front of her lips and shook her head. "Just tell me you're going to be okay."

I smiled weakly. "I'm going to be okay."

Knuckles said glumly, "I'm sorry I let you down, Doc."

"You didn't let me down. There was nothing for you to do."

"I still feel like I should have done something."

I grabbed her hand. "You done good, Knuckles. You can be my wing man anytime."

Turning to Pam. "I guess I have a lot of explaining to do."

She smiled. "Knuckles filled me in. We'll talk about it when you're better, okay? I'm fine."

I let out a deep sigh. I was such a scumbag for lying to such a nice person. I didn't deserve her. I was starting to feel hungry, which was a good sign. I asked, "What time is it?"

Pam replied, "It's almost noon."

"I'm hungry."

Knuckles said, "Me too. I'll go to a deli on Third Avenue and bring you and Pam something back unless you want to eat the hospital slop?"

"A pastrami sandwich would hit the spot."

Pam said, "Yogurt will be fine for me."

As she left, my nurse Jessica, came in with a big smile. "Seeing an awful lot of you these days, Dr. Cesari, aren't we?"

"Yeah, sorry about that."

"I heard your friend was going downstairs to get you lunch. Should I send your tray back to dietary services?"

"Yes, thank you. Who's my doctor, Jess? I don't remember too much." I adjusted myself and felt a bad pain in my chest and my scrotum. I grimaced and said, "Ow!"

I threw my sheets off and looked under my hospital gown spotting a bloody bandage on my scrotum. "What the hell happened?"

Pam said, "John, you don't remember?"

Jessica said, "Maybe I should call the doctor?"

Pam answered, "Please do."

I nodded as my head slowly cleared and the events of last night gradually returned. When the guy in the walking hat got bored, he moved the jumper cables around. I remembered the Spiders pulling my pants and underwear down. I had similar bandages on my nipples and much of the chest pain was from injured ribs. Unless the doctor had some surprises for me I assessed that none of my injuries were life threatening or incapacitating. I would heal up with time.

Jess left to call the doctor and I looked at Pam who was clearly distraught. I said again, "I am so sorry for doing this to you."

She shook her head. "Don't, please."

I nodded.

She said, "Just get better."

I chuckled softly. She was confused by this.

"What's so funny?"

"Well, you wanted a week off."

She smiled and shook her head.

Kilcullen's massive frame suddenly blocked the doorway. He held a large Styrofoam coffee cup in his hand as he entered. He didn't look happy.

I said, "Pam, this is Detective Kilcullen of the Ninth Precinct. Detective Kilcullen, this is Dr. Gottlieb, a professor at NYU in clinical psychology."

He nodded politely at her. "G'day to you, Doctor. I'd be wondering if I might have a wee word alone here with Johnny?"

I turned to Pam who appeared even more worried at this new wrinkle. I said reassuringly, "It's okay. We're practically pals." She gave me a kiss on the cheek and left us alone in the room.

He threw his fedora onto the foot of the bed and sat down next to me, placing his cup down on my table. I smelled whiskey on his breath. He said, "Free-lancing are you, lad?"

"I thought I would have a better chance at getting information if people weren't looking over my shoulder."

He nodded. "You take initiative. I like that. Do you need any more convincing how dangerous these guys are?"

"I'm satisfied."

"Good. Now tell me what you learned."

"Well, I met three more Spiders last night and a very tall, goofy-looking guy. He seemed to be in charge of them. They did all the beating but he did all the interrogating. They were just muscle."

"A goofy looking man? You don't say? Does he have a name or did they just call him, Mr. Goofy Looking Man Sir?"

"I didn't hear any names used and the only reason I saw him at all is because I vomited into the burlap bag over my head and they were afraid I might die, so they removed it. Even then I didn't get a good enough look to identify him. All I can really tell you is that he was tall."

"Okay, lad, I understand you've had a rough go of it but we have to put all of t'at behind us now and prepare for this weekend's meet up with Samuel."

"You're going to make me meet with him again?"

200

He was astonished that I didn't fully comprehend the meaning of all of this. "Son, you don't get it. You've passed their initiation test. You're in like Flynn. Now, they be ready to deal for real. You've only a scratch here and there. You're a strapping young buck. By Saturday you'll be fine. I'd bet me grandmother's dowry on it."

"I don't think you understand. I'm not even sure how many testicles I still have."

"Doctor, don't be misunderstanding my enthusiasm for any lack of sympathy for ya, but if they had cut your shillelagh completely off and shoved it up your arse, I'd still be sending you back in."

He took a long swallow from his "coffee" cup, winced, and belched. "Fine stuff t'at."

Chapter 25

I was discharged later that afternoon once the ICU doctor was convinced that I was okay. I had a mild headache and lots of aches and pains which was to be expected but nothing life threatening; three bruised ribs, a black eye, split lip, and second-degree burns of my nipples and scrotum. I would survive, but somebody was going to pay dearly for this and I was going to start with Samuel and work my way up to the guy in the Irish walking hat.

Pam helped me limp out of the building into a cab. I was sore but knew that once the hospital's narcotics and other pain meds wore off I'd be in agony. They'd given me a three-day prescription of Tylenol with codeine that I knew would barely take the edge off the discomfort. There was nothing to do now but weather the storm. As we rode back to the apartment, I filled Pam in on the Spiders and Kilcullen.

I was barely able to stagger up the stairs and immediately lay on the sofa as Cleo licked my face. Pam sat on the coffee table facing me. She cleared her throat. I didn't say anything. She looked at me, raised her eyebrows up and down in the universal signal women made when they knew they had you by the short ones.

Finally, I broke the ice. "Can you forgive me for deceiving you, Pam?"

"You got me drunk so you could sneak out of the apartment to go meet with the Spiders? Out of curiosity, how do you think I would have felt had they killed you and I woke up to that bit of news?"

I sighed deeply. "Probably not very good."

"No, not good at all. It was bad enough Knuckles calling me in the middle of the night to tell me you were in the emergency room. I was drunk, hungover, exhausted, worried sick, and worst of all, had no idea what was going on. If she hadn't been waiting for you all night to return to the park, we might not even know now what happened."

"She waited all night?"

"Yes, she was worried sick too. She saw those animals throw you out of their car at four in the morning. She called 911 and then she called me."

I was silent and felt ashamed of myself. I'd been playing with other people's feelings and it was wrong. "I owe her."

"Yes, you do."

"And you, too."

"Yes, you do."

I withered under her gaze. She said, "You gave me a phony massage just to put me to sleep. That's terrible."

"I'm a bad person. I know it, but it wasn't phony."

She couldn't help herself and smiled. "Shut up."

I sighed. "Unfortunately, I'm locked in now. Detective Kilcullen has me working for him in Riker's. I couldn't say no. The head of the Spiders is in there and tonight was my initiation into the club. I apologize but there's simply no way for me to back out."

"What makes you think I want you to back out?"

I must have looked confused so she continued. "These scumbags have been selling drugs to young men and women on my campus?"

I nodded. "Lots."

"They killed Justin and beat that girl?"

"Almost certainly."

Anger flashed in her eyes. "Then I want them dead. All of them."

I raised my eyebrows. This is what happened when nice women hung around me too much. "And me?"

She didn't say anything so I added, "Dead?"

"No more lying."

I nodded.

"You rest here quietly with Cleo. I'm going to pick up some groceries and your prescriptions from the pharmacy." She hesitated. "I'm also going to my apartment to pack a small bag. I'm going to stay here with you for a few days until you get back on your feet."

She looked at me expecting resistance but I offered none. I knew when to argue with a woman and when not to. When they catch you in a lie, you have a concussion, and your scrotum is falling off is pretty much the definition of when not to argue. Then again, if she was a big fan of *The Merchant of Venice*, moving in with me might be her pound of flesh. I said, "Thank you."

"You're not going to argue with me?"

"No, I appreciate everything you're doing."

"I'll need a key to your apartment."

"Of course. There's one on a hook in the overhead kitchen cabinet. The one to the right of the stove."

"As a sign of good will, I'll give you a spare key to my apartment."

"You don't have to do that."

"But I want to. It feels right to me."

"All right then."

She stood to leave, but had something else on her mind. Looking at me seriously, she said, "I read Kelly's *Dear John* letter. You left it lying around. We can talk about it later."

I closed my eyes and hoped that when I opened them again I would find out this was all just a bad dream. After she left the apartment, I flung my head back onto the arm of the sofa. I took one of the pillows and covered my face with it. Man, did I mess this up or what? With the pillow on my face, I slept for an hour and felt better when I woke. I limped into the bathroom to pee and saw specks of blood in the urine. I was told to expect that for a few days as a result of trauma from being kicked in the kidneys. Still, it was unnerving to see.

Returning to the sofa, I sat down and saw the pen and legal pad with the numbers we were playing around with last night. I picked them up and stared at them for the thousandth time. There had to be some significance to this. I started jotting down more combinations and even reversing the numbers. I grouped them in a long horizontal row and then again vertically.

Eventually, I separated the numbers into two groups of eight. Then I jotted down one group vertically intersecting with the remaining horizontal numbers in the middle, forming a cross. My heart leaped. That was it. X always marked the spot. The numbers were a location—GPS coordinates. The question was in what order they should be read and which set of numbers represented longitude and which represented latitude. I needed a laptop for this and went into my bedroom to retrieve mine. I was so pumped; the endorphins had suppressed my pain to negligible for the moment.

Cleo watched with great interest as I fired up the laptop on the coffee table and did some preliminary research on GPS coordinates. Basically, every location on Earth could be specified by a set of numbers, letters, and or symbols. I looked at the yellow pad again. The number of combinations was staggering. It was a simple factorial equation; eight times seven times six times five and so on, and I calculated there was somewhere in the neighborhood of 40,000 possibilities. I needed some way of narrowing down the possibilities.

Pam walked in with groceries and a small suitcase and I stood to help her. She saw me and said, "It's okay. I'm fine."

I went to help her anyway and took the suitcase, bringing it into the bedroom. She set the groceries down on the kitchen table and started loading up the refrigerator. She asked, "I hope you like chicken?"

"I love anything that touches your hands."

She chuckled. "All right, don't overdo it."

"What are you doing over there?" she asked, nodding at the coffee table.

"Well, that puzzle I told you about last night wasn't exactly a brain-teaser from work."

She cocked her head and looked at me. "I figured that out this morning when Knuckles told me you have a stolen BMW with a trunk full of heroin or something in a parking garage."

"She told you?"

"Yes, and I'm pissed about that too. Why does Knuckles get to have all these adventures with you and I don't? Besides, I love Italian food more than she does."

We were silent as our eyes met. Then we both started laughing. I groaned in pain from my bruised ribs. She smiled and said, "You deserve to be in pain and lots of it."

Wrapping my arms around her, I said, "I know I do. I'm sorry."

I tried to kiss her and she playfully turned her head away. "No, never again."

I powered through the pain and squeezed her even tighter wiggling my face into hers as she pretended to struggle. Finally arriving at my destination, I kissed her tenderly. She perked up and embraced me just as tightly as I did her. Her eyes watered up. "I was so scared. How could you?" Without thinking, she punched me lightly in the chest in frustration and I backed away gasping in pain.

Alarmed she said, "I'm sorry."

I nodded, and leaned on the counter, catching my breath. "It's okay."

From behind she slipped her arms around me and rested her head on my back. "Don't die on me."

She made me laugh despite the pain. "I'll try not to."

Later, eating chicken stir fry with snow peas, I explained my revelation about the numbers being GPS coordinates and how I thought it might be the key to what's going on.

She thought it over. "Maybe."

I felt deflated. "You don't agree?"

"With what? You haven't proven anything. It's an interesting theory. For all you know it's a combination to a safe or a Swiss bank account number."

Shit. She was right. I needed to rethink it. Still, the coordinate thing was very enticing and fired me up. I went into the living room to get the pad.

"Where are you going?"

I came back and pulled my chair close to hers, placing the pad on the table. "Let's play with the letters for a while."

"Really? While I'm eating?"

"Are you all in or only half-way?"

"You are going to be the death of me. Of course, I'm all in. Let's see what you got."

There were nine groups of two letters; LI, PL, AD, TT, AI, LE, NS, RO, LI and we started arranging them on the pad to see if any relationships would show up. After thirty minutes, we tired and I needed a Tylenol with codeine.

After dinner, we took Cleo for a quick stroll through the park thinking over the puzzle. I was surprised at how easily fatigued I became and sat on one of the benches. Pam sat next to me and giggled softly.

I said, "What?"

"Look at us. Like an old married couple walking the dog and tiring ourselves out."

I laughed. "Yeah. You should consider someone with more stamina while you still got the chance."

"Yeah. Maybe someone who doesn't like to dodge bullets and hang around drug dealers, but gosh darn it, what fun would that be?"

We barely made it back to the apartment when I began to crash and burn from narcotics, injured muscles, and stress. Everything started to swirl around me. I said, "Pam, I don't think I'm going to make it to the bedroom."

Concerned, she hoisted my arm around her shoulder and said, "C'mon sailor, you can do it."

I staggered forward and fell face down on the bed, grabbed a pillow, turned my head, and lay there, groaning in pain and staring at the wall. She sat by my side and looked at me sympathetically while she rubbed my back. "It's only eight. You should try to stay up a little longer or you'll wake up in the middle of the night."

Too late.

Chapter 26

*B*y the time Saturday rolled around I was feeling human again. My chest still hurt a little and the swelling in my eye had gone down considerably. I was off pain medications and my energy had returned. I may not have looked it but I was ready to rumble.

The morning clinic was uneventful; a few bumps and cuts. There was one interesting case. A forty-year-old male in for armed robbery woke with a swollen left leg and shortness of breath. I diagnosed him with a deep venous thrombosis and pulmonary embolus. I had to transfer him out for a CT of the chest and intravenous anticoagulation. I felt bad for the guy but it was a nice change from the mundane. One of Diamond's friends, Alexandrite, came in requesting a pap smear. She argued for an hour about it and wouldn't leave. Just when I thought the guards were going to lose it and start clubbing her, I compromised and told her that I didn't have the proper equipment or exam table, but that I would discuss such purchases with the warden. She finally calmed down and agreed to make a follow up appointment in the near future. After she left, I made a note in her chart that she needed psychiatric evaluation. It was one thing to dress as a woman and another to think you were a woman trapped in a man's body, but to believe that you were actually a woman with a woman's parts was an entirely different ball game.

Oddly, these novelty cases were actually a welcome break in the monotony. After a few months of weekends, I found that the single biggest risk the guards faced was boredom. Almost anything that broke the tedious daily routine was well received here even if it was violence. This was true for the inmates and guards alike.

Lunch time came and I wandered over to Samuel's table holding my plastic tray. The guy sitting next to him dutifully moved to allow me to sit. He studied my injuries carefully without saying anything.

I said, "Lester says hello."

He smirked. "I heard you met Chip?"

Chip? That was the name Kayla had shouted out when she grabbed me in the ICU. "If that was the asshole with the jumper cables then yeah, we met, although he didn't bother to introduce himself."

He nodded. "I hope you don't expect me to feel sorry for you?"

I shook my head. "And I passed your test so I hope we're done with all the bullshit."

"You still have to take care of my problem." He nodded in the direction of a table at the other end of the room where Malcolm sat.

I swallowed a bite of my cheese sandwich and washed it down with skim milk. Leaning over to him I said, "Go fuck yourself. We're even now. I hurt you and you hurt me. I'm here to do business with you and I'm done playing games."

He thought that one over a while. "Fine. We'll meet in the showers later and talk."

"The showers? I thought I already explained to you how I felt about that stuff?"

"It's the only place we can talk freely, asshole. New York State and federal law prohibits the guards from spying on us in there."

I glanced over my shoulder and then around the room. "They're listening to us right now?"

"They could be. You'd never know."

I shook my head. "What time?"

"8:00 p.m."

"Fine, but I'm warning you now. Anybody does anything but talk and you'll be the first casualty."

"Relax, gringo, we're on the same side now."

"Are we?"

"Well, the way I figure it. Anybody who shows up here after what just happened is either totally insane or the real deal and you don't seem totally insane."

I hissed through clenched teeth. "He almost killed me."

"Look around you, dickhead. Everyone at this table has been interviewed by Chip. Now stop your whining and don't be late tonight."

The afternoon came to an end and after the last patient left, Keith handed me my civilian clothes. I said, "May I make a call?"

He looked confused. "Doc, it's almost 5:00 p.m. Once the whistle blows you can get in your car, go wherever you want and make all the calls you want."

Kilcullen had seen the wisdom of letting me out at night to facilitate communication with the Spiders on the outside and he and the D.A. had spoken with the warden. Apparently, she had gotten annoyed because it was what she had wanted to do in the first place until they had stopped her. The problem was now I had to stay for my meeting in the shower.

"You won't let me make one call?"

211

"Rules is rules, Doc. Until five you're on my time. And you don't make calls on my time."

I said, "Fine, but I'm a prisoner until five, right?"

He nodded.

"So I'm staying in my prison suit until exactly five and I'm not leaving this room until exactly five."

He was getting confused. "Doc, are you trying to cause trouble? Because if you are, I should let you know that up until five, I can still whack you with my baton without breaking any rules."

"That won't be necessary if you would just let me make a call."

Shaking his head, he looked at the overhead clock. It was twenty minutes to five. He said, "Come with me." We walked outside the exam room over to the nursing station where there was a landline. "Dial 9 first to get out, and this never happened. You got exactly one minute."

I called Kilcullen, explaining my problem in a hushed voice. I didn't have to worry. Keith was a decent human being and gave me some space. He flipped through a magazine not paying me any attention. All he wanted to do was get home to a hot meal and loving family.

I hung up and thanked him.

"Now will you get dressed?"

"Just wait. The phone's going to ring in a second."

"It is?"

It was more like four minutes when the phone rang. He answered and listened, raising his eyebrows in surprise. "Yes, warden, I understand." He paused for a second and said, "Yes, ma'am, he's right here. I'll put him on."

I said, "Hello."

"Do you want a piece of me, 90157?" she asked angrily.

"No, ma'am."

"Just who the fuck do you think you are? This is my prison. I make the rules not some asshole taking blood pressures on the weekends. I've been trying to be nice to you but if you want to play hardball just say the word," she shouted into the phone and I had to pull the receiver away from my ear.

"I'm just trying to get by, ma'am."

"The hell you are. Now listen carefully 90157. You have until lights out to get your ass out of there and I'd had better not get any more calls from my guards, the NYPD, the D.A., or the damn mayor himself. Do you understand?"

"Roger that. This here's a rubber duck."

"What did you just say?"

"I understand, ma'am."

She hung up and Keith shook his head. "I don't know what's going on and I don't want to, but in twenty years I never heard of anybody asking to spend more time in here than they had to."

"It's complicated."

"I'll bet, but I'll tell you what's not complicated."

"What's that?"

"The warden. You definitely do not want to mess with that woman, Doc. Nobody messes with that woman."

"I'll try not to."

He laughed. "I think you already did. So where to? This is your ballgame now."

"Just drop me off in the cell block, and I'll take it from there. I forgot to ask her, how do I get out of here when I'm done?"

"She told me to stick around, escort you personally to the parking lot and to personally watch you drive off the island and to shoot you if you don't leave."

213

I smiled. "You see. She is nice. Say, Keith, do you think I could make one more call?" I wanted to let Pam know I was going to be late.

He bristled. "What do I look like, a Verizon Wireless representative?"

But he let me make the call and then brought me to a cell where I killed the next few hours by taking a nap and thinking through the numbers and letters I was trying to decipher. Then there was this mysterious nerd, Chip, who liked to torture people. Did he beat Kayla nearly half to death? Who the fuck was he? I'd go talk to Kayla again as soon as I had the chance to see if things were coming back to her.

At 8:00 p.m. I wandered down to the shower room, a place I'd avoided successfully for three months. I entered the large, cold room, painted institutional green and made of cement, tile, and cinder block. Long wood benches lined the room and the grimy floor was still slick with moisture and body oils from earlier use. There was no one here and I looked around for possible escape routes and weapons I might have to use. Not a whole lot. Only one way in and one way out. Everything was tacked down tight. I could always wet a towel and snap it at them.

In a minute, Samuel and two others showed up. He nodded for me to step into the shower with him and I was relieved when he told the others to stand guard where they were. We stood under one of the shower heads and he directed it so that it would spray overhead and past us as we leaned against the tiled wall. He turned on the water full blast and the large room echoed with the sound. It was almost like being under a waterfall. I admired his resourcefulness.

I looked at him and wanted to crush him like the cockroach he was. Peddling drugs to kids who haven't even figured out what life was all about yet was as low on the evolutionary scale as you got. He scratched his chin and tried to avoid getting wet.

"Okay, this is how it works. You bring the messages to Chip and Chip alone. You'll meet him on the sixth floor of the Steinhardt building in one of the empty classrooms. You don't tell anyone else but him what I tell you. You got that so far?"

I nodded. "Who is this guy?"

"That's none of your business. Just do what I say and if you don't disappoint me, maybe I'll let your wop pals in for some sugar."

"Fine, but what's with all the cloak and dagger? Why can't I just call him on the phone when I get out?"

"Once again, that's not your concern, and second of all, you don't ever call Chip unless you'd like to go another round with him and his toys, but as long as you asked, the phones can't be trusted. Everybody is listening in on everybody these days so all important communication is person to person."

"Fair enough. Okay, so what's the message?"

"Are you in a rush?" he asked becoming annoyed.

"No, but I'd rather not be standing here if a guard happens to walk in."

"I'll worry about the guards. Now, because you're in here all weekend, the meeting will be set up for Monday night. You go to Steinhardt at exactly 11:00 p.m., identify yourself, and tell Lester that you're meeting a friend on the sixth floor. That's all you say in case someone is listening. There's a camera on the wall behind you. Don't look at it. Wait in the classroom. Chip will find you. If there's a problem then Lester will let you know. You got all that?"

"Yeah, except I can make it any night now. My lawyer negotiated a deal with the judge and warden. I'll be going home at night, including tonight."

His jaw dropped. "You lucky bastard. You survived Chip and now this." He thought it over and I could see his wheels spinning. "Well, this is good for us for sure. When are they letting you out?"

"I go right from here to the parking lot and return at seven tomorrow morning."

He nodded. "It might be too late to reach Chip tonight but I'll try. You go to Steinhardt tonight and follow the plan. If Chip can't make it the guard will let you know."

"One question."

"What?"

"How do I get into the building without an ID?"

"Tonight, you just knock on the front door and give him the password. I'll get word to him to get an ID for you. Once you have your own ID, you'll go in through the maintenance entrance in the back of the building. There's a key code for the elevator. Lester will give it to you. Once you're in the classroom, you just use the phone there to let the guard know you've arrived."

Simple, yet clever. "All right, you gonna give me the message or we gonna grow old together?"

Chapter 27

I practically flew out of the Riker's Island parking lot, and got caught in heavy traffic on the Grand Central Parkway in Queens heading into Manhattan. It was already after nine and I didn't have much time. I called Pam and told her not to wait up for me. I was totally honest this time about what I was doing and told her I was meeting with the guy who interrogated me. She didn't like it at all.

"Are you serious? Boy, you don't waste any time at all, do you?" she said already worried.

"I have no choice, Pam."

"What if he decides to finish the job?"

"He won't. We're on the same team now."

"Great." I could practically see her rolling her eyes. "By the way, I think I figured out your puzzle. It wasn't that hard."

"Really, what is it?"

"I think it's a set of addresses. One solution to the jumbled letters is Little Plains Road LI, the LI being Long Island. The sixteen numbers may represent four homes on that road. I googled them and there really are four houses on that particular road with those addresses. I'll show you when I see you."

I thought about that. "Are you sure?"

"Of course not, but it works out on paper."

217

"Okay, great job. We'll go over that together later. Would you mind texting me those addresses? How's Cleo?"

"She's fine, but she won't let me work. All she wants to do is play with chew toys, and yes, I'll text you the addresses."

I smiled. That was Cleo. "I guess she likes you. It can't hurt to have a 250-pound mastiff for a friend."

"Sure, it can. She knocked me over twice pulling on the chew toy."

"Sorry about that. Just pet her. She likes that."

"That's what I was doing when you called. So how was your first full day without me to baby you?"

"It sucked, and all the kids made fun of the way I looked."

She laughed. "Well, don't let anything happen to you tonight. You're a tough guy but I don't think your body could handle another beating like that."

"I'll do my best to stay out of trouble."

"Yeah, right," she said wryly.

"Say Pam, I'm sort of pressed for time. I'm supposed to meet this guy at eleven in Steinhardt in the classroom where we found the student. I'll barely have enough time to get there as it is. Can I ask you for a teeny little favor?"

"Don't be silly. Of course, you can."

I hesitated and she said, "Well…?"

"I don't suspect that this guy wants to do anything more than talk, but it wouldn't hurt to have some security measures in place."

"Such as…?"

"Before I tell you, I need to know one thing."

"Go on."

"Are you with me all the way or only half way?"

It took a couple of seconds but she replied, "All the way."

"Beneath my bed is a crowbar in a black duffel bag. Could you bring that over to Steinhardt and leave it in the classroom for me?"

I waited for her to explode, but she didn't. She said, "You keep a crowbar in a duffel bag under your bed?"

"Yeah."

"That doesn't seem smart. Why not keep it on the night table where you could reach it easier in an emergency or at least on the floor by the side of the bed."

I was surprised by that response. "That's a good point."

"That's what I would do."

"So you'll bring it there?"

"Of course."

"Thanks. Do it now, please. I don't want you anywhere near there when these guys show up."

"I'll leave right now. Steinhardt is only a five-minute walk from here."

"Wait a minute. I just thought about something. I don't want you to be alone with that scumbag security guard not even for five minutes."

"I'll call Knuckles. She lives two blocks away on Thompson Street. I'm sure she'll come with me."

"Perfect. Okay then, I'll call you when I'm done."

"You'd better because there's no way I'm going to be able to sleep otherwise."

"I promise."

I was about to take a big risk but I felt that I had to start shaking the tree to see what fell out. Thirty minutes later, I dropped my Toyota off at a garage several blocks from my apartment and gave the attendant the parking ticket for the BMW. He returned promptly with it and I headed over to NYU in style. My phone buzzed with the text message from Pam about the homes on Long Island. I still had a few minutes and an idea came to me so I called Vito.

"Cesari, what's up?"

"What are you doing?"

"I just sat down to eat with my guys at the Café Napoli."

"Hurry up and eat. I need you and your car." I looked at my watch. It was 10:30 p.m.

"Is this life or death? Because after dinner, me and the boys were going to unwind with a cigar and a lap dance at that new place on Broadway."

He was irritating me. "Vito, of course this is serious. Just eat quickly and head over to the Steinhardt building at NYU. Wait for me on the corner of Waverly Place by the park. You should see a silver BMW Alpina B7 parked."

He growled into the phone, "I'll be there, asshole, but this better be good."

"And keep the engine running."

At ten minutes of ten, I pulled the BMW into the maintenance driveway at the back of Steinhardt. I got out and looked toward the park. I had told Vito to wait at the corner a half block away. It was a one-way street so he'd have to be facing in the right direction. So far so good. I walked around to the front of the building and knocked on the glass door. I couldn't see Lester from my vantage point so I knocked again louder. This time his head appeared and seeing me he approached and opened the door a crack.

"Can I help you?" he asked as if he had never seen or met me before. He didn't even blink at my black eye and split lip. He had his *I don't know shit* routine down to a science.

"Samuel sent me."

He nodded. "Lycosa."

I responded, "Tarantula." Samuel changed the password every week to stay one step ahead of the police or one step ahead of his own paranoia.

"I'm meeting a friend on the sixth floor."

"Come on in."

Inside, he handed me a generic ID and the key code to the elevators on an index card. He said, "Don't lose them."

"I won't."

On the sixth floor, I nervously waited for Chip, anticipating that he would probably come with Spider bodyguards. The duffel bag was resting in a corner of the room and I unzipped it to inspect the crowbar. It was made of blackened steel and weighed six pounds. We had been through many adventures together. Your crowbar is your friend. That thought made me smile as I pictured myself wandering through the jungles of Vietnam with a crowbar instead of an M16. I left the bag unzipped with the crowbar out of sight.

Sitting in one of the chairs, I studied all the equipment in the room. If you were interested in learning anything and everything about music this was the place to be. Manhattan was the world's epicenter for music and NYU was Manhattan's epicenter for education. If you were interested in drugs, this was also the place to be. A long and happy life maybe not so much. Why were people drawn to drugs? I never understood it. There was nothing that consumed or obsessed me like that. I chuckled softly. Well, maybe women, but that was good, right? At least they didn't destroy you the way drugs did. And I chuckled again. Well, that was something that was up for debate.

I heard the elevator doors open and readied myself. Two men appeared; Chip in his Irish walking hat and funky sunglasses accompanied by a large ape with a shaved head and a spider web tattoo creeping up out of the neckline of his shirt. What the hell kind of look was Chip going for? Then I got it.

This was some sort of disguise. It wasn't bad and certainly made it difficult to identify him beyond a shadow of a doubt. The hat hid his hair and covered much of his forehead and ears. The sunglasses took care of his eyes.

He wore a brown tweed sport coat with the collar turned up to further obfuscate his appearance. The ape was about 300 pounds of solid muscle. He had that puffed-out appearance that steroids gave people and could barely walk because his thighs were so big they chafed against each other. I'd beat him in a foot race but other than that I didn't have a chance. It didn't matter because when he opened the door, he was holding a .45 Colt semi-auto and pointing it at my chest.

The ape said, "Stand up and turn around."

I did as I was told and he patted me down. Confident that I was unarmed, he ordered, "Turn your chair away to face the wall and sit back down. If you turn around for any reason, you die."

Chip finally entered the room and said, "Thank you, Hezekia. Now stand outside, please. I need to speak to the good doctor in private."

I heard the goon leave the room and close the door behind him. Then I heard Chip sit behind me in the only other chair in the room a few feet away by the control panel.

He said, "How's your dick?"

"It's my scrotum but that's splitting hairs I guess. I'll live."

He tossed a fat envelope over my head. It hit the wall in front of me and landed on the floor. He said, "It's five thousand dollars. No hard feelings, all right?"

I picked it up and nodded. "No hard feelings."

He had a deliberate, cultivated manner of speech. I couldn't tell whether he came from money or just liked to pretend he did.

"So tell me, what does Samuel have to say for himself?"

"Is it safe to talk in here? I mean can that guy hear us? Samuel said to tell you and you alone."

"The room is fully soundproofed. You could press your face against the glass and scream at the top of your lungs for help and he wouldn't hear anything."

I hesitated a second or two and said, "Samuel said, *Cargo coming this Friday. Stay tuned.*"

"That's exactly what he said, nothing more?"

"Verbatim."

He rubbed his chin. "Okay. So, Dr. Cesari, what exactly are we going to do with you? Long term, I mean."

"What do you mean?"

"During our last conversation, you claimed to represent certain criminal elements in Manhattan and yet you're a board-certified gastroenterologist serving time on Riker's. Doesn't that seem odd to you?"

"Why? You think doctors don't break the law?" I chuckled. "You've obviously never worked in a hospital."

I heard him adjust himself in his seat and then there was the unmistakable sound and smell as he struck a match. "Suppose we're not interested in having a partner?"

The sweet perfume of pipe tobacco gently wafted over from his direction. I said, "No harm done. It's just an offer on the table for you to think about. If the time comes that you'd like to discuss the particulars then I would arrange for you to meet the appropriate people. But I have to tell you that the people I represent are very resourceful, generous, and full of surprises, and they only offer their friendship once."

This got his attention and he suddenly sounded very curious. "What kind of surprises?"

"Well, it seems that my friends have come across a certain BMW loaded with goodies. Between the contents of the trunk and the price of the car they estimate the street value at about two million dollars."

Caught off guard, he sat silently for a while. "And—the catch is?"

"No catch. They are willing to return the car and everything in it for nothing more than a sit down with you. They consider it the price of admission to your party. Besides, some of the guys I'm talking about lose five hundred grand on one roll of the dice in Vegas and think nothing of it."

He was silent for just a little too long as he thought it over. I had him. I could feel it and I didn't even need to use the crowbar. I was kind of proud of myself. I was showing maturity and I liked it. He said, "And what do you personally get out of all of this? You seem to be going through an awful lot for these *friends* of yours."

"That's simple. My medical career is over. I need a job."

He said, "I see. Tell me more about these friends of yours."

"I think you'll like them."

Chapter 28

*A*n hour later, they left me in the classroom, my heart pounding with excitement. I grabbed the duffel bag with the crowbar and raced down the stairwell and out the front exit barely acknowledging the guard. Once on the street, I sprinted around the corner and found Vito puffing on a camel in his black Cadillac. I jumped into the passenger side without saying anything and stared down the street. The BMW was still there.

"Well, hello to you too, Cesari," he said sarcastically.

"There they are."

"There who are?"

A black Mercedes had just pulled up next to the BMW. Chip and the ape got out. "The assholes who did this to me."

In the dark, he hadn't noticed my battered face at first, but now as I looked directly at him, he squinted and said, "Shit, what the hell happened to you?"

"Riker's Island is what happened. I'll explain as we drive. See those two guys up there looking in the trunk of that car?"

"Yeah, I see them."

"Follow the guy in the funny hat."

Chip got back in the Mercedes and his bodyguard took the BMW. The bodyguard led the way and I was happy to see that they were following each other rather than splitting up.

Vito hung back enough to give them breathing room and we soon found ourselves in the Queens Midtown Tunnel leaving Manhattan. Driving through Queens toward Long Island, I started filling Vito in on my experiences since I saw him last.

He said, "At least he gave you five big ones for your troubles. That's something."

"Yeah, he's all heart. The next time I try to neuter you I'll be sure to bring along some cash to ease your pain."

"I'm just saying…"

"Well, stop saying and pay attention to the road."

Once on the Long Island Expressway, I became more confident as to our destination and said, "You can lay back a little more now, Vito. I have an idea of where they might be heading."

An hour later, I had brought Vito up to speed on everything, causing him to whistle. "Man, you are really up to your eyeballs in it this time."

"Thanks, but I already figured that part out."

We eventually turned onto the Sunrise Highway toward Southampton and Vito said, "You know, Cesari, if you had told me we were going to drive all night then I might have passed on the second bourbon at dinner."

It was after 1:00 a.m. and we were both tired. "I'll drive back, all right? Cut your lights when we get into town and stay as far back as possible." Traffic had drawn down to an occasional vehicle passing by in the opposite direction and almost no one behind us. We were fifty yards behind and were now driving down secluded country roads in a fairly exclusive part of the country. As an afterthought I asked, "You do have a gun, right?"

"Of course. There's a 9mm Beretta in the glove compartment with a ten-round clip and a .38 strapped to my ankle. Underneath my seat is a fifteen-inch tactical Bowie knife and in the trunk is a 12-gauge Mossberg shotgun."

I smiled. "A Bowie knife? One of those gigantic things?"

"Yeah."

"Let me see it."

He reached under his seat and handed me what had to be the largest and most deadly blade I had ever seen. It was made of blackened steel and had a black rubber grip with hand guard. Its curved edge and size made it seem more like a machete or a small sword.

"Wow! Look at this thing. No one will ever confuse this with a camping knife."

"That's the idea, Cesari. If I have to use that then there's no turning back if you get my drift. Hey, I can't drive much longer without lights. It was bad enough back there in town but out here in nowhere is getting dangerous even with the moon. What do you want to do?"

I put the knife under my seat and thought quickly. "Pull over for a second and let me think it through."

A hundred yards ahead the tail lights of the cars we were following disappeared as they turned down Little Plains Road. Pam was right. I took out my cellphone and plugged in one of the addresses into my GPS. "Cut the engine. The houses are less than half a mile away down the next road up ahead. We're very near the water."

"Okay, but what's the plan. We can't just traipse into a drug ring's hideout."

"No, we can't and that's not what I wanted to do. I needed to confirm where they were going and to do a little reconnoitering for when I return. The big question right now is what are they doing out here … camping? And why are there four addresses? All right, I have an idea. Turn the car around and go back to Main Street and make a left. According to the GPS, Main Street parallels Little Plains Road all the way down to the water. You can cut over at Foster Crossing and park in a secluded spot. I'll go in alone."

Five minutes later, he pulled the car over again and turned the engine off. He reached past me into the glove compartment, grabbed the pistol and shoved it into his waist band. He started to get out of the car and I said, "What are you doing?"

"Shut up and let's get this over with."

He had parked close to the intersection of Foster Crossing and Little Plains Road and we only had about two thousand feet between us and the ocean. The sound of the waves and smell of salt water filled our senses as a quarter moon lit the way. All I really wanted to do was confirm that the houses identified by Pam were the same ones that Chip had driven to.

On Little Plains Road, we found four large homes in a row leading up to a private beach. The houses were on the same side of the road each separated by fifty yards of lawn, shrubs and trees. The one closest to the water had lights on and a Mercedes parked in the driveway. The BMW was out of sight and I presumed it was in the attached garage. The other three homes were completely dark without signs of life. There were no cars parked either out front on the road or in the driveway. The lawns needed mowing. For the sake of completeness, I double checked all the addresses Pam had given me and they matched up.

"What now, Cesari?"

"I say we take a peek inside one of them, like the one furthest from the beach. It's closest to our car and farthest from theirs."

"Or we could go home?"

"That's it? You don't want to go into one of these houses to see what's going on?"

"Think it through, asshole. They're drug dealers. What if there's an alarm, cameras, German shepherds, or armed guards patrolling the property?"

The way he put it made me feel stupid. I wanted to know what was going on here. There had to be a reason that kid Justin had recorded these addresses and tried to hide the fact, but I promised Pam I wouldn't do anything stupid like breaking and entering. It just dawned on me that I had neglected to call her. I took out my phone and saw five missed text messages and two missed calls from her. I called back but she didn't answer so I sent her a text that everything was okay. She must have fallen asleep. She would undoubtedly be worried.

"C'mon Vito. We came all this way. Your car is only a couple of hundred feet away. If anything goes wrong we can make it there in a heartbeat."

Vito took a deep breath and let it out. Shrugging off the last remaining effects of the bourbon he said, "Fine, but just one house, and I agree, it should be the one as far as possible from where they are."

We walked to the house furthest from the beach, and standing on the front lawn we devised a simple plan. I said, "I'll go ring the front doorbell. If no one answers, we break in. If a light goes on or a dog barks, we hightail it out of here. Same thing if we trigger an alarm."

"Fine."

"We'll go in through the garage. I don't want to be seen standing on someone's porch smashing in the front door. Okay, now go back to the car and get my crowbar from the duffel bag."

"I'm not your bitch. Get your own crowbar."

"Don't be stupid. I'm being nice. I was going to wait for you to get halfway to the car and then ring the doorbell. I'm a hell of a lot faster than you if we have to start running, I thought I'd give you a head start."

He saw the wisdom in that, didn't thank me, but started walking toward his car. I said, "Hey, wait a minute."

He turned back to me. "What now?"

"Give me your .38, just in case."

Shaking his head in exasperation, he reached down into his ankle holster, retrieved the gun and handed it to me saying, "Don't lose this one."

I watched him walk away and stepped onto the front porch, glancing around several times. When he was almost out of sight, I pressed the door buzzer and held my breath. I repeated the maneuver several times until I was convinced no one could sleep through that kind of racket.

Several minutes later, Vito returned with the crowbar, and we walked up to the side door leading into the garage and tested it. It was locked but had a paned window on top. We broke one of the panes and reached in to unlock the door. Inside, there were no cars or anything else. It was completely devoid of tools, lawn mowers, ladders; the usual the things you find in a garage. The door leading into the house was similarly locked and I used the crowbar to pry it open.

We went in and crept around as furtively as possible guided only by slivers of moonlight filtering in through large windows. We found sparsely furnished rooms but no real signs that someone lived here. There was a sofa and chairs in the living room but no family pictures, no televisions, and nothing in the refrigerator. There were five large bedrooms with king-sized beds fully made up, but nothing in the dressers or closets.

I stood in the middle of the kitchen and scratched my head. "What do you think?"

Vito said, "I don't know. It's almost like the house is up for sale. I wonder why there's no alarm system. People that own homes like this always have alarm systems."

I thought about that and wasn't 100 percent sure if he was right. In the kitchen, we found a door leading down into the basement. It was made of steel and dead-bolted, which I found odd. I unlocked it, flipped the light switch, and went down the stairs with Vito close behind.

The basement was large and rectangular, finished with wood paneling and an old carpet. There was a flat screen TV in one corner, a bathroom, several children's board games, and a handful of toys lying on the floor including a doll with a blue dress. Two large, filthy mattresses occupied the center of the room. I sniffed the air and looked at Vito. He looked back but didn't say anything. He didn't have to. He smelled it too. It was fear. A chill ran up my spine and I took a deep breath, letting it out slowly. A blood vessel in my temple started to throb.

"Vito, look at this." I knelt down next to the mattress and examined an old stain. "It's blood."

He saw my temperature starting to rise. "Take it easy, Cesari. Let's not jump to any conclusions."

I nodded but my imagination was already flying off the handle as was my blood pressure. You didn't have to be a genius to figure out what was going on here. I leaned down and picked up the doll. The blue dress was dirty and torn. Its brown eyes stared at me and I caught my breath, suddenly very emotional. I tried to imagine what it must be like to lose a child but I couldn't. How do you imagine something like that let alone something as horrible as this? I thought about Kelly and the twins. As strained and unusual as our relationship was, I would still go ballistic if anyone hurt them. I was ready to scream. Anyone that could hurt a child, didn't deserve to live, and they didn't deserve a pleasant death either.

Visibly angry, I said, "I've seen enough. Let's go."

Vito noticed my mounting anger and said, "Take a deep breath first. Losing control isn't going to help anyone."

"You're right except for one thing, Vito. Losing control every now and then for the right reason is a good thing. It means you care, and goddammit, I care. I care about what happened here and I don't need proof. I'm not the fucking FBI."

He raised his hands soothingly trying to calm me down. "All right. I get it, but it's time to go."

We locked the basement door and tried to leave as little a footprint as possible. Of course, they would discover the forced entry and I hoped that they would think it was kids looking for a quick score and not finding anything, left. No harm, no foul. That would prompt them to beef up security but that couldn't be helped.

Standing outside, I wondered aloud if we should check any of the other homes. Vito shot that idea down. "We've been lucky so far, Cesari. Let's not push it. We're just two guys. We have no idea what we're up against. We already know that they have at least one gun and a 300-pound Spider in addition to whatever else, and suppose you're right and there are kids somewhere around here and that's a big if, are you going to take a chance and start a firefight?"

He was right. Better to go somewhere and think it through. We drove home quietly, the mood decidedly soured by the implications of what we had found. "Why did you take the doll, Cesari?" Vito asked noticing me staring at it on my lap.

I couldn't help myself. I was drawn to it and felt a presence that I couldn't explain. "Because when I return I'm going to shove it up somebody's ass."

He nodded, lit a cigarette, and opened a window. "I'd be more than happy to help you."

"Do you mean that, Vito?"

"Sure, I hate guys who hurt kids, and this is the worst kind of hurting. Stealing kids from their parents and doing God knows what to them. There's a special place in hell for people like that."

"I'm glad you feel that way because I feel the same way and I could use your help."

"Go on."

I told him about my meeting with Chip. He said, "You convinced this yahoo that that the mob wants in and is willing to spread some cash around to grow the business in return for a hefty return on their investment?"

"Yes, I did."

"And he believed it?" he asked with incredulity.

"I'm very convincing."

"And since you gave him the drugs and car back he figures it can't hurt to find out what's on the table?"

"Big companies buy up small companies all the time."

"Not in my world, Cesari. You know that. All takeovers are extremely hostile."

"I know that and you know that, but he doesn't know that."

"And I'm the guy you need to sit down with them?"

"I can't think of anyone better."

He took a long drag and blew it out the window as he thought it over. Then he shook his head from side to side as if weighing pros and cons. He coughed, cleared his throat and said, "Yeah, okay. I wouldn't mind slamming these guys. Set it up and give me a call."

"I already told him we'll meet him in the bar at the SoHo Grand on West Broadway, Monday night at seven sharp. He wanted to meet in a public place just in case."

He looked at me suspiciously. "How'd you know I'd agree to do it?"

"Because I know that, despite what everybody says about you behind your back, you're really not a total asshole."

He glanced at me and grinned. "I'm touched. The SoHo Grand? Nice place. Very public."

"Yeah, but not as public as he thinks it will be. I know the bartender there and I think he'll be agreeable to helping us out."

Traffic was light on the way to the city and we shaved twenty minutes off the ride back, arriving at just after three. I entered my apartment quietly, and put the gun in a safe place. Vito had agreed to let me hang on to it. I said hello to Cleo, stripped, and slipped gently under the covers next to Pam.

I stared at the ceiling in the dark. I was exhausted, still in pain, and now furious at the world. As if selling drugs to teenagers wasn't bad enough. Who were these people and from what rock did they crawl out from under? I looked at my watch. I needed to get at least a few hours' sleep. I rolled over toward Pam and jumped back, startled. She was staring at me.

"When did you get home?" she asked.

I laughed. "You scared me. I just walked in the door. Sorry, I tried to call you."

She yawned. "Everything go okay?"

"No, actually, it's much worse than I thought." I told her what I found and what my fears were.

Her eyes went wide now fully awake. "Wow, but maybe it's not what you think?"

Good people always had trouble accepting evil even when it stared at them right in the face. "Maybe, but now I have to find out." I sighed deeply. "I can't tell you how it made me feel to be in that room, Pam. I could sense things. Vito could too."

My voice cracked with emotion and she put her arms around me drawing me near. "You're over tired, John, and you've been under a great deal of stress. How are your wounds? Did you change the bandages today?"

"No, I didn't have time."

She sighed, rolled over, and turned on a light. She got out of bed, went to the bathroom, and came back with a wet cloth, fresh bandages, antibiotic ointment, and a roll of hospital tape.

She knelt on the bed next to me. "Let me change them now so you don't have to worry about it in the morning."

She gently pulled the bandages off my nipples, cleansed the area, applied the ointment, and fixed new gauze in place. "You're healing up pretty good."

"Thanks to you."

She smiled. "Now pull your boxers down and spread your legs." I hated this part. Some things were simply not meant to have tape on them. When she finished, she got back in bed adjusted the comforter over us and snuggled up close.

"Now try to close your eyes. It'll be morning soon."

She laid her head on my chest and I closed my eyes, drifting off uneasily into a world with which I was unfamiliar. I dreamt I was in a dark and depraved place, surrounded on all sides by wicked, vile creatures. I tossed and turned, thinking about who the doll belonged to and the awful things I was going to do to the person who took it from her.

Dark clouds suddenly appeared on the horizon, and as the storm approached, a lightning bolt lit up the sky and thunder shook the ground. I woke in a cold sweat and knew what had to be done.

Chapter 29

Sunday at Riker's came and went uneventfully other than my almost continuous yawning throughout the day. At lunch, I told Samuel that everything had gone according to plan with Chip. He seemed pleased and nodded his approval at me while I suppressed my rage and the urge to stab him in the eye with a fork. But it was two straight days at Riker's that no one attacked me. That was a good weekend.

I didn't even remember driving back to my apartment I was so tired. Pam was out with Cleo and I immediately laid down for a nap. Waking several hours later, I found Pam reading a book, curled up on the sofa in the living room, Cleo at her feet. I liked the way they were getting along. I sat down and rested my head against her shoulder, trying to wake up.

Pam looked at her watch and chuckled. It was almost 8:00 p.m. "Pretty tired, huh?"

"Yup, and hungry."

"I made mac and cheese for dinner. It came out pretty good. I jazzed it up with bacon and smoked gouda. Want me to fix you a plate?"

"Thanks. You keep reading. I'll get it. I need to get my blood circulating. Do you want anything?"

236

"A glass of wine would be nice. I was straightening out your closet this afternoon and found a suitcase full of nice Italian wines so I put them in the wine rack."

Man, I was never going to live that down. I said, "Thank you."

She laughed. "I'm beginning to think whipping you into shape is going to be quite the project."

"Well, you're way ahead of schedule on this matter, according to my internal clock." Instead of going into the kitchen to get my dinner I wrapped my arms around her and kissed her. She dropped her book onto her lap and embraced me.

She said, "Your week's almost up. I'm a tolerant but extremely punctual person in these matters."

It took a minute for me to understand what she was talking about, and then I remembered her self-imposed moratorium on sex. I laughed. My aches and pains had settled down to a dull throbbing. It was mostly a matter of motivation at this point. "Pam, I have something to tell you."

"Speak freely."

I cleared my throat and sang softly with a country twang, "I've been through a lot and I'm not as good as I once was."

She smiled, "But you're as good once, as you ever were. Oh my God, you can't carry a tune at all."

"Cesari's fatal flaw." We both laughed and I asked, "You like country music?"

"I love country music. That's one of my favorite songs. From a psychology point of view, it's a treasure trove of insight into the male psyche. If you recall, the song opens with two girls propositioning a cowboy in a bar for a threesome. He, being a little older, immediately becomes concerned about performance issues and feels he needs to warn them ahead of time. That's hysterical right there but highlights the evolution of the male ego structure. From eighteen to about thirty, most males don't give a hoot about female satisfaction. As long as they get their rocks off, they figure it's all good. As stamina declines, from the thirties on upward, men become increasingly self-conscious about whether they can please a woman and even worse, whether they will be judged or ridiculed by their performance."

"You've really thought this through."

"I've written papers on how male insecurity leads to female oppression."

I glanced down at the cover of the book on her lap, *Fifty Shades of Grey*. "Is that why you're reading that? An educational experience?"

"It's not about oppression. It's about erotic domination, and it's written from the female perspective."

I perked up at that. I didn't know. "Really? How is it?"

"Even sillier the second time around. You haven't read it?"

"No, I've heard about it though, but who hasn't?"

"You really don't know what it's about?"

I shook my head. "Not really. Some girl having sex, right?"

She chuckled. "Basically. The story line is pretty bad, and the writing is horrid, but I have to say, there is a certain something about it that draws me in. So you really don't know?"

"Why don't you tell me?"

"I think I would much rather show you. You seem a little like the guy in the book."

"Now you're beginning to bug me. Is that good or bad?"

She looked at me seriously with an impish grin. "We'll find out. I thought you were going to get me a glass of wine?"

"Did you just change the subject?"

"I need wine."

Unbelievable! I went into the kitchen and opened a bottle of Montepulciano d'Abruzzo, a mellow red from east central Italy. I poured us a couple of glasses and heated up some mac and cheese in the microwave. Handing her a glass, I said, "Where were we?"

Feeling devilish, she continued to string me along. "I can't remember."

After my first bite of mac and cheese I forgot all about *Fifty Shades* of whatever. "My God, Pam, this is great."

She was very pleased. "It's the smoked Gouda. It really makes the dish. I topped it with panko bread crumbs before toasting the whole thing under the broiler."

"It's really good. Okay, this week I have to make you dinner one night. I'm pretty handy in the kitchen too."

She smiled. "This I have to see."

My cellphone rang. "What's up, Vito?"

"Got a sec?"

"Shoot."

"I did some research today on this Spider guy, Samuel Archer, the one you're playing with in Riker's and found out a few things."

"Yeah?"

"Well, according to my sources, he may be a lowlife now but he didn't start out that way. He even went to college. You're going to love this. Guess where?"

I was intrigued and joked. "Harvard?"

"Even better—NYU."

"Get the fuck out of here." I couldn't have been more surprised.

"What's more is he graduated five years ago summa cum laude with a degree in philosophy."

"I can't believe this. Are you sure you got the right guy?"

"Don't insult me like that, okay? His criminal career started in junior year with an arrest for drug possession and resisting arrest. His lawyer got him off with probation. The school decided not to hold it against him. Senior year, he spent six months in

Mexico and Central America ostensibly doing volunteer work, building huts, giving out vaccines, that kind of stuff, but he picked up some bad habits and when he returned was arrested while in the company of a fourteen-year-old prostitute on the streets of some border town in Texas, a place called Pharr. They had him by the balls, but the girl disappeared and they had to let him go. Are you listening to me, Cesari?"

"Unfortunately, yes. Continue."

"When he came back to New York, he took an apartment in the Village near NYU and started dealing to the students. Several arrests and minor jail time followed. It was around this time that the spider tattoo stuff appears, according to arrest records. He began expanding and recruiting, dealing in crack, meth, and heroin, but authorities always felt there was more going on. Whatever connections he had made in Mexico and Central America he maintained and was suspected of bringing in girls from there to pimp out."

"Three years ago, he was arrested for selling marijuana. He had two kilos in the trunk of his car. Bail was set at $10,000, and some girl who didn't speak a word of English came in with a sack of cash to get him out. Now this is where it gets interesting. It was right around this time that the authorities started noticing a spike in drug use at NYU. That's when they think Samuel started infiltrating his men onto campus, taking up key positions, and recruiting students who were financially desperate to distribute for him."

I interjected. "But they couldn't have done that without the help of someone high up in the bureaucracy at NYU to help with the hiring process and to identify students in dire financial straits?"

"You got it."

"Samuel mentioned to me that he had some sort of connection there but he didn't say what or who?"

"Your pal, Chip, maybe?"

"Maybe, I hadn't thought about that, but the dots are starting to connect."

"Well, grab a yearbook and start looking through it for clues. We're still on for tomorrow night?"

"Yes, do you want to get together first to rehearse?"

He thought that was funny. "Not necessary. I live this stuff every day, but I suppose it couldn't hurt. Meet me at my apartment an hour ahead of time. How hard should I press this guy?"

"Grab him by the nuts and squeeze away."

"Got it. One more thing."

"What?"

I traced those houses on Long Island. No luck in linking them together. They have four different owners who live in different parts of the country and have no apparent relationship to NYU. They might be summer homes or rental properties. So whatever was going on in the house we were in can't be linked to the house your pal Chip was in. Could be just a coincidence."

"A coincidence? You can't be serious? Coming home late from work one night and seeing my best friend Vito crawling out my girlfriend's window was just a coincidence. This is real."

"Oh, for Christ's sake are you ever going to let go of that? See a shrink already."

"It hurt Vito, but you know what hurt more?"

"What?"

"Watching her throw your pants out the window after you."

I hung up and turned to Pam who had been listening intently. She started chuckling after that last part. I had a hunch. I cleared my throat and she got serious again. "I need a yearbook from five years ago."

She had heard most of the conversation. "We can go to the library tomorrow. They keep them archived there."

"We can't find one tonight?"

"You have an awful lot of energy all of a sudden."

I did. Vito's news about Samuel having attended NYU had snapped life back into me and I wanted to strike while the iron was hot. The idea that Chip might be his connection on campus also intrigued me. So who was this guy Chip then? Somebody in human resources who could influence hiring and firing on campus in such a way that no one would question his decisions? I said, "Actually, I do feel pretty good right now."

"That's good because then I have something more fun in mind than looking for yearbooks." She put her wine glass down and wiggled close.

I hesitated. "I'm not sure if I'm quite ready, Pam. Even taking a shower hurts pretty good down there."

"Do you have a pair of big boy pants we could put on you?"

"Very cute."

She said, "Open your mouth."

"What?"

"Just do it."

I opened my mouth and she examined inside carefully. Smiling mischievously, she said, "Your tongue looks okay."

I pushed her away laughing as I got her intention. "That's very selfish of you. I'm not feeling well and all you can think about is your personal gratification."

"Isn't that how men are?"

"I wouldn't know. Men don't discuss their sex lives with other men."

She sat back and seemed surprised. "Really?"

"Why would we?"

"I don't believe you."

"It's very unattractive to call your lover a liar."

She smiled thoroughly enjoying this new game. I was having fun myself and started to feel a slight stirring south of the border. She smirked. "Is that what we are—lovers?"

"Or whatever?"

"Whatever?"

"Yeah, whatever."

"I see."

"Do you?"

Our eyes met and we studied each other intently. Without warning, she reached over and tapped the growing bulge in my pants. I caught my breath and flinched, exclaiming, "Hey, what the heck was that?" It didn't really hurt so much as startle me.

"A warning."

"A what?"

Smiling, she said, "You like belts and there are things I like to do as well."

What the hell did that mean? She just let that float around without attaching any specifics to it. We kept staring at each other sending and receiving subliminal messages. I wanted to. I really did but it was too soon. I was still sore everywhere but especially down there. It was going to hurt—a lot, but I was starting to get the feeling that she was okay with that. I sent her a telepathic message that we should wait another week.

In response, she started breathing a little faster and her eyes wouldn't let go of me. She said, "Are you with me all the way or only half way?"

"But…"

"Am I going to have to smack him again?"

I raised my eyes, realizing that I had created a monster. "That won't be necessary."

"Good, because from this point on, I expect strict obedience."

243

Moderately concerned, I said, "I'm not quite sure where we're heading with all of this."

She stood and grabbed my hands, pulling me toward the bedroom. "You're just going to have to trust Officer Pam. Now come along with me. I bought a few things while you were playing jailhouse doc today."

Chapter 30

*D*etective Kilcullen was in unusually good spirits during our Monday morning meeting. "Fine work, lad, but we need more specifics."

I looked at the bottle of Jameson's on his desk. It was down to two fingers. He sipped from his coffee cup and grimaced. I said, "I'm doing my best but they're not stupid. They either speak in code or simple signals. Obviously, something is going down. What, where, and when is the question."

He nodded. I hadn't told him about the four houses on Long Island because to do that I would have had to reveal that I turned a car with a trunk full of narcotics over to drug dealers. He already had enough ammunition on me and I didn't intend on giving him anymore. "So what's next, Johnny boy? We need to know what's next."

"I'm not sure. It's not clear by any stretch who this guy Chip is, so putting a tail on him may not lead us anywhere and may tip them off. Hell, whatever it is that's going down may not even be taking place in New York." I couldn't have the police following Chip, unfortunately, because that would lead them straight to me and Vito, so I had been lobbying hard against it.

Eventually he sided with me and nodded. "You have a good head on your shoulders there, son. You would have made a good cop for sure. I've always thought your people had potential. I used to tell Mary. She be me fourth wife t'at. Done left me for a no-good drunk of a carpenter, she did. I used to say, Mary, them Eyetalian people have potential. Just look at that DaVinci fellow. Now he had a good head on his shoulders also."

I said, "Thank you."

"Maybe I should arrange to have you spend more time at Riker's? You're doing so well there. How would you like a promotion? I could trump up some charge and have you stay all week. Maybe even put you in the same cell with Samuel. Then, if he talks in his sleep we'll have the rat bastard."

I became alarmed. "I don't think that's a good idea at all. This Chip guy is the key. I'm sure of it, but he has to be handled with care and I'm all over it. Samuel isn't going anywhere. Just give me some time and a little latitude."

Please, please, please!

He thought it over. "Aah, you probably be right. Okay, we stay the course for now, but the next time you meet with this Chip character you let me know. It would probably be a good idea to have you wear a wire once he's comfortable with you. No more Lone Ranger and Tonto stuff, understand?"

I nodded. "I would have let you know about Saturday night but I didn't have time. The meeting was set up for less than two hours after I left Riker's, and besides, they frisked me the minute they got there."

"Fine, just remember who's in charge here."

"I will."

"Now tell me about this warden, Garcia. She sounds like a feisty wench on the phone, she does. Told me to go fuck meself, she did. I like a woman with spirit."

"She definitely has spirit, and quite a looker too."

He slapped his knee. "I knew it. I could tell from the sound of her voice."

This was too funny. Might as well throw a little gasoline on this fire. "I didn't notice a wedding ring."

He hesitated a moment and said uncomfortably, almost as if he were talking to himself, "Hmm, now that's interesting."

"That's what I thought."

"Still, there could be a man in her life. You wouldn't happen to know if she has a boyfriend or anything like t'at?" Suddenly getting embarrassed, he straightened his tie and cleared his throat. "Mind you, I'm not interested for meself, but, um, I have a certain friend of mine, a bachelor you see. Nice fella, well-seasoned if you know what I mean, who be fond of the female persuasion himself."

"Well, any friend of yours is a friend of mine so I'd be happy to find out."

Regaining his confidence, he took a long swallow from his "coffee cup" and winced. "T'ats a good lad."

After my debriefing at the precinct, I met Pam in the NYU library to look through yearbooks for clues about Samuel. We sat at a long table and as a starting point picked the yearbook from five years ago when Vito said Samuel had graduated. Searching tediously through every page and picture, we couldn't find his name or any photo that even vaguely resembled him. Taking into account his undoubtedly markedly changed appearance made this very laborious work and after a couple of hours I was seeing double. As a secondary goal, I was also scanning for anybody that resembled Chip. That was a more complicated subject because I couldn't be sure at all he had any ties to NYU. Right now, that was pure speculation.

I said, "Maybe Vito got the year wrong. You take the year after and I'll take the year before."

"But I never met him."

"That's okay, just look for the name."

We grabbed more yearbooks and started flipping through pages and pages of shiny fresh-faced undergraduate pictures. They were all so young and full of hope. I wondered how many of them had turned to the dark side of life like Samuel. After another hour like this, we were frustrated. I said, "What if he never submitted a photo for the yearbook?"

Pam looked up. "Of course, they wouldn't just reserve a blank spot with his name under it. However, at the back of the book, there will be a master list of names listed under the school and degree they graduated with."

We turned to the back of the books with the master listings in alphabetical order of every graduate and eventually found him. Vito was right. There he was in the book from five years ago. Samuel Archer, summa cum laude, Phi Beta Kappa, B.A. in Philosophy. "Pretty smart guy," commented Pam.

I snorted. "If he was really smart he would have left me alone."

"Why is there no picture? I'd really like to see what he looked like."

"The next time I'm at Riker's, I'll take a selfie with him."

She didn't think I was nearly funny as I thought I was and ignored me. "There has to be one somewhere. Nobody goes through four years of college without at least one picture somewhere. He must have belonged to some club or other after school activity." She thought it over for a few seconds. "If he had a degree in philosophy he might be in a group photo. All the departments do that."

Flipping through the departmental photos we found nothing in the year he graduated but kept going backward in time until his freshman year which was nine years ago. I froze looking at the picture. Pam noticed me stiffen up. "You found him?"

"Yeah, that's him. I'm certain of it, but that's not his name under the picture. First row, second from the right. Good looking kid. Look at that hair. He looks like a rock star."

Pam said wistfully, "He so young and innocent there. It's hard to believe what a monster he's become."

"It happens all the time, unfortunately, and everybody always says the same thing, *He was such a nice-looking boy.*"

"Are you sure that's him?"

I studied the picture hard. "That's him. He's been in my face multiple times at Riker's."

She sighed loudly and I continued, "Pam, there's something I want you to start thinking about."

"What's that?"

"The other day when I told you that about these guys dealing drugs on campus. Remember?"

"Yes."

"You said you wanted them all dead."

She didn't say anything. People always said stuff like that in the heat of the moment. In the light of day when justice demanded action it was always different. I added, "Just something to think about."

I stared at the picture some more. Athletic build and sharp eyes, he looked very intelligent. It was his eyes that gave him away. Black as his soul. Even then, he looked like a risk-taker, someone who lived for the thrill. The caption said his name was Seth Ackerman not Samuel Archer, but I was 100 percent certain that was him. I was very good with faces. His initials were S. A.— Samuel Archer? Why would he have changed his name?

For a moment, I considered the possibility that I was wrong and that maybe I just wanted it to be him. This was a good exercise that I practiced all the time when dealing with patients who presented with uncertain diagnoses. It never hurt to take a step back, put your ego aside, assume you were wrong, and take a fresh look.

"What are you thinking about?" Pam asked.

"I'm trying to understand why Samuel would have changed his name."

"Why does anybody change their name?" she asked.

"That's a good question. Actors, musicians, and entertainers change their names to more public friendly names. A difficult Italian name might be changed to one that could be easily pronounced and remembered. A boring name might be changed to one more exotic. People also change their names when they don't want to be found."

"People on the run?"

"Yes, criminals and innocent folks alike such as teenagers, wives, and girlfriends leaving abusive domestic situations. They don't always legally change their names because of the difficulties with social security, driver's licenses, credit reports, and car registration, etcetera. But when they do, it's almost always one that begins with the same first letters of their original name so it's easy for them to remember."

"Where would Samuel figure in?"

"I don't know. Even though I'm convinced it's him, I would like to get some confirmation."

I strummed my fingers on the table as I thought it over. After a few moments, I glanced furtively over my shoulder, then suddenly grabbed the book and carefully tore the page out as Pam looked on in horror. "You can't do that!"

I folded the page neatly and said, "I wish you had told me that before I did it."

She sat there with her mouth open. I said, "I promise to bring it back."

"You are so bad. I can't believe it."

I chuckled. If she thought I was bad now she was going to be horrified at what was coming down the pike. I looked at my watch. "Is there any way we can look up his enrollment records? I'd like to know where he grew up."

"Why, so you can beat up his parents?"

Not a bad idea. "No, not his parents, but his kindergarten teacher for sure." I smiled.

"You'd better not. Let's put these books away and I'll see if I can look it up. I'm not sure if our system was fully online back then but it might have been."

It was and we stared at the screen closely, fascinated by what we saw. Seth Ackerman registered freshman year as an undecided major, and lived a more or less uncolorful life on campus his first two years. There was no registration for Seth for a third year, but Samuel Archer suddenly appears for the first time, registering as a junior. His parents paid all the bills for the first two years and then he picked up the tab himself after that. His parents were Matthew and Linda of 59 Summit Street, New Milford, CT. There was no phone number listed.

This was strange and didn't add up. If it was him, he started school as Seth Ackerman and finished as Samuel Archer. I asked Pam and she couldn't recall if she ever heard of a student doing that. Something happened between the end of his second and beginning of his third year at NYU and I wanted to know what.

"Feel like taking a ride, Pam?"

"Where?"

"Connecticut."

Chapter 31

Summit Street was a beautiful, tree-lined road in the picturesque town of New Milford. The Ackerman home was an old, white clap-board, two-story structure with peeling paint, green wood shutters, and a wraparound porch, complete with wind chimes and rocking chairs. Right next door was a quintessential white-steepled church. A sign out front read, *First Methodist Church of New Milford, founded 1795.*

Pam said, "This town is so beautiful. It's hard to believe we're only an hour north of the city."

"Yeah."

"Look." I turned my head and a bunch of kids were riding their bikes down the quiet street toward us.

I laughed. "I guess we don't see too much of that in Greenwich Village."

"Oh my God. They're adorable." Several of the girl's bikes had colored streamers attached to the handles blowing in the bike's draft. The kids were laughing and yelling as they raced each other.

I said, "Yeah. I'm only here ten minutes and I feel like having kids myself."

She snorted. "You're so cynical. Enjoy the moment."

Enjoy the moment? I came here to see if that asshole Samuel might have thrown any of these kids into the trunk of his car or shown any tendency to wit. I said, "You're right. I need to chill out."

We walked up three porch steps and rang the doorbell. A minute later, a white-haired man in his late sixties answered. He wore black pants and shirt with a white collar. He had a friendly, even kindly face, and I immediately got a bad feeling.

He said, "How may I help you?"

I hesitated. "We're looking for Matthew and Linda Ackerman."

"I'm Matthew Ackerman. My wife Linda is deceased."

"I'm sorry about your wife. May we have a moment of your time, Father?"

He smiled. "It's Reverend usually but Father will do if you can't help yourself. The Methodists and Catholics are close enough that it's not worth quibbling over. Why don't you just call me Matthew? What would you like to discuss?"

I replied, "My name is Dr. John Cesari and this is Dr. Pamela Gottlieb. We're from New York and we were wondering if we might ask you a few questions about your son, Seth?"

The smile disappeared. "I'm afraid you've been misled, doctors. I don't have a son. Good day to you."

He stepped back and as he went to close the door I jammed my foot in it preventing him. "I'm very sorry, Matthew, but I'd really like to talk to you about your son."

He looked at me, quietly sizing me up, and realizing that physically he couldn't resist. He might have had a gun but I doubted he would even think about using it because someone asked to talk to him. He could call the police, and tell them what? His eyes watered up and he suddenly looked small and frail.

Pam stepped forward and with great sympathy said, "Matthew, we don't mean to intrude on your life. We sympathize with your suffering but we just need to ask you a few questions. I promise we won't take up too much of your time."

Sniffling, he opened the door fully and waved us in. We entered his living room and took a seat on his sofa opposite two Queen Anne wingback chairs. He sat in one of them and tears streamed down his face. I looked around the room decorated with vintage wall coverings and furniture. A wood-burning fireplace with a painted mantle was the centerpiece of the room, highlighted with pictures of his wife strategically placed here and there. There were no pictures of Seth.

We quietly waited for him to collect himself. When he did, I asked, "What can you tell me about Seth?"

He sighed deeply. "We tried our best. We really did. I don't think we did anything wrong. Damn drugs just destroy people. They eat at the very soul."

Pam gripped my arm.

"Do you know where he is now, sir?"

"No, I haven't seen or heard from him in seven years, since the summer of his sophomore year when he nearly destroyed this town and us with it."

Pam and I glanced at each other.

"He was attending NYU and home for summer. He was doing well and had his ups and downs like any other kid but that year was very different. He was secretive, angry, staying out late, spending money, and drinking like a sailor. He refused to go to church with us and called us fools for our beliefs. He had several minor run-ins with local law enforcement but because of my standing in town with the congregation they took it easy on him. We thought he was just going through a phase, but deep down Linda and I were concerned about drug use." He paused, his lips quivering and barely audible, he murmured. "And then they found her."

Pam and I caught our breath and waited patiently.

"Christina Middleton. She was thirteen years old. Raped, beaten, her severely decomposed body was discovered in a shallow grave about a half-mile into the woods. She'd been missing for a month. Everyone thought something bad had happened, but for the sake of her family we clung to the hope that she had run away and might come to her senses when she got hungry and lonely."

I said softly, "I gather you think Seth had some knowledge of this?"

He nodded. "Because of his erratic behavior, I was—concerned, and so was his mother. We felt like we couldn't talk to him about anything. Well, one day he passed out on the couch and I decided to check his cellphone. I just wanted to see if he had been in contact with her through text messages or phone calls." He shook his head and began crying. "I found pictures of Christina doing things with him and his friends that no thirteen-year-old girl ought to be doing with anyone, let alone a twenty-year-old man."

"What happened?" Pam asked.

"My wife and I talked it over and decided that we had to give him the benefit of the doubt. So rather than go straight to the police like we ought to have, we confronted him with what we found, thinking maybe some explanation could possibly mitigate our fears. At the time, we considered the possibility that, although he was clearly guilty of rape, maybe, just maybe, he had nothing to do with her death. I know what you're thinking, but put yourselves in our shoes. He was our only child. We needed to believe that he wasn't all bad."

I took a deep breath. "Please continue, Matthew. How did he react?"

"Not well. He got very angry and defended himself by saying that what Christina had done with him was consensual. I told him that there's no such thing as consensual at her age and that it was wrong. When I asked him about her death, he said he didn't know anything about it; that when they parted company she was alive and well. I told him he needed to go to the police and tell them about his relationship with her because there might be something they could learn from him that might help them find her killers. He laughed at me for being a fool. I insisted, and he got even angrier and then…"

Pam asked, "Then what, Matthew?"

"I made the mistake of trying to take his phone from him."

Pam gasped, and uttered under her breath, "Oh God."

"He beat me within an inch of my life right here in this living room, while my poor wife Linda watched helplessly. The poor thing was frozen with terror. That's when we knew—that's when we knew."

He began sobbing and shaking uncontrollably. Pam went over and placed a consoling arm around his shoulder. His voice broke as he spoke. "Do you have any idea what it's like to be a man of the cloth? To really, truly believe in it all and then to suddenly realize that your greatest gift from the Lord is a monster?"

Pam held him tightly and started crying herself. "It's not your fault, Matthew. You mustn't blame yourself."

He nodded and whispered hoarsely. "I was unconscious when he left and Linda was in too much shock to have him arrested. She called an ambulance and told everyone I fell down the stairs. I don't think anyone believed it but in small towns you learn to look the other way. When I was released from the hospital, I tried calling Seth, but he refused any overtures of reconciliation from me and then he went radio silent.

Eventually, I felt I had no recourse and went to the police with my concerns and told them about the pictures I saw on his cellphone. They brought him in for questioning but the cellphone was long gone. He said he'd lost it at a party. There was no forensic evidence linking him to the girl and he denied everything. Told them Linda and I were crazy and abusive of him. They had to let him go. But I know he did it. I know he did. The way he got angry with me, he got angry with her. I could feel it. My God, he almost killed me and I'm a grown man. I had a headache for weeks. I've never spoken with or seen him since."

He was so choked up he could barely get the words out. "He never even came to his mother's funeral. About a year later, she committed suicide because of him—because she couldn't live with the guilt. He might as well be dead as far as I'm concerned. The Bible says I'm supposed to forgive him. It's what I preach every day, and I want to forgive him, I truly do—but I just can't."

I felt awful, worse than awful. This wasn't what I intended to happen here. I stood up and said, "I'm very sorry, Reverend Ackerman. We didn't mean to bring so much pain into your home today. Thank you for your time. We'll be going now."

He looked up. "Are you going to tell me about my son? I thought that's why you came here."

"He's dead, Matthew. I'd rather not go into the details. It will just cause you more grief. Suffice it to say, he won't be coming home."

He hesitated, bowed his head and then buried it in hands as we let ourselves out. We left a shattered man crying in his living room and drove back to Manhattan in a morose silence. Halfway there, Pam said, "John, say something. I need to talk. I feel so bad for that man."

257

I nodded. "I do too, but I feel worse for that girl and her family."

"You don't look upset."

"I internalize a lot. If I don't, I'll be punching holes in the walls when we get back."

"Why did you lie about his son being dead?"

"I didn't lie."

"But he's not dead."

"You mean not yet."

"Please don't talk like that. The law will handle him."

"Yes, eventually, the law will, but I wonder how many more lives will be damaged beyond repair by the time it does?"

"Can we stop somewhere for a drink. I desperately need one."

I looked at my watch. I had to meet with Vito an hour before the main event with Chip to rehearse and update him on everything I had learned since we last spoke. "Sure, but I only have time for one drink."

I garaged the car and we stepped into the Blue Ribbon Brasserie for a cocktail. I was hungry and ordered some hummus to go with my Bud Light. Pam sat with her legs crossed staring into her Manhattan. She asked, "Where is this all heading, John? It just seems like it's getting deeper and deeper."

"That it does. Well, the important thing tonight is to gain Chip's trust and convince him to take us on as partners." I had been completely forthright with Pam about the meeting with Chip. I needed her on my side. "There's more on the line now than just the distribution of drugs to college kids. If these guys are trafficking children, the stakes just went through the roof."

Playing devil's advocate, she said, "I agree with you about the severity of the situation, but shouldn't you let the police know?"

"The problem is that they probably already know to some degree. Kilcullen mentioned to me that he had suspicions about Samuel but couldn't prove anything."

"But what about that house on Long Island?"

"What am I supposed to tell him? I burglarized a house while on probation and found a dirty mattress and a doll? The house doesn't even belong to Chip or Samuel." I shook my head. "I'm no lawyer but it doesn't seem like we have any evidence of wrongdoing at all."

"So, then what?"

"Well, we know there's a shipment of something coming in this week. I want to believe its drugs but after what I found on the Island I'm not so sure. My concerns are even worse now after hearing about Samuel from his father. Then there's the news about him spending time in Mexico and Central America where, because of the extreme poverty, trafficking is simply an alternative career choice for some. He may have learned the nuts and bolts of the trade while he was there."

"You really think it's a shipment of people?"

"Could be. Like I said, possibly drugs, maybe people and more to the point —children. After that conversation we had with his father, I think Samuel has always been a violent predator, and with time has learned to make a living at it."

She nodded and took a sip—a big sip—of her Manhattan. Her hand trembled. I said, "Pam…?"

Her eyes watered up and her voice lowered to a hush. "How can people be so cruel to each other?"

I didn't have an easy answer for that. "I'm not going to pretend I understand humanity on that level, Pam. I'm a little too visceral myself, but I suspect that not all of us are evolved to the same degree you are."

She gave me a funny look. "I hope you're not lumping yourself in with these animals because I would have to disagree."

"Thanks. No, I'm a bit different. Let me explain in medical terms. Cancer research has revealed several mechanisms for tumor growth. One of the big ones is defects in DNA repair. We believe that our DNA is subject to damage either naturally or from exposure to toxins in our diets or environment. These defects in our DNA lead to abnormal growth of cells eventually leading to cancer. The good news is that the body has specialized proteins that run around repairing these defects in our chromosomes. These proteins are coded for by special DNA repair genes."

Pam looked at me confused, "What are you saying?"

"Samuel and Chip are defective DNA and I'm the repair gene."

Chapter 32

The SoHo Grand was elegant and reeked of wealth and splendor. This was a place where people came to see and be seen. The long wood bar with leather chairs faced a massive mirrored wall lined with high-end scotch and whiskey. Surrounding that were multiple tables, well-dressed with linen tablecloths and crystal vases. Two men in sport coats sat at the bar engaged in quiet conversation hunched over their drinks. Two other men sat three tables away, out of hearing range.

Chip glanced around nervously. Now that he wasn't wearing his funny- looking Irish walking hat and sunglasses, he seemed vaguely familiar, but I couldn't place him. He said, "I thought there would be more people here."

"Relax, it'll start filling up soon. Besides, we need to be able to talk freely without hundreds of people listening in. What are you worried about anyway? You're in the middle of friggin' Manhattan at the SoHo Grand. Counting the bartender, there are five witnesses and more on the way. What could happen?"

We had agreed on a very public place for the meeting so that if he felt uncomfortable, he could leave at any time. He seemed to relax a bit. "I guess you're right."

What he didn't know was that the other patrons in the bar worked for Vito and I had paid the bartender, Bennie, a thousand dollars to close the bar for a couple of hours so we could conduct our business privately. I gave him another thousand to give to his manager to mind his own business and another thousand to leave a 20 year old bottle of Pappy Van Winkle bourbon on the table. As soon as Vito arrived, he was to high-tail it out of here and lock the doors.

Chip had come alone. I had advised him that would be less confrontational and more conducive to meaningful dialogue. Despite some minor pre-game jitters, Chip was in exceedingly good humor and fairly excited about the meeting. He was moving on up and he knew it. Getting his BMW back along with a couple of million in drugs had really bolstered his confidence.

Fashionably late, Vito cut a striking figure as he appeared in the bar wearing a two-piece, beige Armani suit, diamond-and-onyx pinky ring, and alligator shoes. Bennie the bartender saw him and scurried away on cue, closing the door behind him.

Vito sauntered up to the table nonchalantly, letting his great size and impressive physique send a not-so-subtle message that the alpha male had just arrived. His thick, wavy, black hair accented his huge head and sharp features. He had a fearsome countenance as if he belonged on some ancient battlefield rather than in a sophisticated lounge in Manhattan. He was 260 pounds of pure muscle and even pushing forty, worked out fanatically. As he scanned the room, the muscles in his neck and shoulders strained to punch through his clothing.

Chip and I stood to greet him as he neared, and I made the introductions. Chip was taller than Vito by about two inches but lighter by about sixty pounds. I was somewhere in between. Vito extended his huge hand to Chip, revealing diamond cufflinks and a $10,000 Rolex watch.

They shook hands and Vito sat, signaling to Chip and me to follow suit, symbolically taking charge of the meeting. Chip didn't understand this very practiced move, and allowed the quiet shift in control.

I poured Vito two fingers of bourbon and, without thanking me, he took the glass and studied Chip, who was clearly not sure how to proceed. When Vito was in full form, as he was now, he could unnerve even the best of them. He had the look of someone who could be your best friend one minute or rip your throat out the next. In his low rumbling voice, he said, "I've heard a lot about you."

It was an observation that didn't require explanation. It was a way of letting Chip know that he was now on the radar of something much bigger than himself. Implicit in this was that once you were on this particular radar, there was no easy way of getting off. Chip seemed to grasp that part and said, "All good, I trust?"

I was relieved by Chip's tone. He sounded like he was on a job interview. Vito nodded. "Mostly, but there are a few things from a security point of view we need to work on if our relationship is to move forward."

Chip looked at me and then back at Vito. He hesitated, not wishing to misspeak. "I didn't know that it was decided yet whether we were going to move forward."

What Chip didn't realize is that meetings like this were never casual. A rabbit sitting next to a lion can hope for the best but better prepare for the worst. By agreeing to meet with Vito he had surrendered all rights to his business, his property and perhaps even his life. Vito sipped his bourbon and stared Chip down with cold gray eyes.

Vito growled, "I hope you didn't bring me here to waste my time."

Off balance, Chip stammered, sensing the delicate nature of this type of negotiation. "I didn't mean to imply that I'm not interested in what you have to say. It's just that I was hoping to hear what you had to offer and then I would have to discuss

it with my business associates and sort of take a vote on it."
He shrugged, smiling. "I hope you understand. I really can't
commit to anything today. It's a process."

Vito sat back in his chair, pulled out a pack of Camels
from his suitcoat, shook out a cigarette, and lit it with a lighter.
Silently, he took a long drag and blew it out of the side of his
mouth as Chip fidgeted in his seat.

Finally, Vito broke the silence. "Look, Chip, I think
there's been a misunderstanding. I'm not really in the business
of mergers and acquisitions. I'm simply in the business of
acquisitions and although you may not realize it just yet, you've
just been acquired. I know you have a lucrative drug distribution
business on NYU's campus and I also know what's been going
on in those houses on Long Island. We've been watching the
Spiders for quite some time and we want in. This meeting was
for you to give me details and for me to explain to you what is
going to happen next."

As Vito spoke, one of his men walked up to our table
handing him a plastic bag and then took up position behind Chip.
From the bag, Vito retrieved an ordinary hammer. He placed
it on the table in front of Chip who looked on with growing
consternation. Chip was well-versed in dishing it out so he
knew what this meant, but his mind couldn't accept that this
could be happening in such a sophisticated and public place. He
looked around to see if anyone else noticed the growing crisis.
Frustrated by the lack of public concern, Chip said, "What are
you going to do?"

"Establish trust. The way you established trust with my
friend, Cesari. Remember?"

Chip gulped and glanced at me. "I think I've heard enough
for one day. I should be on my way." He stood to leave and
Vito's guy put two massive hands on his shoulders and forced
him back down into his chair.

Vito said, "But we're just starting to get to know each other."

Chip was speechless and beads of sweat appeared on his brow. He whined, "There's no need for this."

Vito replied, "I disagree. Now hand me your wallet."

Chip shouted, "Help! Somebody help me."

The other guys in the bar stood and came over to the table. The largest of them asked with a Spanish accent, "Is everything all right, Mr. Vito?"

"We're good, Carlos. Thanks. Just keep an eye on the door."

Chips eyes went wide and he started to shake. Vito said again. "Your wallet."

Chip reached into his back pocket and placed it on the table in front of him. Vito went through it, found Chip's driver's license and studied it. "I see you live in a nice neighborhood. I'll hang onto this just in case I need to find you in a hurry. Now put your left hand on the table." He pocketed the driver's license and Chip soaked in the implication of someone like Vito knowing his personal address.

Silence fell heavy on the room as Chip hesitated, now clearly alarmed. Vito took the opportunity to signal his guy who pulled out a pistol and pressed the tip of it into the side of Chip's temple. Vito said, "Put your left hand on the table."

The gun was nudged harder into the side of his head and Chip slowly placed his hand palm down on the table. Vito picked up the hammer and explained. "I'm not doing this to be mean or because I enjoy suffering but there can be no doubt in your mind about who I am, who I represent, and who you now work for. Now spread your fingers wide."

"Please don't," Chip pleaded.

"I ask a question and you answer it, quickly and truthfully. You're going to tell me right here and now everything about your drug distribution operation at NYU. More importantly, I want to know about Long Island. I know you're trafficking. I want to know where they come from, who your contacts are, how you bring them in, and where they go. If I believe you, then we can be friends and I will be very generous."

In desperation, Chip stammered, "How do I know you're not a cop?"

Vito nodded at his man who wrapped a massive arm around Chip's head covering his mouth with his hand. Vito stood suddenly, grabbed Chip firmly by the wrist and smashed the hammer down hard on his pinky. As surprised as Chip, I flinched at the sight of blood splattering on the tablecloth. Vito hadn't told me about this part. I thought tonight was just supposed to be a little intimidation. Looking at the finger, I doubted he would ever be able to use it again. Chip writhed uselessly, now drenched in perspiration, and nearly fainted in the grip of his captor.

Vito sat back down and calmly said, "Would a cop do that?"

An hour later, as I left the bar, I gave Bennie an extra thousand dollars for his cooperation and explained that I needed to take one of the table cloths and a few napkins. They were soiled from blood and I didn't see any point in leaving hard evidence about what had just happened. He looked confused as Chip staggered past him, pale and shaky, holding his hand wrapped in a bloody cloth napkin. Bennie knew it was none of his business. He had just made $3,000 without having to kiss up to anyone pouring drinks, so he thanked me and walked away. Later, I caught up with Vito in his apartment on Mulberry Street. He was stretched out in a leather recliner.

"You might have warned me, brother Vito."

"You're a big boy, Cesari. You'll get over it. Besides, we got what we wanted."

I nodded. "Are you sure about that? You forgot to ask him who hires the Spiders at NYU."

"Who gives a shit? They probably just pay off somebody in Human Resources. That's what I would do. We got enough to blow the whole thing apart. You can pull the trigger on these guys any time you want and that's what's important."

He had a point. "Yeah, I know, but do you believe everything he said?"

He sat up. "Well, I was a little skeptical after the first finger but not after the second. He was definitely all in after that."

I sat down on his sofa. He said, "It's up to you now, Cesari. I got you in the door. You have to bring it home. I'm not sure what else I can do to help."

I nodded. "Well, thanks. You've done plenty, but if I think of anything I'll holler. Hopefully, I'll live long enough. I'm sure as soon as his pain improves, Chip will start thinking about putting a bullet in my brain."

He chuckled. "I have no doubt about that, but I think he will suppress that notion for a while. I thought I impressed upon him pretty well that you work for me and will be overseeing the business on my behalf from now on, and if anything untoward befalls you it will reflect poorly on our relationship. I know he was crying and all that and may not have heard everything clearly. Maybe I should give him a follow up call in a couple of days just to make sure." He laughed. "Even better, maybe I'll just go visit him in his apartment on Fifth Avenue. I'm sure he'll get a kick out of that."

I smiled. "Priceless, in fact, but it might be counterproductive to push him too far. After what you just did to him I wouldn't be completely shocked if he took off like a rabbit."

"You're probably right about that. Maybe we should just push him off a cliff?"

"Can't do that yet. Samuel is the real freak. We remove Chip and it definitely puts a damper on things, but Samuel will just regroup somewhere else. You heard him. Samuel controls the flow of everything from his prison cell. He just tells Chip where and when."

"Still, it'd slow things down a bit."

"Yeah, it would." I admitted.

"And killing him would make me feel better."

I smiled. "Me too, but I prefer a more permanent solution. I want to know where these kids are coming from and who's bringing them in. It has to be someone Samuel met in his travels."

"You don't know that, Cesari. It could be someone he met in prison or maybe no one at all. He could've just been born the asshole he is now."

Thinking it over I said, "Do you really want to help, Vito?"

"I thought I just did?"

"Even more, I mean?"

"Like what?"

"I'm thinking about that shipment of kids coming in. We can't let them get off loaded to the house in Long Island. Once there, they'll be in too much danger."

"I agree. So you want to intercept them before they make the exchange? That's a tall order, not knowing where the drop-off is. Even Chip didn't know. It's a pretty clever system they developed."

"I know. I need to think it over. Keep your cellphone on."

I stood to leave and he said, "Here, take this." He reached into his pocket and handed me Chip's driver's license.

I looked at it. His real name was Charles Ippolito. Chip was simply a combination of the first two letters of his first and last name. Clever, but not clever enough. I got you by the balls, Chip, and now I'm going to squeeze.

Chapter 33

The next morning Pam and I sat in the park sipping Starbucks coffee discussing recent events. Cleo strained at the leash I had tied to the leg of the bench. She tried to say hello to everyone who walked by. Most gave her a wide berth, but the braver ones jumped in, only to find out that having a 250-pound dog push you around with her head wasn't as much fun as it looked.

It was 10:00 a.m. and sunny. Pam wore shorts, sandals, and sunglasses. Her hair was in a ponytail. She looked cute. I had just filled her in on the meeting with Chip minus the part about breaking his fingers. I didn't see any point in telling her and I didn't think it would go over well. So, without actually lying, I let her believe that Vito had simply frightened Chip into submission.

She said, "This guy Vito sounds a little scary."

"Believe it or not, he's not that bad a guy. It's just that he doesn't believe in rules."

"Nice."

"So who's in charge, Chip or Samuel?"

"According to Chip, Samuel is the ultimate boss, although it sounds like he relies heavily on Chip's counsel. Unfortunately, in the heat of the moment, with so much going on, we forgot to ask how they knew each other in the first place or how Chip fit in at NYU or whether he did at all."

"Is Chip a pervert too?"

I looked at her and she added. "I guess that was a dumb question. So put it together for me."

"Well, I've been thinking about it a lot. Here it goes. He goes to school and is the model student for the first two years as far as anyone can tell, but there's a lot brewing underneath the surface. He probably realizes he is a sexual deviant and is attracted to children. Maybe drugs were his way of dealing with the internal conflict this posed, especially with very religious parents. Maybe I'm being too kind. In any event, it all comes to a head with the death of that girl during the summer of his sophomore year and the subsequent blow-up with his parents.

"It is now obvious that he is a true sociopath and could give a crap about anyone but himself. He changed his name probably as a metaphor for disowning his family and previous life. It probably gave him a sense of freedom and relief that he could now lead his life the way he wanted. How am I doing so far?"

"Freud would be proud. Continue."

"With his newfound freedom came a set of new problems."

"Like tuition, rent, and food?"

"Exactly. Now cash-strapped, he started dealing drugs to pay the bills. One thing led to another and now here we are. He was a very bright kid but, unfortunately, he channeled all his intellect into destructive behavior."

Pam shook her head in frustration. "Just awful."

I nodded. "Yes, it is, and I believe he took that trip to Mexico his senior year not only to look for more reliable suppliers to feed his growing drug business, but to satisfy his other needs as well. Once there, he learned how easy and profitable it was to traffic children and how little interest either government had in stopping the trade. The rest, as they say, is history."

Pam shook her head. "This is so hard to believe. How could something like that be easy?"

"Because you don't understand real poverty, Pam. Americans think being poor is not being able to afford the NFL package through their cable supplier. There are parts of Mexico and Central America where there are families with nine and ten children who can barely afford to feed one. They drink water out of puddles when it rains and pick through garbage for dinner. Children willingly prostitute themselves on the streets to buy a piece of candy."

Pam was getting upset. "Stop, please stop."

"And that's the other part of this. What is happening is so monstrous that people can't think or talk about it because it makes their heads want to explode. At any rate, when Samuel returned to the States, he recruited a partner, Chip, who is mostly on the distribution end. According to Chip, Samuel is the mastermind. He also claims that Samuel has kept him in the dark about who supplies the drugs and kids. Since Samuel's incarceration, Chip has had to step up to the plate and assume more responsibility, but still takes his marching orders from Samuel.

The spider web tattoo idea came from Mexico when Samuel became fascinated with tarantulas. It also made for easy differentiation of friends from foes and ensured a certain amount of commitment from his followers. The Spiders are everywhere and recruit students who they find are in financial difficulties. They gradually suck them in until they're up to their eyeballs and can't get out."

"Is that what happened to that student, Justin and his girlfriend?"

"Seems like it."

Sipping her coffee, she glanced around the park. "What are you thinking?" I asked.

"We really are lucky, aren't we? Look at everything we have and we take so much of it for granted."

I nodded in agreement. "Yes, we do. We're so busy arguing about how to spend trillion-dollar budgets and which bathrooms girls and boys should use that we don't even realize what a luxury it is to have these kinds of arguments."

Pam looked depressed. "Will we become like them or will they eventually rise up to become like us? The bad guys, I mean."

"No way of knowing but history teaches us that all great societies eventually collapse for one reason or another. The greatest of them all, the Romans, at their zenith had it all just like we do. They ruled most of the known world for half of a millennia. I'm sure had you asked any one of them if they could conceive of their own demise they would have scoffed at the notion. They were so successful for so long it was literally beyond their comprehension that anything could change."

"But it did change."

"Yes, and when the end came, it came so fast and so furious it defied all logic, leaving nothing but ruins, abandoned villas and farms in its wake. Did you know that the population of ancient Rome at its height approached five million people, and yet, within fifty to one hundred years of the date commonly accepted as the collapse of the empire, the population had dwindled to less than fifty thousand? Think about that."

"What happened?"

"Many things—corruption, over-expansion, moral decrepitude, foreign invasions, plagues, lack of fresh water. It's not entirely clear but mostly, in my humble opinion, they lost the will to do whatever it takes to succeed. The Romans were some of the most, practical, tenacious, and pugnacious people the world has ever known, Pam. There was a time in their history when they wouldn't hesitate to march a hundred thousand men thousands of miles away to fight to the last man for no better reason than to prove their might. They never, ever, turned down a challenge to their authority. Yet, by the time of the fall of their empire, less than ten percent of the Roman legions were made up of actual Romans. With time, they became soft, fat, and lazy and came to rely heavily on foreign recruits who had no loyalty to Rome."

"Soft, fat, and lazy."

"Sound familiar?" I asked.

She nodded. "It does."

"We have to be willing to fight our own battles, Pam. We have to be willing to work and struggle on our own and to accept with grace our successes and our failures. Did you know what the Roman games were really all about?"

She shook her head.

"They started out as paid gladiatorial combats to honor the dead. At first the combats were ritualistic and no one was supposed to die. No one knows exactly when it started, but eventually politicians seized on the popularity of the combats to gain votes. Soon the combats grew in size and scope. Eventually, blood was drawn and someone died, and guess what?"

"What?"

"The people loved it. It was all downhill from that moment on. Death, death, death. Arenas starting springing up all over the empire to watch people die for entertainment. The Colosseum in Rome gets built, and before you know it, all sorts of horrors start taking place on an almost daily basis. Elephants, tigers, slaves, prisoners of war, and gladiators start dying, sometimes hundreds per day. All the while free food, wine, and prostitutes are provided by the government to curry favor with the mob."

"Did it work?"

"Very much so, but the government also became trapped by it. What they found is that once they got caught up in this cycle of depravity, they couldn't stop it. Eighty thousand people filled the stadiums twice daily for free food, wine, and entertainment. They couldn't stop the games because the people would riot. And the people didn't feel the need to work, and why would they? Slaves did all the manual labor in Rome and the government fed and amused the citizens. They could party all day every day if they so chose and many of them did."

"At least we don't have slaves."

"Don't we? Close to twenty million illegal aliens living in poverty within our borders doing all the menial jobs our soft, fat, and lazy citizens think are beneath their dignity to do, and then they have the nerve to complain about it."

"So, am I to assume that you see some parallels between the decline and fall of the Roman Empire and what is taking place in our society?"

"You tell me. Have you ever heard of people rioting because they wanted free stuff from the government? Do you think kids would rather work a forty-hour week in the hot sun or sit at home and play video games? Do you think teachers that do drugs with students qualify for the expression 'moral decrepitude'? You've been teaching for a number of years. How many students have you met here at NYU that plan to serve in the armed forces or would even consider serving their country?"

She sighed, "Not many, but aren't you being a little judgmental?"

"Am I? I have a question for you. Think about it before you answer. If I went up to some random individual and offered him or her a choice: free tickets to the Super Bowl or a year's worth of health insurance, which do you think they would pick?"

She didn't say anything so I continued. "We have our priorities screwed up on so many levels. We are living off the fat of the land, the labors of those who came before us. No one appreciates how we arrived at where we are and so they are willing to throw it all away. We don't seem to care anymore about achieving anything other than our next high or orgasm."

"Are you quite done?"

"Almost. Whatever happened to *ask not what your country can do for you but rather what can you do for your country?*"

"JFK's inauguration speech?"

"Yes, one of the most moving speeches ever given. Right up there with Lincoln's "Gettysburg Address" and Martin Luther King's "I Have a Dream" speech. Those were the days when Democrats were Democrats and Republicans could kiss my ass. If I were to stand up in front of an auditorium filled with NYU students today and repeat that quote, I would probably be stoned to death."

She seemed taken aback. "Probably. You're a fan of John F. Kennedy?"

I nodded. "Of course. He was a great man. Why are you surprised?"

"I don't know. You seem so—primitive."

I chuckled, "Thanks. One of these days I'm going to figure out who really ordered his assassination. Sometimes, I can't even sleep at night it bothers me so much."

"You really think big, don't you?"

"His death led the country down a dark path from which we still haven't completely recovered."

"You're depressing me."

I sighed. "I'm sorry. I'm finished. Thanks for listening."

She smiled. "So what now?"

I stretched my arms over my head and grunted. "Now I save the God damned world." Our eyes met, we held each other's gaze for a moment, and then she laughed.

"Can it wait until after lunch?"

Chapter 34

*L*ater, while Pam attended a faculty meeting, I decided to act on a hunch about something. I entered St. Matt's, hopped the elevator to the fifth-floor rehab center, identified myself to the nurses, and found Kayla in her room watching TV. She had just returned from physical therapy and looked a thousand times better than when I saw her in the ICU last week. The bruising and swelling in her face was much improved. I put my duffel bag on the floor and sat down.

I said, "Hi, Kayla."

She muted the television and replied, "Hi."

"Do you remember me, Kayla?"

She studied me carefully and shook her head. "No, I don't. I'm sorry."

"It's okay. I'm Dr. Cesari. You can call me John. I came to see you last week. I was one of the people who found you and called the police."

"I don't remember that either, but thank you."

I looked at her bandaged hand and wondered how she was handling missing her thumb. She saw me and said, "Don't ask what happened. I can't remember."

Damn.

"Where are your parents?"

"They're staying in a hotel. They're making arrangements to fly me back to Dallas. I'll be leaving in a day or two."

I nodded. "Well, that's good."

"Yes, it is. You look like you were in an accident, too."

I smiled. I had almost forgotten about that. In fact, Kayla and I probably received our injuries from the same guy or at least on his orders. "Yes, I was, sort of."

"I'm sorry."

"Thank you. Kayla, would you mind if I asked you a few questions concerning what happened to you?"

"I don't mind, but I won't be able to tell you a whole lot."

"The last time I came here, you said the name, Chip. Do you remember saying that?"

She thought it over and shook her head. "No, I don't."

"What about the name, Maria?"

She furrowed her brow in thought. I waited patiently while the wheels spun inside her contused brain. Maybe it was a good thing she couldn't remember. Sometimes impaired cognition was a blessing. She said, "I'm not sure. I feel like I should remember but just can't."

"It's okay. How are you feeling in general?"

"Much better, but the doctors tell me I have a long way to go. I don't like the antidepressants. They make me sleepy all the time even in the middle of the day."

"Yes, drowsiness can be an unfortunate side effect." I paused, deciding whether I should go to the next level or not. If I was barking up the wrong tree, no harm done, but if I was right, it might push her right off the edge.

I reached down into the duffel bag by my feet. "Kayla, I was exploring an old house and found this. I was wondering if you knew who it belonged to." I showed her the doll with the blue dress I had found in the house on Long Island.

She looked at the doll long and hard, filled with curiosity and then … recognition. Her eyes suddenly reddened and watered up as she reached out to hold it. I handed it to her as tears streamed down her face. She clutched it tightly and started rocking back and forth. Choked up, she could barely speak. "Is she okay?"

"Who?"

"Maria, this is Maria's doll."

***

I had lot to think about as I left the hospital several hours later. Kayla's memory was still spotty but the neurologists were impressed and pleased by her sudden turnaround. Her parents were euphoric and the police would return to take a statement. I was disheartened and upset at what I had learned but was happy that Kayla would be leaving the state on an upbeat note. I called Vito as I hopped in a cab.

"What's up?" he barked into the receiver.

"New wrinkle with some extra urgency. I just left the girl in the hospital. Her memory is starting to come around. She wasn't that dead kid's girlfriend after all. She was being held captive by the Spiders in one of those houses. He befriended her there and helped her escape. The Spiders found out and he tried to ransom his way out using the car full of drugs as leverage. They didn't go for it."

"Damn, the kid had moxie, didn't he?"

"He's a fucking hero, Vito."

"A dead hero."

"Yeah, but there's something else. Apparently, there was another girl, an eight-year-old Mexican kid named Maria. It was her doll I found in the basement. That kid Justin managed to get them both out in the middle of the night."

"And where's the kid?"

"That's just it. Kayla thinks the Spiders took her back to Long Island."

"Fuck, what are we going to do?"

"I don't know yet. There's a lot on the line. If we act too soon we risk losing the kids coming in this Friday and if we do nothing we may lose this girl, Maria."

"You mean if she's still alive."

"You're right, but I think she's still alive or else why would they bring her back to the house. They could have just left her for dead like they did with Kayla. I have a feeling they weren't finished with her."

"I'm getting angry, Cesari."

"Good, I need you angry. Now start thinking of a plan. I'm on the way to meet Pam for dinner. Call me if you think of anything."

The taxi let me off in front of John's Pizzeria in the Village. I had an idea that might work and it involved Pam and her friends. It was fraught with risks and not well thought out, but I was in crisis mode and some sort of action had to be taken soon. The question was how did I bring it up with her? Through the window, I saw Pam, Liz, and Knuckles sitting at a corner table with a half-empty carafe of red wine on the table. I looked at my watch. It was after six and I was a little late.

Sitting next to Pam, I placed the duffel bag with the doll on the floor beside me, and said hello to everyone as I poured myself some wine. Pam said, "I invited Knuckles and Liz to join us. I hope you don't mind?"

Funny question to ask with them sitting right there. "Of course not." I took a long swallow of the inexpensive, chianti-like house wine.

Knuckles said, "Wine is for sipping, Doc."

I smiled. "I was thirsty. Did we order yet?"

Pam said, "There's a large meatball pizza on the way."

"Great. So how did the faculty meeting go?"

"Boring as always. Mostly administrative B.S. as we're getting close to the new year. You know, dot your I's and cross your T's kind of stuff."

"Our department got a visit from the president of the university," piped in Liz.

The pizza came on a large metal serving dish and was placed in the middle of the table. The waiter handed us plates and said bon appetit. Pam handed me a slice and said, "That's impressive, Liz. He almost never comes out of his ivory tower. What did you do to deserve that honor?"

"Women's studies are receiving a special grant from the Department of Education. It's half a million dollars earmarked to study male aggression on campus. Not nearly enough to do the job, but it's a start. We took a photo with him and everything. It may be in the papers tomorrow. I was standing right next to him. He's a pretty nice guy."

I raised my eyebrows at that and before I could stop my lips from moving said, "Why does he rate as such a nice guy and I don't?"

Pam said, "John…"

Knuckles said, "Geez, Doc."

Liz smirked, "He's not like you. He's sensitive and understands that for 25,000 years, half the human population has been oppressed by the other half. He's devoted much of his life and the school's resources to rectifying the inequality between men and women. What have you done?"

The color rose in my cheeks as the table went silent and I regretted opening my mouth. Pam cleared her throat. "More wine, anyone?"

We all chuckled and I said, "Sure, fill it to the top if you don't mind."

Liz added, "Anyway, I took a selfie with him if anybody wants to see it?"

Knuckles and Pam enthusiastically nodded and said yes. I just kept chewing. It was really good pizza. Knuckles looked first and then handed the phone to Pam. She said, "Nice photo, Liz. He's so tall."

"Yes, he is. I felt like such a shrimp standing next to him. It's only the second time I met him. I was pretty nervous."

Knuckles said, "Well, that's one more time than me."

"Maybe you should come to more departmental meetings. You really shouldn't have missed this one," Liz said sarcastically.

"I was working out." Knuckles said, defending herself.

Liz rolled her eyes and Pam added, "Well that's two more times than me. Want to see, John?"

I almost gagged and shook my head no. "That's okay. You've never met the president of your school? That's hard to believe."

She shrugged. "NYU is enormous. There are more than 7,000 active faculty members."

"But still…"

"Okay, to be fair, that's not exactly true. When he was made president five years ago there was a grand celebration in his honor and I waited on a long receiving line to shake his hand. It was only for half a minute but I guess that counts as meeting him."

I chuckled. "The truth comes out."

She smiled at me as she reached across the table to hand the phone back to Liz who said, "Speaking of hands. Did you see the bandage on his hand in the photo?"

Pam hadn't quite let go of the phone, and abruptly pulled it back to look at the picture again more carefully. "Yes, I see it now. What happened?"

"He was at a fundraiser for the mayor's re-election last night and some jerk slammed the bathroom door on his hand by accident. He thinks it was a Republican. Broke two fingers."

I raised my eyebrows.

Knuckles said, "Ouch. Which hand? Not that it matters."

Liz said, "His left, pinky and ring fingers."

My eyebrows went even higher.

Pam added, "Ouch is right. Where was the fundraiser? Here on campus? I didn't hear about it."

"No, not here. It was at the SoHo Grand."

"Can I see the picture, Pam?" I asked, suddenly very interested in it.

She handed me the phone and I stared in disbelief at the image. There he was, towering over diminutive Liz, that asshole Chip, the God damned president of NYU. I was in shock and it must have shown.

Pam said, "Hey, are you all right? You look like you've just seen a ghost."

Recovering my composure, and thinking quickly, I nixed the idea of telling everyone what I knew. This was something I would confide to Pam when we were alone. I said, "I'm fine. I just never realized how photogenic Liz was. You look great here, Liz."

Without making eye contact, Liz snapped back. "Don't even think about it, all right? I'm not susceptible to guys like you."

Knuckles jumped in. "Geez, Doc. Pam, then me, and now, Liz. Are you sure you don't have a problem?"

Pam chuckled. "C'mon guys. Take it easy on him. He's Italian and can't help himself. I promise to keep an eye on him if that will make everyone feel safer."

Liz couldn't help herself and had to add, "You should try to be more like the president of our university."

That was the last straw. She just pushed me over the edge and I had enough. I said, "Liz, I have some really bad news for you about your wonderful president."

Chapter 35

"*I*'m going over there and punch his face in," Knuckles snarled.

"No, you're not," I said.

Liz folded her arms in defiance and angrily declared, "I don't believe any of it."

Pam was speechless. It took the better part of half an hour to bring them up to speed on everything including who Chip really was and how I knew it. A lot of raw nerve endings had just been exposed and their emotions were supercharged. Needless to say, they were incredulous.

Knuckles looked at Liz. "You can't be serious, Liz. You don't think the doc would make up a story like that?"

"He's a felon for God's sake."

I desperately wanted to beat her up, but managed to sit there quietly while she vented. Pam took a deep breath and said soothingly, "John, try to understand how shocking this is to hear. I believe you, and yet I can't believe my ears. The president of NYU is trafficking in drugs and human beings? This is beyond comprehension."

"I understand. Nonetheless, I was there when his fingers were smashed and it had nothing to do with a political fundraiser. Furthermore, Liz, if I were making it up why would I have this?" I reached into my trousers, retrieved Chip's driver's license and tossed it across the table at her. Knuckles grabbed it and whistled as she saw who it was.

Liz and Pam then studied it in turn. Liz covered her face and groaned. Pam said, "Shit. How'd you get this?"

"We took it from him as insurance that he better not try to pull a fast one on us."

Knuckles said, "I swear to God. I'm going over there and punch his face in."

"No, you're not," I repeated. "We need him for now, so control yourself."

"But it pisses me off."

"I'm just as pissed off, but right now we all need to stay calm. There are lives on the line. Children's lives."

Liz pushed her plate away, tears forming in the corners of her eyes.

Knuckles slammed her hand down on the table in frustration. "Fine, but as soon as this is done I'm going to kick his ass."

I said, "Agreed, but for now, let's keep it together, all right? No one can repeat a word of this to anybody. Understood?"

She nodded and I continued, "Well, as long as you all know the full extent of what's going on, is there any chance I can ask for your help to stop these monsters?"

Pam murmured, "Of course." She was still in shock.

Knuckles said, "You can count on me, Doc."

For the first time since I met her, Liz looked me right in the eyes and nodded.

"That's good. This is all hot off the presses, mind you, so the plan is fluid and subject to change, but I know this. There's a shipment of children coming in this Friday. I intend to intercept it. There's going to be an undetermined number of them and they are going to be frightened and confused. I don't know how many will speak English or what they expect when they arrive. Remember, these bastards don't tell anyone what they're really getting into until it's too late. Some of them undoubtedly believe they are coming here to be with relatives or to get jobs. When they see us, they're going to be scared and may even resist our help. Believe it or not, they may think we're the bad guys. The situation is going to be very delicate and must be handled with kid gloves. Do any of you speak Spanish?"

Reverting back to her usual self, Liz looked away as she spoke. "I speak Spanish fluently."

Knuckles added, "I'm not bad myself. Not fluent but I'll be able to communicate with them easily, but why not just call the police or child protective services when we get them?"

"If any of them need medical care, of course, we bring them to the nearest emergency room. Other than that, I'd rather not alert the authorities until we have that asshole, Samuel, hogtied for justice. If the situation blows up too soon, he'll simply relocate his operation. For the time being, I need him to believe everything is going smoothly."

I took a breath and continued. "Okay, there are four of us. That's four apartments we can house them in. Are we all in agreement with that?"

Everyone nodded and Liz wrote something on a piece of paper and slipped it across the table to Pam. Knuckles and I pretended not to notice as Pam read it and mouthed thank you to her. Knuckles said, "What about Bob and Stan? I'm sure they'd want to help."

"I know, but they're married and are clearly having difficulties with their spouses. It might be better if we didn't embroil them in this; the same for Todd. Besides, I'd rather not have news of what we're doing spread beyond this table. "I took out my wallet and handed my American Express card to Knuckles. "This is for you and Liz to buy supplies. They're going to need food, toys, pillows, blankets etcetera."

Knuckles handed the card back to me. "Thanks, but I don't need your money. I consider this my civic duty. By the way, I may not look it but I can handle kids. Love them in fact."

That was more than I could say. "I know you'll be fine. Liz?"

"Ditto."

"What about that girl, Maria, the one Kayla told you about?" Pam asked.

"Unfortunately, we have to wait until after we rescue the group coming in this Friday. If we act prematurely, the Spiders will be tipped off and we risk losing them all. We don't even know if she's out there in one of those houses. That's pure speculation right now."

She nodded in agreement.

I turned to Knuckles and Liz. "Okay then, as soon as I know more, I'll give you a call. Keep your cellphones charged. Stock up your refrigerators because once they're tucked in I don't want anybody leaving them alone for any reason."

Knuckles seemed to be perking up. She wasn't as personally hurt as Liz was by the news of Chip being a scumbag. She was just plain angry, "Roger that, Jimbo."

"Jimbo?"

"Jim Phelps—Mission Impossible…"

I shook my head. We were back to that again. "Got it."

After dinner, Knuckles and Liz left while Pam and I waited for the bill. As she walked by Pam, Liz whispered, "Call me for anything."

Once they were out of sight, I asked, "What was that all about?"

"Nothing. Forget about it."

I looked at her. "What was in that note she passed to you?"

"Oh that…"

"Yeah, that. What's going on?"

"You don't want to know."

"But I do."

She sighed. "All right, but you asked for it. It was the NYU sexual assault hotline number."

I shook my head. "I hope you realize that she's totally insane."

"She means well. She just can't help herself when it comes to you, and you really burst her bubble with all this stuff about Chip. Mine too, I might add."

"It had to be done. I'm sorry."

"You did the right thing. I'd rather know the truth."

"Just keep an eye on Liz, all right? I have a feeling I'm going to let my guard down one of these days and get a face full of mace for no reason."

"Well, I can't promise you that won't happen, but if it's any consolation I think she will feel bad when she does."

"I suppose I should be happy with that."

"You should. By the way, she gave me a small present the other day."

"I'm afraid to ask."

"Pepper spray."

I rolled my eyes. "Okay, I'll pay the bill and then you and I need to talk about your role."

"My role?"

I signaled the waitress, glanced at my watch, and handed her some cash. "C'mon, let's go. We'll talk on the way."

Walking down Broadway. She said, "I simply can't wrap my head around this. The president of NYU?"

"I know but at least the dots are starting to connect and would explain how the Spiders were able to infiltrate the campus to the degree they have. Chip probably met Samuel when he

288

was a student and Chip was still a professor. What did Chip teach before becoming president?"

Her eyes lit up with sudden comprehension as she said, "Philosophy."

"Bingo. Samuel majored in philosophy. I'm going to have to look at that group photo from Samuel's yearbook again. I'll bet Chip is in it somewhere. We weren't looking for him so we didn't notice, but I knew there was something familiar about him when I met him at the SoHo Grand."

Pam let out a big sigh. "What is it you wanted to talk about? You said something about my role."

I said, "I have a big favor to ask and if you say no, I'll understand."

Her curiosity piqued, she asked, "What is it? Spit it out."

"The only thing we couldn't get out of Chip last night was where and when the kids will be arriving. Friday night sometime is all he knew. He said that the final destination rotates between five different drop-off locations for security reasons. The final price depends on the number and age of the kids. That information he receives usually within hours of the appointment."

"How does he know how much money to bring?"

"He doesn't bring money. He is told the price and wires it to an offshore account. We're talking big money here, not the kind you can carry in a suitcase. Millions. Once the transfer is confirmed, he is told where and when to get the kids."

"So presumably, he receives a phone call or text, maybe an email."

I nodded. "The Spiders pick up the kids in a van and transport them to Long Island. They have those four houses out there that they use and rotate around between them. He didn't know who owns them. He is told which house to use on a monthly or bi-monthly basis. That's another thing. Shipments like this don't come in on a regular schedule. It all depends on what's going on at the other end. At any rate, the house I broke into hadn't been used in several months, which is why there was no security. That will be different in the house where they keep the kids. They have Dobermans patrolling the grounds and armed Spiders."

Pam turned pale. "That's not good."

"No, it's not. Anyway, while we were talking back there, I thought of a way we might find out where the kids are being delivered in time to save them." I paused for a moment before continuing. "Are you with me all the way, Pam? Because it will involve some risk on your part."

She stopped to face me. "Although, I'm upset and having trouble with Chip being involved, I believe everything you said and more importantly, I believe in you. If I have to take a risk to save innocent children then so be it, and I am most definitely with you all the way."

"Thank you for saying so. You said that you only met Chip the one time. Would he recognize you?"

"I doubt it. I was on a long reception line. I shook his hand briefly, congratulated him, and moved on. NYU is so big. At commencement ceremonies, I use binoculars to watch him talk. So what do you want me to do?"

"I'd like you to provide a distraction for Chip and maybe find out the drop-off point ahead of time so that I can make arrangements to get there before the Spiders."

She was quiet for a moment. "You want me to seduce the president of NYU?"

"It's for a good cause."

"You're going to offer me to him like a piece of candy?"

"No, more like dangle you in front of him in such a way that he won't be able to ignore you."

"Liz is wrong about you."

"She was?"

"You're much worse than she thinks."

"That's not fair."

"Tell me more about the kids. What happens to them after they get to the house on Long Island?"

I hesitated. "I'd rather not talk about that, if you don't mind. It will make me angry and cloud my judgment. Like I said to Knuckles, I want to get them to safety first and then I'll afford myself the luxury of getting pissed off, but you can use your imagination."

"I understand. It can't be anything good. All right, so, I'm supposed to use my charm to get Chip to drop his guard and then what? I hope you're not expecting me to sleep with this asshole?"

"Not at all, but it wouldn't hurt to allow his imagination to wander in that direction. You don't have to do anything you don't want, but keeping an open mind, might help us achieve our objective."

She frowned.

I continued. "It was just a thought. Nothing clouds a man's thinking more than the thought of sex. Anyway, what I'm hoping is that after the call comes in telling him where the kids are, you'll be able to either find out directly from him or access his phone and send me the information. There will only be a two, maybe three, hour window for us to mobilize in time."

"Who's us?"

"Vito has agreed to help me."

She was quiet for a while before saying, "Suppose my charm doesn't work on him?"

I smiled. "Then use body language."

She liked that. "I'm glad you have so much confidence in me. What happens to Chip if all goes well?"

"That's when the fun starts. If things go right, Chip will find out from the Spiders that something went wrong. He'll freak out because he will have already wired the money. Back in prison, I'll plant the seeds of doubt in Samuel's mind about Chip, that maybe he double crossed him. Since the next shipment won't be for at least another month, maybe two, that will buy us time to figure out our next move."

"I have a couple of questions, Jimbo."

Grinning, I said, "Go ahead, Ethan."

"Ethan?"

"That was Tom Cruise's name in the Mission Impossible movies. Ethan Hunt. He was the super spy."

She chuckled despite her rising concerns and the gravity of the situation. "Okay, if you're planning on intercepting the truck or van with the kids doesn't that represent a certain amount of risk to the children? I assume the transport people aren't going to give up without a fight."

"Chip said it's a van and usually between six and twelve kids in the back, occasionally a few more. There is usually one adult woman with them to keep them calm. Two guys driving, unknown whether they are armed or not. The subject never came up, but you're right. It's better to assume they are. If we hustle and get the drop on them would they be willing to risk their lives for their boss, whoever he is? Good question and I don't have an answer. I do know that once the children arrive in Long Island, the horror will begin in earnest. At that point, we will have no choice but to call the police and that will send Samuel on high alert. Assuming the police will agree to raid a house without any evidence but the word of a felon is also a big assumption. But to be honest, even if we involved law enforcement, the way the system and bureaucracy works, they'd never mobilize in time."

I sighed deeply and continued. "It's risky, but I don't think we have a choice. According to Chip, once the kids are brought to the house there's not that much time before the buyers come to haul them off like cattle. At that point, we may never see them again.

Pam let out a deep breath.

I said, "Yes, it's pretty bad and Chip is lucky to be alive right now. When he told us what went on out there, I thought Vito was going to beat him to death right there in the middle of the SoHo Grand."

"What should I do if Chip gets out of control? I guess I always have my pepper spray."

I thought it over. "When I see him, I'll do my best to convince him what a mistake that would be, but it's a risk for sure. I would definitely bring the pepper spray. If at any point you feel you have to abort, then just do it. I don't want you to get hurt."

She looked at me seriously and with grit and determination in her voice, said, "If it's the last thing I do, I'll find out what you need."

Chapter 36

*F*riday came and Pam was modeling for me in her apartment when my cellphone rang. It was Harry, the pathologist at St. Matt's.

"Good afternoon, Harry. What's up?"

"Hey, Cesari. Remember that kid from NYU?"

"Sure do."

"Well, you said to call you if something came up."

"I'm listening."

"Well you and that cop, Kilcullen, voiced concerns about whether the kid died of natural causes or not. Since I couldn't find any real explanation for his death, I had just assumed he died of a sudden cardiac arrhythmia and I signed it off as that."

"I remember, his drug tests were negative and there was no physical evidence to suggest it was a homicide."

"That's right, and the kid's in the ground now somewhere in Buffalo where he came from. Well, I was reading a book about WWII over the weekend and came across something that made me start re-thinking the case."

"A book about WWII made you start re-thinking the case?"

"Yes, it did." He paused for effect and then continued. "Well, there is a possible explanation for the kid's death other than natural causes and it's one that could easily be missed unless you were specifically looking for it and I wasn't—air embolism."

"Air embolism?"

"Yeah, it's an extraordinarily rare cause of death and in twenty years on the job I can't remember even once making that diagnosis."

"What did you read that made you think of it now?"

"Well toward the end of the war as the Nazis got increasingly desperate, they started investing heavily in wonder weapons and advanced technologies to turn the growing tide against them. One of them was massive sound machines. They were gigantic speakers to be placed on the battlefield and create noise at a sufficient level to disrupt enemy effectiveness. They claimed they could kill with sound but since they were never deployed in battle it is unknown. The thing is this, in an open-air setting, sound waves dissipate too quickly to be used as a weapon. But…"

"But what, Harry?"

Pam came out of her bedroom wearing high heels and black thigh-high stockings, spinning around in front of me. My eyes popped open and I gasped because she wasn't wearing much else. I pointed at the phone, gave her a thumbs up, and turned away before I lost track of what Harry and I were talking about. Smiling at her success, she returned to her bedroom.

"But in a small room like the one the kid was found in, all bets are off. No one really knows what happens if the decibel range goes beyond human capacity to tolerate, but the first thing is undoubtedly perforated ear drums."

"Like the kid had."

"Yes, we talked about that, but what I didn't know at the time is that if it got loud enough the pressure from the sound waves could potentially force air out of the lungs into the blood stream. At least that's what some people postulate."

I thought about that. "What would it look like on an autopsy?"

"Well, air emboli can cause areas of ischemia, that is, tissue damage from lack of blood flow. Also, if I had been looking for it, I would have performed thin slices of his myocardium hoping to find pockets of air trapped in the ventricles. One theory is that if there is enough of an air bubble it could prevent the heart valves from opening and closing properly."

"Well, I have to say this is interesting but there's no way to prove it without exhuming the body I assume?"

"Even that won't do it. The air will have been reabsorbed by now. It wouldn't just sit there waiting for us to come find it. I feel bad for not thinking about it."

"Don't knock yourself out, Harry. Maybe there's no harm done. The family is already upset just thinking he died of natural causes. The only thing that could possibly make it worse is for them to think he was murdered because of his involvement with drugs. The good news is that the police suspected foul play all along and have been investigating it as such."

"I still feel stupid, but thanks for the pep talk. Look, I have to go. I hope that helps your understanding of things."

"It does, Harry. Thanks."

I hung up and thought it over for a minute. If he had died like that, it would explain the lack of physical trauma other than his perforated ear drums, but what a way to go. I tried to imagine what it must have been like. Severe ear pain, difficulty breathing, heart pounding, helplessness, fear. Your killers, wearing noise cancellation headsets, stare at you, waiting for your ultimate collapse, enjoying your suffering. I let out a deep breath.

Pam returned wearing a short, tight skirt and button-down white blouse. She wore gold, dangly earrings, and blue-framed eyeglasses. Noticing her bare legs, I asked, "What happened to the stockings?"

She shrugged. "I thought it would be a little strange to wear black stockings in late August. Even hookers have a sense of fashion, don't they? How do you like the shoes? I bought them for a wedding two years ago and haven't worn them since." Standing in front of me she modeled the black high heels and flashed me some leg.

"Irresistible, especially the glasses."

"You like them? I figured he might go for this look more. It's just a teeny bit more subtle, and I needed a break from my contacts."

"It's a good look, sexy, but not overly slutty. A man would have to be made of stone to resist you."

She smiled. "Thank you. So when do we spring into action?"

"As soon as you're ready. I left off with Chip that I was going to drop by his apartment to review a few things before the shipment arrives tonight. He wasn't thrilled about a home invasion like this, but Vito and I felt it was important to stress to him that we could reach out and touch him whenever we chose. Bringing you along will soften the blow."

"There won't be anyone else in his apartment like a wife and kids?"

"Nope, he's divorced and his ex-wife lives in L.A. No kids."

"What about Spiders?"

"I doubt it. We warned him not to say anything to anyone about the new arrangements and I think he's smart enough to know which way the wind is blowing. Right now, his best friend is continued silence until he can figure a way out for himself. I'm betting they know nothing about me or Vito and he wants to keep it that way."

She smiled thinking about that. "He's really in a tough spot, isn't he?"

"That's good for us. The pressure will keep him in line, at least for the short term. C'mon, we should head over there soon."

"Give me a couple of minutes to finish my makeup and I'll be ready."

"Don't forget the pepper spray."

We left her apartment at ten of six and took a cab over to the Flatiron District where Chip had a two-bedroom apartment on the tenth floor of an exclusive building on Fifth Avenue. Pam had hiked her skirt up way too high for public consumption so she wore a lightweight raincoat to keep prying eyes away.

Glancing over at her, I noticed her giggling quietly. "Thinking of something funny?" I asked.

"Yeah, I was imagining if we broke down with me dressed like this. They'd have to call a *hoe-truck* to come get us."

I chuckled. "Well, I'm glad you're in a good mood."

"And you're not?"

"No, I'm not. I don't like what we're doing at all. I don't like the idea of putting you in this position, but I just can't think of any other way on such short notice."

On the tenth floor, I knocked on his door. The apartment was handsomely furnished with antique furniture, period paintings and Persian rugs. A large, old steamer trunk off to the side looked like it had been rescued from the Titanic. Chip's appearance was very different than when I last saw him. His hand had been casted; he hadn't shaved in a few days, and looked exhausted. His eyes were glazed and I suspected he'd been taking pain meds along with hefty doses of scotch to ease the stress. There was a half-empty bottle of Glenlivet on his desk next to a bunch of tiny pills that had spilled out from a tipped-over prescription container. From my vantage point, they looked like Vicodin. Confused and a little high from the narcotics, he stared at Pam but waited for my cue. Pam checked out the apartment and, without waiting for an invitation, sat on his sofa with her raincoat on.

I nodded at him but didn't proffer a hand. We weren't friends. He got it. His world was being turned upside down and he couldn't do a thing about it. I wondered what he must be feeling, but then realized that I didn't care. I sat in an armchair and waited for him.

He sat next to me and opposite Pam. I said, "We haven't really talked since earlier in the week, so let's get something out of the way, all right?"

He didn't say anything so I continued. "You're in pain. You're frightened. You're pissed off. You're wondering what to do next." I paused for effect. "First of all, I don't give a fuck how much pain you're in. As far as I'm concerned we're even." I softened my tone and sat back in the chair. "If it's any consolation, I had no idea Mr. Giannelli was going to do that to you, but now that it's done, we move on or things can only get worse. I hope you understand. Don't just sit there looking pathetic. Nod your head or something."

He nodded and said slowly. "I understand, but you know I have a partner. You met him, remember? His name is Samuel, and he's not a nice guy."

I looked at him very severely. "Yeah, I met him, but everybody now works for Mr. Giannelli, understood? Even Samuel."

He gulped and nodded. "He's not going to take this well."

I continued. "I'll talk to Samuel and he'll be given the option to cash out or join in. It will be his choice, but we had better not find out that you tried to communicate with him in any way shape or form until we tell you to. We're watching you every minute of every day. Nod your fucking head if you understand."

You couldn't look more glum than he did at this moment. I glanced over at Pam. "Okay, this is Pam. She's a friend of Mr. Giannelli's. Pam, say hello to Chip."

Pam stood up and took her raincoat off, shook her hair and spun slowly around for Chip to get a complete view. She was breathtaking, and I saw Chip's eyes and mouth open unconsciously.

She smiled coyly and said, "Hi, Chip."

He looked at me even more confused. I said, "She's a present from Mr. Giannelli. It's his way of saying, welcome to the team. No hard feelings about the fingers, all right?"

Pam sat down and crossed her long legs. Chip was mesmerized and I could practically feel his heart rate pick up. "I hope you like girls?" I asked, smiling at him.

Bewildered, he finally cracked a grin. "Yes, I do."

"Okay, then. We have an understanding. I know you and Pam are going to hit it off but let me make something clear. She is one of Mr. Giannelli's favorites. She can make you very happy, and I mean very, very happy, but if you hurt her in any way, you'll have to answer directly to him—and me. So if it wasn't in your vocabulary before, look up what the word 'no' means. She makes all the decisions. Got it?"

He stared at her and nodded. "I understand."

I stood up and walked in front of him. He looked up at me. I said, "Tell me that you understand again."

"I understand."

"All right, is there somewhere we can talk more privately?" I asked nodding at Pam. She smiled and winked at Chip.

"Come with me."

We walked into his private study with leather chairs and wall to wall bookcases. I was still hoping I could keep Pam out of it and said, "Mr. Giannelli wants me to tag along with you for the pick-up to see how things work from the ground up."

He said, "But I don't go personally to get them. I told you and Mr. Giannelli that. The Spiders get them and bring them out to Long Island. I usually go out there in the morning with a doctor to examine them and do an invoice check."

"A doctor?"

"Yeah, it's going to be long night for them once the Spiders get them. They'll need exams, medications, sedatives, and stuff like that. The older ones will need birth control pills."

I controlled a sudden impulse to throw him out the window. "Can't you tell the Spiders there's been a change of plans and that you'll make the pick-up?"

"Wouldn't work. They use passwords with the delivery crew and I don't know them. Besides, if I suddenly changed the routine without Samuel giving them a heads up, they'll get suspicious and tell him. If he finds out I have new friends without his approval, he'll fly off the handle. Not a great way to start off a partnership. He won't like it at all. It's his system. He's never let me in on the supply side. I manage the houses and the buyers."

"Fine. So tell me again what the process is from your end."

"Later tonight, the suppliers will text me the exact price. I have exactly one hour to wire the money to the account number they send. Once they receive confirmation, they'll send me the drop-off location and time, and then I let the Spiders know. Generally, the kids arrive in a van between midnight and one."

"Okay, I'll leave you to take care of business. You have my number. Call me if there's a problem. Have a good time with Pam and remember what I said."

"I will. Does she get paid or anything?"

"It's all taken care of, but a tip wouldn't hurt."

Chapter 37

At 8:00 p.m., I left his apartment and hustled over to Broadway arriving just as Vito pulled up to the curb in his Cadillac with tinted windows and two goons in the back seat. They held short-barreled shotguns with pistol grips on their laps and unforgiving expressions on their faces. I nodded at them and buckled up. Vito said, "That's Carlos and Tommy back there. Carlos speaks Spanish. From what you told me, I thought it might come in handy."

I waved to them and they waved back. I remembered Carlos from the meeting at the SoHo Grand with Chip.

"Good thinking, Vito."

"Now what?" he asked.

"Now we wait." I filled him in on my plan so he understood the anxious look on my face.

"Relax, Cesari. She's a big girl. She'll be all right."

"I keep telling myself that."

"Tell me more about these NYU professors that we're taking the kids to. Can they be trusted?"

"Yes, they're very nice people; a little goofy, but harmless and well-intentioned. They really want to help."

"You said one's a dyke?"

"Knuckles, yes, and hardcore no less. Takes no prisoners. Wants to go a few rounds with me in the gym to see if she can take me."

He chuckled. "No kidding?"

"She gonna be all right taking care of kids?"

"Better than you or me, I have no doubt. Why?"

He nodded. "I'm just concerned what my boys are going to think when they meet her."

"Who, these two in the back seat?"

"Yeah."

I turned back to the Tommy and Carlos. "You guys have any problems with lesbians?"

They looked at each other then back at me. Carlos said, "None at all." Tommy agreed.

I said to Vito, "What are you talking about?"

"Ask them if they know any."

"Do you guys know any lesbians?"

Tommy said, "Not personally but we've seen plenty of videos. Great stuff."

I rolled my eyes and Vito grinned. "I told you."

"Shut up. They'll be fine. Out of the handful of faculty I've met, except for Pam, Knuckles is the most normal."

"Are you getting sucked into that world, Cesari?"

I thought about that. "Maybe a little."

At 10:30 p.m., my phone buzzed with a call from Pam. I put her on speaker phone. Her voice was nervous and frightened. "John, something terrible has happened. "I'm still in the apartment. I don't know what to do. I think he's dead."

"Who?"

"Chip, I mean Professor Ippolito. You know."

I was stunned. "What happened? Never mind. I'll be right there. Do you have the drop-off information?"

"Yes, the Shea Stadium parking garage in Queens. Midnight on the top level. The gate will be up. He already told the Spiders."

"Don't move. I'm coming." I hung up and turned to Vito. "You get all that?"

He looked at his watch. "Midnight, top level of the Shea Stadium parking garage. Got it. What happened?"

"I don't know. You heard what I heard. I'm going back, but you go, go, go, and call me later. Be careful. The Spiders are on the way also."

I jumped out of the car and he took off, tires squealing and burning rubber. With my heart pounding and adrenaline pumping, I sprinted back to Chip's apartment. Pam buzzed me in, and sucking wind, I rode the elevator to the tenth floor where she greeted me, tears streaming down her face. She wore a white bathrobe and was practically frozen with terror. She trembled as I hugged her.

"Where is he?"

She pointed to an open door. "The bedroom bathroom."

He lay on the tiled floor naked staring up at the ceiling, mouth open, a smattering of blood behind his head. There were two broken scotch glasses nearby. "What happened?" I asked as I knelt beside him, checking for a pulse.

"He recognized me."

"So you killed him?"

"No, I pepper sprayed him and he slipped backward and hit his head on the edge of the tub."

"Shit."

She continued. "He got the call and made the money transfer in the living room. That was around 10:00 p.m. I talked him into taking a bath to buy some time. When he got in the tub, I went to get us a scotch so I could grab his phone off the coffee table."

"He called out to me to hurry back so I didn't have time to text you at that moment. When I returned to him, he was sitting in the tub and started yakking about how important he was. I had the pepper spray in my robe pocket as a precaution. I was totally focused on how I was going to text you that I wasn't thinking about what I was saying to him."

"I don't understand."

"He was trying to impress me I guess, and mentioned how he had bestowed an honorary doctorate of letters on the secretary of education and I absent-mindedly told him that I remembered the event because as faculty I was invited. As soon as the words left my lips I knew I had screwed up. I could see it in his eyes. He became angry and climbed out of the tub. I panicked, dropped the scotches, and pepper-sprayed him. He staggered around blind, walked into the door, slipped, and fell back. I called you immediately."

"Oh man. Well, he has a strong pulse and he's breathing. Put your clothes on and we'll get out of here. There's nothing more we can do right now. I can't be sure, but he'll probably be all right."

"We're just going to leave him?"

"Want me to finish him off?"

"No! I didn't mean that. It's just that I feel terrible. Shouldn't we call 911?"

"Not a chance. Just remember, we were never here. Besides, he's a piece of trash who sells children and drugs to the highest bidder, Pam. Don't think of him as an educator. He wasted his chance to be a good person and I won't lift a finger to help him."

As she dressed, I walked around the apartment wiping down anything we might have touched just in case he didn't survive and this became a criminal case. He fell and hit his head. It could happen to anyone but you never knew with this stuff, and he was a big enough fish that some people might not be satisfied with the obvious explanation, especially if we were seen leaving the apartment. What would happen if he recovered was a different story, but there wasn't much I could do about that now–or was there?

Pam came rushing out of the bedroom, grabbed her raincoat off the sofa and said, "I'm ready. Let's go. He's starting to groan in there. That's a good thing, right?"

"If you're hoping he's going to make it, yeah, but I'm starting to have second thoughts about leaving."

"What do you mean?"

"Well, for starters, if he wakes up too fast, he may piece things together and warn his friends that something's up even if he doesn't know what. Then there's the issue of his recognizing you. I'm not comfortable with a bunch of Spiders coming to visit you in the middle of the night."

She raised her eyebrows in consternation at that thought. "Then what are we going to do?"

"I think we're going to have to stay for a while until I figure it out. C'mon, let's go back in there and secure him."

"Secure him?"

"I'll put him in the bed. Go through his closet and bring me some ties and belts."

"I have a pair of handcuffs in my bag."

I looked at her confused. "Why?"

"Liz gave them to me."

"To play with Chip?"

"No, they were for you."

"What are you talking about?"

"If you ever got out of control, Plan A is I pepper spray you and then handcuff you."

"What's plan B?"

"You don't want to know."

"Why does she hate me so much? You know, I think she and I need to have a serious chat. She's starting to bug me."

"Relax, let's focus on the here and now."

I shook my head and we went back to Chip. He was still out cold and I noticed a lump the size of a baseball in the back of his head. Dragging him out of the bathroom I hoisted him up onto the bed and blindfolded him with one of his ties and cuffed his hands behind his back.

Pam said, "What about his legs?"

He wasn't going anywhere but why risk a well-timed kick, so I restrained each ankle to its respective bedpost using leather belts we found. When I finished I threw a sheet over him. I spared him a gag for now but had one ready.

I walked Pam into the living room and we sat on his sofa. "Now we wait and think."

The stress of the evening had taken its toll on Pam and she snuggled close, her eyes watering up. I placed an arm around her. "It's going to be all right, Pam. You did a great job."

She sniffled. "Will your friends get to the children in time?"

I looked at my watch. "I hope so."

The die was cast and there was nothing more anyone could do except wait it out. After an hour, the anticipation was making me edgy. Pam was deteriorating and looked at me with swollen red eyes. I said, "How about a drink?"

She nodded and I poured her four fingers of Chip's best bourbon. She took a big gulp and sat back in the sofa. Finally, at 12:30 a.m., just as I was ready to jump out of my skin, my cellphone rang with an unknown number. It was Vito. "How'd it go and what phone are you using?" I asked.

"We got'em. Heading over to your professor friends' apartments. I already called them and they're waiting. I picked up a throw away phone at Walmart so no one can listen in. How'd it go with your girlfriend?"

"She'll be okay. Some unexpected stuff went down that shook her up. Any casualties on your end?"

He was silent.

"Well?"

"There was a dead kid."

I bit my lip. "What happened?"

"The two drivers pulled over enroute sometime last night and took turns assaulting her in the back of the van in front of all the other kids. She became hysterical and wouldn't stop screaming so the woman in the van got nervous and covered her mouth until she stopped."

"You're kidding?"

"She looks to be about ten years old."

"Shit! Did the drivers put up a fight?"

"No, we got the drop on them good and Carlos calmed everybody down but you're not going to be happy with me."

"Why?"

"Remember how you told me not to lose my temper?"

"What happened?"

"Well, I lost my temper."

"How bad?"

"Both drivers. I couldn't help it. When I heard what they did to that girl I lost it."

Shit!

"Vito...I needed them."

"I know, but we still have the woman. When she saw what happened to her friends she became a fountain of information."

"Where are the drivers now?"

"In the trunk of the caddie with the dead kid. I'll figure out something to do with them. Carlos is in the back seat interrogating the woman. Tommy's behind us driving the van with the kids. We'll be there in thirty minutes."

"Anybody speak English?"

"The drivers spoke a little. The kids are from out of the way villages in Mexico and Central America. We'll know more later. Carlos is just scratching the surface right now."

"No Spiders?"

"No, they probably got caught up in traffic. It's a zoo right now in both directions but much worse if they were coming in from the island. There was an overturned tractor-trailer on the LIE coming into Queens. Stop and go for miles, even at this hour. We didn't dawdle up there either. We got there early and the van was already waiting. One, two, three and we were out of there."

I thought it over for a moment. "Okay, good work. I'll catch up with you tomorrow. How are the kids?"

"Scared, hungry. There were six of them, all girls, eight to twelve years old. The van was also loaded with heroin, maybe a hundred kilos. What should we do with the woman?"

"I got a situation at Chip's apartment that I'm going to need help with. Tell Carlos to find out everything she knows. I want details. Write down everything she says about who she works for. I want names and places. When you're sure she has nothing left to say, bring her to one of the apartments and restrain her. I'll deal with her later."

"Anything else?"

I told him about what happened to Chip and said, "After you drop off the kids, swing by with the van and we'll put Chip in it. I think I want to hang on to him for a while."

"How are we going to get him out of there without being seen?"

I looked around the room and spotted the antique steamer trunk against the wall. I replied. "I got it covered. See you soon."

I hung up and noticed Pam looking at me quizzically. "We're going to kidnap Chip?"

I pretended to be shocked. "Kidnapping is a felony, Pam. I would never do that. The poor man's suffered a significant head injury. I'm just going to keep him under observation for a couple of days. It's the ethically correct thing to do."

She was quiet for a minute and then said, "Am I going to prison with you?"

Smiling, I couldn't help myself and said, "No. They have separate prisons for pretty girls."

She was definitely not in the joking mood. "I heard about the child. That's so awful. Your friend has a very loud voice."

"Yes, he does. I'm sorry."

"John, please hold me."

Chapter 38

The next day at Riker's, I was wound up and couldn't wait for the clinic to end for my pre-arranged meeting with Samuel in the shower. When I arrived, he wasn't in a good mood. "What happened?" he whispered.

"What do you mean?" I asked wiping water from my face.

"Something went wrong—very wrong, and I want to know what."

I feigned innocence. "I have no idea what you're talking about."

"Don't fuck with me. I sent you to give Chip a message and now nobody knows where he is and something very valuable that belongs to me is missing. Tell me everything—every word that took place between you and him, and I'm warning you, don't leave anything out."

The fact that he knew what happened already indicated to me that he must have had at least one other way of communicating with the outside that I didn't know about. I'd have to be careful. I gave him the Cesari version and his features darkened with anger. "Are you telling me he set up a meeting with your guinea friends without telling me?"

"I don't know what to say," I stammered. "He insisted on it. I'm sorry. I didn't think I was doing anything wrong. Chip made it sound like he was your boss."

"Oh, he did, did he?"

I nodded timidly.

He continued, "So what happened at this meeting?"

"I wasn't in the actual meeting. I don't rank that high. I introduced him and then had to leave. It lasted about three hours, though."

"Three hours? What the hell did they talk about for three hours?" Samuel was getting seriously agitated.

"I don't know, but I can tell you this. Chip was smiling ear to ear when he came out. He looked like a kid on Christmas."

"And he didn't say anything at all about what they talked about?"

"Not a word and I wasn't about to ask."

He nodded. He was frustrated. "That makes sense, I guess, and then what happened?"

"Nothing. Chip thanked me for setting up the meeting and we separated. Here I am. I haven't heard from him since then and that was almost a week ago."

He slapped the cement wall in anger. He gritted his teeth and spit. I backed away cautiously not knowing where this was heading. Finally, he growled, "That scumbag. Just like that he thinks he can go into business for himself."

"Maybe, it's not what you think. Maybe he's just sick in bed or something. I know it sounds stupid but it could happen."

He snickered. "Yeah, right. I already sent guys to his apartment. He's not there. Besides, if it was something as simple as that he would have gotten word to my men. He knows the rules. No, Chip's smart. He's jumping ship and upgrading his portfolio with your grease-ball friends. Thanks for nothing, Cesari."

I tried my best to look offended. "Whoa, I had no idea what was going to happen. In fact, I still don't know what happened, but I do know one thing for sure about my people. They wouldn't disrupt a smoothly running operation like yours. It's not their style and it makes no sense economically. If Chip betrayed you then it was his idea not theirs—guaranteed. I thought he was a little too enthusiastic. I mean, when I brought the subject up he jumped on it. I even suggested we wait to talk to you first and he said it wasn't necessary. Look, I'm not happy about this either, but you never told me not to talk about it with him."

The seed was planted. All it needed was a little nurturing. He let out a deep breath. "I can't believe it. That's millions of dollars of my money. If he thinks he's going to cut me out and get away with it he's got another thing coming. And you—I should just finish you now."

He suddenly wheeled to face me pulling out of his pocket a four-inch shiv made of rusted metal. I squared away defensively, my heart racing. "Wait, Samuel. Listen to me. I know you're upset and I'm sorry about what happened with Chip but don't blame me."

He took a step closer and I backed away, looking around for a weapon. I blurted out. "Give me a chance. I can help you figure things out."

He hesitated and said, "How?"

"It's a long shot, but I can get you out of here."

He relaxed a bit. "I'm listening, asshole."

Thirty minutes later, I left Riker's, my brain on fire thinking of moves and counter moves. As I drove to my apartment I called Vito. It was almost 8:00 p.m.

"Cesari, you just get out?"

"Yeah, where are you?" I heard a lot of noise in the background.

313

"The Café Amalfi, it's on the corner of Prince and Mulberry. What's up? How'd you make out with Samuel?"

"Touch and go, but he's willing to hold off on my execution for a while."

"Why was he so generous?"

"Because I promised to break him out of Riker's so he can go after Chip."

Vito chuckled and took a bite of something. "Did you know it's a sin to lie?"

"I didn't lie. We're going to get him out."

"We?"

"Yes, we. Do you know where we could borrow an ambulance?"

"Yeah, let me see. Oh, there it is. I have one up my ass."

"Very funny. Even a medical transport van will suffice."

Chewing loudly into the phone, he said, "Let me think about it. You can't just jack one from a hospital, but there are tons of nursing homes that may have one sitting around. There's almost no security at those places either. What are you going to do with him if, and that's a big if, you're able to get him out. You're not seriously going to let a guy like that run loose?"

"No, of course not, and I haven't decided yet, but using him as a hostage to trade for the girl, Maria, crossed my mind."

"If she's alive."

"Stop saying that."

"Fine, and when is this prison break going to take place?"

"I was aiming for tomorrow night."

"For Chrissake. What do I look like, a magician?"

"Well, start looking tonight. Time is a factor, and as long as you're at it, grab a couple of medical-looking uniforms if you can."

"You make small requests, did you know that?"

"I'm not done either. Could you send Tommy or Carlos over to my place to keep an eye on Chip tonight? I have errands to run and this really isn't a job for Pam."

"You're a pain in the ass. I'll send Carlos."

"Thanks, I got to go. Tell him I'll leave the key under the mat, and make sure he knows about Cleo. By the way, don't talk when you're chewing your food. It's better for your digestion."

I hung up, parked in my garage, and found Pam sitting on the sofa in my apartment with Cleo nearby. I said hello to both of them.

"How's our guest?" I asked nodding my head in the direction of the bedroom.

She stood up to hug me and I saw that she was swimming in a pair of my jeans and one of my shirts. We hadn't had time last night to swing by her apartment for clothes. "He was a good boy so I fed him and let him watch TV. Potty breaks were a little awkward, but the gun and Cleo kept him cooperative, more Cleo than the gun. She doesn't like him at all."

A .38 Smith and Wesson rested on the coffee table. The second one I had borrowed from Vito in less than two weeks. I said "Don't tell anybody about the gun. I'm a felon."

"What different does it make? Handguns are illegal in New York City for everyone, not just felons."

I grinned. "Yeah, but a handgun with the serial number scratched off and possibly traceable to a homicide could really land one of us in hot water."

"One of us? You would throw me under the bus?"

"Sure, you're a kidnapper."

She laughed. "You son of a bitch."

I smiled, "So no trouble?"

"He cursed and threatened a little but whenever he raised his voice Cleo started growling and that shut him right up. I wouldn't talk to him and that really pissed him off."

"Really, not at all?"

"Not a word. I just let him babble and speculate. He has no idea what's going on. Did you eat?"

"No, prison seems to take my appetite away. I'll grab whatever's in the refrigerator. I'm going to say hello to our guest first, okay?"

"Fine, but keep it civil in there."

I walked into the bedroom and closed the door behind me. Chip sat naked on the bed leaning back against the headboard with his hands cuffed behind him and one ankle tied with a length of rope to the bedframe. He had enough slack to reach the bathroom. I made a mental note to get new sheets when he was gone. There was a bottle of water on the night table with a straw in it for him to sip from.

He looked at me with disgust and said, "You have no idea what's going to happen to you—and to Pam. The Spiders are going to have a field day with her."

"You should be more concerned about what's going to happen to you, Chip. Now lean forward. I want to see that lump on the back of your head. How's your headache? Any double vision?"

"Like you care?"

"I just don't want you to die, not here, and not yet. Now lean forward, asshole."

I examined the back of his head. He had a good-sized lump but otherwise he seemed okay. "Why did you bring me here anyway?" he asked.

"Between me and you, I would have just killed you last night, but since Pam and I are—you know—involved." I winked at him. "I felt it might have led her to think less of me, and since I couldn't kill you proper and didn't want you ratting us out to the Spiders about what we're up to... Well, here we are."

"What exactly are you up to?"

"Oh right. You don't know. It seems that I was able to snatch the van with the kids, but don't worry they're all safe. The heroin, too. Samuel, however, is totally pissed. Told me so himself. Seems he's under the impression you betrayed him. Thinks you might have found new friends you like better than him. Not to mention all the money that's now missing from the bank account that you wired away. Yeah, he's pretty upset."

He turned pale and didn't say anything as his mind raced. Finally, he said, "I still don't get it. Was this about the kids or the drugs or both? Either way, it's stupid. The kids are where the real money is. I was going to cut you in. Now you got nothing. I had buyers all lined up, at least two million a kid. Now what are you going to do? Do you even know how to process them? There's a lot that goes into this business."

He still didn't understand what was going on. That was good. I suddenly had an idea. Why not drain the swamp if I could? I looked at him. "So, why don't you be a good guy and tell me all about it?"

"It's all about the clients. I have access to many rich and powerful people. The kind who don't mind paying top dollar for their entertainment and that's what you need."

"You mean because of your position as president of NYU?"

"Of course, that's what I mean."

"I don't suppose you would care to tell me the names of your clients?"

He smirked. "It doesn't work that way."

"I could break a few more of your fingers if that will help."

He gulped. "That's not what I meant. I know a few names off the top of my head but most of the time I'm approached through intermediaries. There's a list of contacts but it's encrypted on a laptop at the house in Long Island guarded by the Spiders."

I looked down at him quietly trying to decide what to do. Misunderstanding my silence, he said. "Look, if all you want is to take over the business from us there's a smarter way of doing it. Why not just work with me instead? We already have a very smooth and efficient operation. I could show you all the ins and outs. I could be very useful, and Samuel, well, he's in prison for at least two more years."

It was hard for me to believe that someone this highly educated could have sunk so low. I mean, this wasn't just one of the guys in the ivory tower. He was the ringmaster. Then again, maybe I could use his temerity against him, but first I needed to suppress the rage I felt rising in my chest.

Thinking his arguments were swaying me he continued, "C'mon, give me a chance to prove myself to you. There's a whole process to this business that you don't understand. There's nutrition, medical consults, GYN procedures, training..."

Glaring down at him, I was torn between the rational side of my brain that wanted to use him and the side that wanted to tear his arms out of his sockets and watch him bleed to death.

I said, "Let me think about it."

He breathed an audible sigh of relief. "Thanks. You won't regret it. By the way, how did you manage to get a tenured professor like Pam involved in all of this?"

"I could ask the same question about you. Now turn onto your stomach."

Without moving he said, "What are you going to do?"

Suddenly, and with extreme violence borne of repressed fury, I punched him in the face. His head snapped backward and his eyes rolled up in his head as he went limp. I rolled him onto his stomach and using the rope, hogtied his ankles to his manacled wrists. It looked very uncomfortable. For good measure I decided to gag him with one of my socks.

318

Back in the living room Pam asked, "Everything okay?"

"Yes, but he needs to rest now and so do you. I've already asked Vito to send one of his men over here to keep an eye on him. We'll go sleep at your apartment tonight. This couch isn't that comfortable, and you'll need clothes."

"How long are you going to keep him?"

"Not a second longer than I have to."

Tucking Cleo in her bed, I pocketed the .38, and found my duffel bag with the crowbar. Pam grabbed her bag and cellphone and we headed toward the door. Just as we were about to leave, I spotted the doll with the blue dress sitting on the credenza by the door. Kayla had wanted to keep it but I needed it. It kept me focused. I hesitated, picked it up and placed it in the duffel bag.

Pam asked, "Why did you do that?"

"Motivation."

Chapter 39

*P*am and I took a cab to her apartment in the West Village. I said, "You look cute in my clothes."

"Thanks. You must be tired. Are sure you sure you don't want to come in?"

"I am tired, but I really have to run an errand. I won't be more than an hour. Wait up for me."

"I will. I'll probably call Knuckles and Liz again to see how they're holding up. I spoke to them several times today. Everybody's doing fine. Eating like horses and playing games or watching cartoons."

I smiled and nodded. "What about the woman?"

"Knuckles has two bathrooms. The witch is locked up in one of them. Liz bought a PlayStation and they're all mesmerized at her place, including her." She chuckled. "They may never be the same."

"Any of them—damaged—physically?"

"According to Liz, who's pretty fluent, no. The woman, whose name is Rosa, said they weren't supposed to harm the children in any way. The other night, the drivers got high or drunk and lost control of themselves. The kids confirmed that."

I grunted. "I guess that's something."

"I know. That poor child."

"Yeah."

The taxi pulled to a stop and Pam got out and I handed her my duffel bag. "I'll see you later then?" she asked.

"An hour."

I watched her walk into her building and then had the driver take me over to St. Matt's on Third Avenue. I paid him, walked through the main entrance, and waved to the old security guard sitting at his desk. It was almost 10:00 p.m.

"Hi, Frank."

"Hello, Dr. Cesari. What brings you here at this hour?"

"A friend of mine is in the ICU. I just wanted to stop in to say hello. I won't be long."

Frank had known me a long time. He also knew what a mess my life had become. He looked at me sympathetically, but spared me any personal comments. "Sure, go ahead, Doc."

I made a mental note to be very gentle if I ever got the chance to do his colonoscopy. I rode the elevators to the third floor where the OR was, not the ICU. The hallway was dark and no one was around. Saturday night in any OR was a lonely place. The main doors were locked, which was good because it meant no one was inside. I went to the male locker-room, pulled out my wallet and retrieved my St. Matt's ID and held my breath. I swiped the magnetic strip in the receptacle and was gratified when the light turned green and the lock clicked open. When it came to hospital security, the word oxymoron came to mind. Pushing through the door, I found a pair of scrubs and changed into them, donning a surgical hat and mask. I didn't want to contaminate the OR.

At the other end of the locker-room was an entrance into the OR's central work area and nursing station. I flipped on the lights and searched each operating room for what I needed. I found it in room 2, a three-foot green metal canister with a valve at the top. It was marked "Enflurane." Enflurane was a potent gaseous anesthetic. Most of the OR's gasses such as oxygen, nitrous oxide, and Enflurane were delivered via hoses from a central storage area in the basement of the hospital where large tanks were kept. The OR kept smaller, portable versions around in case a problem developed with the delivery system in the middle of a case.

I picked it up and estimated it weighed twenty to twenty-five pounds. A small hose attached to it gave it the appearance of a green fire extinguisher. How to get it out of the hospital was the question now. I carried it into the locker room and changed back into civilian clothes. Furtively opening the locker-room door, I peered both ways down the corridor. Finding no one there, I stepped into the hallway carrying the Enflurane like a baby, knowing that I was committing yet another felony. Once on the elevator, I said a small prayer and pressed the button to the basement. If I could make it into the morgue undetected, I had a chance.

As I got off the elevator, my cellphone buzzed and I almost jumped out of my skin. I rested the canister on the floor and answered it. "Vito, what is it?"

"I got one—a transport van. The best part is they won't even know it's missing for a couple of days. It was in a garage on Second Avenue getting a new transmission, which they finished last night. Nobody's supposed to come for it until Monday at the earliest."

"What about uniforms?"

"Hey fuck off. How about a thank you?"

I rolled my eyes. "Thank you."

"I'm working on the uniforms."

"Where are you right now?"

"I'm test driving the van to make sure we don't have any screw ups tomorrow night. I'm coming up Houston."

"Great. You're not too far from St. Matt's."

"Why's that great?"

"Because I need a lift and I want to check out the van. Come to the back of the hospital. There's an ambulance port by the morgue where they drop bodies for autopsy. It's well marked."

"Are you insane? I'm driving a stolen medical transport van. I'm not going to pull up to a hospital with it."

"Why not? You just said yourself no one will even miss it until Monday."

He thought it over. "I guess not. It just doesn't seem smart. Look, fine, I'll be there in ten. Don't make me wait."

I hung up and made my way down the corridor to the morgue. The wood door was locked and I kicked myself for not bringing the crowbar. I glanced in every direction trying to determine if there was another way in but there wasn't. I then tried unsuccessfully to power the door open with my shoulder and then a few well-placed kicks. It was a solid oak door with a good lock. Time passed and I started to sweat. Vito would be here any minute. There had to be some way to open this friggin' door without a proper lock-pick tool set. Then I remembered I had my .38 in my pocket. Could I blow the lock out without being discovered? Probably not. Gun shots ringing out in the middle of the night were sure to attract attention, but I had an idea. If I triggered the fire alarm down here in the basement, the noise would certainly cover the sound of a .38, but it would also give away my location.

I left the canister on the floor in front of the morgue and took the elevator back up to the OR. In the hallway outside the elevator, I found a fire alarm and pulled it, quickly stepping back in and returning to the morgue as the screeching of the alarm resounded throughout the building. Moving the Enflurane safely out of the way, I aimed the .38 at the door's lock and fired twice. Wood splintered, gunsmoke filled the hall, and the door opened. I picked up the gas tank and raced to the exit at the back of the morgue. Vito was just pulling into the port when I came rushing out. I placed the tank in the back of the van and hopped into the passenger seat, breathless.

I said, "Let's get out of here."

"What's all the noise?"

"I pulled a fire alarm. I needed a distraction."

He shook his head. "You're such an asshole."

"Just drive. So how's it feel?"

"Not bad. I thought it was going to have more buttons and stuff, but it's just an ordinary van. What was that you tossed in the back?"

"A little surprise for tomorrow night."

I looked back and was relieved to see a panel separating the driver's compartment from the rear of the van. There was a four-inch window to see into the back of the vehicle. It wasn't air tight but I could fix that with some duct tape.

"What are you looking at?"

"We'll have to fix the van up a little. I'll need you to have your guys drill a one-inch hole into this back panel so I can slip a hose into it and then we'll have to seal the whole thing tightly with duct tape."

"Is that what the gas tank is for?"

"Yeah."

"Jesus, you're on a rampage, aren't you?"

"Short of shooting the guards, I don't have a better way and I'd rather not do that. They haven't treated me badly."

"When they wake, won't they remember us?"

"When they wake from this stuff, they may not even remember their own names."

He nodded, slightly reassured. "Okay, and then what?"

"I haven't gotten that far yet. Drop me off on Barrow Street in the West Village, all right?"

"What's in the West Village?"

"Pam's apartment."

"How's she holding up?"

"She's pretty strong. That was a rough night for her and she had to babysit that jerk all day."

"Yeah, I give her credit for that. So, I'm not going to hear from you tomorrow at all?"

"Not during the day, no. I'm not allowed to make calls. Show up at 5:00 p.m. sharp. I don't want to give them any time to think things through. Remember, you're a private transport service sent by Queens County hospital because all their ambulances were tied up. You have all day to come up with a phony or stolen ID."

"Got it. Okay, here we are. I'll see you tomorrow afternoon."

"Thanks, and tell your guys not to play with the gas."

I got out of the van and waved him goodbye. Pam was waiting for me, scotch in hand, wearing a terrycloth robe and fuzzy slippers. She said, "Hi, get everything done you needed to?"

"Yeah."

"Scotch?"

I looked at my watch. It was after eleven and I was exhausted. "Sure."

"Have a seat and I'll pour you a glass."

I sat on the sofa and closed my eyes. A few minutes later, Pam led me into the bedroom half asleep and undressed me. At two, I awoke to pee. Pam was asleep and I felt—different. In the bathroom, I looked down and found that she had removed the bandage and decided I didn't need another one. The area was still red but healing well and didn't hurt that much anymore. The same for the nipples. Something else wasn't right though.

I got back in bed and the jostling woke Pam. She said sleepily, "Hey, is everything all right?"

"Yeah, I had to go to the bathroom."

She flung her arm and head onto my chest and curled into me. "Oh, I thought maybe you wanted to go for round two."

Round two? I couldn't remember round one. "Did we do something tonight?"

She giggled. "I did something. You slept through the whole thing."

"Is that possible?"

With her eyes closed and already mostly asleep she whispered. "I filmed it all. I'll show you tomorrow."

I snorted and gave her a kiss.

Chapter 40

Sunday morning at Riker's was a zoo. Everybody was in a foul mood. The first five patients had minor cuts, abrasions, and puncture wounds. The sixth had a concussion. I felt bad for the 11:30 a.m. patient. There was nothing quite as awkward as telling a man who had been locked up for six months that he had gonorrhea.

Keith poked his head in on me as I finished my charts for the morning. "Just received a call from the warden, Doc. She wants to see you in her office."

I looked up puzzled. "On Sunday? What did I do?"

He shook his head. "She didn't say."

I walked to her office in shackles and took a seat. On her desk was a vase with three dozen long-stemmed red roses. The room was filled with their fragrance. As I admired them, Warden Garcia entered wearing a business length black skirt and white blouse. She nodded at me and took a seat behind her desk, moving the vase slightly to see me better.

"Dr. Cesari."

"Warden."

She tapped her hands nervously on her desk before clasping them in front of her. "Did you notice the flowers?"

"Yes, they're quite beautiful."

She nodded. "They came to my home last night. My private home. Do you know who sent them?"

I shook my head.

"Detective Terrence Kilcullen of the Ninth Precinct. The same detective who keeps calling me repetitively about updates concerning you."

I cleared my throat in surprise. "I don't know what to say. What's this got to do with me?"

She opened a small envelope and pulled out the card. "This came with the roses. 'Dear Lucinda, I know we haven't met but in talking to you these last few weeks I feel like I have known you my whole life. Dr. Cesari tells me you are a passionate woman of exquisite beauty and grace. It would give me the greatest honor if you would consider sharing a pint with me in the near future.'"

Jesus Christ!

He jumped the gun. My face colored. "I can explain."

"I'm listening."

"He's not a bad guy. A little impulsive, maybe, but definitely not a bad guy."

"Tell me about him."

Hmm, I detected a note of interest in her voice. "Fiftyish, tall, full head of hair, decent shape. He can still handle himself is my guess. I wouldn't want to get on the wrong side of him if you know what I mean."

She nodded. "Single, divorced, widowed?"

"Divorced."

"And so what does this mean?" She pointed at the flowers. "Does he think I'm desperate or that any yahoo with a credit card can bed me?"

"I don't think so. He's just, um—enthusiastic?"

She thought it over. "Well you let him know I don't appreciate advances from elderly men and I don't like convicts discussing my personal attributes with anyone."

I gulped as she spoke.

She went on. "I can handle my own love life just fine and he'd better not start stalking me or I'll report him to Internal Affairs."

Ouch!

"But..."

She continued. "You can also let him know that once in a great while I've been known to grab a margarita at Muldoon's Saloon after work like maybe this coming Friday between five and seven. It's a cop bar in Astoria. He'll know it. Also, I don't speak to men unless they're clean-shaved and wearing a tie. If I like what I see, we'll take it from there. If I don't show up, he'd better not cry about it and make it clear that I'm always armed with a .40 Sig."

She grabbed a handful of roses and sniffed them as I sat there speechless. She looked up at me. "Now, get out."

By the time we finished, I didn't have time to make it to the mess hall for lunch. Keith had mercy on me and bought me a yogurt from a vending machine. Afternoon clinic began promptly and was a lot more of the same until 4:00 p.m., when our VIP and last patient arrived.

Samuel came shuffling in doubled over in abdominal pain. He looked to be in agony and grimaced as I assisted him onto the exam table. Once he was in a more or less comfortable position sitting down, I asked him a few questions.

"Tell me what's wrong?"

"My stomach hurts and I've been puking all night."

I glanced at Keith, who watched Samuel carefully. "Any diarrhea or rectal bleeding?"

He shook his head. "No, but I can't eat. The pain is getting worse."

"Okay, lie down and let me examine you."

He did as I directed and I took his temperature. It read 98.6 but I said, "Whoa, 102 degrees. You're burning up my friend."

"I told you, Doc. I'm not right."

"All right. I believe you. Look, I'm going to press on your abdomen. It's going to hurt and I'm sorry but I need to localize the pain so don't jump off the table."

"I'll try not to."

I palpated his abdomen counter clockwise beginning in the left lower quadrant. When I reached the right side, I glanced in his direction and he jumped on cue yelling, "Oh my God! That hurts."

I backed away. "I'm sorry. Take it easy. Do you still have your appendix?"

He nodded, still wincing.

I went over to Keith. "I think he has appendicitis. He's going to need to go to the hospital."

He looked at his watch and sighed. "C'mon, call the medical director and explain it."

Opening the door, he told the other guard outside. "I'll watch the prisoner. He needs to call the doctor in charge about a transfer to the hospital."

Outside the exam room, I was led to the nursing station where the guard dialed the number for me. "Hey, Dave, sorry to bother you."

Sounding quite annoyed, he said, "No problem, Cesari. I love being disturbed while I'm at a Yankee game and it's the bottom of the ninth and the winning run is on base. Whatcha got?"

I smiled, listening to the crowd roar in the background. "Couldn't be helped. I have a thirty-year old piece of garbage here with right lower quadrant pain and fever. On exam, he has rebound tenderness. I think he has appendicitis."

"How sick is he?"

"Pretty sick. Temp's 102 and he's diaphoretic."

He sighed deeply into the phone and I understood his frustration. Making the necessary arrangements would take at least thirty minutes of phone calls, most of that spent waiting on hold while the appropriate people at the hospital were contacted. I had no intention of letting that happen anyway so I interceded. "I'll call the hospital, Dave. Why don't you get back to the game?"

This was a slight breach of protocol. Not a massive one, mind you, but since he knew me pretty well by now, I figured he'd be okay with it. I also guessed that if it was the bottom of the ninth and he was a typical Yankee fan, he was probably well into his seventh or eighth beer. He said, "Are you sure you don't mind?"

"Not at all. I'll leave a detailed note in the patient's chart for you to review in the morning."

"Thanks, put me on the phone with the guards and I'll let them know I approve the transfer."

The guards were informed of the transfer and I pretended to call the hospital, calling Vito instead to get his ass over here quickly. Keith let the front gate know that a medical transport was on the way. So far, this was all routine and had been done just like this many times before.

Walking up to Samuel, I said, "You're going to the ER, prisoner, and you're probably going to need surgery tonight."

He looked at me and I could tell he was trying hard not to smile. "I don't care what they do just as long as they stop the pain."

"I understand. In the meanwhile, we wait quietly for the transport vehicle. I don't have anything to give you for the pain. I'm sorry."

"It's okay."

Time seemed to slow down as Samuel writhed theatrically on the exam table. Keith discussed transfer protocol with the other guard and I rehearsed in my mind all the myriad of things that could go wrong. They gave me my civilian clothes to change into, and finally, at just after five, Vito and Tommy came strolling in wheeling the gurney from the van. They looked absolutely ridiculous wearing white uniforms and caps. Vito obviously didn't know what an EMT was supposed to look like so he chose the Maytag repairman appearance.

The guards didn't seem to notice or perhaps they didn't care. They were supposed to go home at five and now they were stuck transporting Samuel to the hospital. It was overtime for them but it still sucked. I helped Vito and Tommy strap Samuel securely into the stretcher and walked with them out to the van. They loaded him into the back, followed by the guards.

I said, "Good luck, guys."

Vito closed the door tightly behind them and locked it. He went to the driver's side and I followed Tommy to the passenger side. Once they were in, I inspected the setup as Vito started the engine. The gas tank now lay propped between the two seats with its hose plugged into the hole I had Vito drill into the panel. Duct tape sealed the opening and was stripped up and down every joint leading to the back compartment.

I whispered to Vito. "Remember, keep an eye on them through the window. The minute they go out, turn off the tank. Too much gas could kill them all."

He nodded, "See you on the other side."

I watched them pull away and went to my car. I stopped at the security gate and made a big deal about asking the guard directions to some restaurant in Brooklyn. I wanted to make sure he remembered me leaving long after the van. Once on the road, I drove back to Pam's apartment and was fortunate enough to find a parking spot on the street. Vito would call me once he was done. The plan was to gas them into unconsciousness, offload the guards someplace relatively safe and bring Samuel to one of Vito's safe-houses where he would be kept under lock and key until I got there to set him straight on a few things. In the meanwhile, Pam and I were going to check on Knuckles and Liz.

I found Pam in her apartment putting toys and games into shopping bags lined up on her living room floor. She was smiling ear to ear. She said, "Hi, I'm almost ready. I thought we could drop these off at Knuckles and then go out to eat. I already made my delivery to Liz. These kids are so cute. You can't believe it. Liz is beside herself she's having so much fun."

I smiled. "She's handling it well, then?"

"Boy, is she ever. When I got there, she was running around with a red towel across her back pretending to be Superman."

"Oh boy!"

"Yeah, and from what I hear Knuckles also has everything under control."

"Let's go find out. They each got three girls and Knuckles has the woman?"

"Yes. How'd it go at the prison?"

I glanced nervously at my watch. "The first part went very well. I'm waiting to hear about the second part. Vito should call me within an hour."

We finished packing the bags and walked over to Knuckles' apartment by NYU. She let us in and we smelled pizza. The three girls were crowded around the television watching the Disney channel. Toys, board games and dolls lay strewn about the living room floor. The girls wore new clothes and were giggling at something.

Paper plates with half-eaten slices lay here and there. A Pepsi bottle was half empty on the kitchen table. It looked like a pajama party. Knuckles looked at the bags. "More toys and dolls?"

"Books, too—in Spanish."

Knuckles laughed. "These kids are going to get the wrong impression."

Pam countered, "So let them. After what they've been through they deserve a break."

I nodded in agreement. "Absolutely. Well, why don't you hand out presents while Knuckles introduces me to Rosa?"

"Sure."

Knuckles and I headed off into one of her bedrooms. A queen bed was neatly made, and pictures of Rocky Marciano adorned the wall. She said, "I keep the bitch locked in the bathroom."

She opened the bathroom door and I found Rosa sitting on the floor leaning back against the tub. A pillow and blanket were in the tub. She was about forty, dark skinned, with shoulder-length black hair. She appeared to be exhausted and had been crying. She looked up at me and said something in Spanish. Knuckles said, "She says she's sorry."

"Yeah, they always are after they're caught. How good's your Spanish?"

"Good enough to know if she lies to you."

"Good. Tell her my name and then translate word for word everything I say and don't leave anything out."

Knuckles nodded at me and spoke to the woman who listened attentively.

"Now tell her that I'm going to ask her a bunch of questions, some of which she may have been asked already."

Waiting for Knuckles to translate, I watched Rosa's facial expression carefully. I was pretty good at being able to tell when someone was lying. "Now tell her that if she doesn't answer me truthfully the very first time I ask a question, I will cut her head off with a rusty knife."

Knuckles' eyes went wide and she hesitated. "Tell her," I repeated sternly.

She told her and Rosa shrank back in fear, suddenly becoming pale. She stammered nervously.

Knuckles said, "She says she won't lie."

"Okay then." I sat on the toilet seat and glared at her. "Start from the beginning. Where are the children from? Who is her boss? Who pays her? Where is she from? I want to know everything."

Tearful and contrite, she spilled her guts and thirty minutes later, I was convinced she had told me everything she knew. She still had to pay for her crimes but I was now willing to consider jail time as an option.

I turned to Knuckles. "Keep her locked up. I'll get her out of here soon, maybe tonight."

"She's got to pay, Doc."

"A lot of people are going to pay, Knuckles."

"Understood."

We went back out to find Pam sitting at the kitchen table sipping from a glass. "Everything all right?" she asked.

I sat next to her and grabbed a slice of cold pizza. Knuckles started cleaning up. I said, "Yeah, she was cooperative, but really didn't know a whole lot. Spent most of the time trying to convince me that she's just as much of a victim as the girls."

"Is it possible?"

"Anything's possible."

As we talked, one of the girls came into the kitchen, and stood right next to me, staring at me with her big brown eyes. She was maybe six or seven years old with long dark hair and a sweet smile. Her name was Sofia and Knuckles asked her in Spanish if everything was all right.

She pointed at me and said something that made Knuckles grow quiet. Pam asked, "What did she say?"

Knuckles smiled and replied, "She says the doc looks like her father."

Sofia and I looked at each other for a long time before I finally broke. My lip started to quiver and my eyes watered up. Overcome with emotion, I couldn't speak. Pam touched my shoulder reassuringly and Sofia wrapped her arms around me. My whole body started to shake uncontrollably and I just couldn't stop it.

I couldn't believe it. I had survived the animals at Riker's and a little girl I didn't know brought me to my knees.

Chapter 41

Pam and I left Knuckles' apartment and walked arm in arm in silence. She asked, "Are you okay?"

I was still quietly crying. "Do I look okay?"

Very softly, she said, "It's okay to be in touch with your feelings sometimes. Men should really try it more often."

I turned to face her. "How could anyone even think of hurting a little girl like that? That's all I could think of when I was looking at her. I can't believe I lost it like that and Knuckles saw the whole thing."

Pam grinned. "And that bothers you … that Knuckles saw?"

I hadn't thought about it like that and hesitated for a moment. "No, not really … I guess."

"Are you concerned she might tell someone you have feelings?"

"Well, if you put it that way…"

"John, you may not realize it but what happened in there was very healthy and normal. You've been under a lot of stress both mentally and physically. Sofia simply put a face on what this is all about. Up until tonight, it's been third person for you. They've been children, kids, cargo, and shipments. Now, it's personal. It's Sofia."

337

"And Maria."

She nodded. "And Maria."

We continued walking until we reached my building on the corner of Avenue of the Americas and Waverly Place. I was quiet, deep in thought and Pam let me have my space. At the doorway, before entering, I said, "Pam, I have something to tell you and you're not going to like it, but I've made up my mind."

"I'm listening," she said soothingly.

"I … I don't know how to say this."

"Take a deep breath and just say it."

"You don't know me, Pam. You don't really know me. You don't know the things I've done, the people I call friends. They're not Fifth Avenue types."

"John, whatever you're getting at…"

"I'm going to kill them, Pam. I'm going to kill them all, and I'm not just saying it to blow off steam. I'm going to hunt them down wherever they are and slaughter them one by one. There will be no survivors."

She took a deep breath and quietly studied me before sliding her arms around my waist and pressing her head into my chest. We held each other tightly for a few moments, and then I stroked her head gently and looked into her eyes. "I'm sorry, but this is going to put a real damper on our relationship."

"John, I know you're upset, but think about what you're saying. You're either going to get yourself killed or go to prison for real."

"I don't care. It needs to be done."

"How about we sleep on it?"

"Nothing's going to change."

"There's no way I can talk you out of this?"

I shook my head. "I've made up my mind."

She nodded and was quiet. Sighing deeply, she said, "Then we're going to be very busy."

It took me a second to get her meaning. "No, Pam, you can't be part of it. In fact, you need to put as much distance between yourself and me as you can."

She smiled. "As Liz would say, 'There he goes again. Telling all the women what to do.'"

Despite my mood, I chuckled at the Liz-ism. She was spot on with it. I said, "How on earth do you see yourself participating in what I just said I'm going to do?"

She squared away in front of me and said, "I don't know, but I know this. I'm not just with you half way. I'm with you all the way, so get used to it."

As I was trying to come up with a response to that, she giggled. I asked, "Which part of this do you find amusing?"

"I don't think I've ever seen a guinea cry like that. I'm going to have to watch the Godfather again. I must have missed that part."

She caught me off guard with that and despite my mood, I laughed. "Now that wasn't very nice."

Shaking her head and smiling, she said, "No, it wasn't. I agree, but it does beg the question: If a little girl can make you fall to pieces, what can a big girl do?"

With her index finger, she playfully jabbed me in the abdomen and added, "You better watch out."

I looked down at her finger and suddenly remembered what my mother used to say. *Stay away from girls. They're nothing but trouble… all of them.*

In my apartment, we found Carlos watching TV, petting Cleo. He jumped to attention when we entered. We said hello. "Any problems with Chip, Carlos?"

"No, none. He was quiet."

I didn't think there would be. Carlos was about twice my size, well over 350 pounds and looked like a sumo wrestler.

"Why don't you take a break, Carlos? Pam and I can watch him the rest of the night."

"Are you sure? Mr. Vito told me to stay."

"We'll be okay. I'll clear it with him. I have your number if we need anything."

"Thanks." He left the apartment while I put on a pot of coffee. I was starting to get a little apprehensive about Vito. I should have heard from him by now. I had no choice but to sit tight and wait. I checked on Chip. He was sleeping so I let him be.

Thirty minutes later while Pam and I were watching TV my cellphone rang. It was Vito and I breathed a sigh of relief.

He was very agitated. "Cesari, everything's fucked."

I felt my spine stiffen. Pam turned the TV off. "What happened? Where are you?"

"In Queens. In the middle of the Calvary Cemetery. The Spiders ambushed us." He sounded hurt.

"The Spiders?! How the fuck...?"

"Don't ask me. They must have been waiting for us when we left Riker's. I noticed a tail ten minutes after we left and tried to give them the slip. We've been running around Queens for the last hour. I drove under the BQE as it passes over the cemetery. It's deserted there and I thought it would be a good spot to hide and gas everybody in the back of the van. The corrections officers knew something was wrong and I could hear them getting agitated back there. I was sure they were going to start shooting when suddenly two Suburbans filled with Spiders pulled up and started spraying lead. They killed Tommy."

"Shit, what about the guards?"

"I don't know. I was too busy running for my life through fields of headstones with bullets buzzing by my head."

"Are you okay?"

"I took one in the shoulder. I'm bleeding pretty good but I think it went right through. Samuel must have sent word out to head us off. I guess he didn't trust you as much as you thought he did."

I thought about that and concluded that there must be a guard on the take. Someone Samuel couldn't rely on enough to send to NYU as a messenger boy, but who might have let him make a private phone call for the right price. The feds couldn't have every phone in Riker's tapped and the guards would likely know which ones were safe. Samuel wouldn't have wanted to call in a favor like this often but this was an emergency. Shit.

I said, "I guess not. Why'd it take you so long to call?"

"I made it to an open mausoleum and passed out. I called as soon as I woke. There are freaking cops everywhere. You got to come get me."

"Okay, hang tight. I'm on the way."

"Hurry, I'm in section eight by the 49th Street entrance. Big honker of a mausoleum with a wrought iron gate in front. You can't miss it."

I turned to Pam. She heard everything, "Oh my God. That animal is on the loose?"

"I'm afraid so. He must have suspected I wasn't on the up and up. Somehow, he managed to contact his men and set up an ambush. Probably has a corrections officer on the payroll. Vito never had a chance. Look, I have to go. Not sure when I'll be back. Depends on how bad he is."

"Why doesn't he just call an ambulance?"

"Because then he'll have to explain why he was impersonating an EMT in a stolen ambulette that's now missing a Riker's inmate with possibly two dead corrections officers."

"What about his own men?"

"Good question. It's a tough business he's in. Most of his men respect him and are loyal, but it would only take one guy

341

trying to move up in the ranks to see this as an opportunity for advancement, and all they would have to do is dial 911. Vito knows that when the chips are down he can always count on me no matter what."

She nodded. "I understand. Be careful."

"I will. It's getting dark and hopefully by the time I get there the cops will have moved on. Sounds like he made it a significant distance from the ambush site. I'm just not sure what I'm going to do about his blood loss yet. He's not going to be happy about it but I may have to take him to an emergency room. I'll bring some sterile gauze and antibiotic cream with me. That should at least help and I still have plenty of that in the bathroom."

I made a care package including water and a bottle of Jack Daniel's and said goodbye to Pam. "I'll call you as soon as I can."

As I turned to leave, I hesitated and turned back to Pam. "Did you forget something?" she asked.

"I left the gun Vito gave me in your apartment."

"I have it here." Reaching into her bag, she retrieved the .38 and went to hand it to me saying, "I didn't like the idea of leaving a loaded gun lying around."

I declined the weapon. "No, I want you to have it. Just remember, it's a small caliber pistol so if you have to fire it, fire all five rounds. Remember that, okay? At this point, it's kill or be killed."

Her eyes went wide, but she didn't say anything. I'd just given her a lot to think about. I left in a hurry and concerned with Vito's health, I failed to lock the door or to consider thoroughly the full ramifications of the recent news. My car was parked by Pam's apartment and I practically ran the whole way there. It was a thirty-minute drive minimum to the cemetery and I hoped I wasn't too late.

Pulling into the cemetery from the opposite end of where the incident occurred, I drove slowly to section eight where Vito was hiding. It was after 9:00 p.m. and dark. I was far from the scene but could see the flashing lights of police and emergency vehicles. I parked the car as close as I could to the large mausoleum. It was unmistakable in its size and grandeur. Probably built in the late 1800s, it housed several generations of the Gates family. The massive, rusted wrought-iron gate creaked loudly as I let myself through and walked up to the large metal door. I had brought a small flashlight but hadn't turned it on yet for fear of attracting attention.

The heavy door scraped open and once inside, I flicked on the light. Vito was lying flat on his back on the floor with blood pooling beneath him. He was semiconscious and I raced to kneel beside him.

"Hey, buddy, I'm here."

He looked at me. "What took you so long?" His lips were parched and I propped his head holding the water bottle to his lips. He drank half of it and started coughing. I examined his wound. It was a small, clean-entry wound, entering his right shoulder and exiting just as cleanly through the back. The bleeding was already well coagulated, at least on the outside.

As I dabbed it with a whiskey-doused gauze, he winced, and I gave him the Jack Daniels to drink. I said, "It looks like a 9mm. You're lucky they weren't hollow points."

"Am I going to make it?"

I nodded. "Unless, it hit a major internal vessel. My guess is yeah, unfortunately for the Spiders, you're going to make it."

He smiled weakly. "Damn right about that. They're going to regret this."

I placed a fresh four-by-four bandage on the entry wound and fastened it in place with strips of duct tape, repeating the process on the exit wound.

He looked at me. "Seriously, duct tape? No wonder they took your license away."

"I'm glad to see you still have your sense of humor. Now finish the water bottle and we'll get out of here. Think you can stand?"

Feeling stronger with the water and whiskey he said, "Yeah, let's go."

He put his arm around my shoulder and I hoisted him up to his feet. We staggered out to my Camry and I laid him out in the back seat as best I could, given his great size.

"All right, sit tight. I'll bring you back to my apartment."

"No, not your place. Carlos is there."

"No, I sent him home."

He thought it over. "Yeah, but he may come back at some point. I ordered him to keep tabs on your apartment. I trust him, but I don't want word getting out about my condition until I'm strong enough to defend myself. My world is different from the doctor world, Cesari. In my world, they eat their young."

I turned on the ignition and laughed. "Trust me, it's the same thing in the doctor world."

Chapter 42

I took him to Pam's apartment and was thankful she had the forethought to give me a spare key. Practically carrying him from the car up to her door was no easy feat. He was a big guy and I worked up quite a sweat. By the time I heaved him onto Pam's bed, it was after eleven and I was panting heavily. In the light of the room, he was pale and pasty. He had lost a lot of blood, but he was relatively young, in good health, and the bleeding seemed to have subsided. A couple of juicy rare steaks ought to bring him back. If he didn't get infected, that is. Overall, it was my considered medical opinion that he would survive. If his condition worsened, I'd bite the bullet and take him to the emergency room and let the shit fly wherever it may.

I checked his wound again and tucked him in, leaving two water bottles on the night table beside him. "Your phone's on the table here. I'll bring you back food and antibiotics later. Try not to move around too much and drink as much water as you can."

He was weak and whispered, "Thanks."

"Get some rest."

I called Pam twice but she didn't answer. I took a deep breath and let it out slowly in frustration trying not to be overly paranoid. Suddenly, I got a sinking feeling in my stomach. If I

345

was Samuel and I didn't trust me and I just got busted out of prison where would be the first place I'd go? My heart skipped a beat and I ran to the door.

Shit!

I didn't want to waste time parking so I hailed a passing yellow cab and told the driver I'd double his fee if he hustled. Five minutes later I tossed a fifty at him and bolted up the stairs to my apartment. I caught my breath as I saw a trail of blood leading out of my apartment into the hallway. The door was wide open and I felt as if my heart was going to burst as I lunged through the doorway. There was blood everywhere in the center of the room, and most of it came from a large dead Spider lying on the floor with his throat ripped open. Cleo lay motionless on top of him. It was Luther, the security guard at Steinhardt. He held a gun in one hand and I smelled gun smoke. A quick inspection revealed both were quite dead, Cleo from close range bullet wounds. I suppressed the urge to scream.

The bedroom!

I grabbed Luther's pistol, rushed in ready for combat and saw more blood on the carpet. Chip lay motionless on the bed, a wide-eyed witness to whatever took place. He looked terrified but unharmed. He nodded toward the closed bathroom door and stammered, "She's in there. She shot him. She shot Samuel."

The bathroom door was closed and I noticed four bullet holes through it. The .38. That meant she had one shot left. I called out to her, "Pam, it's me, John. Don't shoot."

No answer. I approached slowly. "Pam, it's me, John. Are you all right?"

No answer. I said, "I'm going to open the door. Please don't shoot."

Slowly I turned the knob ready to jump. I peaked in through a slit I made and saw Pam curled up on the floor trembling all over and holding the .38 with both hands pointed at me. When she saw it was me she dropped the gun and covered her face in her hands, sobbing. I sat next to her and wrapped my arms around her.

"It's going to be all right," I said.

She nodded. "Cleo—it was terrible."

"I know."

"Is she…?"

"Yes, she is."

She shuddered but didn't say anything. "C'mon, let's go. We can't stay here anymore. We'll talk about what happened later. I'm just glad you're okay."

I helped her up and we walked back into the bedroom. Chip was frantic. He said, "We have to get out of here. He's going to come back. He said so."

"How badly was he hit?" I asked.

"She got him in the leg. It didn't look too bad to me, but I don't know anything about that stuff. I mean, he was limping but he was able to run out of here. He was pissed."

"Why did he leave you here?"

"Are you kidding? With her shooting like crazy through the door and the dog going wild on his friend in the other room, he was as rattled as I've ever seen him. Besides, he was as surprised to see me as I was to see him. Maybe seeing me like this confused him. I don't know but I know him. He'll want to interrogate me for sure to find out what the hell is going on and what I've told you. We have to get out of here before he comes back with more Spiders."

"Why shouldn't I just leave you here for him?"

"Because I'm ready to help. Whatever you want. Get me to a cop. I want protection. I'll tell everything I know."

"I want all the names of your buyers that are on that laptop in Long Island."

"You get the laptop and I'll give you everything, just get me out of here before he returns."

I nodded and said, "One wrong move and I'll beat you to death. Understand?"

"Yes."

I released him and he dressed quickly in a pair of my jeans and a sweatshirt. He was a lot taller than me and looked just a little silly. As we left the apartment, I paused momentarily by Cleo's body. The full impact of her loss hadn't registered yet. Pam touched my arm for support. She was about to say something and I shook my head and said under my breath, "Later."

We took a quick cab back to Pam's apartment. Chip sat in between Pam and me and was cooperative, but Luther's pistol in his rib cage helped with that. Up in the apartment, I had Chip sit on the floor and cuffed him to the old metal radiator in Pam's kitchen. She said, "I'm going to shower."

I called Carlos and filled him in on what happened in my apartment. He agreed to send men to sanitize the place and get rid of the bodies. I also hesitantly told him about Vito's condition and asked him to come to Pam's apartment. Vito would be pissed, but I had a sixth sense about Carlos and felt he could be trusted to keep the information to himself. Besides, I needed help.

Carlos arrived a half hour later and I gave him a status update on Vito and a list of supplies I needed from the drugstore and supermarket. I brought him in to say hello to Vito, but he was sleeping. Carlos saw how weak he looked and nodded. We went back to the living room to converse.

"You understand how important it is to keep this quiet, right?"

"I understand. Is no problem. Mr. Vito very good to me. I very loyal."

"Thank you, Carlos."

"Who did this? The same men who bring the children?"

I nodded. "Yes."

"Very bad."

"Yes, they are."

He looked at me directly in the eyes and I could see how angry he was. "We finish this, yes?"

"Yes, we will. I promise."

He turned and left to get supplies. I went back in to peek at Vito. He was breathing comfortably. I figured as long as he could drink and eat he should be okay. Carlos would come back with broad spectrum antibiotics, Gatorade, lots of high-protein food and a few other things I needed.

The problem was that Vito couldn't be missing from the streets for more than a day or two before people began to speculate. One day fine, two days borderline, three would be disastrous. It was Sunday. If I could get him up and walking by Tuesday morning all should bode well for his criminal empire, but time was running out. Samuel and the Spiders would be on high alert. That was one problem. The other was Maria. If Samuel decided to cut his losses, she might be the first casualty.

When Carlos returned, Vito was still out cold. Carlos graciously offered to pan fry some burgers for all of us and we accepted. Fifteen minutes later, we ate ravenously. I almost threw a scrap of food at Chip on the floor but decided I didn't like him enough.

Afterward, I cleared the table, released Chip, and made him sit next to me. Pam went to lie down and Carlos went to check on his boss again. He was very concerned and I could tell that his loyalty and respect for Vito was genuine. Carlos had brought me a handheld recorder and I now put some batteries in it as Chip watched. Placing stationery in front of him, I handed him a pen and said, "Starting with your full name, date of birth, and position at NYU, I want you to write a full and detailed account of your relationship and business activities with Samuel. Don't leave anything out. I'll guide you with what's important to say and what's not. I have a knack for this sort of thing. Then, when I think we're done you're going to dictate verbatim everything you just wrote. If I think you're lying to save your ass, I'll drop you off on the front porch of that house on Long Island for Samuel. I'd have to break your legs and arms first but I think you'll understand that. Okay?"

He nodded. Defeated and truly scared for his life, he cooperated fully. We finished at just after 1:00 a.m. I cuffed him back to the radiator and read through his confession one last time. It was pretty complete, but I was curious about something.

I said, "Tell me about Justin, the NYU student that you and the Spiders killed."

"I put it all down in writing."

"I see that, but you were kind of terse. Help me fill in the gaps. He was selling drugs to other students to make ends meet, but when he found out what was going on in those houses on the Island, he was horrified. He met Kayla and Maria, felt sorry for them and helped them escape. He used the heroin as a bargaining chip to get you to leave them alone but you didn't go for it. Am I warm?"

"Very. He was naïve to think he could leverage us like that. The Spiders wanted blood."

I nodded. "Well, I understand why you killed him. It's the where I don't get. It's a minor point, but why did you do it in Steinhardt? I mean why not in a dark alley somewhere?"

"He was the one who chose the place. He was comfortable with it because that was where he usually sold drugs to the other students. He called a meeting to discuss the situation and to buy his way out with the drugs. He figured we wouldn't touch him right on NYU property, especially with a security guard downstairs."

"He didn't know the guard was a Spider?"

He shook his head. "No, he didn't, but they knew him."

"When did he find out about the girls?"

"Just a few weeks ago. The Spiders felt it was time to reward him for his service. I think they were grooming him to join them one day, the tattoo and everything. Anyway, to answer your question, after he died, we thought about moving him, but figured everybody would interpret his death as a drug overdose, not murder. I mean, it's well known there's an epidemic on college campuses. The real benefit to leaving him there was to serve as a warning to the other dealers working for us. Even though they didn't know for sure what happened, they suspected the truth."

I stared at him for about half a minute digesting the cold, hard facts of life. Justin was probably a good kid and smart academically, but like so many others these days, didn't see the danger in drugs. He starts using, then dealing, and before he knew what was happening, his life had spiraled out of control. I let out a deep breath and without another word, left Chip sitting there on the floor. On my way to see Vito, I saw Carlos in the living room on his cellphone talking animatedly with someone. Vito was awake and whispered hoarsely, "Cesari."

I came close, and sat on the edge of the bed. "Hey, pal, how are you feeling?"

"Pissed off, what do you think?"

"I bet."

"Cesari—I just wanted to say…"

"You don't have to say anything. Just get better."

He nodded. "Thank you."

"You'd do the same for me."

"You know I would." He paused for a moment. "These guys have to be exterminated."

Nodding, I said, "Yes, I agree."

"I told Carlos to get the rest of the crew for a war meeting. I want to hit them hard and fast before they know we're coming for them."

"You mean the house in Long Island?"

"That's exactly what I mean and I mean tonight before these scumbags have a chance to understand what they started. I'm also going to pick off that guard at Steinhardt tonight too while we're at it."

"He's already dead. He came with Samuel to my place. Cleo got to him, but he got to her too, unfortunately."

His eyes registered surprise and dismay. "She's…?"

"Yeah, she took five 9mm rounds at close range and still ripped his throat out."

"Oh my God, Cesari, I'm so sorry. Carlos filled me in about what happened at your apartment but he forgot to mention the dog. Fuck, you must be beside yourself. I know how much you loved her."

"Thanks, and I still love her. Death will never change that, but you should rest, Vito. The Spiders will still be here tomorrow and the next day. Give yourself at least twenty-four hours to gain some of your strength back. Besides, what happened to not wanting your men to see you like this?"

"No, it has to be now. They won't be expecting retaliation so soon. If we wait until tomorrow, they'll have time to beef up their defenses or they might even decide to clear out. And now that I think about it, this is the best way for my men to see me for what I really am—a warrior."

I grinned. He was right. "I guess you're not pissed I called Carlos?"

"No, you did the right thing. He's a good man."

"You sure you want to drive out to the Island tonight?"

"Yes, I'm fine. Pass me the bottle of Gatorade over there."

I handed him a bottle Carlos had placed on his night table and he took a long swallow. I said, "Well, if we're going to war tonight then let me change your bandage and re-clean the wound with hydrogen peroxide. And I want you to take some antibiotics I had Carlos pick up."

He nodded and I worked on him. I gave him ibuprofen and a thousand milligrams of amoxicillin. "I'm coming with you, Vito."

"You're a doctor, Cesari. You don't want to be part of this. We're going to burn that house down to the ground after we eliminate everyone in it."

"Like I said, I'm coming, and I have my reasons. First of all, there might be a little girl in there. Your boys are going to need somebody to remind them of that when the shooting starts. Secondly, there's a laptop in the house with a master list of all the rich scumbags who buy these kids. I need that laptop to expose them so I'm going in whether you like it or not. I can't take a chance on your guys accidentally destroying it."

He nodded. "Fine. You can come with us, but I'll let you know when you can go in. I can't have you getting in the way or being a distraction. Okay, they'll be here in less than an hour and then we'll go. It's going to be a long night so let me catch a few z's before they arrive."

"One more thing. You need to leave at least one guy here with Pam to keep an eye on Chip."

He nodded and closed his eyes. I shook my head and went to find Pam. She looked like she was already asleep, but I didn't want to leave her without saying something, especially after the night she'd had. Sensing my presence, she opened her eyes. I said, "Hi."

"Why aren't you getting in bed?"

"I have to go out."

She nodded. She was a quick study. "The Spiders?"

"Yes, it's starting."

"Be careful."

"Vito's going to leave one of his men to watch Chip."

"I was just dreaming about Cleo."

As she spoke a tear came to her eye and I leaned down to kiss her. I couldn't let myself get emotional over Cleo right now. I'd mourn later. I said, "She was a good dog."

"She saved my life. If it wasn't for her I wouldn't have been able to escape to the bathroom. I'd be dead now—or worse."

I nodded.

Chapter 43

We piled into three vehicles. Vito's black caddie led the caravan, followed by two Suburbans loaded with dangerous, angry men, shotguns, pistols, and Molotov cocktails. I had a crowbar next to me and Vito held a double-barreled, sawed-off shotgun in his lap. ETA was approximately 3:00 a.m. I drove and Vito rode shotgun. He looked pale, but he was a good patient, and kept sucking on a water bottle for hydration. Carlos and another guy sat in the back.

Vito said, "This isn't going to be subtle, Cesari."

"I understand. Just give me a chance to find the laptop before you torch the house, and warn your men again about the girl."

Vito turned to Carlos, "You listening?"

"Yes, we will be careful."

"You're sure about how many Spiders there are?" Vito asked returning to me.

I shrugged. "Chip said anywhere between four and ten. Not counting me and you, we have ten guys and the element of surprise. Unless they have a machine gun mounted on the roof, we should be okay."

"You don't think that's a possibility, do you?"

"No, I don't."

"I hope that asshole, Samuel, is in there."

I nodded. "Me too. Let's keep our fingers crossed on that, but I'm not going to hold my breath. I'd love to talk to him personally about Cleo among other things, but he's wounded and may have had no choice but to find a doctor. It doesn't matter though because tonight will send a good message no matter what."

"I agree about the message. Vermin should stick to the shadows where they belong. Well, if he's in there, don't get upset if he catches one in the lungs before you have your chat."

I nodded. "There's nothing you could do to him that would upset me."

As we turned down the road toward the house, all the cars cut their lights and we parked about one hundred feet away, but I kept the engine running. A half-moon and a few lights on in the house gave us decent visibility, enough to tell that there were no outside patrols or Dobermans running around the front lawn. The garage door was open and several cars and SUVs were parked on the street.

Vito's men organized into two groups of four. One group would enter from the rear of the house, clear the main floor, and then head to the basement. The other group entering through the front door would clear the upstairs. Carlos and another guy would remain outside in case anyone managed to escape. Everyone had orders to kill on sight. If they could manage to capture one alive for interrogation purposes, great, if not, don't worry about it.

Sitting in the car watching the scene unfold I said, "The Spiders don't seem to be on high alert here, do they?"

Vito replied, "Do you have any idea how many wars and battles I've survived, Cesari?"

"Many?"

"That's right. Trust me when I say these guys are amateurs. They pick on college kids and children. My guess is they're mostly druggies without any discipline. I wouldn't be surprised if they were all high in there. They don't even know what they've gotten into tonight fucking with me, but they're going to find out."

I nodded and was glad he was on my side. He tapped my arm. "It's about to start."

Captivated, we saw his men creep into position at the front door. Using a pre-arranged signal with the group in back, they suddenly crashed into the house. Gunfire abruptly lit up the night like flashes of lightning and claps of thunder followed by desperate screams. Then quiet, then more gunfire as Vito's men moved methodically toward their objectives. Half a minute later, an upstairs bedroom glowed brightly from several shotgun blasts. Then all was quiet again.

I looked at Vito nervously. His face showed no expression. I said, "You think I should go in now?"

Before he could answer, car lights suddenly flashed on from inside the garage and a powerful engine roared. Rubber burned and tires squealed as the BMW shot out of its resting place like a rocket. Vito's guy was standing in the driveway and didn't have time to react as the B7 hit him head on, flinging him onto the hood and then onto the road where he bounced and rolled to a stop. Carlos fired several wild and futile shots at it, and as the car careened past, I saw Samuel in the driver's seat.

Shit!

I threw the caddie into drive, and slammed on the accelerator making a wild U-turn in hot pursuit. "Buckle up, Vito, and get the shotgun ready."

The B7 was a hot car and could easily outrace us on the open road, but in this part of Long Island, the roads were dark, narrow and winding, and I was able to keep pace with it at least

357

for a while. The caddie didn't handle as well and I gradually began to lose ground with every curve in the road. Vito held the sawed-off waiting for an opportunity to blow out his tires, which was looking less likely as time went on. After five full minutes, he had increased his lead from about fifty feet to close to a hundred.

Vito yelled over the roar of the engines and wind. "C'mon, Cesari, give it some gas."

"I'm trying. Who told you to buy a damn caddie? It handles like shit."

"Press on the God damn pedal, for crying out loud."

I was doing fifty around thirty-mile an hour curves, but Samuel was doing sixty around the same bends in the road. I pressed further on the accelerator just as the BMW disappeared around yet another curve. I saw the speedometer inch up past sixty-five, and braced myself as we approached the same curve. Just then, we heard tires screeching, a horn blasting and the unmistakable sound of a car crashing into an immovable object, which I guessed was a tree.

Coming around the turn, I saw the B7 too late to slow down. It had hit a deer which lay dead or dying in the middle of the road. The B7 had lost control and hit a large tree, crunching in its front end almost to the windshield. Steam and smoke poured out into the night sky. I swerved to avoid its rear end, which was sticking out, and wound up running over the buck. It was like hitting a gigantic speed bump at too high a speed. The caddie rammed into the deer and went airborne. The front tires blew out on impact, the airbags deployed and its forward movement brought us smack into a tree on the other side of the road from the B7.

I lost consciousness for just a minute or two and when I woke saw Vito out cold next to me. My face hurt but nothing was broken. Looking back, the BMW sat there quietly, smoke wafting from the engine block. Its trunk was open. I didn't notice any movement from within or around the car. Shaking Vito vigorously until he roused, I said, "Are you okay?"

He nodded, "Yeah, damn, am I gonna be sore tomorrow or what?"

He was fine. "I'm going to check on Samuel."

Stretching, he groaned, "I'm coming with you."

Grabbing the crowbar, I ran over to the B7 with Vito close behind. Samuel was gone. In the open trunk, I spotted multiple kilo-sized bricks of heroin. I scanned around quickly. The area was heavily wooded and sparsely populated. The ocean and dead Spiders lay behind us, the town miles ahead. He'd have to stay off the main road so I guessed that he plunged headfirst into the woods for cover. He needed time to come up with a plan. The problem was that he was out of time. I said, "Call your guys and have them pick you up. I think Samuel ducked into the woods and I'm going after him.

He nodded and sat down on the grass, leaning back against the BMW. He looked like shit as he reached into his pocket for his phone. I took off at a jog into the woods trying to follow the only reasonable semblance of a path I could find. In the dark, with only the light of a partial moon, the going was tough, but I was deeply motivated.

Running with a six-pound crowbar, tripping over roots and bramble wasn't easy, and I was soon panting and sweating. He couldn't be that far ahead. He had a wounded leg and was just in a head-on collision. On the other hand, he was deeply motivated as well. His survival was on the line. Even though he couldn't be 100 percent sure who was after him, I'd bet he had a pretty good idea.

As I entered a clearing, a small figure on the ground caught my attention and I stopped dead in my tracks. In the shadow of a large oak, the figure lay motionless. I stepped toward it trying to make it out. Ten feet away, I could see it was child, a girl.

Maria!

She was unconscious, her hands tied, and she had a strip of duct tape across her mouth. That was why the trunk of the car was wide open. He had hidden her in there. Vito was right. He and the Spiders must have been getting ready to clear out when we arrived. As I moved toward her, I was struck in the back of the head. I fell to the ground in pain, and rolled quickly to face Samuel who was coming in fast for a second blow. Fortunately, he hadn't had much time to look for a proper weapon, or I might have already been knocked unconscious.

As the small branch came down, I raised the crowbar up, deflecting the force of the blow. He was close enough now and I kicked him hard on the inside of his right knee. He grunted and his leg buckled under him. As he staggered, I jumped quickly to my feet and delivered a hard crack to his left clavicle with the crowbar. He screamed as something broke and I kicked him in the face. He tumbled backward, staring up at the forest canopy, momentarily stunned.

I sat on him and he wiggled and squirmed so I hit him repetitively with the crowbar in the side of the face until he stopped struggling. He spit out a tooth and blood. Anybody else would have been ready to surrender, but the fire in his eyes told me otherwise.

We stared at each other, both breathless and pumped up on adrenaline. This is what it was all about. Primordial combat between two males fighting for dominance. It felt good.

Dazed but not out of it, he hissed at me, "What do you want?"

I hissed through clenched teeth, "I told your father that you were dead. I don't want you to make a liar out of me."

He showed neither surprise nor that he cared in the slightest that I had been in contact with his father. Drenched in sweat, with blood and drool running down his chin, he was still defiant. "Just do it and get it over with, asshole."

"I plan on it, but first, you're going to tell me a few things."

"I'm not going to tell you shit."

"Wrong answer."

Chapter 44

The next morning, I was exhausted and running on just two hours' sleep. I showed up an hour late for my meeting with Kilcullen and yawned loudly as I waited for him in his office. It was 11:00 a.m. and a lot had happened since I last met with him. I was working on my second cup of black coffee when he entered the room, thoroughly flustered and rather grumpy.

"Where've you been, Cesari? I've been trying to reach you all night."

He sat behind his desk, reached into one of the drawers and came out with a new bottle of Jameson's. He opened it and poured some into his coffee mug. I said, "I'm sorry. I was exhausted and turned my phone off."

"Humph. T'is a fine thing that happened. I suppose you heard?"

"You mean Samuel's escape from Riker's?"

"Of course, t'at's what I mean. The whole city is exploding over it."

"Yes, I heard this morning. It's all over the news."

"T'at scumbag. I don't know how he did it. Two dead corrections officers and some bloke who got in way over his head for sure. Then a house full of Spiders gets wasted in the wee hours this morning. Did you hear about t'at too?"

"I saw something on the news this morning about it. There was a big house fire out in the Hamptons."

"House fire, my arse. The place was riddled with bullets and shotgun shells and they found empty five-gallon cans of gasoline on the front lawn. I'm telling you lad, we have a full-scale turf war going on. If I didn't know you were on my team, I might have thought you were involved somehow."

"Me?! Why would you think that?"

"Why? You were the one t'at gave Samuel the medical clearance to go to the hospital, which resulted in his escape. In the detective business t'at's called suspicious."

I feigned outrage. "Bullshit! I did the right thing. I'd swear to it on a stack of bibles; he had appendicitis. You can't fake that. He had a fever. I did the medically correct thing and I would do it again. I would never help that scumbag."

"Calm down, son. I'm just thinking out loud. There's only one way they could have arranged t'at ambush anyway."

"How is that?"

"One of the guards at Riker's must have been on Samuel's payroll and tipped off the Spiders the ambulance was coming for him. That warden has her hands full for sure over there."

"Well, she already knew that, but Samuel won't get far."

"And why's t'at?"

"I have every confidence in New York's finest."

He took a long swallow from his mug. "Humph."

As we spoke a uniformed officer came into the office and whispered something in his ear. His eyes grew wide. "You don't say? Unbelievable. Where'd they find him?"

The officer whispered a few more words and was dismissed by Kilcullen. He turned back to me, a shocked look on his face. "T'is a fine thing. They just found Samuel's body in the woods a couple of miles from the Spider house t'at burned down."

"I knew he wouldn't get far."

"Beaten almost beyond recognition, he was, with a crowbar shoved right through his heart like a stake through a vampire in some old movie."

"I guess somebody was pretty upset with him."

"I'll say."

Ten minutes later, the uniformed officer returned holding a laptop and a large manila envelope. He placed both down on the desk in front of Kilcullen and again whispered in his ear too low for me to hear. This conversation went on for a much longer period. Kilcullen's face revealed more surprise and confusion. "Is there a full moon out, Sean? Okay, thank you, lad, and keep me posted."

After he left, Kilcullen said, "If you don't mind, doctor, I'll be needing a moment to look at this."

He opened the manila envelope. Inside were several sheets of paper and a tape recorder. He whistled as he read the hand-written, signed confession from Chip, and let out a long loud sigh.

"I don't be meaning to give you the bum's rush, son, but I have some urgent business to tend to. It seems the president of NYU was just found naked in an old steamer trunk t'at was thrown out of the back of an SUV as it sped past the Bellevue emergency room. Apparently, the professor would like to take responsibility for all sorts of heinous criminal activity including aiding and abetting our lately departed friend, Samuel, in dealing drugs and trafficking minors. This here is his signed confession t'at was hand delivered by courier to the station, along with a voice recording of this same affidavit. Rather than demanding clothes and medical care, which would have been his right, he is insisting on speaking to me in person and is demanding police protection from the remaining Spiders. According to what he is telling my people in the emergency room, this laptop contains a financial paper trail and lists of all the people t'at have participated in these illicit activities. Needless to say, I have to get ahead of this so I'll be taking leave of you for now, but keep your phone on."

I said, "Wow! Sounds like the next time I see you, you'll be commissioner."

"Or mayor. Think big, lad."

We both stood to leave and I said, "Oh, one more thing. I spoke to Warden Garcia about you..."

He grinned. "Ah yes, I've spoken to her several times meself this morning about this mess but I—uh—steered clear of the elephant in the living room."

"Well, there's no need to steer clear of it anymore. She was impressed by the flowers you sent and told me to give you a thumb's up. She said to show up spit-shined this Friday at Muldoon's Saloon in Queens and buy her a margarita."

He looked stunned. "No way. She said t'at?" I nodded and a big smile gradually spread across his face. "Margaritas, eh?"

"She also said to tell you that she wears a .38 in her garter belt."

"No..."

"Actually, it's .40 Sig in a shoulder holster, but you get the idea."

"A fiery lass for sure. I would expect no less. Either way, it sounds like it may be fun trying to disarm her."

I cleared my throat. "I would go slow there if I were you."

He thought it over for a moment. "You're right. A spirited filly needs to be coaxed along right proper. Well, thank you, lad. I have to be going now but don't be surprised if I call you for some more tips."

"In Riker's, they call me the doctor of love."

"To be sure, but they may not be calling you that much longer if the warden has her way."

I still had two months to go on my sentence. He continued, "Warden Garcia is furious over Samuel's escape and while she doesn't necessarily blame you, she thinks that maybe you were too easily duped, perhaps even that you are medically incompetent. She's petitioning the judge to have your sentence cut or at least have you finish it doing some other form of community service. In her own words, she doesn't ever want to see your sorry ass in her jail again. So I'm afraid that if you forgot to say goodbye to anyone there, it's too late now."

On that note, we walked out of the precinct together and I took a quick cab back to Pam's apartment and found her on the sofa. Vito was out cold in her bedroom, snoring loudly. I sat next to her. She asked, "Is it over?"

"Not quite, but it's time that Knuckles and Liz called child protective services."

"I'll let them know. What about the woman, Rosa?"

"I don't know what to do about her. If she doesn't confess, then there's little we can do unless the children testify and think about the quagmire that will cause."

"Not to mention stress. These kids have been through enough. For what it's worth, she told Knuckles that she was forced into helping them by her boyfriend, one of the dead drivers. She said she never meant to hurt the little girl but was afraid her crying was going to make the men come back and hurt her even more."

I got kind of snotty. "Yeah, well, for what it's worth, I couldn't care less about any excuses she has to offer."

Pam nodded and I said, "I'm sorry. I didn't mean to talk to you like that. I'm very tired."

"I understand. Why don't you try to sleep for a few hours? You must be exhausted."

"I am." I thought about the woman and it burned me up that she might conceivably get away with it. She was a minor player,

I knew, but still, everybody who had a hand in this needed to burn in hell. I sighed, but then a thought came to me how she could possibly mitigate her culpability.

As I sat there, I started to slouch toward Pam. I was very tired and needed to sleep but my mind raced. I rested my head against her shoulder and put my legs up on her coffee table.

She said, "Wouldn't the bed be more comfortable?"

Yawning I said, "No, I'm fine right here."

"And what am I supposed to do? Just sit here and act as your pillow?"

"Exactly."

She chuckled. "My friends would never forgive me if they knew I let a man treat me like this."

My eyes were half-closed. "I don't mean to be politically incorrect but maybe your friends need to get laid more."

"As long as it's not by you."

"Say Pam…?"

"What?"

"Have you ever been to Texas?"

Chapter 45

The Suburban rumbled along the interstate uneventfully. We were just a few miles out from Pharr, Texas. It was eighty degrees and the sky was clear. Palm trees and citrus orchards fed by irrigation from the Rio Grande dominated the landscape. Looking in the rear-view mirror, I saw the other two Suburbans in single file behind us. I smiled inwardly. We looked like a Secret Service motorcade. I had cautioned everybody to stay within the speed limit.

I turned to Carlos and said, "I know I've asked you this before, but do you really think we can trust Rosa?"

He thought about it for a second. "I think so. She seemed truly remorseful. She did not know what she was getting into. She says if God saves her she will join a convent and spend the rest of her life taking care of the poor to atone for her sins."

"And you believe her?"

"Maybe. I told her that if she betrays me, she will get the first bullet."

Pam and I had decided together that, rather than let the children get caught up in the bureaucracy of New York's child protective services, possibly causing an international incident, we would let Rosa guide them back to their homes in Mexico accompanied by Carlos, who had dual citizenship. They were in the Suburban directly behind ours.

I said, "Well, for what it's worth, I want to believe to her. About being truly sorry, I mean."

The big man was brooding. "What are you thinking about?" I asked.

"Is no right that men do these things."

I nodded. "No, it's not right."

"But why then?"

"There's no easy answer to that one, Carlos, but I think about these things a lot. A famous Irish philosopher once said, 'The only thing necessary for evil to triumph is for good men to do nothing.' He was right. I have a theory that if enough good men stood up for what is right and were willing to make sacrifices, then people who do things like this, men like the Spiders, and men like their clients, would crawl back under the rocks from which they came."

He nodded. "I am very angry, especially at those in Mexico who sold these children to the Spiders. They are Mexican and I am Mexican. I was brought to California when I was ten years old to live with my aunt and my uncle. I worked hard in the orchards and sent what little money I made back to my family. When I saw the children in the van, all I could think about was how that could have been me."

"You're right, it could've been."

He looked at me. "What does it take to stop it?"

I thought about that and said, "It starts with caring about little things. Caring about the old lady you see having trouble carrying her grocery bag. It starts with caring when you see teenagers smoking pot instead of studying. It starts with caring when you hear one man denigrating another man because of

369

the color of his skin, or because of his beliefs. It starts when you decide you can't look away when you see something that you know is wrong even if your brain tells you it doesn't concern you. When men like you and me care enough that they are willing to take risks for no personal gain is when it starts."

"You are good man, Mr. John, like Mr. Vito."

"How did you meet him anyway?"

"Mr. Vito? I leave California five, maybe six years ago. They say New York is more interesting. I work in kitchen in one of Mr. Vito's restaurants. He see me one day and says 'What you do here? You come work with me, Carlos. I make you big star.' And now I am big star."

I smiled. "Yes, you are."

He grinned. "Mr. Vito say you are big star also, big doctor."

"Yeah, big doctor," I added wryly.

"I am sorry I will not be able to help the others. I would have liked to join them."

"You're doing a very important job for us, Carlos. These kids need someone to protect them until they're back in the arms of their loved ones. You're about the only one I trust at this point."

"Gracias. This is going to make the news. I hope you know that. Killing a high-ranking border patrol agent is going to raise a few eyebrows."

"He's a scumbag, Carlos, and I don't care whose nose gets bent out of shape. Besides, we got fifty kilos of the Spider's heroin that we're going to plant in his house and car. That should cast quite a cloud on his character. I think we'll be fine."

Using crowbar enhanced interrogation technique, I had convinced Samuel to reveal to me the identity of the border patrol agent on his payroll. He would let the traffickers know ahead of time where the patrols were so that they could make safe passage into the U.S. Sometimes, they would pay him with money, sometimes with drugs, and sometimes with girls. There was a special place in hell for a guy like him and Vito's men were going to send him there tonight. They were in the third Suburban with the heroin.

My phone buzzed. It was Vito.

"Hey, Vito. How are you feeling?"

"Stronger every day. How's it going down there?"

"Good. We're entering Pharr now and the border crossing is just a few miles away. We're going to split up soon. How's Chip doing?"

"Oh, man. He's been getting reamed out on the news, day and night, and there have been massive protests in the park almost continuously. Thousands of students, faculty, and parents have been protesting, even burning him in effigy. Several class-action suits have already been filed against the university for lack of oversight, and the U.S. attorney general has announced a separate investigation. The smart money is that he'll commit suicide before he ever makes it to trial."

"Good."

"How's Maria?"

"As well as can be expected. She's going to need time and lots of love. It's the only real remedy for what she's been through. I think we're off to a good start though. She desperately wanted to see Kayla again, and Kayla felt the same way, so we're all meeting at a hotel down here before Carlos takes them across the border. It was nice of Kayla's parents to agree to it."

"I hope things work out for her and for all of them. They've been through enough. Say 'Hi' for me and I'll see you when you get back."

"Ciao."

I turned to look into the back seat. Pam was listening to me talk and when our eyes met, she smiled. She had her arm around Maria, who slept peacefully snuggled in close, with her head laying on Pam's chest. Like a tired angel, Maria hugged the doll with the blue dress.

Chapter 46

Two Weeks Later

I came out of the locker room and found Pam waiting for me along with twelve NYU students who clapped at my appearance. Shorts, sneakers, and no shirt made several girls cheer their approval. Pam studied my chest and abs.

She said, "Not bad."

"Thanks."

"Are you sure you want to do this?"

"I don't want to do this at all, especially not in front of my students."

"Then you shouldn't have agreed to it."

"Oh please, Pam. You were there. Knuckles challenged me right in front of the whole class. She called me a cry baby and started clucking like a chicken. I've never been so embarrassed."

As we approached the boxing ring, I saw Knuckles shadow boxing in preparation. Liz was in her corner, of course. Pam helped me tie my gloves on and I stepped into the ring very concerned about the next few minutes of my life. This was one of those situations no male ever wants to be in—a fight with a girl. Beating her was no honor and losing would be the height of humiliation. I had the longer reach and planned on keeping as much distance between me and her as I could. Thank God she agreed to gloves. The idea of bare-knuckle boxing with her made me cringe.

Bob had agreed to referee the three-round, three minute-per-round match. Stan was the timekeeper. He sat seriously at the side of the ring holding his stop watch.

Pam whispered in my ear, "Good luck. By the way, in the eight years I've been teaching here, I've never seen any students this excited about any sporting event."

Knuckles wore protective head gear and a mouth guard, which I had declined. She was dancing around like a professional and I was starting to get a little edgy. Bob signaled us to the center of the ring and we approached each other. I smiled and Knuckles grunted in reply.

Bob said, "Keep it clean and above the belt. If I say break, you break, understood? When someone goes down, you go to your corner."

Geez, they were taking this very seriously.

He continued, "Okay, touch gloves and when the bell rings, come out swinging."

I went to my corner and Pam reached over the ropes to give me a kiss. More cheers from the students. Clearly, I was the crowd favorite, but getting challenged to a fight on my first day teaching probably got me the sympathy vote.

Stan rang the bell and I took several steps toward the center of the ring. Knuckles came charging out of her corner like a bull to meet me. Coming at me fast, it appeared she was going to tackle me and I back-pedaled, tripped, and fell back into the ropes by my corner. A roar of laughter erupted from the students as Pam helped me to my feet.

She whispered. "If you survive, I'll let you do that thing to me with your tongue again."

I looked at her and smiled. "That's not going to help my concentration."

Turning back, I found Knuckles standing right in front of me. She gave me a quick left jab to my cheek, followed by a right cross that caught me off guard. I fell back into Pam's arms again. I heard Liz yell from across the ring, "Give it to him!"

Knuckles took out her mouth guard and said, "Seriously, Doc, is that the best you got?"

I turned to Pam again. "Do you mind if I beat up your friend?"

"Not at all. She asked for it, just don't kill her."

The rest of the round I bobbed and weaved, exchanging light jabs with her while she worked up a sweat chasing me around for the kill. I decided the best course was to wait for her to throw a punch and try to meet her glove with a counter punch. This frustrated her greatly and I could tell she perceived it as an insult to her manhood. The bell rang and we went to our corners. It was the longest three minutes of my life.

Waiting for the second round, I asked Pam, "How am I doing?"

"Well, it's pretty obvious you're trying not to hit her."

"Don't worry. I'm just toying with her. She's going down in the next round."

She laughed. "This, I have to see."

As the bell for the second round clanged, I saw Vito and Carlos walk in. Oh brother. This, I didn't need. I looked at Pam and she shrugged, smiling. I said, "Thanks."

Out of one eye I watched Vito approach the ring smirking. Suddenly, he lifted both hands and I saw he was holding a camera. Distracted, I didn't see Knuckles coming up on my other side. She landed a big one and I staggered back as Vito clicked away.

Shit!

Knuckles decided this was her best chance to finish me off. She came in close as the students cheered, giving me rapid-fire

375

body blows, and then I saw her wind up for a massive upper cut. There are two ways to handle an all-out punch. You can try to get away as fast as you can or move in close to reduce its effectiveness. With the ropes directly behind me I decided to move in close so she couldn't deliver the blow.

Big mistake.

Since she was at least six inches shorter than me the upswing of the blow caught me between the legs. It all happened so quick, no one caught it, not even Knuckles. I grimaced, held my breath, and slowly crumpled to my knees.

Knuckles went to her corner waving her arms over her head in victory. Pam realized something was wrong and came into the ring as I sucked wind in pain. I never heard Vito laugh that hard and, somehow, I knew NYU would never be the same.

Bob started counting to ten, and Pam just waved him off. "It's over, Bob. Can't you see he's hurt?"

He went over to Knuckles and raised her arm over her head, declaring her the winner. Vito stepped into the ring and came over to me. Kneeling down close, and still chuckling, he said, "Jesus, Cesari, I haven't had a good laugh like this in ages. Just wait until the guys hear about this. You'll be famous."

"Thanks. Now how about helping me up."

I put my arm around his shoulder and he assisted me up. Pam put her arm around my waist. "I got it from here, Vito."

"Sure thing, Pam. Thanks for inviting me. I'm glad I got here in time."

Knuckles came over and said, "No hard feelings, Doc?"

I was starting to feel better. "None at all. You won fair and square."

"Well, you put up quite a fight. For a couple of minutes, I was worried."

"Well, the better man won."

Pam walked me to the locker room and insisted on coming in to help me change. I said, "I'm all right, Pam."

"You've got to be kidding me. She cleaned your clock."

"She punched me in the balls."

"Did she order you to not wear a cup?"

"No."

"Well, then it's your own fault."

Jesus. I wasn't even safe in the locker room. She continued. "I have a lot of emotional investment in your nether region and I don't like the idea of you not taking care of the equipment properly."

I laughed. "Thanks for your concern."

Smiling mischievously, she said, "Now let me see how much damage she did." Standing in front of me she tugged on the elastic waistband of my shorts and looked down inside. "Everything in there looks fine to me." She grinned and let the elastic band snap back.

I smiled and sat down on a bench. "Is that your considered opinion as a doctor of psychology?"

She sat next to me, nodding. "Yes, it is. Want to make something of it?"

"No, one woman beating me up per day is my limit."

"You are getting smart, aren't you?" She held my hand. "So, what's the plan now?"

"I was going to take a shower."

She smirked and squeezed my hand. "I meant what's the plan after you shower?"

"The same plan as every day, Pam."

"And that is…?"

"To save the world."

She chuckled and said, "Again?"

I looked at her seriously. "I need to know something, Pam. Are you all in with me or just half way?"

She got serious too and put her arms around me, snuggling close. Her face was an inch from mine as she stared into my eyes. "I've never been more all in with any man than the way I've been all in with you."

We kissed for a long, long time.

The End

In 2012, the U.N. crime-fighting office reported that 2.4 million people across the globe are victims of human trafficking at any one time, and 80% of them are being exploited as sexual slaves.

Only one out of 100 victims of trafficking is ever rescued.

About the Author

𝒥 ohn Avanzato grew up in the Bronx. After receiving a bachelor's degree in biology from Fordham University, he went on to earn his medical degree at the State University of New York at Buffalo, School of Medicine. He is currently a board-certified gastroenterologist practicing in upstate, New York, where he lives with his wife of thirty years. Dr. Avanzato co-teaches a course on pulp fiction at Hobart and William Smith Colleges in Geneva, New York.

Inspired by authors like Tom Clancy, John Grisham, and Lee Child, John writes about strong but flawed heroes.

His first five novels, Hostile Hospital, Prescription for Disaster, Temperature Rising, Claimed Denied and The Gas Man Cometh have been received well.

Author's Note

Dear Reader,

I hope you enjoyed reading Jailhouse Doc as much as I enjoyed writing it. Please do me a favor and write a review on amazon.com. The reviews are important and your support is greatly appreciated.

Thank you,

John Avanzato

Hostile Hospital

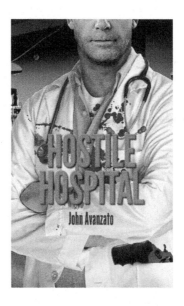

When former mob thug turned doctor, John Cesari, takes a job as a gastroenterologist at a small hospital in upstate New York, he assumes he's outrun his past and started life anew. But trouble has a way of finding the scrappy Bronx native.

Things go awry one night at a bar when he punches out an obnoxious drunk who won't leave his date alone. Unbeknownst to Dr. Cesari, that drunk is his date's stalker ex-boyfriend—and a crooked cop.

Over the course of several action-packed days, Cesari uncovers the dirty little secrets of a small town hospital. As the bodies pile up, he is forced to confront his own bloody past.

Hostile Hospital is a fast-paced journey that is not only entertaining but maintains an interesting view on the philosophy of healthcare. If you aren't too scared after reading, get the sequel, Prescription for Disaster.

Prescription for Disaster

Dr. John Cesari is a gastroenterologist employed at Saint Matt's Hospital in Manhattan. He tries to escape his unsavory past on the Bronx streets by settling into a Greenwich Village apartment with his girlfriend, Kelly. After his adventures in Hostile Hospital, Cesari wants to stay under the radar of his many enemies.

Through no fault of his own, Cesari winds up in the wrong place at the wrong time. A chance encounter with a mugger turns on its head when Cesari watches his assailant get murdered right before his eyes.

After being framed for the crime, he attempts to unravel the mystery, propelling himself deeply into the world of international diamond smuggling. He is surrounded by bad guys at every turn and behind it all are Russian and Italian mobsters determined to ensure Cesari has an untimely and unpleasant demise.

His prescription is to beat them at their own game, but before he can do that he must deal with a corrupt boss and an environment filled with temptation and danger from all sides. Everywhere Cesari goes, someone is watching. The dramatic climax will leave you breathless and wanting more.

Temperature Rising

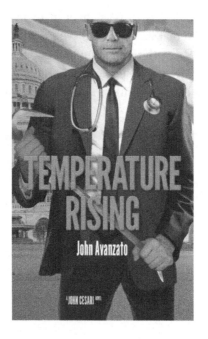

John Cesari is a gangster turned doctor living in Manhattan saving lives one colonoscopy at a time. While on a well-deserved vacation, he stumbles upon a murder scene and becomes embroiled in political intrigue involving the world's oldest profession.

His hot pursuit of the truth leads him to the highest levels of government, where individuals operate above the law. As always, girl trouble hounds him along the way making his already edgy life that much more complex.

The bad guys are ruthless, powerful and nasty but they are no match for this tough, street-smart doctor from the Bronx who is as comfortable with a crowbar as he is with a stethoscope. Get ready for a wild ride in Temperature Rising. The exciting and unexpected conclusion will leave you on the edge of your seat.

Claim Denied

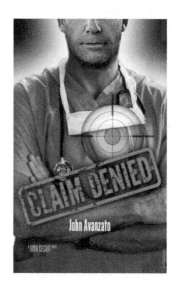

In Manhattan, a cancer ridden patient commits suicide rather than become a financial burden to his family. Accusations of malfeasance are leveled against his caregivers. Rogue gastroenterologist, part-time mobster, John Cesari, is tasked to look into the matter on behalf of St. Matt's hospital.

The chaos and inequities of a healthcare system run amok, driven by corporate greed and endless bureaucratic red tape, become all too apparent to him as his inquiry into this tragedy proceeds. On his way to interview the wife of the dead man, Cesari is the victim of seemingly random gun violence and finds himself on life support.

Recovering from his wounds, he finds that both he and his world are a very different place. His journey back to normalcy rouses in him a burning desire for justice, placing him in constant danger as evil forces conspire to keep him in the dark.

The Gas Man Cometh

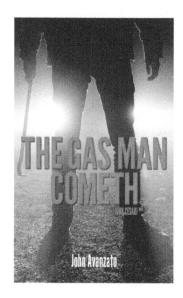

A deranged anesthesiologist with unnatural desires lures innocent women to his brownstone in a swank section of Manhattan. All was going well until John Cesari M.D. came along becoming a thorn in his side.

Known as The Gas Man, his hatred of Cesari reaches the boiling point. He plots to take him down once and for all turning an ordinary medical conference into a Las Vegas bloodbath.

Hungover and disoriented, Cesari awakens next to a mobster's dead girlfriend in a high-end brothel. Wanted dead or alive by more than a few people, Cesari is on the run with gangsters and the police hot on his trail.

There is never a dull moment in this new thriller as Cesari blazes a trail from Sin City to lower Manhattan desperately trying to stay one step ahead of The Gas Man.

KCM Publishing
a division of KCM Digital Media, LLC